HARBOUR

Paul House

Dragon International Independent Arts

This novel is entirely a work of fiction. The names, characters, and incidents portrayed in it are the work of the author's imagination. Any resemblance to actual persons, living or dead, events or localities is entirely coincidental.

First published in 2006 by lulu.com
This edition published 2009 by
Dragon International Independent Arts

ISBN 978-1-907386-02-2

Available from www.diiarts.com, all major online retailers
and available to order through all UK bookshops

Or contact:
Dragon International Independent Arts
Suite 133, 80 High Street
Winchester, Hampshire SO23 9AT
0845 643 6480
books@diiarts.com
www.diiarts.com

Printed in the UK

1

"When three people journey together,
their number decreases by one.
When one man journeys alone,
he finds a companion."

(i)

They came down out of the mountains with the flat plain of Kwantung stretching away before them to the horizon, unaltering and immense. The cultivated, alluvial green of the fields was broken only by the dove-grey line of a river which split the plain in two from East to West. The three taut sails of a junk moved slowly along the river. Molly watched the junk from the sedan chair, resting her hand on the bamboo window frame and her chin on her hand. The chair swayed unevenly as the bearers' bare feet slid over the loose stones on the path. At the bottom of the hill, the roughly trodden mud and pebbles of the path became a causeway of flat paving stones that stretched out across the plain. An old man was driving a pig along the causeway towards them. He was calling out in a high-pitched whine, trying to get the pig to the mountain path before the sedan chair descended onto the plain. There was no room for them both to pass and if he did not manage to get off the flat stones and onto the gravel path of the hillside, the laws of class and respect would force him into the monsoon drain which had been dug into the earth beside the causeway. The monsoon drain was filled with foul-smelling stagnant water and the long, thin leaves of weeds.

Molly turned her eyes away from the junk and glanced at her mother, Suyong, who was lying beneath a grey blanket on the seat opposite. Her eyelids had fallen across her pupils and her eyes were glazed and unseeing. She stared past Molly's head at the slatted bamboo of the sedan chair, and she looked through her fever at the dying sunlight.

Her face had been hollowed out by cholera. Her skin was grey, her lips almost blue. There was no trace of the striking Chinese beauty that had so captivated Molly's father that he had been willing to face the wrath and indignation of the American authorities rather than lose her.

Molly looked at her mother's drained, exhausted face. Her life was ebbing, seeping away. Every step the bearers made took them a little closer to Hong Kong, but every step they made jolted the chair and took a little more life away from Suyong. Although she was only fourteen, Molly had seen death before and she knew her mother would die soon. She carried some water across to her on the tips of her fingers. She ran her fingers along Suyong's lips and they felt dry and gritty. Molly moved the flimsy bamboo curtains of the window and looked back towards the junk. Some phlegm hissed and bubbled in her mother's throat, but she was used to that by now. She rubbed her fingers together to rid them of the last traces of water. Because of the water her mother would die, but without the water she would already be dead.

Three coolies edged past them on the causeway, heading North. They carried wicker baskets on bamboo poles. The baskets were filled with chickens. Molly looked at the chickens. They were headed for the market in Lungchan where, in the morning, they would be sold and slaughtered. But they would live longer than her mother. She knew that her mother would die that night. She knew it, just as she knew that the junk in the distance was heading, like they were, for Hong Kong.

Molly thought of her father as she watched the flat, brown sails of the junk. He would already be waiting for them. Had they been able to make the whole journey by train as he had planned, they would have arrived at almost the same time, but near the lakes a little to the north of Nanchang the train had stopped, the tracks impassable beneath five metres of water. Suyong had spent almost half the money Russell had given them for the journey buying the sedan chair and hiring the bearers, and since then, they had continued on foot, her mother, Ah Chien, the amah, and the six bearers. No one had mentioned sabotage, but everyone knew that Nanchang was an important logistic centre for the Kuomintang and that it had a munitions factory. The railway was the lifeline for the numerous guerrilla forces in the field.

Willard Russell had stayed behind in Nanking to close down his office before getting himself shipped out of Shanghai and making for Hong Kong to meet up with his wife and daughter. Molly still tried to imagine them all living together again although she knew it was impossible. Suyong had first shown the signs of cholera, paradoxically, in the town of Hoping. It was only years later that the Western half of Molly's character would see the irony and the ridiculous inappropriateness of the name. Now, though, her Chinese education dominated her feelings and she tried to accept what she had been taught, that everything in life happened at its appointed time. It was quite simply the moment for her mother to die and, not only was there no point in fighting it, there was nothing to fight. Molly had heard her father say that, for the Chinese, the shortest distance between two points was not a straight line, but the line of least resistance. But Ah Chien said that it was not that. It was just that you could not change the natural order of the world. Her mother would die, because she had to. But, said Ah Chien, the reference for all changes was the unchanging and it was there that we had to live.

Molly was still watching the almost stationary sails of the junk when Ah Chien's face appeared at the window of the sedan chair. Her gold teeth flashed as she spoke. For years Ah Chien had been replacing her stunted teeth with perfect gold replicas. It was an investment for her old age. When she had no money, she would simply have her teeth pulled.

"Soldiers, missie," she said, pointing off along the causeway.

Molly leaned her head further from the window and saw four soldiers blocking their path. They were standing in the middle of the causeway with blankets over their shoulders. In the absence of her mother, Molly was in command. Molly accepted the responsibility as calmly as she accepted the inevitability of her mother's death.

The soldiers held their rifles trained on the bearers as they approached. There was a neurosis and a nervousness in the country even this far south and it was not only caused by the recent Japanese invasion of Manchuria. Although news was sketchy and mostly through word of mouth, it was generally accepted that the Chinese Civil War had temporarily stopped and that the rival factions, Mao Zedong and the Communists and Chiang Kai Shek and the Kuomintang, had joined forces against the Japanese, but nobody could be sure yet whether it was true or not. Any movement on the roads was still looked on as a potential threat. One of the soldiers, a thin, undernourished boy of no more than sixteen, waved his rifle nervously towards them and shuffled round to the side of the chair on broken leather sandals. He poked his sharp face in at the window then recoiled quickly as he recognised the signs of cholera in Suyong's washed out face. He ordered the bearers to move on and waved his rifle butt at his three companions. They all stepped obligingly into the mud and slime of the monsoon drain to let them pass.

Ah Chien ran for a while beside the window of the sedan chair.

"If there are soldiers, missie," she said, "There will be a settlement. If there is a settlement, there might be a mission."

Molly nodded. She was tired, but she knew their only hope of getting food and shelter was at a French or English mission. The Chinese would have nothing to do with them once they had seen Suyong.

"Send one of the coolies on ahead, Ah Chien, to find somewhere to sleep," she said.

When she stepped down from the sedan chair, Molly could see the straggling atap roofs of a village stretching away behind the stone walls of a half-ruined watchtower. To the left of the tower was a hill covered by the small mounds of recently dug graves, each one marked by a white Christian cross. The missionaries, though, had been unable to rid the Chinese of the tradition of burying their dead on the side of a hill and the recent rains had caused one or two of the crosses to totter and fall as the soft earth had been washed away. The dull brown of a skull resisted burial at the very top of the hill. Molly could hear the grunting of pigs and the crying of a child, but could see no sign of life. She looked at the brown skull and noticed there was a flake of dry, leathery skin clinging to the bone behind the temple.

She looked past the tower and the huts of the village and she watched the sun dropping down behind the sails of the junk. A small amber light swayed and flickered at the bows and reflected in the dull waters of the river as a mist began to settle over the plain. Behind her, Ah Chien was knocking on the door of the tower.

Finally, a French nun came to the door. She gave a nervous glance towards Molly, Ah Chien and the bearers, then closed the door again. Ah Chien grumbled beneath her breath and banged on the door. This time, they were received by a young priest. As he opened the door he had already begun to give excuses.

"Christians!" said Ah Chien, and spat on the ground at the priest's feet. What she really meant was "Europeans".

"My mother is ill," said Molly in English, pointing back towards the bearers and the sedan chair. Responding to their common language, the priest stepped stiffly forwards and pulled the curtain aside. He looked at Suyong's agonising face which was a deathly grey in the half light.

"We have more than our fair share of illness already," said the priest. He was complaining to justify his unchristian impulse to just turn them away. "Malaria, dysentery, typhoid. We have brought all the children of the village here, into the tower. To protect them. There is no more room." He looked sadly towards Molly and spoke, but more to himself. "The Chinese, they just throw them out, the children. When they're ill, they just let them die." He looked absently off along the road for a moment and then turned back to them. "I'm sorry," he said, "I can let you shelter round the back. We have so many children, you see? But I'll send food. Some rice. Perhaps a little broth." And he closed the door.

"Men!" said Ah Chien, spitting again in disgust. "In this country, it is even more of a sin to be a woman than it is to be Chinese. If we'd had a man with us, he'd've changed his tune." The bearers were merely beasts of burden, little more than animals. They had no man to protect them and would have to make do with an animal's pen.

Molly went back to the sedan chair and took a small bag of belongings from beside her mother. She pulled the grey blanket up beneath her mother's chin and followed the bearers round to the back of the tower. They settled beneath a bamboo shelter, the roof of which leant at a sharp angle against the whitewashed walls of the mission.

Ah Chien gathered her skirts between her knees and crouched down, sitting on her heels, her feet splayed flat on the floor. She wagged her head from side to side.

"I suppose we cannot blame the priest," she said finally, a note of resignation in her voice. "They are always being attacked. So many of them have been killed. By bandits. By the rebels."

"They shouldn't be here, should they?" said Molly.

Ah Chien said nothing but she had, by now, forgiven the priest not only his nationality, but also his sex and his religion. One of the bearers lit a lamp and placed it on the packed earth before them. Molly watched the wick floating in the oil of the clay dish.

"We're going into the village," the bearer said, and the men left.

"They'll get drunk," said Ah Chien. Her voice was flat and unemotional. It was obvious that she did not care what they did.

Darkness fell across the village and Molly and Ah Chien sat beneath the shelter in silence, watching the dim pool of light spilling over the ground from the oil lamp. There was nothing else for them to look at. Molly listened to the creaking of wood and the sound of the wind blowing across the plain. Ah Chien watched the flame and began to breathe deeply. Molly closed her eyes. She knew the cycle by heart but, even so, she had to listen. The amah controlled her breathing until it became deep and regular. Molly counted first thirty-six breaths, then a pause, and then twenty-four breaths. Ah Chien was meditating, concentrating on the positive and negative elements of the inner fire. Molly felt the trodden floor clammy and damp beneath her. She pushed her hands into the earth and gripped tightly to the soil. In the night, she suddenly needed something more tangible than religion to explain things to her.

Molly was woken twice during the night. The first time was with the drunken return of the bearers who, not content with the restless fatigue induced by alcohol, squatted together in a circle to smoke several soft pellets of opium.

She got up, her back stiff from lying on the hard earth, and walked behind the bearers out to the sedan chair which stood propped against the tower just beyond the shelter. She drew the curtain aside and stepped in beside her mother. Suyong's breath was coming in a hoarse crackle, an echo of the opium pellets being scorched beyond the window. She was delirious, neither sleeping nor awake, and when Molly carried a few drops of water to her mouth in her cupped hands, Suyong pulled her lips away from her teeth but did not have enough energy even to swallow. Molly took a blue silk scarf from her neck and soaked it in the water. She wiped the sweat from her mother's forehead and was frightened by a sudden look of terror in her eyes. Suyong had let her head fall to one side and with the first touch of the cold silk she had snapped her head back to face Molly. She had drawn her eyes wide in fear. Molly snatched her hand away and squeezed the scarf tightly between her fingers. She had to look away from the empty horror in her mother's face because she did not want to see it. She looked at an embroidered dragon and tiger on the curtain and counted to ten. She remembered her mother saying once, "You must be like the tiger, Molly. A positive spirit." She looked at the pattern on the curtain and ran her finger over the raised stitching that marked the tiger's back. When she turned back towards her mother Suyong was slumped again against the corner of the chair where it joined the front wall. Her eyes were closed and she was breathing thickly from deep in her throat. Molly left the sedan chair quietly and walked back to the shelter. Ah Chien stirred slightly in her sleep as Molly lay down again on the packed earth. She listened to the bearers' sporadic conversation and turned onto her side to watch the red points of burning opium as they smoked. The heady smell of the drug wafted into the shelter and she soon drifted off to sleep again, the sweet smoke prickling in her nose.

It was still not light when she woke a second time. Ah Chien was bending over her and calling her name softly. Ah Chien pulled her to her feet and spoke in a reverent whisper.

"Her spirit has left her, missie," she said, and she led her out of the shelter and round to the sedan chair. Molly looked at the corpse beneath the grey blanket.

"The leap into the great emptiness," Ah Chien whispered at her shoulder. She looked up at the dark sky and the stars. "Her spirit will appear now in the heavenly bodies of space," she said with a confidence based on certainty. It was, it seemed, a moment to celebrate. But Molly could not forget her mother's momentary horror and not even Ah Chien with her forty-seven centuries of Taoist teachings would convince her that she should be happy. She began to cry. Ah Chien placed her arm round Molly's shoulder and turned her away from the chair.

"Patience, missie," she said, offering up the only comfort she had. "Patience and endurance."

"She was frightened," said Molly, and the idea of it was terrible.

"No," said Ah Chien, "She has joined the void—the void which is not empty." And she kicked one of the bearers in the ribs. "Let's go!" she said.

They were just under a day's march from the New Territories, Kowloon and Hong Kong and, despite the fact that the priest had reluctantly offered them his burial mound, Molly decided that Suyong's corpse should be delivered up to her father. The priest protested, but half-heartedly. He was glad to be rid of them and their diseased body and, anyway, as he would later explain to the nuns, they were Chinese. Their behaviour was, at best, illogical. Giving them the usual warnings against bandits, he had waved them off, happy to see the back of them.

Molly was uncomfortable in the sedan chair with her mother's lifeless body lying opposite her. She could not bring herself to pull the blanket up over Suyong's face and, although her mother's eyes were closed, she did not look as though she were sleeping. She looked as though she were dead.

Molly tried to, but could not even envisage the void, still less place her mother there. She felt lonely and abandoned and her mother's dead silence only emphasised the finality of existence. She could only think that she was loading her already physically disabled father with the added burden of bringing up a motherless child. And if that were not sufficient, one who did not even resemble him. He would not even have the evidence any more of his Chinese wife to explain away her features.

(ii)

Willard Russell was drinking in the bar of The Parisian Grill on Hong Kong Island when he heard the news that his family was arriving. He was not informed directly. The bearer Molly and Ah Chien had sent on ahead to find him had been stopped at the Chinese border and refused entrance. Even had he managed to overcome this obstacle, he would have had no idea where to look amongst the other 800,000 inhabitants of the Colony and, even if he had been lucky enough to locate Russell, he would never have been allowed inside the European confines of the Parisian Grill. Willard Russell learned of his family's arrival by accident.

He was drinking a gin and water and listlessly thumbing through a two-day-old copy of *The South China Morning Post.* He could not concentrate on reading the news, but at the bottom of the page there was an advertisement which he had read now three or four times:

IMPERIAL AIRWAYS

Fly to England
for the Coronation
in 10 days

£160 single fare

Russell's priorities did not include the new King of England, but what struck him about the advertisement was the fact that you could now get to Europe in ten days. His own journey East had taken the best part of six months.

Suddenly, a group of British soldiers burst noisily into the bar. They called out to Harry Osbourne, a reporter for the Post, who was drinking a Tiger beer half way along the bar between Russell and the soldiers.

"Story for you, Osbourne!" said one of the soldiers. "Bit of a rumpus at the checkpoint out in the New Territories."

"I'm off-duty, Fletcher. I'm not interested," said Harry Osbourne and he continued with his beer.

Ignoring him, Sergeant John Fletcher talked out to no one in particular but to everyone at once. "Three Chinese," he said. "Two women, one corpse, rolled up in a sedan chair, happy as you like. Said they'd started down from Nanking by train but that they'd walked from as far North as Nanchang!"

Willard Russell put down his newspaper and wheeled himself a little closer to the group of soldiers. "Three women?" he asked.

"No," said Fletcher with a grin. "Three Chinese. One of them a young girl! One of them dead!"

Russell drew level with the reporter. "Take me out there with you—Osbourne, is it?"

Harry Osbourne sniffed. "I'm not going out there, mate," he said.

"The Chinese aren't news."

"I'll pay you to take me," said Willard Russell quickly. He did not need to be told that it was his family.

Osbourne stopped drinking and looked at the American. "Pay me?" he said. It was not clear from his tone of voice whether he was offended or considering the offer.

Russell corrected himself quickly: "I mean, buy you a drink, or something."

"I said: I'm off duty," said Osbourne again. He turned his back on Russell, but the American insisted.

"It's my wife," he said. "I know it's my wife."

Osbourne looked again at the American. He had learnt early in life that there was little benefit to be made in worrying about anyone's plight but his own, but something in Russell's desperate expression, or perhaps merely the fact that he was in a wheelchair, prompted him to say, much to the surprise of Sergeant Fletcher, "Go on, then, get me another beer and I'll take you out there. I've got nothing better to do."

"I'd given them up for dead," Russell confessed to Harry Osbourne as they crossed from Hong Kong Island to Kowloon on the Star Ferry.

"Really?" said Osbourne, but he was not listening. He was already regretting his generosity. The sympathy evoked by the wheelchair had not lasted and Osbourne was soon bored by Russell's gushing expressions of love. The sooner he got him to the New Territories and dumped him the better.

"And now they have been brought back to life!" Willard Russell had become talkative in his excitement. He did not care that the reporter was not interested. He thanked God and talked out to the choppy waters of the harbour. "It's over six months since I last saw them. As soon as I'd put them on the train, I knew I'd done the wrong thing. I've been blaming myself ever since. Thought they'd been killed by bandits, or Nationalists or something."

Osbourne was already thinking of what he would do once he was rid of Russell. He was a thirty-four-year-old Englishman. He had a mediocre talent as a writer and he covered the social and sports news of Hong Kong, consisting mainly of horse racing at The Happy Valley Racecourse and polo. He spent most of his time in the bar of the Parisian Grill or in the Glory Hole talking to taxi-girls. He would rather have been there now than gallivanting about the New Territories with a cripple.

As they approached Kowloon the surface of the water became greasy with oil and spattered with refuse. Willard Russell looked off along the lines of sampans which were moored together up to six deep in places. They were the homes for thousands of Chinese who would never step ashore in their lives. They were fishing families, mainly Tanka, but some Hokio. Russell looked across the squalor of the bobbing sampans. The lowest of the low, he said to himself. Banished from the earth. Descendants, the Chinese say, of traitors, all of them unworthy to live on dry land. Persecuted if they tried. Forgive and forget was not, it seemed, a quality of the Chinese.

Osbourne breathed the thick pungent air with distaste. "It's the bloody Chinese," he said, cupping his hands to light a cigarette. "They just tip their waste into the harbour. You'd think they couldn't smell it, wouldn't you? Think they didn't have to live amongst it all."

"It's the same all over," said Russell. He did not like the Englishman's attitude and had no desire to hear his brash opinions. But Osbourne was now speaking about a subject which was dear to his heart.

"Too bloody true, mate!" he said. "I've been there. I've seen it. It's the same bleeding filth in Shanghai, Macao, Singapore—you name it, and it's filthy fucking dirty!"

"I meant, all over the world, Mr Osbourne. London, Marseilles, Lisbon. Anywhere where you have a port and poverty you get the same smells."

Osbourne flicked his cigarette out towards the dark waters of the harbour.

"Smells, maybe," he conceded. "But not this bloody smell!"

Willard Russell decided to ignore him. There was no point in arguing with someone who was so utterly convinced that he was right.

But Osbourne had not finished.

"And they've got the nerve to say that we—the Europeans—are the ones that pong! Bloody cheek that is!"

Willard Russell closed his eyes and thought of Suyong and Molly. He had been living at the Parisian Grill since his arrival in Hong Kong two weeks ago, but now he would have to find them all a house and himself a job. Kowloon was the best bet. It was cheaper and it was away from these damned Europeans.

As the engines of the ferry began to churn the water into an oily froth of dead leaves and cardboard, Osbourne suddenly realised he was going to have to push the American along the steep ramp and onto the quay. He grabbed the handles of the wheelchair bad-temperedly.

"How do you manage with this contraption, mate, when you've got no friends with you?" he asked grumpily.

"The Chinese have always been very kind to me," said Russell, wishing he could have chosen a more agreeable companion to bring him out, but the anticipation he felt at seeing Suyong and Molly again outweighed any disgust he felt at Osbourne's company. And the Englishman was moaning again.

"Can't stand Kowloon!" he was saying, sniffing at the foul stench of rotting fruit and seawater. "Never come here if I can help it."

Willard Russell, though, recognised something else in the smells. They held the pulse of life. Once he had been bundled into the back of a taxi, he settled back to watch the passing shops, run-down, dilapidated shacks, with piles of food still spilling into the street despite the time. Oil lamps flickered softly in the backs of the shops and on the narrow balconies above the street. Osbourne looked straight ahead at the back of the driver's neck, already convinced that they were being cheated.

"He thinks we don't know the way," he said almost smugly, nodding his head towards the driver and he was surprised when Russell addressed the man in Chinese. The driver turned and grinned at the American.

"They're making fun of me," Osbourne thought to himself angrily. "The bastards are laughing at me." He turned to Russell. "Don't speak the lingo, myself," he grunted. "Can't see the point. After all, what the hell could they say that might be of interest?"

The taxi pulled away from the shacks and tenements of Kowloon and out into the New Territories. Darkness had fallen and it was impossible to see the plain which led off into China and Guangzhou to the right of the road. Osbourne wondered again why he had let himself become involved, why he had allowed himself to be dragged out to the New Territories, and he looked across at the American in the back of the car. He could see his sharp profile in the moonlight and was vaguely disconcerted to notice that Willard Russell was smiling. Still, everyone in Hong Kong seemed either to be crazy or a misfit, thought Osbourne, himself included. Willard Russell was just one more.

(iii)

Molly and Ah Chien were waiting on the Chinese side of the border when the headlights from Russell's taxi appeared at the end of the road. Molly paid no attention to the approaching lights. She was staring fixedly at the wall of the Chinese border post. Closed, unvarnished, wooden shutters covered the windows behind the jagged remains of six square panes of glass. Above the window the rotted struts of an elaborate wooden lattice had been replaced by bits of string tied in a criss-cross pattern. Over an hour ago, a young Chinese soldier had slammed the shutters closed and disappeared into the building. Molly had been sent back by the British soldiers to dispose of her mother's body but all the Chinese border guard had said was that it was not a Chinese problem. It was Ah Chien who recognised Willard Russell's voice drifting down to them through the darkness. She pulled Molly towards her and, with an expression which suggested that she expected no less, she said, "Missie, it is your father, at last."

Two British soldiers had called across the narrow strip of no-man's-land between the borders and as Molly began to walk towards the wandering beam of a torch that was coming towards them from about a hundred yards away, the soldiers passed her and walked on towards the barrier. She could hear them talking to the Chinese guards but she was not listening to them. She was concentrating on the wavering light on the road before her. She could hear her father calling her name and calling for Suyong, his voice clear and echoing through the night.

As soon as she could make out her father's shape, Molly ran towards him, throwing herself round his shoulders. Russell squeezed his daughter to him and kissed the top of her head. But when he saw Ah Chien approaching his face fell.

"Ah Chien," he said quietly. "Oh, Christ! Who would have thought...?" And Molly felt him slump back in the wheelchair, his arms limp. "Oh, God!" he hissed in her ear and his head fell forwards. He buried his face in his hands. "I told Osbourne, the soldiers, to dump the body. I mean, I thought...Oh Jesus Christ!"

Molly suddenly realised what was going to happen. She pushed herself away from her father and began to run back down the hill towards the Chinese border.

"I didn't know, you see?" Her father was shouting from behind her. He was more frightened by what he had thought than by the enormity of what he had done. "Molly! I didn't know! I thought it was Ah Chien that was dead!" His voice sounded unnatural and ugly.

Molly reached the barrier across the road in time to see two of her bearers obediently tipping Suyong's lifeless body out of the sedan chair onto a small mound of smouldering refuse beside the rotting corpse of a dead dog.

(iv)

Miss Ruth Dekyvere was making a minestrone. Earlier in the day, she had sent her amah out to buy one carrot, one onion and two cabbage leaves and she was just finishing her frugal boiling of vegetables when Osbourne began to bang on the door of her house. Although he had little more than a nodding acquaintance with Miss Dekyvere,

Osbourne knew that she was the one person in Hong Kong who would not turn them away. She had worked on a mission in Canton until the Nationalist Revolution had caused her belief in God to weaken. There were too many deaths, she said. No God could explain them away. She had arrived in Hong Kong with the sole intention of boarding a P&O liner and returning to her hometown of Bridport but, on her way down to the P&O ticket offices, she had realised that she had nothing and no one to go back to, not even God. She had stayed on in Hong Kong in a bungalow on Victoria Peak like a relic from a different age.

When Miss Dekyvere opened the door of her bungalow she was surprised to see Osbourne, a man she could not recall ever having spoken to, clutching a young Chinese girl in his arms. At first, she did not notice Willard Russell, crumpled and pale in his wheelchair. Her first impulse was to tell them to go away, but her religious training, though debilitated, was still stronger than her intuition.

"Do come in, my dear," she said to Osbourne, stepping away from the door to let him pass. Osbourne sniffed at the faint smell of boiling vegetables and, without asking, located the bedroom, carried Molly through, and dropped her heavily onto the bed. A crucifix hung above the bed, but it had been turned to face the wall. Osbourne looked at the smooth sides of the cross and turned the figure back out to face the room. He grunted self-consciously before returning to the front door. He was dying to get down to the Glory Hole for a drink and a dance or two. Miss Dekyvere and Ah Chien had manoeuvred the wheelchair over the two stone steps of the doorway and parked Russell by a bay window where he could gaze down at the lights of the city of Victoria falling away to the harbour. Osbourne coughed but only Miss Dekyvere seemed to notice.

"Well, my man," she said, insinuating that he was to blame for the whole situation. "I think an explanation is called for."

Osbourne made his explanation as brief as possible and was not disappointed when Miss Dekyvere turfed him out into the street. As he walked down the steep, luxurious, residential street with its high walled gardens and expansive lawns, Osbourne could hear the swishing of hoses watering the lawns while the sun was down. The city itself seemed a long way away. He stopped and looked down the hillside where the lights of the buildings were haphazard and jumbled together, and then on to the harbour and the wide expanse of dark water with the occasional, intermittent, flashing of a police launch or the clutch of yellow that marked out the lozenge shape of one of the Star ferries, and over to the almost uniform chain of lights hugging the opposite shore which was Kowloon. He lit a cigarette, lost in thoughts of what he could have been doing if only he had had more luck in his life, but all his thoughts, whether of the insurance office in Darlington where his father had been a clerk or the rubber plantation in Malaya run by a distant second cousin, seemed to lead him finally to the taxi-tables, the 50 cent vouchers and the dancers at the Glory Hole. Harry Osbourne flicked the stub of his cigarette over to the opposite side of the road and began to walk down the hill towards the harbour. A white Bentley was coming towards him, its headlights on full beam. Osbourne shielded his eyes from the glare and waited as the Bentley turned into the drive next door to Miss Dekyvere's narrow crazy-paving footpath.

"Crazy is right!" Osbourne muttered to himself and he plunged his hands sulkily into his trouser pockets before heading off to the bar.

Miss Dekyvere handed Willard Russell a glass of gin and water.

"It has been rather unfortunate, my dear, hasn't it?" she said, she hoped, kindly.

Willard Russell took the gin. "Is Molly all right?" he asked, twisting in his chair to find her.

"She's sleeping," said Miss Dekyvere, nodding towards the bedroom.

"Some place you got yourself here," said Russell, looking back to the window.

"Yes," said Miss Dekyvere. "It's a nice view."

"Got to see about getting myself a job now," said Willard Russell.

Miss Dekyvere felt she should respond positively.

"Yes," she said. "A job is not only important for the money it gives you. It keeps the mind active, helps us to forget, at least momentarily, the unpleasant things that have happened."

Willard Russell looked across at the old woman. He could not imagine anything unpleasant happening to Miss Dekyvere.

"I must go back tomorrow and try to bury the body at least," he said, sipping at his gin and running his tongue along his bottom lip. Miss Dekyvere, he noticed, finally sat down. She clasped her hands round her knees and leaned forwards as if about to impart a confidence.

"The girl, then, shall stay with me," she said, adding as an afterthought, "Poor little mite!"

Russell did not know whether he should accept or protest. Finally, he just grunted. Miss Dekyvere stood up again and ran her hands down the front of her loose, cotton dress. She bent slightly towards him as though talking to a small child.

"And besides which," she said with a smile, "We have a wedding tomorrow. My neighbour, Chen Liew, is marrying—oh, dear, what is her name?—some girl from Kowloon, a beautiful girl, but not the same class at all, it seems." Nor the same age, she might have added. She walked across to a small, delicately carved, walnut coffee table in the centre of the room and picked up the stiff gilded card of a wedding invitation. "Tung Nien!" she said triumphantly.

"The stirring of a thought," Russell said absently.

"What's that?"

"Tung Nien. It means 'the Stirring of a Thought'."

Miss Dekyvere was impressed. Not many Westerners ever bothered to master even the most simple phrases. "You speak Chinese?"

"Cantonese," said Russell, "And a little Tanka."

"Well," said Miss Dekyvere, replacing the card on the table, "That is nice. But, now, I think it is time for bed."

Willard Russell lay awake for a long time listening to the insects whistling and hissing in the garden and the trees beyond his window. He lay watching the slow ceiling fan because every time he closed his eyes he could see Suyong's lifeless body falling onto the smouldering tip beside the fly-infested corpse of the dog. He could not see her beautiful and alive no matter how hard he tried and the only way to rid himself of her dead was to lie awake watching the fan. He felt an enormous emptiness somewhere between the pit of his stomach and his chest that engulfed him. He found he began to repeat her name to himself over and over again, as though that might somehow take him nearer to her or bring her back to him, but even as he lay there mouthing her name he knew that it was partly remorse, partly the fact that he blamed himself for sending her on such a journey. Had he not sent her, she would not have died. And every time he turned over in the bed to sleep, the welling sadness began again in his chest and forced him to open his eyes. There were moments when it all seemed unreal, when he could not believe that it had actually happened, when he could think that he would wake in the morning and find that there had been some dreadful mistake and that Suyong was still with him. If only I could see her alive just once more, he said to himself. Though what would be the point of that? What could he possibly do with her to atone for sending her on such a perilous journey? What would he say or do? No. There was nothing except the emptiness of her no longer being there and the regret for all the things he should have done. He should have been with her when she had died. At least he might have comforted her in some way, held her close to him, spoken to her. He watched the shadow of the fan moving slowly across the ceiling and tried to remember things about her to take forward with him in his life without her. He wished he could cry and have done with it but his tears stuck in his throat. Molly has not even realised it has happened, he said to himself, thinking of his daughter's calm brown eyes looking up at him on the dusty road above the border crossing. She knows it has happened because it was she who saw it, she who travelled with Suyong when she was sick, and she who brought him the body. But she does not know it as a reality. It is a gap as it is for me, but I know that, no matter what else happens, it will never be filled again. And what shall I say to her when she asks, "Why did she have to die?"

Willard Russell turned away from the fan. Suyong, Suyong, Suyong, he said to himself over and over again.

The preparations for the wedding in the garden next door had already begun by the time Willard Russell finally abandoned any attempt at sleeping. He pushed himself to a seated position in the bed and propped a pillow at the small of his back. He looked morosely through the bedroom window as first light picked out the damp petals of the flowers in the high part of Miss Dekyvere's tidy and meticulously planted garden. He looked across the flowers to a small square lawn which led away to a high wooden fence. He could see enough of the garden to notice that it was only where Chen Liew's property bordered Miss Dekyvere's that it ceased to be protected by a white-washed stone wall worthy of Stanley Prison itself. In his present mood the fact did not strike him as anything more than slightly odd. That a wooden gate communicated the two gardens went, at first, unnoticed as he watched the turbaned heads of half-a-dozen Indian servants struggling with a huge tarpaulin at the far end of Chen Liew's garden where it began to climb away and disappear into the luxuriously rich foliage of Victoria Peak.

(v)

In the front room on the fourth floor of a crowded flat in one of the teeming tenements in The Walled City of Kowloon, Tung Nien was being dressed in a red cheongsam made of shot silk. Rather than look past the rotting, but ornately carved, balustrade of the balcony where she would see only misery and poverty, Tung Nien looked at the very beautiful reflection of herself which seemed to glow with a soft silver light of its own from within the tarnished glass of a mirror being held by one of her six younger sisters. The face that looked back at her was quietly confident and certain that what was about to happen—her marriage with Chen Liew—was no more than she deserved. Her dark hair had been pulled away from her face and was tied in a tight bun beneath a head-dress made from a sweeping loop of black velvet decorated with pink orchids and pearls. Three small rough river pearls laced with fishing wire had been plaited through her hair above her right temple and, hanging from the left corner of her head-dress, joined by seven perfect pear-shaped pearls threaded onto a gold chain, was a cascade of round pearls of varying sizes that clicked together as she moved her head from side to side.

"Like an abacus," said her sister.

Tung Nien ignored the comment, although her sister had not meant to insult her. The chain of pearls lay across her breast and rose and fell with her breathing.

They had wanted to whiten her face but Tung Nien had refused. Now, free of make-up save for a little colouring on her lips, her face, framed by the pink orchids and the creamy whiteness of the pearls, glowed with dignity, youth and beauty. She had, she knew, no need of artifice.

It was her mother who brought the small leather box containing the gold filigree earrings. She chattered excitedly as she clumsily tried to thread the clip—the curled tongue of a dragon—through Tung Nien's pierced ears. She had no idea of the value of the jewellery—it might have been a sliver of bamboo between her rheumy fingers—but she was entranced by the reflected light and almost liquid colour of the gold. Tung Nien smiled kindly at all of them and accepted their unspoken adulation because she deserved it. It was not just anyone who could be plucked from the seething beehive of The Walled City, with its labyrinth of narrow, rat-infested streets, and be whisked away to the exuberant luxury of The Peak. Indeed, it was doubtful whether any of Tung Nien's family had actually seen The Peak as anything more important than a green mountain on the other side of the harbour. How could she expect them to understand the tremendous significance of this twenty-minute trip across the water? And anyway, what did it matter? When she left The Walled City this morning she would be leaving it, not as the daughter of a poor rickshaw owner, but as the wife of Chen Liew, one of the most important men in the Colony and owner of one of its oldest businesses.

Although Chen Liew had made no secret of Tung Nien's penurious background, one condition of the wedding was that she should turn her back forever on her family. Instead of being invited to the ceremony, Tung Nien's parents, her six sisters and three brothers, would, later in the day, be shipped out to Cheung Chau, one of the outlying islands, where they would begin a new life, the sons as fishermen on a junk which Chen Liew had provided for them and moored at the quay in Cheung Chau harbour, and Fu Yuen, her father, as keeper of the Temple of the Jade Vacuity, the main purpose of which was, perhaps appropriately, to exorcise wandering and malicious ghosts. The arrangement suited everybody.

When she stood up and asked her sister to incline the mirror a little, Tung Nien had already begun to live in a different world. The jewellery on her head-dress alone was worth more than her father had managed to scrape together in his entire life. Yet her family danced and bowed around her. Far from resenting her good fortune or regretting the fact that they would never see her again, they revered her. She felt powerful. And why not? she thought. After all, she had brought them all solace and comfort; she had, by marrying Chen Liew, not only resolved her own future but she had assured for them a life of relative ease.

And so it was not a tearful farewell. Fu Yuen even consented to use his rickshaw for one last, short journey. He pulled his radiant daughter, momentarily covered from head to foot by a cautious, plain green cloth, from the confines of The Walled City out to Chen Liew's waiting Bentley where, with a casual wave of his hand and a grin of genuine pleasure, he said good-bye to her forever.

(vi)

From the sanctuary of his sprawling house above The Happy Valley Racecourse, higher even on The Peak than Chen Liew's respectable mansion, Eliot Rodmell, his mind only half-concentrating on the neat row of printed figures before him on his desk, called out bad-temperedly to his wife, Margaret.

"You'd think they'd make less of a show about it, wouldn't you?"

But his wife, who was arranging a bridge four for the evening, was not really listening.

"And when you think about it," Eliot Rodmell went on, wetting his lips as though in preparation for an important announcement, "She is basically no more than a tart."

Rodmell disliked on principle anything which took the attention of the Colony away from his own carefully chosen and select circle.

"A very beautiful tart," his wife called back from the other room, rather too breezily, he thought.

"You'd think he'd have enough on his mind," Rodmell turned his eyes back to the rows of neat, black numbers, "without lumbering himself with a wife as well."

Margaret Rodmell did not notice the insult but she stopped struggling with the improbable pairings she had made for her evening party and put her head round the door of her husband's study.

"Whatever do you mean, Eliot?" she asked, though he could tell she did not really care.

"I mean," he said, pausing again in his scrutiny of the figures, and making it patent by the stiff way in which he turned to face her that he was, at the very least, put out at having to answer her at all, let alone enter into details. "I mean with these figures." And he shook the paper ominously.

Margaret Rodmell shrugged. "I think you are just upset because he didn't invite you, us, rather, to the wedding," she said over her shoulder.

"I would have refused had he had the audacity to do so," said Eliot Rodmell as though stating an obvious and irrefutable fact.

"You would have loved it!" His wife's voice sang back from the distant reaches of the house, somewhere from the direction of the kitchen. Eliot Rodmell satisfied himself with a grunt which brought a faint taste of bacon to his mouth. He swallowed quickly before it also became poached egg and looked down again at the rows of numbers before him on his desk. Opium sales into China were down by fifteen per cent on figures from the last quarter. If his sales had fallen off by fifteen per cent he could safely say that Chen Liew's losses would be as great, if not greater. Of course, it was easy to blame the Japanese. It was easy to blame the unrest and the uncertainty caused by the recent bombing of Shanghai and whether or not it would stop at that, or might they not now continue to move south? Who would stop them? Chiang Kai Shek and his Kuomintang? Mao Zedong and his Communists? No. Even if they had decided to stop fighting each other, they were unlikely to be a match for the Imperial Japanese Army. The international community through its fragile mouthpiece The League of Nations? No. Anyway, it was not that. The Japanese had very little to do with it. New competition, that was the only explanation. Chen Liew and he were suddenly being faced by a common enemy, an intruder in their carefully guarded monopoly. Since the Second Opium War of 1860, the selling of opium to China had been virtually the exclusive right of two families, the Rodmells and the Liews, and it had lived a relatively untroubled existence. Eliot Rodmell found he was grinding his teeth as he thought perhaps he had been over hasty in tearing the stiff card of the wedding invitation into thin strips to use for lighting his pipe.

(vii)

Not all the European community had refused to attend the wedding, for not all of them shared either Eliot Rodmell's prejudice or his knowledge as to the source of Chen Liew's fortune. Dr Alfred Laughton and his wife, Mary, were quite happy to believe it all came from a large factory near Prince Edward Road in Sanpokong which manufactured propelling pencils. Of course, they had, like everyone else on the island, heard the rumours which referred to Chen Liew as the Head of the Dragon, the leader of a Triad Group but, like everyone else, they preferred to ignore them. "Leave well alone," was the unspoken motto of the European community when referring to anything Chinese.

Laughton and his wife were standing at the bottom of the garden by the high stone wall and drinking champagne when they noticed Miss Deyvere walking purposefully across the lawn towards the house, pulling a young Chinese girl along behind her by the hand. Dr Alfred Laughton smiled to himself at this flagrant breach of Colonial etiquette, but his wife was not amused. It was well known that Miss Dekyvere mixed not only with the rich Chinese, which was not to be encouraged but could be tolerated, but also with those whose social standing was far from acceptable. It was also rumoured that she allowed her Indian gardener into the house to shower after his day's work. Such flaunting of the established order could only give rise to problems sooner or later, thought Mary Laughton.

"It wouldn't matter quite so much if she didn't always insist on being so public," she decided finally, and they watched as Miss Dekyvere actually kissed Chen Liew on the cheek. More as a result of emotional inertia, from an unwillingness to contradict, Alfred Laughton shared his wife's offence and tutted. He clicked his tongue against the back of his teeth. In fact, however, his attitude to the Chinese was far more liberal than his wife could have imagined. More than once he had managed to escape from the claustrophobic, imperialistic atmosphere of the Chess Federation or the Royal Hong Kong Golf Club at Deep Water Bay and he had crossed the harbour to Kowloon to seek out the more lively company of the British soldiers in the Bottoms Up Club or the Glory Hole. But, finally, even that bored him and it was then that he would walk alone along Ferry Street and into the Yau Ma Tei District to find one of the tiny, open sampans where, with the clicking of Mah-jongg tiles from the other sampans moored around him accompanying his efforts, he would satisfy his lust and try to ease his loneliness with one of the young girls from the floating city. He sometimes thought that, more than the sex, he enjoyed the obvious danger entailed in returning to dry land, hopping from one sampan to another, knowing that, at any moment, he might be set upon and killed and that no one would be any the wiser. The Floating City of Yau Ma Tei not only had its one-girl sampans. It was, as its name suggested, a city. It had dentists, schools, barbers, and apothecaries. It had its own particularly ruthless law-enforcement brigade. Alfred Laughton knew of at least three cases of Europeans who had last been seen gingerly stepping across the bobbing sampans in the company of a young girl.

"And you know what she said the other day, don't you?" His wife's voice brought him back to the wedding party rather more suddenly and stridently than he would have liked. "It was quite funny, really. I was out walking with Beth Hartley—of course, she couldn't see the funny side!—and her two children and we bumped into old Miss Dekyvere." Mary Laughton almost gulped at her champagne and swallowed quickly as she sensed her husband's attention wandering. "She bent down," she went on, choking back the bubbles that were rising in her throat, "and said, if you please, to Beth: 'Oh, how nice! One dark one and one blond one! Both from the same father?'"

Alfred Laughton smiled but could not see the relevance.

"But of course she knew!" said his wife emphatically.

"I'm only surprised the Rodmells aren't here," Dr Laughton said yawning and looking for a suitable place to dispose of his half-empty champagne glass. "Shall we?" he said, and offered his wife his arm so that they should mingle. Miss Dekyvere saw them coming and pushed Molly away inside the house.

Molly felt awkward. She pulled off the pink tasselled and tinselled head-dress that Miss Dekyvere had miraculously, but unnecessarily, resurrected that morning from a leather trunk, and began to walk off down a long, empty corridor that ran the entire length of the house. After the noise of the garden party the house seemed unnaturally quiet. She could hear a woman's voice coming from somewhere near the end of the corridor.

Thousands of red papers had been pinned for luck along the whole length of the corridor. The corners of the papers curled outward as though they were damp, and the red Chinese characters all proclaimed the same message of congratulation and goodwill. Half way along the corridor in a gap in the seemingly endless stream of papers and set in its own perfumed forest of joss sticks was a *pat kwa* octagonal mirror. It had been placed there to keep away evil spirits and to keep Chen Liew and his family from harm. Molly stood on tiptoe and looked at herself in the round circle at the centre of the three octagonal rows of the gilt framework. What she saw did not please her. Miss Dekyvere had given her a pair of dangling pearl ear-rings, had swept her long hair into a bun and painted her lips in a raspberry coloured lipstick. Molly scowled into the *pat kwa* mirror and continued on along the corridor. She could hear the woman's voice clearly now. It was coming from an open door at the far end of the corridor.

"I want to know why he is not happy," the voice was saying calmly, but with a potential for sudden anger. A man's voice, soft and subservient to the point of being indistinct, answered in a muffled whisper. Molly crept a little closer to the open door. She saw, seated inside at what seemed to be an elaborately decorated shrine, the most beautiful woman she had ever seen. Her face was turned slightly away from the door and the light from the window settled on her cheek like a faint dusting of talcum powder. It was the bride—Tung Nien. Molly stood at the door, transfixed by the vision of beauty that she saw before her. She was immediately surprised that the old man, Chen Liew, was marrying such a young bride. She did not notice a cold, even cruel glint of determination in Tung Nien's eyes because it was already beginning to melt to match the soft glow of her cheeks when she stood up and, on seeing Molly, began to walk towards the door, her hands outstretched to grasp her by the cheeks.

"But what have we here, Ying? She's so lovely she could be my sister!"

Ying, Chen Liew's fifty-year-old housekeeper, remained inscrutable. He did not even turn to look at her.

"The daughter of a *gweilo*,"[1] he said coldly.

"But look, Ying!" Tung Nien insisted that he turn to see. "She could be my sister. Look! Even down to the pearls!"

Ying turned obediently, placed his hands together before his chest and bowed.

"Your sister," he agreed. "Yes."

It was not his place to point out that not one of Tung Nien's six

---

[1] Gweilo—Foreign devil —used as an insult.

sisters bared even the slightest resemblance to Molly, but it was true that neither did they resemble Tung Nien. Molly, bedecked in pearls and painted raspberry lipstick, her dark hair tight on the back of her head, did, on the other hand, look like the bride.

"But what is she doing here?" Tung Nien continued to speak to Ying whilst holding Molly's face in her hands. Before Ying could reply, Molly, carefully taking Tung Nien's hands in her own and lowering them to her sides, said, "I am with the *saiyahn*,[2] Miss Dekyvere. My father has gone to bury my mother in the New Territories. Ah Chien says she will not be buried well. She will not have favourable breezes if my father does it because, you see, my father does not know." She thought for a moment and then added by way of explanation, "And besides, he is upset."

"Your father does not know what?" asked Tung Nien softly.

"My father is American," said Molly. "Ah Chien says he does not understand the winds. My mother will not be buried well, she says, because for them, for the gweilos, it is not important. They bury them like dogs, she says, or worse."

"Ying!" Tung Nien called, although he stood at her shoulder. "Something must be done!"

And so Ying was dispatched to look for Willard Russell and the hapless Harry Osbourne, who had once more been roped in as wheelchair pusher—"Feel like a flaming rickshaw boy," he had moaned—and to ensure that Suyong was given a fitting burial site. By the time he and Russell were brought back to the party, the celebrations had disintegrated and the guests had formed isolated groups. The Chinese were involved in noisy games of mah-jongg, the ivory bricks clacking and banging on the wrought-iron garden tables, and the Europeans had drifted into aimless groups which were trying to communicate and which, in the absence of anything more important than the Japanese aggressions as a subject, were getting steadily more and more drunk, losing, at the same time, that colonial dignity which defined

[2] Saiyahn —Western person

all of their excursions into the outside world. Dr Alfred Laughton having, as always, Mary said, had just one whisky too many, was even on the point of becoming downright objectionable—he was going to launch into a defence of Mao's Communists—when he was stunned into silence by the unexpected appearance of Osbourne staggering out of the white Bentley, a glass of champagne already in his hand.

"My God!" he hissed at his wife and then with a grin at Nurse Gemmell. "What the hell is he doing here? We wouldn't even invite him to the annual dinner and dance of the Bird Watching Society!"

Mary Laughton wondered whether her husband were attempting a joke, albeit, to her mind, a feeble one. Still unsure as to his intentions, she decided to ignore the comment but she cast a disapproving eye anyway over the unfortunate Osbourne. Antonia Gemmell, who had travelled to the Far East in search of a husband, did likewise. And then a limp figure was lifted bodily from the car.

"What in God's name...?" Mary Laughton began, but seeing it was an invalid, fell into an embarrassed silence and turned her attention to the flowerbed nestling beneath the wall. Nurse Gemmell was not so cautious.

"The poor man!" she said, grabbing, as she did so, Dr Alfred Laughton by the arm. Once extricated from Nurse Gemmell's impulsive and clammy grasp, Alfred Laughton excused himself.

"I need a bloody drink!" he said. "This damned Chinese food—it sticks your gums together!"

"Personally, I like it," Antonia Gemmell said to his back but her attention was focussed firmly on Willard Russell and his wheelchair. She thought he looked washed out and grey, as though he might have spent the night travelling somewhere, and she immediately felt sorry for him. His disability was a trigger for deep emotions. Harry Osbourne was, she regretted, brash and as unwelcome as ever. You could even see where he had sweated into his shirt. Dark stains looped beneath his arms and had settled into the small of his back. And he did not seem to care, for here he was, a beery grin on his face, loping towards them across the grass.

"Quite a hullabaloo!" he said, evidently pleased at something. "A

Chinese stabbed on the Kowloon to Canton railway! Talk about all go! We nearly couldn't get through. Harland's soldier boys are out, the Chinese have taken it into their own hands and cordoned off the station. If it hadn't been for old Ying they'd never've let us through onto the ferry."

"They are always killing each other," said Mary Laughton cautiously, and she looked up at Nurse Gemmell and added for reassurance, "Aren't they?"

"This one worked for Tang!" said Osbourne, touching the side of his nose. The importance of this fact was lost on the women. Osbourne insisted. "The Tangs of Kat Him Wai!" Picking up Laughton's discarded champagne glass and tipping the remnants into his own he continued. "Rumour has it," he said, in a confidential whisper, "that the Tangs have moved into the opium market!"

"Do you think I could have a scotch and soda to wash this down?" Dr Laughton had gravitated towards the house and was picking at a bowl of prawn crackers. Whilst waiting for his drink he cast his eyes languidly over the crowded garden. "Quite a turn out!" he said to himself, hooking his tongue into his teeth and chewing thoughtfully. Even the Chairman of the Hong Kong and Shanghai Bank had come, he noticed, for there was Sir Vandeleur Grayburn himself by the hibiscus talking to Major Harland, Walker, the Colonial Secretary, and Da Souza, the Portuguese Consul from Macao.

Laughton looked away from this little group which represented the most illustrious guests, for he suddenly saw that a little wizened Chinese with tired eyes was toiling up the drive, seemingly unaware of the attention he was drawing to himself. He was wearing the traditional dark *samfoo* of the Hakka people and he looked totally out of place so far from the paddy fields of the New Territories. The wedding guests turned to stare at the little man as though they might never have seen a Chinese peasant before and the conversations and pleasantries they had until so recently been sharing suddenly died out to be replaced by an expectant and heavy silence.

"Damnedest thing!" said Laughton taking his whisky and soda and stepping forward slightly, unable to take his eyes away from the incongruous visitor.

The Hakka took an interminably long time to struggle up the steep drive to the house and this was so emphasised by the silence that accompanied him that Laughton was inclined to think that perhaps the little man had always been there, caught in mid-stride half-way up the hill, but that he had just failed to notice him until now. He looked at the clear blue sky and then back to the baking concrete drive and he willed the Chinaman to arrive so that he might continue with his drink without drawing attention to himself for any sudden movement would, he knew, break the strange, timeless spell that had settled over the garden and held it still as a photograph or a painted scene from the Chinese opera. The Hakka drew his thin lips away from his mouth and his breath caught in harsh gasps at his throat. You would have been forgiven for thinking he had walked the twenty miles from Kat Him Wai although in the silence the soft purring of a car engine could be heard from beyond the garden wall.

As he neared the veranda and the arched entrance to the house where Chen Liew waited, flanked by two obvious bodyguards, the Hakka took a creased paper from the pocket of his pyjama-like jacket and flipped it open with a surprisingly agile flick of his wrist. He waved it towards Chen Liew and said something which Laughton's non-existent knowledge of Cantonese did not allow him to understand. He did notice, however, as did all the other guests, that the paper was not the traditional lucky red. Without knowing quite why, Laughton felt uncomfortable and he was pleased to see that Harland, Walker and Da Souza looked equally embarrassed. Only Harry Osbourne drank on regardless.

One of Chen Liew's men took the piece of paper from the Hakka's hand and walked with it back into the shade of the veranda. The Hakka turned and began his long descent towards the waiting car. Laughton found he was letting out a huge sigh of relief as though he himself might have been instrumental in averting some moment of almost tangible danger. Now, the danger past, he drank greedily at his whisky and soda, quite happy to be ignorant as to its cause and eager to return to his wife to discuss the significance of what had just happened.

A buzz of excitement swept around the garden. Each group of guests exploded into conversation. It was as if a line of firecrackers had been set off round the garden until the initial overloud voices died down a little, order was restored and the party continued its natural course where congratulations were dropped like confetti on the happy couple and the guests, a little the worse for drink, finally drifted away to their own isolated bungalows and houses on the lower slopes of the Victoria Peak for an afternoon's sleep before having to face the rigours of the evening.

(viii)

Tung Nien was watching her husband as he undressed for bed. The love and romance she had anticipated for her wedding night had slowly evaporated during the day as Chen Liew's face had grown steadily more sullen. The strange Miss Dekyvere had taken her to one side before leaving with the young Chinese girl and her father, late in the afternoon, long after all the other guests had gone and had said, her face at the same time serious and gentle, "People tend to think, my dear, that Chen Liew has sacrificed the passion and passionate flow of life to the subtleties of the intellect—the heart to the head, as it were. I do not believe this to be true. Indeed, the very fact that he has chosen you to be his bride gives me a very good indication that his heart is very much at the centre of his actions. Do try to treat it well." She might think differently if she could see him now, thought Tung Nien to herself but, in an effort to at least draw herself closer to her husband and whatever it was that was so upsetting him, she said, "Shall I prepare you a pipe?" already reaching for the small needle and pasty pellet of opium that lay in an open ivory box on the bedside table.

Chen Liew turned towards her and his face looked old and tired. Slowly, it softened for the first time since the unexpected visit of the Hakka peasant. He walked over to the bed, smiled, took her face in his hands and kissed her on the lips. "No," he said softly. "I have had enough of opium for one day. And besides which, drugs dull your sense and your desire. I want to be aware of everything, to go into every corner of your body. I want to be like the lamp which illuminates everything, which lights up even the backs of the petals of the plum flowers."

Tung Nien relaxed in his arms and lay back unashamedly naked on the bed. "Is that a poem?" she asked laughing. The words had sounded uncomfortable in his mouth.

"I think it was once," he said laughing too. "Until I changed it. I have been practising saying it for days. It sounded better when I was alone." He began to run his fingers over her stomach and kissed her again on the lips.

"I was never alone at home," she said, returning his kisses. "I even had to sleep with my sisters. One of my greatest dreams has always been to have a room of my own. To be able to sit and listen to the silence, with no one to tell me what to do, and nothing to be done. I think I should like it."

Chen Liew pulled himself away from her slightly and, still caressing her body with the tips of his fingers, he shook his head. "I lived alone in a village with only my shadow for company," he said. "Who was there then to listen to my orders?"

Tung Nien smiled but she was hardly listening to him. She closed her eyes and allowed his hands to roam across her body a little nervously at first and then with more conviction. She raised her back slightly from the bed and led his hand down and between her legs, pulling his mouth up to her breasts and squeezing his head to her with both hands. "Now I am here to give your orders for you," she whispered in his ear. "And all you have to worry about is me."

She felt powerful and strong. She could almost taste his submission to her in his mouth as they kissed. She could feel his dependence on her in the grubbing of his fingers as he rushed and strained to push himself inside her, clumsily prising into her until she felt she would split apart before accepting him. Then suddenly he was gentle and tender and small and she could feel her body contract and mould itself to him until it seemed to be about to engulf him utterly in a shuddering rush of passion. But he was already pulling away from her.

Chen Liew rubbed his hands over his eyes. "I'm sorry," he said in embarrassment, covering his nakedness with the sheet. He looked at her for a moment and then shook his head before standing and making for the door. Before leaving the room he turned to face her. "I am not used to such beauty," he said simply.

Tung Nien lay back on the bed and felt hot. A sticky breeze blew in through the slatted blinds of the window and settled the perspiration on her body. The bed had been made with a single silk sheet and he had taken it with him, not realising in his haste to leave that she would be left naked. She listened to the sounds in the house, a clock down the hall and, from somewhere out towards the inner courtyard, the tinny, tinkling bells to keep away evil. It was so silent compared to the massive noise she was used to in the tenement that she knew that the lack of human sounds would keep her from sleeping. She got up from the bed and slipped a silk kimono around her shoulders, tying it loosely at her waist.

"So many things have happened today," she told herself as she walked quietly to the bedroom window and pulled the bamboo blind away from the glass, just enough to look out obliquely into the darkness of the garden, "that it is not surprising that you cannot sleep." But as she walked around the long empty corridors of the enormous house and as she peeked into more rooms than she could have imagined existed beneath one roof, it was not the excitement of the new life she could see stretching away before her that was foremost in her mind, nor the difficulties she would have in adapting, not only to this new life of luxury, but also to the customs of the strange foreigners she had seen in the garden—what she most worried about as she crept through the darkened mansion was the fact that she had realised that she hardly knew her husband at all. She stopped where Molly had stopped earlier in the day, half way down the main corridor that led away from the front door of the house, and stood in front of the *pat kwa* mirror. If she moved her head a little below the height of the mirror she could see the full moon reflected in its three octagonal bands. She stood, then, to her full height and looked into the central circle of the mirror. She smiled at her reflection, but it was more a smile of resignation than of happiness.

2

"Sun and Moon follow their course
and it is now hot, now cold."

(i)

Life on The Peak was unaffected by the wedding and virtually unaffected by the nearby war in China. Every evening during the Spring of 1938 the elevated train, the Peak Tramway, was filled with hot English businessmen and rich Chinese making their way home up to the cooler slopes above the city where they shared the hillside with the military and their flags and uniforms. The Australian jockeys still won all the races at The Happy Valley Racecourse, the English Civil Servants played tennis in the afternoons and the Rodmells entertained lavishly on Sundays after Evensong. The wild monkeys in the bamboo and stunted pine forests round Bowen Road could still sometimes be heard screeching out to each other at dusk and the sparrowhawks and kites floated elegantly out over the harbour towards Stonecutters Island. The Great Men of Hong Kong followed the course of the birds and crossed the water to meet at The Peninsula Hotel. There, they continued to take afternoon tea as though the Japanese forces were not already dangerously close, just across the border. Their only concession to the nearby war was a disinterested discussion of the emergency regulations recently issued by the Governor which were designed to ensure the Colony's neutrality. The Governor's communiqué had made it plain that neither Japanese nor Chinese ships were to be repaired or welcomed in the harbour. The Government had passed legislation which gave it the power to ban meetings and processions if they were suspected of being seditious. This meant that the Chinese had to meet each other in groups of fewer than six people. At the same time, the Chinese newspapers began to suffer heavy censorship and any reference to the nearby war, its illnesses and refugees was automatically deleted for the common good. As Major Harland pointed out, "It would only provoke undue and unnecessary nervousness amongst the civil population." Food prices were officially controlled and the Government had assumed the power to intern Chinese and Japanese combatants who attempted to take refuge in the colony.

The Great Men looked at the steam launches and the motor boats pulling away from the wharf outside the Peninsula Hotel, and they yawned and decided that, however difficult, life must go on. Further along the waterfront, the red brick tower of the railway station stood out amidst the cluttered buildings like a Victorian cathedral and the trains chugged through the suburbs of Kowloon, carrying their freight first into Canton and then on into the heart of unoccupied China. The Sikh policemen and the Punjabi soldiers kept guard outside the barracks and the Japanese barber at The Peninsula Hotel drank sake and recited haiku when he had drawn the shutters down before his shop.

The fortune tellers, the geomancers and the fung shui men, the calligraphers, the smugglers and the apothecaries worked through the hours of daylight in the packed, secretive tenements of Kowloon, and the whores and the taxi-girls took ingenuous soldiers to their beds and boats for a few grubby dollars.

Out in the New Territories, the walled villages, the monasteries and the temples lay impenetrable and silent while on the plains the peasants watered their crops and stood knee-deep in the stagnant mud of the paddy fields. But beneath this apparent normality, the underworld was seething. Eliot Rodmell knew it, but he told his wife that it was a problem for the Chinese to solve. Which they did.

The knifing of the Chinese on the train, which so nearly prevented Russell and Osbourne arriving at the wedding, and the strange and unexpected visit of the Hakka peasant, had been two sides of the same coin and had borne out Eliot Rodmell's suspicion that a new competitor had joined the opium trade. Tang had chosen the day of Chen Liew's wedding to send him an ultimatum. There could either be an agreement between the two of them or an underground war. Pride, at first, had made Chen Liew resist, but finally, seeing that the only person who would benefit from a Chinese struggle for power would be Rodmell, he had called a meeting with Tang and a temporary truce had been arranged.

Chen Liew was particularly happy on the morning of April 19th, 1938, because he had resolved the last of his differences with the Tangs of Kat Him Wai. The drug trade into China was now divided into three parts, weighted in favour of Rodmell and himself, but including Tang. But, at least, he said to himself, they had avoided yet another Opium War which could only ever lead to killing and unrest.

Tung Nien had never believed that propelling pencils kept them in the lap of luxury but neither had she stopped to wonder overmuch where their money came from. After all, nobody lived on The Peak if they had only one string to their bow. What was it Miss Dekyvere had said the other day?—"Rich people are seldom as rich as they make out they are, except here in Hong Kong, where they are richer."

When Chen Liew had picked her out that night from the cloud of girls clustered around his table, she had expected, at most, a small jade ornament for her favours. But he had not even wanted to take her to bed. Walking along the quay by the Peninsula Hotel, two bodyguards half-a-dozen paces behind them, he had said only, "We are two small people in this world. How extraordinary that we should have met at all!" And she had been more impressed by the bodyguards than by him. Although his age demanded her respect, he was a small, serious man who did not invite passion. Now, though, his face was alive. He had forgotten to treat her with the distant sensitivity of a poem and he was talking to her as an equal, someone who shared his problems and his success.

"Of course, Rodmell was reluctant at first," he was saying, "But when I offered him an extra five per cent..."

"From where?" she asked suddenly.

"We have more than enough with less," he said, reaching his hand out to touch her cheek. He smiled indulgently, wanting her to share in his happiness.

But she frowned and said, "So, the Taipan won!"

"It is not a question of winning, Tung Nien," he said, "It is a question of survival."

She was slightly amused by the sincere expression on his face but because she still wanted more than anything else to please him she decided to drop the subject of Eliot Rodmell and she leaned forward to accept a kiss.

Her indignation, she knew, was principally a product of boredom. She had not left The Peak since her marriage for her husband had forbidden it. "You have everything you need here," Chen Liew had said to her, "And what you don't have, I shall bring for you." She had lived eight months of exactly the kind of inactivity she had always dreamed about during the years she had lived in the crowded tenements of Kowloon, with only sporadic interruptions from Miss Dekyvere to break the monotony. Now, though, she had grown tired of it. Her mind was in danger of atrophying. She no longer got the same simple pleasure from merely sitting beneath a sunshade and watching the minutes tick away, allowing the sticky heat of midday to almost hypnotise her into a waking void with the minutes still ticking away somewhere at the back of her mind but swallowed occasionally by the buzzing of insects. She needed now to begin to think again, she needed to concentrate her attention on something or someone. She needed, more than anything, company.

"But surely, you have Miss Dekyvere!" Chen Liew was genuinely surprised at her complaint. He looked into her eyes and tried to see more than just the reflection of himself looking at her.

"Miss Dekyvere! What kind of company do you suppose she can give me?"

So as not to lose the tenuous hold of love, he kissed her again. She did not pull away, but neither did she surrender herself to him as he would have liked. He was concerned because he had taken it for granted that she was happy and that she would always be so. And he was confused because he did not understand why she was not.

"Miss Dekyvere is an extraordinary woman," was all he could think of to say.

Tung Nien sighed and said, "I want to go out." She pointed across the lawn to the huge white walls and the closed gate. "I want to walk through there and shop, or visit, or just have tea. I want to go to that little bar in Mongkok where the old men take their birds down in cages and hang them on the walls. I want to be able to sit there in the shade, listen to the birds sing, and see that life is still going on—even if it is without me."

It was Chen Liew now who sighed. "I don't think you quite understand the complications," he began. "Or perhaps the dangers." He thought for a moment and looked with her towards the gate. "Let us compromise," he said finally. "I shall bring you the company you choose."

Tung Nien knew that Chen Liew, despite his generosity and will to please her, would refuse to accept any of the girls she had known before.

"Bring me Molly," she said, because she could think of no one else.

Chen Liew merely stood up and said, "Molly. The girl Miss Dekyvere took under her wing for a while." He found it neither a strange request nor a subject worthy of further discussion.

(ii)

With the death of his wife, Willard Russell had begun to drink heavily. He had found a squalid tenement block where he set up home for Molly and himself. The little money he had managed to smuggle south to Nanking was soon squandered, but he scraped together enough to buy them food by setting himself up as a scribe in the compound. He sat outside the tenement in the street in his wheelchair, an old Remington type-writer on a folding table before him, and three bottles of bright inks with three feathery pens lined up on the table beside the type-writer for the work he might have to do in Cantonese. It was almost as though, not content to escape from his misery in an alcoholic negation of any future happiness, he felt the need to inflict further pain in the present by living amongst abject poverty and filth.

Ah Chien took Molly off to a local Chinese school every morning and picked her up again in the late afternoon. During the day Molly learnt what it was to have been born a woman in China and she was teased mercilessly by the other children because she was a gweilo. She hated school, but she hated her home more. She dreaded going back and finding her father slumped in his wheelchair, an empty bottle beside him and an incontinent stain over the legs of his trousers. Ah Chien, who lived in a windowless scullery at the back of the flat, refused to clean but she did cook them boiled rice and vegetables which tasted blandly of the earth and she gave them cloudy glasses of water drawn from a well in the street. Molly drank the water and prayed that she might get cholera like her mother and die. She drank the water greedily, taking a vicious pleasure in knowing it had not been boiled.

And then, one morning, on a sudden impulse and with the vague thought that fresh air would clear his head of a tremendous hangover, Willard Russell paid a sixty-year-old rickshaw boy to abandon his work for the day and, instead of the rickshaw, to pull his wheelchair. They went all over Kowloon drinking from Russell's hipflask and ended up in the foyer of The Peninsula Hotel, the rickshaw boy embarrassed by such opulence in his blue shorts and white shirt, holding his round straw hat between his fingers and excusing himself to the Indian doorman in a language neither Russell nor the doorman could understand. Finally, the Chinese was pushed out onto the pavement outside and Russell was wheeled in to the Japanese barber, Kenji, for a haircut.

Kenji would speak to all his customers in the same quiet, serious voice. He had heard the tragic story of the crippled American and his dead wife and as he cut Russell's hair he said, "Mount Fuji is very big and the snail climbing its side is very slow. Which is you and which is your grief? The mountain or the snail?" And so it was that Russell understood that his grief would always be there and that it was stupid of him to consciously try to overcome it because, no matter what he did, he would always be the snail and his grief the mountain.

"So, what do you do then?" he asked Kenji. "I mean, to escape back into life?" He realised the sentence sounded awkward and coughed to hide his embarrassment. But Kenji did not notice, accustomed as he was to the sometimes forced intricacies of meditation.

"Yoga," he said quietly. "Ch'ien i, Heavenly Oneness, the Great Emptiness. You will see that there is always a reason for everything."

But Willard Russell continued to drink, to lose himself in his own personal great emptiness although he recognised in Kenji an inner strength and a noble honesty of thought which attracted him. Soon he was paying the rickshaw boy to take him out every Friday, and every Friday he went to the hotel for a haircut. Sometimes, his hair was already so short that Kenji limited himself to a discreet snipping around his ears, but they both knew by then that it was Russell's need for conversation which drew them together. Russell soon came to realise that Kenji was not trying to give him advice. He was just certain that what he said was right. Russell had, at first, begun to offer up objections by countering Kenji's cryptic Taoist pronouncements with parables until he saw that the Japanese was quietly laughing at the simplicity of his arguments. Because Kenji was self-sufficient. When he spoke of Hsuan kuan—the Mysterious Gate—he was not telling Russell about it because he wanted to convince him of anything. There was no need. Mostly he was just speaking for himself.

One morning, Russell was feeling particularly belligerent. He had what he called a migraine, although it was a hangover, and to add to the discomfort of his headache, bile kept rising into his throat each time he coughed, which he did frequently.

"Tell me, Kenji," he said. "How come you're accepted here, what with all the anti-Japanese feeling that's about?"

Kenji smiled. "They think I'm Chinese," he said.

"Oh, yes! The Europeans, maybe. But what about the Chinese themselves? They must know, surely? And, after all, it's they who hate the Japanese, not the rest of us."

"The Chinese know the facts but choose to ignore them. You would not understand."

That night, Russell went to the Glory Hole and bought himself a bottle of whisky. Harry Osbourne was there with some of his soldier friends.

"Lend us a couple of dollars," Osbourne was pawing his friend's shoulder and was already beginning to slur his words. "Lend us a couple of dollars and I'll buy you a drink! Come on, Fletch!"

Sergeant John Fletcher pushed the insistent Osbourne to one side just a little too firmly with the result that he happened to land in the chair opposite Willard Russell, a rickety rattan table between them where the bottle of whisky stood half-empty. Osbourne reached for the bottle and looked at the American with bleary, bloodshot eyes.

"Lend us a couple of dollars...," he began, but Russell silenced him by pouring him a drink. Osbourne felt he ought to say something. "Golf competition, you know?" he said. "Open to all-comers, not just the bleeding nobs. First prize is a second free round of golf." He belched and poured himself another scotch. "They do say, mind you, that you get a free round with the President of the Golf Club's wife too! Ha! Ha!"

Willard Russell decided he preferred Kenji's mysticism to Osbourne's vulgarity and, the following day, he reached an agreement with the Japanese. When he was not working, Kenji would wheel him through the city and, in return, Willard Russell would set out with him in search of the Absolute Void.

(iii)

Miss Dekyvere had come to bridge rather late in life but she was a careful and skilful player. This was, she knew, the only reason her eccentric presence was requested at the Rodmells' dinner parties. Tonight, it seemed her partner was first to be Dr Alfred Laughton. She could not help liking him. At least he had a bit of spunk. And he liked Mao and his Communists! That upset all of them, though why he liked the Communists Miss Dekyvere had yet to hear him explain. It was quite possible, she decided, that Alfred Laughton did not actually know himself.

The wireless was playing as they sat down at the card table. The BBC Empire Service.

"A taste of home," suggested Miss Dekyvere politely.

"Eliot has to hear the news," Margaret Rodmell corrected her.

He could do it at a different time, thought Miss Dekyvere, smiling to herself at the man's apparent need to appear pompous and self-important at all times.

"Have you noticed," Rodmell was not even listening to the news anyway, "how, for the Chinese, there never seems to exist the excitement of surprise? I see it time and time again. Can you imagine a life where everything is always as you expect it to be?"

"I don't quite follow you, Eliot," Laughton said. He had not been listening to either the news or his host. He had, instead, been thinking of a rumour he had heard at the hospital earlier in the day, when yet another Chinese peasant had been brought into Casualty suffering from various knife wounds. And so, rather than wait for a reply, he went on quickly, "I'm told your rival, Chen Liew, has had his boys out again."

Eliot Rodmell intensely disliked any reference to business at his card table, but he had heard nothing of Chen Liew for some weeks now. Unlike the Chinese, he was surprised, and he did not like it.

"Why do you say that, Alfred?" he asked, trying his best not to appear too interested. He adopted his school teacher tone of voice and raised his eyebrows as he dealt the cards. This, coupled with an almost imperceptible but, once perceived, definitely stern way of handling the cards, had the desired effect on Laughton who now wished he had said nothing.

"No," he said, to fill a silence. He picked his cards from the table before they had all been dealt, another thing which was sure to infuriate his host. 2♦ 4♠ 5♠ 8♣ 4♣[1]. He grunted. "No," he said again, "It was just another victim, I suppose, of the senseless street violence that seems to be so prevalent, these days, I mean, I thought..." Laughton's voice dropped away. He did not really know now what he might have thought.

"Oh, that!" said Eliot Rodmell, successfully dismissing the matter as if of no importance, at the same time placing the last card neatly before him on the table. "Is that all?" Any further thought of Chen Liew was immediately overshadowed by a handful of red cards. Ace, King, Queen, Jack and Ten of Diamonds! Plus the Eight, the Seven and the Five! He could not believe his luck. A couple more picture cards, too. Eliot Rodmell could not wait for the bidding to begin. Laughton, on the other hand, looked at a solitary, insulting King. Every other card he had was lower than Eight.

"Come along, Alfred!" Eliot Rodmell boomed happily. "Your bid!"

"Pass," Laughton grunted and reached for his whisky and soda. Mary Laughton bid One Heart and scowled a warning towards her husband which said, at least so Alfred Laughton interpreted it: You should not be drinking at all and that is already your second! To get drunk at the Rodmells'! I shall never speak to you again if you drink that!

"Oh dear! I don't know how to say this," Miss Dekyvere began, her voice an apologetic whisper.

Laughton sipped his whisky and thought: I shall drink as much as I damned well like. And with cards like these there is not a soul on God's earth who would blame me for it.

"You see, I don't think I shall make any tricks," Miss Dekyvere continued quietly.

"Well, the best thing for you to do is pass, Ruth," Margaret Rodmell suggested as kindly as she could. She was not playing, but sitting by the wireless in case of interference. Miss Dekyvere smiled and looked again at her cards.

"I mean," she said in the same quiet voice, "That I want to bid 'One Under'."

"Three Diamonds!" said Eliot Rodmell with a flourish. He did not care what the old trout wanted to bid.

Alfred Laughton sighed and wondered why he ever allowed his wife to talk him into coming to these dull evenings in the first place. It is an honour, Alfred, his wife told him. Not any old Tom, Dick or Harry is invited. You should be proud. Proud! thought Laughton, and sipped his drink.

"Four Clubs!" chirped in his wife. She was enjoying herself, anyway.

"Five Diamonds!" said Rodmell sternly, looking across the table at Mary Laughton and daring her to contradict.

"Excuse me," said Miss Dekyvere, "But don't I have a go?"

Rodmell ignored her. "Come on, Laughton!" he growled. "Get on with it!"

"Pass," said Laughton wearily.

"Pass," said his wife.

"Five Under," said Miss Dekyvere.

Alfred Laughton looked up suddenly from his whisky and soda. She was actually going to challenge the great man in his own house!

"Five No Trumps!" Eliot Rodmell almost shouted, and Alfred Laughton could not resist.

"Six Under, or whatever it is you're supposed to say!" he said, unable to resist a little chuckle of pleasure.

"Pass," said Mary Laughton meekly.

"Pass," said Miss Dekyvere.

"Double!" Eliot Rodmell pronounced the word somehow with three syllables. "Now, Miss Dekyvere," he said, managing to make it sound like a threat, "Woe betide you if you get more than one trick!" And he rubbed his hands together in anticipation of failure.

"Well done, Eliot!" Margaret Rodmell congratulated her husband on his masterful bidding.

Before he played his first card, the Six of Diamonds, Alfred Laughton could have sworn that Miss Dekyvere winked at him. When he laid his cards on the table, she actually dared to smile. But then she smiled at each of them in turn. Given that Eliot Rodmell never expected sense from a woman, he was able to beam back at her, confident and undaunted. Laughton was only vaguely interested in the game, in part due to the fact that he was sure they would lose. He leant back in his chair, clasped his hands behind his head and watched the small lizards on the ceiling. You are getting into a rut, he told himself. Forty years old and acting as though you were already an old man. Perhaps if we'd had children there would be another interest. And he looked as his wife took a trick with the Eight of Spades. It was two-nil.

Mary Laughton glanced a little nervously at Eliot Rodmell and led the Nine of Spades. Rodmell shook his head. Two people alone with each other for twenty years, Laughton continued to mull over the causes for his actual feeling of inertia. Got to be a bad thing. At least with children... and he looked at Rodmell ...or excitement. For you had to admit Rodmell had that.

"Oh, dear!" said Miss Dekyvere.

"Ha!" said Rodmell triumphantly.

Laughton glanced at the card table. His King of Spades had won their first trick.

"Now we'll have some fun," Rodmell grinned and patted his wife on the knee.

There is a cruel streak there though, thought Laughton, examining the elder man's almost exultant profile. It was a sharp profile and although it was ageing, beginning to sag a little beneath the chin, it was elegant. And a little cruel, Laughton insisted to himself. He can't wait for us to lose. And when we do, he will take an almost manic pleasure in explaining what we did wrong. I have seen it before. When Nurse Gemmell, poor thing, was brought to tears for having led the wrong suit. She was not invited again after that either. That she had had no cards to lead back into Rodmell's hand had been unimportant once he had decided to publicly humiliate her.

"That's six-one," said Miss Dekyvere from across the table. "Do pay attention, Alfred! At least some moral support."

Alfred Laughton looked reluctantly at the cards. His wife played the Four of Hearts.

"Oh, good lead, Mary!" Rodmell boomed, a glint of light catching in the corner of his eye. He looked expectantly towards Miss Dekyvere and would have rubbed his hands, but she played the Two. As Eliot Rodmell pulled the trick across the table towards him and placed it against the other six, Ruth Dekyvere placed her cards face up on the table.

"And the rest are yours, dear, I think," she said to Rodmell.

Alfred Laughton found he was suddenly laughing out loud. They had beaten the smug old bastard! His wife was guiltily offering up the Ace, King, Queen, Jack and Ten of Hearts. Margaret Rodmell looked slightly offended and coaxed a strident whistle from the wireless.

"Turn the damned thing off, Margaret!" Rodmell had exchanged the School Teacher for the Head Master. Managing, but only just, to control his anger, he turned to Miss Dekyvere. "Fine game," he muttered. "Fine game, indeed!" And he pushed himself to his feet. There would be no more cards tonight. He would wait for his revenge. "Yes," he said again, more to himself now, almost as a self-congratulation, "Fine game."

Laughton could not take the grin from his face and so buried it in his whisky glass. Miss Dekyvere walked round the table to take his arm and lead him out behind the Rodmells to the veranda.

"I've been wanting to do that for years," she whispered to him. And she gave his arm a squeeze. "I'm so glad you were here to enjoy it too. I don't expect many people would have done."

As they walked out onto the veranda, Eliot Rodmell turned on him. "I say, Laughton!" he commanded. "What was all that about Chen Liew?"

Miss Dekyvere released Laughton's arm and walked over to the wives who were looking absently down at the lights of the city. A monkey cried out from above them on The Peak, the sound suddenly shrill and piercing.

"Nothing, Eliot," said Laughton casually. Something had changed during the game of bridge. He would not, he decided, allow himself to be in awe of the Great Man anymore. He and Miss Dekyvere had won! "Just trying to make conversation," he said. "That was all." Laughton accepted one of Rodmell's cigars.

"Not like you, Laughton," Rodmell snapped, "Not like you at all!"

Laughton shrugged and puffed on his cigar. "The excitement of surprise, Eliot!" he replied with a grin. Eliot Rodmell scowled and then decided to be pleasant. He needed information.

"Laughton," he said. "Alfred."

Alfred Laughton blew a cloud of cigar smoke into the night sky between them. Twelve-one! He smiled to himself. Wait until I tell them at the Cricket Club! Rodmell had placed his hand on Laughton's shoulder.

"Do try to think about this very carefully," he said, exerting a slight, but nonetheless threatening, pressure with his fingers. "What do you know about Chen Liew?"

Laughton would have confessed the truth despite his recent resolution for courage that he knew only what he had said before, but it was Miss Dekyvere who spoke.

"He's looking for a young girl," she told them.

Eliot Rodmell was all but leaning his entire weight on Laughton's shoulder and Laughton could have sworn that he could feel the Taipan's heart miss a beat and then begin to race.

"A young girl," said Miss Dekyvere. "Tragic story. Really tragic. But she has disappeared."

There was silence as they all looked at the lights of the city. Laughton felt they were perhaps all trying to locate the girl in the twinkling, anonymous expanse that stretched away beneath them to the sea. Again the monkey shrieked high up on the hill.

"God! I wish they wouldn't do that!" said Eliot Rodmell. "They sound like people in pain!"

(iv)

Even had Willard Russell been behaving more discreetly than he was, it would not have taken Chen Liew's bodyguard, Chan, long to find him. As it was, the new friendship between Russell and Kenji was soon a topic of conversation from The Peninsula Hotel, where it was frowned upon, to the Glory Hole, where it was misunderstood.

"Mind you, they deserve each other," said Osbourne. He was talking to an only vaguely interested Sergeant Fletcher.

"You're just sour because he kept roping you into going with him out to the New Territories," said Fletcher.

"No, it's not that," said Osbourne. "There's something funny about that Kenji-bloke. And, as for our American friend! Well! It stands to reason, doesn't it? I mean, what the hell kind of man would marry a Chinese!"

Fletcher shrugged. "Why do Chinese women have two holes in their knickers?" he asked with a grin. Osbourne's eyes sparkled behind their alcoholic haze as he went through myriad vulgar possibilities.

"Dunno, Fletch," he conceded finally.

"To put their legs through!" replied Fletcher smugly.

Osbourne's shoulders heaved with laughter and were then stilled by the pressure of two large hands. Osbourne turned and found himself looking straight into the immovable, inscrutable face of the bodyguard, Chan. Chan leaned his face still closer to Osbourne's.

"What are you writing?" Chan asked. Even this simple question seemed to contain a hidden threat. Osbourne glanced towards the blank pages of his grubby notebook where the only thing he had written for days was the word "Catinat," the name of a horse, a sure winner for the weekend.

"A little piece on the war in China," he said nervously. Chan touched the notebook with the tips of his fingers as though it were unclean, and pushed it slightly further into the centre of the table.

The Glory Hole was filled with soldiers exchanging vouchers with the taxi-girls. A rowdy group of sailors leaned against the small bar in the corner. Their merchant ship had docked the day before and, having already satisfied their thirst for sex, they were now slowly drifting towards a noisy and anti-social drunkenness. The air was thick with cigarette smoke and opium and from the rooms upstairs came the sudden gasping sigh of a faked orgasm or the very real cry of a child.

"Drink, Chan?" said Osbourne, pulling a chair towards the table. He was desperately trying to think of all that he had done over the last week, trying to locate at what point he might have done something to upset Chen Liew. But Chen Liew was a reasonable man, not like some of the others. Osbourne could feel the sweat trickling from beneath his arms and his hand was shaking.

Chan did not even smile. He neither refused nor accepted Osbourne's offer of a drink. Instead, he pointed out the word "Catinat" and shook his head gravely.

"No chance!" he said simply.

With anyone else, Osbourne would have argued. As it was, he grabbed the notebook from the table, tore out the page, screwed it into a tight ball, and dropped it onto the floor beneath the table.

"Paddy White's horse will win," said Chan.

Osbourne was certain that he had done nothing to deserve Chan's visit, which meant that he was going to be asked to do something. He hated doing things for Chan, but Chan was not the kind of person you refused. The last time, he had been asked to tail one of the Tangs and to write down everything he did. That had not been a problem until he had been led out into the New Territories and the walled village of Kat Him Wai. He had never been so frightened before in his life. Four watchtowers protected the village and on each watchtower stood a six-foot Chinese armed with a machine-gun. There was only one entrance into the village through a small gateway which Osbourne had stupidly tried to cross. He had been stopped at gunpoint and they had asked him who he wanted to see. When he had said "Tang", the watchmen had begun to laugh in the same humourless, evil way that Chan laughed and, pushing him back out of the village with the butts of their rifles, they had told him that everybody in Kat Him Wai was called Tang! Now, the last thing he wanted was to have to do another little job for Chen Liew.

"You know Miss Dekyvere?" Chan was saying, sitting now at their table but not drinking. "It is because of her that I am here."

Osbourne felt suddenly so relieved that he found he had started to grin. Chan looked at him and said quietly, "I don't see why that should make you laugh, Mr Osbourne."

"No," said Osbourne hurriedly, "It was a joke. Fletch told me. " he said.

"You have been asked, Osbourne, or rather, you are being asked to transmit a message to the American, Russell. We know you drink with him from time to time." Chan looked round the stuffy room almost as though he half-expected to see Russell himself slumped in his chair in a corner. Osbourne nodded.

"Tell him," said Chan, "That Miss Dekyvere has expressed an interest in seeing the child, Molly." And with that, Chan had apparently finished, for he pushed himself to his feet. Sergeant Fletcher and Osbourne watched Chan's immense back as it pushed a way easily through the crowded room. At the door, Chan stopped. A drunk soldier was gently mauling one of the girls, a Russian refugee. Chan examined the girl's flaming red hair, first with his eyes, and then with the tips of his fingers. He pushed the soldier to one side and, without saying a word, took the Russian girl with him and out to the waiting Bentley.

"Why does he want you to be his go-between, Harry?" Fletcher asked. He was still looking at the space which Chan's enormous form had, until a moment ago, occupied so completely that now something actually appeared to be lacking in the room.

"It's a test, Fletch," said Osbourne, sniffing. He might almost have been proud of the fact. "They like to know that they're still in charge." He took a well-chewed pencil-stub from his pocket and scribbled 'Paddy White' on a clean page of his notebook. After a moment's thought, he underlined the name and wrote 'Catinat' beside it. "It *is* bloody Paddy White's mount!" he explained to a disinterested Fletcher. Fletcher grinned although he had found nothing to amuse him. On the contrary, he had found the whole incident with Chan profoundly disturbing.

"The way he just took that Russian girl!" Fletcher said indignantly, reaching for his beer.

"They take more than bloody tarts, Fletch!" said Osbourne ominously. "This isn't the Old Kent Road, mate! This is Hong Kong!" And with a final dismissive gulp at his beer, Osbourne stood up. He ran a finger round the inside of his frayed and smutty collar. "I'd best be making tracks," he said emphatically.

"I thought we were going to have a hand of crib," said Fletcher.

Osbourne pushed his thickset face towards Fletcher and blinked behind his glasses. "Look, mate!" he said. "When they tell you to do something, you better jump to it! Our friend Chan is a 426, a Red Pole!"

It meant nothing to Fletcher. "He is a trained killer, Fletch, for the Triads. If I don't get hold of that soppy yank by this time tomorrow, I might as well start booking my passage home!"

Fletcher glanced quickly round the room. The soldiers and the whores and the noise depressed him. A child was crying upstairs, its voice barely audible above the masculine din in the stuffiness of the bar.

"What about if I just tag along?" he suggested, standing.

Osbourne shook his head very slowly. "You stay out of this, Fletch!" he said, looking at the table as though he had lost something. "You don't owe him anything."

"And you do?" Fletcher had not meant to say it but, perhaps driven on by the prospect of being alone, he had been unable to resist. Besides which, sometimes there is a need to hurt.

"That's none of your bloody business, is it?" said Osbourne bluntly.

Fletcher laughed, but it was partly embarrassment. "That's tantamount to saying you do," he said.

"You can think what you like, sunshine," said Osbourne. And, stuffing his notebook into his jacket pocket, he left.

Alone in The Glory Hole, Sergeant John Fletcher felt morose. Whilst Harry Osbourne was not the most likeable of men, at least he was company. He looked a little sadly at the young, gaudily painted Chinese girls standing round the walls of the bar. Some of them could not have been more than fifteen. This, however, did not stop him beckoning to the nearest girl to his table and allowing himself to be led away upstairs.

As he took off his trousers, folded them neatly and placed them over the bamboo rungs of the bedstead John Fletcher could hear the plaintive cries of the child quite clearly, coming, it seemed, from the next room along the passage. But he was not about to let that ruin his enjoyment.

(v)

"But you are neither considering the girl's feelings, nor her father's."

Miss Dekyvere felt she ought to protest. "Besides which, you know the British Government banned Mui Tsai[3] years ago."

"This is not Mui Tsai," said Chen Liew quietly. "I am not buying the girl, not as such, and, anyway, so as not to provoke unnecessary gossip, she shall live with you." He could not see where the problem lay. "She will have everything. She will attend the best schools. And Tung Nien shall be like an elder sister to her. There is not much difference in their ages, after all. It will make them both happier than they are now and no one shall be any the worse off."

Miss Dekyvere glanced into her garden. "You remind me," she said with a cough which revealed the misgivings she felt in saying anything which Chen Liew might interpret as a criticism, "You remind me of the old Buddhist woman who was converted to Catholicism on her death-bed because she had learnt that the Christian graveyard had better fung shui than the Buddhist burial ground."

"And what is that supposed to mean?" asked Chen Liew a little testily.

"It means, my dear," said Miss Dekyvere standing now and walking across to the window, the better to observe the riot of colour in her garden where a flame-of-the-forest tree dominated the landscape, "that you bend the rules to suit yourself. You have decided what is best and you will not see things any other way."

"And what would you have me do?" Chen Liew was genuinely at a loss to see what he had done wrong.

"You might consider the feelings of other people," said Miss Dekyvere with an exasperated tug at her skirt as she turned to face him. "What if the girl does not want to live with a stuffy spinster like me?"

"But she will."

"What if I don't want her?"

"But you will do it. For me."

"Do you really think that money can solve all your problems?"

---

[3] Miu Tsai: the buying of children for adoption, or for selling them into service or prostitution. It was declared illegal in 1922.

"Experience has shown me that that is generally the case."

"You should begin to consider the place emotions have in your life or you shall end up being most unhappy."

"This is a question of emotions. My wife's emotions."

"I just don't see the point," said Miss Dekyvere, "in uprooting this poor girl..."

Chen Liew held up his hands and then stood. "For her it will be like winning the lottery," he said. "What has she now? Nothing! What am I offering her?"

"But her father?"

"He may see her whenever he wishes."

"You have no idea, Chen Liew, have you, of the deeper feelings?"

Chen Liew walked slowly towards the door. He wondered how he could explain that were it not for the deeper feelings, the problem would never have existed in the first place.

"I love my wife," he said, but it only sounded like an excuse.

"I shall accept only with the father's consent," Miss Dekyvere said, but she spoke so softly that it was almost as though she did not really want him to hear it. But he did.

"I don't see that he has much of a choice," he said.

When Chen Liew had gone, Miss Dekyvere was left alone to consider what right she had to object. For certainly the girl's life, at least in its material aspect, would see itself greatly improved. And from the little she knew of Tung Nien, Miss Dekyvere judged her to be kind. There was a calculating, even ambitious streak to Tung Nien's character which had bubbled irrepressibly to the normally tranquil surface on one or two occasions. Miss Dekyvere remembered a discussion about money. She had been invited for afternoon tea, one of the few occidental customs which Chen Liew approved of. "It was," he would say, to excuse this momentary lapse in his rejection of all things foreign, and in reference to a valuable set of painted silk scrolls, "not uncommon for the Manchu Overlords of the seventeenth century to take tea." But Tung Nien, who had never seen the scrolls which depicted 'The Four Pleasures of Bo Juyi' (none of which, in fact, showed anybody drinking tea) had had the nerve to ask to be given money of her own. Miss Dekyvere had been about to ask Chen Liew what the Manchu Overlords would have felt had they known that Manchuria would one day be invaded by the hated Japanese when Chen Liew, raising both his voice and his hands in a mixture of anger and incomprehension, had said, or rather shouted, that she had no need of money. Tung Nien had looked at her husband with an expression of fierce determination.

"I am not the kind of woman," she had said slowly, "who will be content to allow my life just to drift on placidly like some kind of pale reflection of your own. I did not agree to leave the Walled City to come up here and vegetate, to do no more than to sit about making myself look pretty and to wait for you to have time to notice me. I want to have a life of my own and I want to live it."

As far as Miss Dekyvere knew, however, she had not managed to convince Chen Liew to give her anything, nor had she managed to find any life other than that which her husband meticulously planned out for her. She had merely, it seemed, exchanged the Walled City in the slums of Kowloon for the walled gardens of Chen Liew's mansion on The Peak.

(vi)

Osbourne's search for Willard Russell was not a complicated one. He left the Glory Hole and went directly to The Pen. Although it was late, the foyer and the bar of The Peninsula Hotel were filled with people. In the bar, the gentlemen of the city were sitting around only half-heartedly discussing the problems of smallpox and cholera brought about by the tremendous influx of refugees who were flooding across the border to escape from the war in China. At least most of them stay on this side of the water, they said. But Osbourne was stopped before he could go any further. He was not wearing a tie.

"I only want to see the Yank, I'm not going to have dinner, mate!" he said to the stern-faced Sikh who was barring his way.

"Mr Russell?" asked the Indian, who knew perfectly well. "In that case, would you wait here, please?" And he indicated a hard chair which was partially hidden by the voluminous leaves of a palm. Osbourne watched the Sikh's light blue turban as it weaved its way above the neatly combed European heads thronging the bar. "Bastards!" he said to himself, and sat down to wait.

When he saw Russell being wheeled towards him by the Japanese, Osbourne snickered. They both looked totally out of place in the ostentatious luxury of The Pen and, from the way the American was lolling to one side, it was obvious he had been drinking. He had a confused expression on his face, as though he might just have been woken from a deep sleep. Kenji was poorly but immaculately dressed in a high-collared grey suit at the neck of which a tight black bow tie protruded. It reminded Osbourne of a small bat. As they came into the colonnaded entrance hall, Osbourne stood and shuffled a couple of places towards them. He jerked his hand out towards the American in greeting, but Willard Russell frowned and kept his own hands firmly folded in his lap.

"What do you want, Osbourne?" he asked gruffly.

Osbourne grinned. "Miss Dekyvere wants to see your girl, Molly," he said, replacing his hand in his trouser pocket.

"And?" said Russell.

"And I've come to tell you," Osbourne replied. He could not decide whether or not the American had been drinking. He leaned forwards for a hint of whisky, but Russell's breath was sweet with the smell of camomile. A little disappointed that he appeared to be alone in his alcoholic excess, Osbourne rubbed his hand over his unshaven chin and turned to leave. "Well?" he all but demanded.

"Tell Miss Dekyvere I shall send her up tomorrow."

"You're not even going to ask what she wants?"

"She would not have told the likes of you, Osbourne. What would be the point?"

Osbourne had to agree that that was true. "See you around," he said. None of it had anything to with him anyway. Why should he bother his head about it? Let the old Yank dig his own grave if that was what he wanted. Or his daughter's, come to that. And without waiting for a reply—in the event, Russell merely raised his hand slightly, but said nothing—Osbourne walked as elegantly as he could back out into the sticky night air. He grabbed a rickshaw which was heading west along Salisbury Road and looked absently across the harbour to the twinkling lights on The Peak.

"Bugger them!" he said.

(vii)

"A Russian prostitute has been strangled. Her body was found by the quay of the Floating City."

Miss Dekyvere looked up at Tung Nien and scowled. "I don't know why you read that nonsense!" she said, and she offered up her own copy of *The South China Morning Post.* "I have read it," she explained.

Tung Nien took the newspaper and frowned at the front page which proclaimed:

"MAO ZEDONG AND CHIANG KAI SHEK FORM ALLIANCE TO FIGHT THE JAPANESE"

Miss Dekyvere smiled to herself before saying, "Mind you, I don't suppose it's that much of an improvement. One Russian whore, or hundreds of Chinese peasants. There is so little, these days, that is happy."

Tung Nien was still looking blankly at the front page of the newspaper. "They look so funny," she said.

Miss Dekyvere, who had found nothing amusing in the paper, leaned forwards. "What's that?" she asked, putting her glasses onto the end of her nose.

"Your letters," said Tung Nien. "They look so funny. I don't think I shall ever be able to decipher them."

Miss Dekyvere sat back in her chair and sighed. It had been a stupid thing to have done. Thoughtless. She always spoke Cantonese to Tung Nien but, then, you took it for granted that the educated classes spoke English too. And, now, she had inadvertently brought to light a failing, a weakness, in her neighbour. To make amends, or to hide her embarrassment, she moved quickly on to the subject which had brought them together that morning.

"Molly, I suppose, will soon be here," she said.

Tung Nien's face brightened and she dropped *The South China Morning Post* onto the grass. She pulled a red envelope from her silk sleeve. "I have prepared this for her," she said, smiling.

Miss Dekyvere could not help thinking how young and beautiful she was. She was not thinking about the red envelope as she leaned forward to take it between her fingers. It swung heavily. The bottom of the envelope seemed to have been filled with tiny pebbles.

"And what is this, my dear?" she asked.

"Lai see," said Tung Nien, still smiling in the same apparently innocent way. "Lucky money. For luck and prosperity."

Miss Dekyvere carefully lifted the flap of the envelope and peered inside. A necklace had been dismembered and the envelope had been filled with the pearls.

"I had no money," Tung Nien explained quickly, "Either lucky or otherwise!"

Miss Dekyvere folded the flap back into the envelope and handed it across the table to Tung Nien as the huge metal doors away at the bottom of the garden opened and the long bonnet of the white Bentley appeared.

Molly could see the two women from where she was sitting in the car. Her father slumped, rather than sat, beside her. Preferring to ignore his presence, she looked through the window of the car, across the lush green lawn which climbed away to form a small mound before the house, to the two women. She recognised both of them and some of the apprehension she had been feeling fell away. The name "Miss Dekyvere" had meant nothing, but the kind old face was a symbol of hope. It had rescued her before and might do so again.

The younger woman, Tung Nien, was a far more vivid memory for her. She could still see her quite clearly, on the day of her wedding, sitting before the shrine-like dressing-table bedecked in silk and pearls, pretty and peaceful, her skin as smooth as a porcelain doll. Molly had found, then, her ideal of beauty and as she looked, now, from the car, she saw it again, floating down towards her over the grass as though she belonged to another world.

The sun was hot through the car window and Willard Russell flipped the back of his hand at a fly. With his other hand, he held tightly onto Molly's arm. He felt an unreasonable sense of foreboding and imagined for a moment that the reason they had been summoned was for him to be interrogated and found guilty for being a bad father. But seeing that both women were smiling as they walked towards the car, which was now crunching to a standstill on the gravel drive before the house, Russell decided, not without a small sigh of relief, that they knew nothing of his debauchery.

"Mr Russell!" It was Miss Dekyvere stepping forward in a bright cotton dress to greet them. "And Molly! How nice!"

Shang-Chih Su, the chauffeur, helped Russell into his wheelchair and pushed him over to the table where breakfast had, until recently, been in the place now occupied by Miss Dekyvere's carefully folded copy of *The South China Morning Post.* Willard Russell gave the newspaper a cursory glance, although he knew what it said, and he cleared his throat before saying, "The longer the war lasts, the better it will be for the Japanese. You don't seriously believe in an alliance between the Communists and the Kuomintang..." He stopped because he sensed that the two women were looking at him. "I know China," he said, instead. "I worked there." He looked at Miss Dekyvere's sincere expression and smiled. "Quite beautiful in its way," he said dreamily, reliving, perhaps, thought Miss Dekyvere somewhat romantically, afternoons beneath the peach blossom with his wife. Until she suddenly found that she was still wearing her glasses. She removed them quickly and, as she was searching in her handbag for her glasses case, she said in a kind of forced whisper,

"If we could speak in Cantonese, Willard?"

Russell nodded in agreement and glanced at Tung Nien. She was looking fixedly at Molly and smiling. Molly returned her smile.

"I do not imagine," said Russell finally to break a silence that was in danger of becoming, at least, for him, embarrassing, "that we have been invited here for morning coffee." And then he added with a laconic smile himself, "Although coffee would be most welcome."

"We were worried about you," said Miss Dekyvere. "You hear such stories." She wished she could have been more specific.

"Stories?" said Russell.

"Rumours," Miss Dekyvere corrected herself.

Tung Nien had not been listening to them. She took the red envelope again from her sleeve and pressed it into Molly's hand.

"Lai see," she said. "For you."

Molly took the envelope but did not open it. After the squalor of their tenement flat, where the air was always thick with the stench of rotting vegetables and laced faintly with the smell of fried fish, she was enjoying the heavy, scented smells of the flowers. After the rows on rows of bamboo poles and damp, washing forever dripping into the dank central well of the flats, after the truncated view offered by their small balcony which was merely the dull sockets of a darkened row of windows in the flat opposite, she was enjoying the immense green open spaces of the garden and the hard blue of the sky. She held the red envelope in her hands and rolled her fingers round the pellets of the pearls through the paper.

Tung Nien was speaking to her father. "It's not because I am in any way altruistic, Mr Russell, that I have made this suggestion."

Russell's first reaction upon being informed that they wanted to all but adopt his daughter had been to laugh. The idea was preposterous!

"Is it not?" he asked quietly. His thoughts were racing, though. In a way, it was a godsend. He, a cripple, could not look after her properly. (For the time being, he would not also say drunkard. Anyway, he would stop drinking altogether soon. That was not a problem.). And he would still see her. It was not as though they wanted to take Molly away from him. He had not considered sending her away to boarding school, but if he had? What would be the difference? In fact, she would be better off here, by far. He realised, rather guiltily, that he was already trying to give himself reasons as to why he should accept. But Tung Nien was still speaking to him. She had rested a lovely soft hand on his and she looked at him with her calm almond eyes that looked, he decided, like two brown leaves floating in a pond.

"No," said Tung Nien firmly. "I must learn English and Molly will teach me. In return, I shall giver her the kind of life she could never even have dreamed of."

"Why Molly?" asked Russell. It was a logical question, but the reply was far from logical.

"Because she, too, is beautiful."

Willard Russell had lived long enough among the Chinese to know he would never understand them. He had loved his wife, he had known her better than any other person in his life, but he had never wholly understood her. Molly had inherited enough from Suyong to be somewhat of an enigma to him. There were times when her thoughts would go down a path that he could never follow. So, he said, "I don't understand!" Because it was true. When he spoke to Miss Dekyvere, he found he had reverted to English.

"What the hell kind of reasoning is that?"

Miss Dekyvere, too, was at a loss. "I know her very little," she said. "Too little to imagine what she might be thinking. But I can assure you that your daughter will want for nothing. I, myself, can guarantee you that."

Willard Russell attempted a more comfortable position which, unfortunately, turned into a slouch. "And what do you stand to gain from all this?" he asked.

Most people would have been offended by the question, but Miss Dekyvere accepted it as she accepted most things in life. Her own personal philosophy was not so far removed from the Chinese. There was nothing she could do to change the unexpected and strange incidents in life, so why should she fight pointlessly against them.

"I?" she asked quietly. "I shall gain, if anything, the experience of seeing this girl become a woman. Nothing else. Unless it is a certain friendship."

Willard Russell was confused. A part of him had already agreed to the arrangement as being the best thing for both him and Molly, but upbringing, rather than emotion, rebelled.

"It is as good as admitting that I am not capable of looking after her myself!" he complained. But he was almost willing Miss Dekyvere to convince him otherwise. She would not, however, do that.

"I am very sorry if that is how you see it, Mr Russell. You see, it is not that at all."

"I wish I knew what the hell it was, then!"

"Willard! Why try to look for deeper reasons when they don't exist? I must confess that I had my own misgivings. I had suspected that perhaps Tung Nien and Chen Liew were incapable of..." But she stopped, unwilling, even in thought, to intrude upon another's intimacy. "And that would indeed have worried me. But as it is..." she concluded.

Tung Nien and Molly had left the table and were walking across the lawns up behind the house to where the grass disappeared into a tangle of ferns and palms that rose almost vertically up the side of the mountain. Molly felt as though she were living out a dream. She would have agreed to anything, but Tung Nien was careful to speak no more about it. Instead, she spoke of the "Bun Festival" on the island of Cheung Chau.

"We shall go together," she said. "And we shall take your father, if he wishes to come."

Molly knew he would not, but the idea of mountains of edible buns pinned to huge bamboo frames appealed to her. Anything to escape from the endless bowls of earthy rice which Ah Chien prepared every night. She looked down the steep rise of the lawn and she could see her father talking earnestly to Miss Dekyvere.

"Let him say yes!" she said to herself. "Please, let him say yes!"

"So long as I can see her whenever I want and so long as I can break the contract the moment that I am not happy with it," Willard

Russell decided, "I don't see that it will do her any harm. But she must, of course, still go to school."

Miss Dekyvere nodded. "I shall see to it that she goes to the Forces' school."

"An English school?" grunted Russell.

"Quite so, Willard!" Miss Dekyvere countered.

As he was being driven away, Willard Russell felt strangely relieved. He drank slowly on his hip flask of whisky and felt as though a great weight had been taken from his shoulders. Yet, at the same time, there was an emptiness with Molly gone.

"Take me to The Pen," he told Shang-Chih. "I need a drink!"

(viii)

Dr Alfred Laughton felt tired. He was tired of the heat, tired of his work at the hospital where the flow of refugees from China had brought endless cases of typhoid and smallpox, tired of the hospital itself, tired of the company his wife forced him to keep and tired, he realised with a sentimental pang of regret, of his wife. From his bungalow on the lower slopes of The Peak, he watched Chen Liew's Bentley roll slowly past the end of his driveway.

"Now that's a woman for you!" he said beneath his breath, erroneously imagining the identity of the passenger behind the tinted windows. Normally reticent in allowing any sign of passion to emerge, Alfred Laughton could not help but let his desire surface when he thought of Tung Nien. Ever since the wedding, when he had first seen her, he had imagined himself making love to her each time his wife had reluctantly allowed his clumsy gropings to reach fruition. Sterile as she was, he thought, she might have let him do it more often. Of course, it might have been he and not she who were sterile, but what did that matter now? There were no children. There was no life for them together. What little it had been which had brought them together in the first place had long since dried up. There was nothing. But just seeing

Tung Nien's car made his heart race.

Alfred Laughton poured himself a whisky and soda although it was only half past eleven. He rattled the ice against the side of the glass and walked back to the small veranda of his bungalow. Mary was out shopping with Margaret Rodmell. "Now we are going up in the world, Alfred!" she had said. At that moment, he should really have been playing cricket but he had cried off at the last minute. He could think of nothing more pointless than the sound of willow against leather and Eliot Rodmell's pompous "Shot, sir!" as their Punjabi openers scored yet another boundary, with the sun beating down mercilessly, the flies moaning annoyingly in his ear, the glass of orange juice (orange juice!) somehow always sticky in his hands, and the ladies, having finished shopping, wittering behind him in the clubhouse, his pads cutting into the backs of his knees and his "box" cutting into his testicles. It was time for a change.

Alfred Laughton sat down heavily in a rattan chair and picked up a magazine he had taken home the day before from his surgery at the hospital. "What's on in Hong Kong and Macao." He flipped through the pages listlessly and sipped at his drink. And, suddenly, there they were! He had to smile.

The Kowloon Cricket Club Austin Road 10.30 The Royal Hong Kong Cricket Club Vs A combined RAF/Army XI

He flipped the pages. "Cheung Chau," he read, "used to be the island home of pirates. Cheung Po Chai was one of the greatest pirates in Chinese history and he used the island as his hide-out. Many deaths and ritual tortures down the centuries have sullied the land to such an extent that, once a year, the whole island community comes together for a big Bun Festival, a celebration held to exorcise wandering and malicious ghosts who have been unable to find rest in this world. The festival is held between the last 10 days of the third moon and the first 10 days of the fourth moon (the end of April, beginning of May)."

"Pirates." said Laughton to himself. "Well, it beats bloody cricket."

(ix)

There were many small motor boats to take people across to Cheung Chau from the piers on Connaught Road, but Tung Nien and Molly had no need of them. Chen Liew had arranged for them to be picked up from Blake Pier in a motor launch that he normally used to do the opium run into She-k'ou, in China. As they waited on the wharf, Tung Nien and Molly spoke of confetti and firecrackers. They could have been two sisters on their way to a birthday party, enjoying each other's company the more for what they were about to share together. Tung Nien explained to Molly the legend of the skeletons, the origin of the feast. How the island of Cheung Chau had suffered and been persecuted following the discovery of a pile of skeletons. Some years after the find, a Taoist priest had visited the island and explained that as the dead had been murdered they would have to be placated every year with offerings. With buns and fireworks and confetti.

"But does it work?" asked Molly.

"Does what work?" said Tung Nien.

"Do the buns get rid of the evil spirits?"

"I don't know," said Tung Nien. "I've never been before. I suppose so. Why else would they do it?"

"Maybe they just like to have a party."

Molly looked across the waters of the harbour towards Kowloon. Beyond the clustered buildings of the city, the New Territories stretched away into the distance.

"Do you suppose my mother is a wandering ghost?" she asked, with no hint of emotion, only a childish desire to know.

"Why ever should she be?" she asked in return.

Molly thought for a moment and then said, "I shall get a special bun for her, just in case."

Alfred Laughton, from his vantage point on the terrace of a small bar slightly to the east of Blake Pier, saw Molly before he saw Tung Nien. His heart missed a beat. She was, he thought, an exact version in miniature of the older woman. But then he saw Tung Nien herself. She was even more strikingly beautiful than the image he had fostered of her from his memory of the wedding. He stood on the terrace, his whisky and soda caught at the point of touching his lips, and he could not, indeed he did not want to, take his eyes away from her. Two men pushed past him, rudely knocking into his arm and suddenly bringing his attention back to his drink. He looked at it in some surprise, not that he did not remember ordering it, but that he did not remember ever having wanted it. Or anything else, for that matter. Except her. He slumped back in a bamboo and rattan armchair.

"She's young enough to be your daughter!" he sighed, resigning himself to sipping at his whisky. It was a sad state of affairs when even his lust brought him full circle and back to the greatest tragedy of his life. When so many had children without ever wanting them. Of course, Mary had suggested adoption. That had caused another argument. He could not understand how for her the child would be theirs, and she could not understand why he did not want one which was not his. "It's nothing as banal as seeing the name 'Laughton' continuing on for generations, stretching away into the future. It's just the idea of a part of me (he forgot to include her, but not out of malice or lack of affection) growing into a separate being, with its own feelings, ideas and prejudices, and me, all the time, having to live up to the ideal of being a father. I can't see the bond being the same, being so automatic, if you adopt."

"That is because you are a self-centred, insensitive brute."

That is because you are a man, she had meant to say.

And perhaps, she was not too far away from the mark at that, he admitted, juggling the ice in the watery remains of whisky.

A small, brown motor launch with an inboard motor was slowly approaching the wharf of Blake Pier. At the bows the enormous Chan was shouting orders and swaying from side to side on the deck like a guard dog pulling against a restraining chain. Laughton realised the futility of his infatuation. It would, he thought sourly, be easier to go to bed with anyone else in Hong Kong than her! As Chan waved his arms and ordered previously unseen, or at least unnoticed, minions into action, to clear a path through the bustling crowd, Tung Nien took Molly by the arm and Laughton watched as the two most beautiful things he had ever seen were first swallowed up by the bobbing heads and hats before the pier and then emerged to take their seats in front of the wooden cabin of the launch. If he had only previously been in half a mind to visit the Bun Festival when he had ordered his whisky and soda, he was now convinced that fate or destiny had decided he should go. If only to have the chance of being on the same island as her. Hong Kong would be empty with her gone. It would be unbearable to think of her across the water on Cheung Chau, with anonymous eyes looking at her, whilst he sat in the company of these rude Europeans, drinking drinks he did not want and thinking about the children he could never have.

Molly and Tung Nien watched the lush, green foliage of The Victoria Peak darken through blue to almost purple as the launch bounced over the choppy waves of the harbour and took them west and around the point of Pok Fu Lam. On the nearest tip of the island of Lantau, they could see the green and ochre tiles of a white pagoda, half-hidden in the dry, scrubby bushes that climbed the hills around it.

Chan walked towards them from the little cabin, his body swaying from side to side in time with the rocking of the launch, carrying a silver tray of Dim Sun, small, heart-shaped dumplings and pastry triangles filled with pork, shrimps, bamboo shoots or liver and steamed fried rice wrapped in lotus leaves. For Molly, used to food which tasted of the earth, the Dim Sun were like little parcels of heaven. Tung Nien picked at her food and looked out over the bows of the launch at the approaching island. By now she could make out the low, four-storey houses along the waterfront of Cheung Chau harbour. Each one was painted a different colour—yellow, red, blue, brown and green—over whitewashed walls and brown wooden balconies. Behind the buildings, the trees were dark green and thick as thunder clouds. Sampans and launches rocked on the green water of the bay and away to the right a rickety fishing pier stretched out into the sea, its dark, wooden struts standing out against the light like the teeth of a comb. Molly bit into a steamed dumpling filled with tiny shrimps and the spicy, fishy sauce dripped onto her chin. As she looked with Tung Nien towards the island, she could make out the garish, multi-coloured, rippling cloth of a dragon dance weaving off along the quay and she knew that she had never been so happy in her life before.

Laughton was dropped off, along with some twenty excited Chinese families, not at Cheung Chau Harbour but on the other side of the island at Tung Wan Beach. He and the other passengers had to wade through the water to the beach as there was no pier for their motor boat to moor at. None of the Chinese seemed to mind and even the oldest among them leapt with surprising agility into the sea. Laughton leaned against the hot, splintering wood of the side of the boat and removed his shoes and socks before lowering himself gingerly into the warm, soupy water. Although it came only to just above his knees, Laughton winced in displeasure and instinctively pulled his genitals away from and over an incoming wave. He struggled onto the beach and sat down to brush the wet sand from his feet and to replace his socks and shoes. With his trousers flapping wetly against his legs, he set off across the small strip of island which separated him from Cheung Chau Harbour. He could already hear the deafening chain of explosions as strings of firecrackers were set off to scare away the evil spirits before the festivities could begin. Through the trees before him, and from over the roofs of the village, he could see the 60 foot bamboo towers covered with buns which had been erected all along the coastal path, for all the world like watchtowers to look out for the distant Japanese army divisions which were at that very moment making their way slowly and inexorably south along the Chinese coast. A huge papier-mâché effigy of a grotesque red face loomed occasionally above the heads of the crowd. Laughton walked out of the narrow strip of palm trees which separated the two sides of the island and found himself suddenly in the narrow alleyways of the town. A child, no more than five years of age, walked beside him, balancing on his hands. Laughton knew that this was supposed to represent some kind of human vice, he had read as much in the guide book earlier that morning, but he could not for the life of him think how. All he saw was a strangely red-faced child—an echo of the red-faced effigy of Shang Shaang, the Earth God—smiling innocently up at him from upside down. He had an urge to tickle the child's bare feet but resisted for no other reason than that he felt sure that it would be the wrong thing to do. "A man is the less, is somehow incomplete if he is childless," he said to himself, concerned by the fact that he did not know what to do in the presence of the little acrobat. He had no idea what he could do to make himself friendly and so he did nothing. Suddenly, the child tipped himself forwards and ran off into the crowd. Laughton noticed that he made a rude sign at him before he disappeared among the milling backs of adults. He sighed and began to look for somewhere to have a drink. The real festival would not begin until nightfall.

In a small square which had somehow been hollowed out from the tangle of narrow, twisting streets, Laughton stumbled upon a hastily erected, make-shift bamboo and mat theatre. People had already begun to crowd into the square and were sitting cross-legged before the stage, patiently waiting for the show to begin. Laughton had experienced the tuneless, incomprehensible whining of Chinese opera soon after his arrival in Hong Kong and nothing would have induced him to sit for three hours watching a white-faced man in an elaborate head-dress prancing across the stage and making noises like a cat on heat, had he not suddenly seen Tung Nien and Molly looking out at the stage from a balcony at the back of the square.

Laughton glanced behind him at the brilliant reds, blues and golds of the painted bamboo scenery and noticed that the musicians had already taken up their positions, the percussion instruments on one side of the stage, the wind and string instruments on the other. He sat down like the Chinese, cross-legged on the floor, but in such a way that with the slightest movement of his head he would be able to turn his attention from the actors on the stage and rest his eyes instead on the calm but eerie beauty of Tung Nien.

Molly was excited. She had never seen the opera before and she was none too sure what to expect. Tung Nien was doing her best to explain, but her own knowledge was limited to the most basic facts.

"If the actor is wearing green," she said, "It means he represents a person of high rank."

"Like Chen Liew!" said Molly.

"I suppose so," Tung Nien agreed and continued, "Purple is the colour worn by Barbarian Generals."

"Like the Japanese!" laughed Molly.

"A red-faced actor represents a courageous but dim-witted man."

"My father," said Molly quietly. Tung Nien took Molly's hand and decided she had explained enough. As they looked together over the heads of the people sitting in the square below them, Tung Nien thought that perhaps she should have defended Russell before his daughter. But she knew so little about him. What could she have said? Something stupid and grown-up like, "That's no way to speak about your father!" Besides which, maybe Molly was right.

Most of the people in the square were wearing round, pointed straw hats and it was not long before Laughton's beige panama attracted Molly's attention. She pointed towards the Englishman with a shriek of pleasure.

"Look!" she called out to Tung Nien, tugging onto her sleeve. "Doesn't he look silly sitting there in those stupid clothes!" It was unusual for a European to venture so far from Hong Kong. Not many of them were interested in native culture and most of them would have been too frightened to sit, as Laughton was doing, alone amongst the

Chinese.

"That is your courageous but dim-witted man," Tung Nien said, laughing, but she could not help finding the situation curious. What on earth was a gweilo doing at the Bun Festival? As she looked towards him over the heads of the crowd, Laughton turned his face and looked up at the balcony. Their eyes met. Laughton, far from dropping his eyes in embarrassment, as she would have expected him to do, smiled and moved his hand towards his panama. He was going to take it off as a sign of greeting! Tung Nien snapped her eyes away to the floor and then up to Molly.

"Dim-witted, certainly!" she said, but it was half to herself.

"Do you know him?" Molly was asking.

Tung Nien shook her head. She would not look at the man again to find out.

"I know no Europeans," she said, and she raised her chin to make it obvious to anyone who was watching that Chinese Opera was one of her passions, a passion from which nothing could distract her.

A flat gong sounded to indicate that the opera was about to begin and the musicians began what for Laughton was the most horrendous, tuneless noise imaginable. The Chinese around him continued to talk as though the opera had not begun. Indeed, one man had stood up and was weaving his way through the seated crowd, making for a far corner of the square from where he could make good his escape. Laughton did his best to catch some hint of melody but found it impossible. He tried to pick out the beat, drumming his fingers on his knees, but there did not seem to be one. When a man loped across the matting dressed in an elaborate red and gold silk costume with matching head-dress to take up centre-stage and sing in a piercing, falsetto voice, it was almost too much for Laughton. It was all he could do to stop putting his fingers in his ears to block out the appalling racket. He looked up at the balcony. Tung Nien was looking at the stage and was smiling. She actually seemed to be enjoying it! Beside her, Molly had screwed her face into a frown and a grimace, as though she had bitten on something sour. Tung Nien leaned towards her, said something and the frown vanished, although Laughton noticed a bitter taste still lingered on at the corner of her mouth.

The falsetto voice rose slightly in pitch as though demanding Laughton's attention, but what was going on on the stage was totally beyond the bounds of his comprehension. A man was trotting from one side of the stage to the other with precise and measured steps chasing, it appeared, two squares of brightly embroidered silk, but never getting any closer to them. A white-faced man appeared at his shoulder and the Chinese sitting beside Laughton drew back his lips and hissed between his teeth in displeasure. Laughton searched the actor's expression for some hint as to what was going on, but the white make-up remained as immobile as a mask. Laughton looked at his watch. Only ten minutes had passed. He hoped this was not one of the operas Miss Dekyvere had mentioned once over bridge. "There are some of them which last all day," she had said, before adding with a smile, "But in those cases, it is acceptable for the audience to talk, to have luncheon or, indeed, to leave at any given moment, if they so desire." Laughton would certainly have left immediately had Tung Nien not held him spellbound in his place.

"That man with the hat keeps on looking at you," said Molly, who found Laughton's antics more interesting than the man chasing, but never catching, the embroidered silk.

"He is not chasing the silk, Molly. The silk represents a sedan chair. It means he is being carried in a sedan chair. And the European gentleman does not keep looking at me."

"Oh, yes, he does! And he has taken off his hat."

"What is he like?" Tung Nien asked quietly.

"For one of them," said Molly, "He's very handsome."

And so she would have to look after all.

At that moment, Laughton was watching the stage. His profile was soft in the sun, although his nose was large in comparison with the snub-nosed Chinese sitting around him. He was holding his hat by the brim between surprisingly long and feminine fingers.

"He has a gentle face," said Tung Nien, but Molly snorted.

"He looks like he was made from stone!" she said.

When Laughton caught her eye for a second time, he could have sworn that she smiled at him. It made the torture of the opera worthwhile. The tuneless music, the unrhythmical percussion, the high, falsetto voices and the garishly made-up faces all faded into insignificance with the faintest movement of her lips. It did not occur to Laughton to examine the other faces of the audience. Had he done so, he would have found that everyone was looking across at him and that all of them were treating him to the same quizzical smile which, in Tung Nien, he had taken for affection. And the reason that they were all looking at him was that the man who had been chasing the silk squares had arrived at his destination, put away his sedan-chair and was now pointing his sword at Laughton and singing a very angry song in a most strident squeak. Laughton would have felt mortified had he realised he was the centre of attention, but Tung Nien's smile protected him from baser feelings. When she looked away and released him, the moment had passed and it was only the insistent nudgings and leers of his hissing neighbour which gave Laughton the uncomfortable suspicion that something else had happened.

And then Tung Nien and Molly left the balcony. One minute they had been there, laughing, and the next, they had gone. Laughton would not have felt more devastated had he been told that the Japanese had reached Kowloon and were preparing an invasion of Hong Kong itself. He stood up immediately and began to climb over the seated bodies in an effort to reach the corner of the square in time to see where they were going. He fell a couple of times and banged against the spectators' backs with his knees but they seemed to forgive him his clumsiness because he was European.

When he reached the alleyway, it was empty. A solitary bamboo pole of white washing dripped from a balcony to his right and a small puddle formed in the path before him. Laughton wandered the streets aimlessly for a while until he came out on the waterfront of the harbour and there he found a bar in which to hide himself away along with half a dozen old men. Watching people scrambling up bamboo poles and grabbing at edible buns with which to assuage the anger of the dead did not seem such a good idea any more.

No sooner had he sat down with the only drink he had ever been able to pronounce in Cantonese, a rather malodorous brandy (whisky was not available on the outlying islands), than he was approached by a young boy of about fifteen with bright, piercing, black eyes. The boy sat down uninvited at Laughton's small, rattan table. He held out his hand and Laughton obligingly shook it.

"Wu Tang," said the child and, seeing no reaction in Laughton, added proudly, "The Tangs of Kat Him Wai."

"Sorry, young fellow," Laughton said smiling, "The only Chinese I know is Mao Zedong!"

The boy grinned and clasped Laughton's knee as he repeated with a grin, "Mao Zedong!" He shook his head happily. "You Communist!" He said in English.

Laughton leaned back in his chair. Communist? He had never stopped to think about it before. He sipped the brandy. It was so disgusting that, without thinking what he was doing, he spat it straight back into the glass.

"My God!" he said to the boy, his face involuntarily showing his disgust. Wu Tang grabbed the glass and ran with it back to the bar. After some gesticulating and a little laughter, the boy returned to the table with a glass of clear, but yellowy, liquid which smelled of petrol or paraffin, Laughton could not decide which. The taste was fiery but surprisingly palatable. Laughton smiled at the boy and took a second mouthful of the drink.

Outside in the streets, darkness was falling and paper lanterns were being lighted and hoisted onto long poles. They were being carried towards the harbour as the people made their way slowly down to the waterfront and the bamboo bun towers.

"You come!" said Wu, pointing towards the lanterns. "You watch!"

Laughton shook his head.

"I don't think so," he said. Wu frowned, shrugged and left the bar. Laughton was again made aware of how clumsy he was in the presence of children. He felt angry with himself for not having simply agreed with the boy. He watched the soft yellow glow of the lanterns bobbing past in the street and sipped at his yellow drink. He listened to the birds singing in their cages at the door of the bar and he began to relax, preparing himself for an evening's drinking. He had lost Tung Nien. For all he knew she might have already left the island, and he had lost his little Communist companion. All he felt like doing was sitting apart from the crowd and looking on as the strange festival ran its course. But Wu Tang had returned.

He had changed his clothes and he stood now arrogantly in the doorway of the bar, silhouetted by the dancing lights of the passing lanterns. He was wearing a white T-shirt covered in red Chinese characters, a green, silk band at his waist, and baggy, red trousers with a flash of white just below the knee. Wu Tang stood with his hands on his hips and beckoned to Laughton with a surly tilt of his head.

"You come!" he demanded.

Laughton stood up. He recognised the uniform of the dragon dancers. He placed a hand on Wu's shoulder.

"Are you going to be the one who carries the ball for the dragon to chase?" he asked. It seemed the most logical thing, given the boy's size, but Wu tossed his head back and said, "I am head of dragon!"

"Well," said Laughton, "In that case, I should be delighted to come and watch."

When the dance began, although Wu was apparently thrusting the dragon's head as high as he could into the air, his face remained hidden beneath the huge grinning mouth of the dragon. The head was mostly red, although the edges of its mouth formed an elaborate pattern of intertwined blues and greens. Inside the mouth, four white fangs and a pointed red tongue tried to make its lolling grin more fierce. Two red and white horns wobbled on the top of its head and its green and yellow eyes seemed to be set on springs. The striped silks of the dragon's body flowed out behind Wu like an enormous centipede, floating and twisting and rippling through the air. A deafening crash of firecrackers echoed along the street and died in the tight alleyways of the village and hundreds of children ran towards the bamboo towers in search of buns. Somewhere, gaudy floats were being prepared and hoisted aloft on bamboo poles.

Laughton felt suddenly exhilarated in the presence of such unfettered energy. He breathed in deeply, the remains of burnt gunpowder and the smoke from thousands of joss sticks stinging in his nose. The dragon continued its mad, frenetic dance and another string of firecrackers exploded somewhere away to Laughton's right. Everywhere he looked, he saw happy faces reflected in the soft glow of the paper lanterns, all of them chewing on small buns.

"I got three!" said an excited voice behind him in English. Laughton turned quickly and saw Molly repeating her message in Cantonese to Tung Nien. "Three!" she said again, counting out the buns on her fingers. Tung Nien smiled and pushed Molly past Laughton to the front of the crowd from where she would have an unobstructed view of the dragon dance. Laughton placed himself directly behind them and breathed in the intoxicating smell of jasmine perfume. He opened his eyes and saw that the dragon was careening towards them, racing and twisting its way across the open ground, heading straight towards where they were standing at the front of the crowd. In a mad cacophony of exploding firecrackers, Wu jumped up onto the man's shoulders who had been in charge of the furry ball which teased the dragon. He pushed the dragon's head high up into the air, holding it stiffly up into the night on the end of two long poles. He stood immobile on the man's shoulders and stared fixedly down into the crowd, his face fulfilled and still, with a faint smile playing along his lips, as though in a trance. He was staring straight into Molly's eyes.

3

"A spring wells up at the foot of the mountain.
It is not I who seek the young fool.
The young fool seeks me."

(i)

Since leaving his wife and since allowing his daughter to be taken away from him, Willard Russell had drifted aimlessly from one alcoholic daze to the next. His life had no purpose. His only two reasons for living had disappeared. At first, he had spent long hours tormenting himself with the meaningless nature, not only of what his life had become, but, more than ever now, what it had always been. He had always been led into events, never confronting situations to bring about change, but accepting them meekly and convincing himself later that he had decided. Even marrying Suyong had been her decision. "I'll give you twelve months to make up your mind," she had said. "And then either you marry me, or I'll leave you."

He was sitting in the Tea Room of the Peninsula Hotel with Kenji and he looked at the Japanese barber, the eyes two scalpel slits in the soft putty of his face. The droning of a propeller drifted into the room from the clear blue sky outside. Russell listened absently to the sound of the 'plane. He thought himself into the cockpit, the earth below spread out small and flat like the pages in an atlas. His life had once been like that, mapped out and clear, the roads leading away to the distant horizon of his future. But then a mist had blown in from the sea and with the mist the darkness of night. He had banked his 'plane once, climbed away from the sea, and then banked again to resume the mundane course of his destiny, unaware that his horizon had slipped away and the 'plane had begun to plunge towards the sea. Thinking he was flying true to the co-ordinates he had mapped out for himself, pulling the wings of his fragile craft steady, he had accelerated into the darkness heading straight towards, not the open sky, but the solid sheet of the choppy sea below. He had not realised his mistake because he had not to his knowledge lost his sense of direction. Maybe the 'plane had broken up before the impact that had taken his family and allowed him to survive, but that would have taken the blame for disaster away from Willard Russell himself and, more than anything else, he needed to feel that he was to blame. So he had flown blindly on into the sea believing he was still heading over the distant horizon where all his dreams lay like fields of cherries waiting to be picked.

And so, although he was often bored by it and almost always confused, he embraced Kenji's mysticism with a manic conviction, desperate to find something which might justify his existence and fill the emptiness which his life had become and which could no longer be filled satisfactorily by alcohol and self-pity. But today, he was finding it difficult to concentrate.

"There are two forces in Taoist Yoga, Willard," said Kenji, "Negative vitality and positive vitality, two opposites. The negative vitality is represented by the Dragon, the positive vitality is represented by the Tiger."

Willard Russell thought of the wispy shapes of animals on Chinese prints. The last thing he could think of was vitality and he could not imagine vitality being negative. It seemed a contradiction in terms. But then so much of life was a contradiction. What did one more matter?

"Immortality," said Kenji, "which is our final goal, is Spirit plus Vitality." He looked seriously at Willard Russell, about to reprimand him for not listening, but Russell was leaning slightly forwards in his wheelchair and watching the Japanese intently. Kenji swallowed quickly and continued, "Spirit leads to the realisation of Essential Nature and Vitality leads to Eternal Life."

It is as though he is reciting a poem, thought Russell, allowing the sounds of the words to wash over him. It reminded him of the sermons he had sat through as a child, the interminable flow of complicated, archaic words spoken in a reverent monotone, words which seemed to both threaten him and lift him up. The feeling was not dissimilar now. Perhaps the only difference, he thought, was that he had lost the innocent belief in the world and the hereafter that he had had as a child. Maybe the first step was to get that back.

"Vitality manifests itself as a white light," said Kenji. "It is like moonlight. When the light is full, it is equivalent to only one half of a whole. When Vitality is full and descends to unite with Eternal Life, the golden light manifests itself. This light is reddish yellow and when it is full, it is equivalent to the other, to the missing half. The union of these two lights produces the whole, and this whole is the Immortal Seed."

Willard Russell loved the sound of the words. But he loved the shapes of words too. Perhaps that was why he had ended up as a calligrapher, tracing the feathery shapes onto rice paper with the delicate tip of his pen. He had never learnt to draw the Chinese symbols quickly, but would painstakingly sketch them out as though the slightest wavery line might steal some meaning from the whole. He thought how beautiful the Chinese symbols were and yet how ugly and flat the language was because it was the words he liked, not language. He thought how difficult it had always been for him in any language to put one word next to another and to build a meaning that would truly reflect what he felt. Russell yawned and sat forwards a little.

"Let's call it a day, Kenji, eh? I can't seem to concentrate."

One or two curious heads in the Tea Room turned.

"The cavity of the dragon is the seat of the element of water," said Kenji, although it was now more to himself than to Russell.

"Can't concentrate," said Russell again.

"Man loses the power of concentration once he has fallen into the post-natal state," said Kenji simply, stating a fact now rather than teaching.

"I sometimes wonder if I ever had any powers of concentration," said Russell morosely.

"But that is the whole point, Willard," continued Kenji patiently. "You haven't. We must first return to our prenatal state..."

Russell held up his hands. "Forget it, Kenji!" he insisted. "Not today. No more today, eh?" He sipped at a cup of weak camomile tea. "What I'd like to do today is go out to the frontier."

Kenji had begun to clear away the empty plates from their table. "Why?" he asked, looking up with a slight frown. "There's nothing there."

"My wife is there," said Russell. "It's one year today since she died."

Kenji shook his head. "Your wife is not there, Willard, just her remains."

Russell smiled sadly, recognising the truth in what Kenji was saying. "You know some of the Chinese polish the bones of their dead, don't you, dig them up and polish them once a year? I kind of like that."

Kenji moved round the table and eased Russell's wheelchair out into the passage that led through the potted ferns to the foyer.

"I just don't want to forget her," said Russell.

Kenji hailed a taxi and helped Russell into the back of the car.

Russell looked through the window of the car and out over the plain which separated the New Territories from China. It was, he thought, almost as though he had left his life behind there among the steep gorges and river valleys, the sculptured hilltops carved into the flat watery strips of paddy-fields, the junks almost motionless on the lakes where the villages were hoisted up on wooden struts and the sampans bobbed and rocked on the water. Since leaving China one year ago, he had lost everything. His wife, his daughter, his job and his self-respect. He looked across the plain with a melancholy longing. China seemed to symbolise all the good that he had left behind. And somewhere, not so very far to the north, they were fighting.

"How do you reconcile your country's attack on the Chinese with all your noble thoughts, Kenji?" Willard Russell asked suddenly, a desire to hurt welling up from his own sense of inadequacy.

"People always look for the bad things, Willard. That's the problem."

"What's that supposed to mean?"

For a while Kenji was silent. A funeral procession was blocking the road before them and the taxi drew to a stop beneath the fanning leaves of a banana palm. Willard Russell looked absently at the long purple sheath of the seedpod at the centre of the palm and then away down the road to the mourners who were draped in sackcloth and marching slowly behind a coffin.

"Think for a minute, Willard. The Japanese invasion has brought the Chinese together. They have stopped fighting amongst themselves," Kenji observed quietly. He too was looking at the straggling line of mourners.

"But the atrocities," Russell complained weakly.

"There must always be some who do not make it," said Kenji. He leant forward and dropped his voice to an almost confidential whisper. "But you have to consider it all on a grand scale, Willard. You can't narrow things down to one or two isolated events. We, the Japanese, are thinking and acting for the good of the rest of the Far East. The Greater East Asia Co-prosperity Sphere. Think of it, Willard. A ring from the Aleutian Islands all the way down to Burma, all working together for the common good."

Russell was shocked. It was the first time that he had been forced to consider that the problems in China were not part of some local scuffle for power which would eventually blow over. The Japanese Imperial Army intended to sweep through China and across the rest of Asia as far as the Indian Ocean. Russell looked towards the horizon to the north as though, perhaps, he expected to see some evidence, some cloud of dust caused by the massive moving of troops.

Although he himself felt no stirrings of patriotism other than the mixed melancholy of his memories of China, Willard Russell would not blame Kenji for the fact that he had pronounced the ominous words "Greater East Asia Co-prosperity Sphere" with more than a hint of nationalistic pride. The idea of it, though, was horrific, and the implications were obvious. Russell found it hard to reconcile the attitude of the gentle mystic beside him with the stories of torture and depravation that had drifted down to them first from Manchuria, then Shanghai and finally Nanking, where the Chinese, it was said, were not even allowed to eat the rice they grew in their own fields. All of it went to feed the Japanese occupying forces.

"So, they will continue to advance," he said, not even bothering to make it a question.

Kenji smiled a little sadly and spoke reluctantly. "They have to, Willard," he said. " People have to eat. And Japan is very small."

"Tell the Chinese that," said Russell bitterly.

The taxi had drawn level with the coffin and a framed photograph of the deceased dressed in ceremonial robes and a hard, rectangular hat stared blankly back at Russell. A soft wailing, which was coming from the professional mourners behind the coffin, accompanied the passage of the taxi as it made its way bumpily back towards the open road. Kenji turned away from Russell and looked out into the darkness.

When they reached the border post Willard Russell was still more concerned with the Japanese aggression than he was with the purpose of his visit. He felt that Kenji had cheated him out of his grief and he tried hard to push all thoughts of war out of his mind, to replace them with just one clear image of Suyong. Sadly, the only clear image left him was that of her lifeless body falling onto the rubbish dump beside the rotting dog. Still, he pointed across the frontier and to his right towards a small clump of trees.

"They buried her over there," he said, but he could not rid his mind of all the families that had been slaughtered away to the north, or that had died from starvation, exhaustion or the cold whilst trying to escape, all the people who had had no formal burial at all.

"She was lucky," said Kenji as though reading his thoughts.

Russell shook his head. "Not lucky," he said. "Chen Liew's chauffeur seemed to have a certain influence with the border guards. They might almost have been brothers."

Kenji could not be bothered to explain. "No, Willard," he said to himself. "She was lucky. She died. She will not have to see it."

(ii)

"Of course, an escalation in hostilities across the border can only benefit us in the long run," said Eliot Rodmell leaning across the table and picking up a small parcel of fried Wun Tun.

"Oh, come on, Eliot! You can't seriously wish suffering on other people just to further your own ends?" As soon as he had said it, Alfred Laughton knew the question was redundant. Rodmell was already replying, elbows on the table. He took in all the diners with a long sweeping glance of his watery blue eyes.

"I'm not speaking for myself, Laughton, I was referring to the Colony as a whole. You won't have read it, of course,—why should you?—but the Hong Kong Chamber of Commerce recently published a memorandum listing all goods processed or manufactured here in Hong Kong."

Laughton yawned and looked through the window of the floating restaurant to the dark waters of the harbour. Rodmell continued, counting on his puffy fingers as he spoke.

"Preserved and dried ginger, soya products, sugar refining, knitted wear, rattan furniture, rubber shoes, rope, cement, perfumes, soap and, naturally, fire crackers! Now, then," he said, somehow seeming to lean towards each of them at the same time, "Mark my words, within a matter of months, if they were to publish a similar list, it would include steel helmets, gas masks, army radio transmitters," he shook his head as though amazed at the possibilities stretching away before them, "and other miscellaneous items which are an integral part of warfare, less obvious maybe but, for all that, equally indispensable: nails, bicycles, torches, batteries, water bottles, vacuum flasks—just think about it for a moment! "

An uncomfortable silence settled over the table which was broken by Eliot Rodmell's insensitive admission that he had already branched out into tobacco.

"Soldiers always need cigarettes," he added rather needlessly. "Isn't that right, Major?"

Major Harold Harland, who was sitting opposite Rodmell, nodded in agreement. Harland was well known in the colony due to his impeccable organisation every weekend of the Fanling Hunt where, in the absence of foxes, a bag of aniseed was trailed along the ground by a Chinese coolie to provide a scent for the dogs to follow. Rodmell was a regular and assiduous member of the Hunt.

"I think it's disgusting that you can even talk about it in these terms," said Laughton. "What about morality?"

Rodmell would have laughed, but the question was too ridiculous even for that.

"Come, come, Doctor! We are talking about the Chinese," he said, and he smiled complacently round the table. "It's not the same thing at all. You must remember that we, the British, are a superior race. And it is not just I who think so. The Chinese think of us like that too. It is the nature of things."

It made Laughton feel sick but a glance from his wife was sufficient to stop him saying anything that might endanger their future presence among the elite of Hong Kong society. Laughton knew that he could offer his wife little else and so he ignored Rodmell and his bigotry and, instead, he gave his undivided attention to a glass of whisky and soda which was becoming more insipid by the second as the ice melted in the sticky heat of the evening.

The only recent excitement in the tedium Laughton's life had become had been the moving of the hospital down to Pok Fu Lam on the west coast of the island. It would now be known majestically as Queen Mary Hospital. The new hospital was, however, of little importance when compared to the fatuous plans for the new offices of the Hong Kong and Shanghai Bank which were, it was already obvious, going to dwarf the Golden Jubilee statue of Queen Victoria into insignificance. Laughton felt it somewhat apposite that money and commerce were so blatantly going to overshadow the Empire for it was becoming increasingly clear to anyone who wished to notice that the Empire was now no more than a vanishing dream. True, they were still there as a physical presence. They had the Indian garrisons, the Punjabis and the Rajputs, they had the Governor and they had the P&O liners in the harbour to remind them of their connection with Britain and the far flung reaches of its Empire, but more than ever now, it was an illusion. There had recently been a clear example of this. What had happened when the Japanese had bombed the HMS Ladybird on the Yangzi River? Nothing! They had apologised! And yet, in the same attack, they had sunk the American ship, the USS Panay. There had been no casual apology then. There had been a profound admission of guilt followed by the immediate payment of a huge indemnity! No, thought Laughton, British power in the Far East only lives on in the likes of Rodmell. And a good thing too, at that! Laughton continued to mull over his thoughts, Sir Vandeleur Grayburn, the President of the Hong Kong and Shanghai Bank, has more power in Hong Kong than the poor old King, God bless him!

"And, of course..." Rodmell continued to dominate and monopolise the conversation. It was his privilege. When all was said and done, he paid for the meals that brought them together. "You remember the changes in the currency regulations? Well, it stands to reason that the situation as it was, was untenable—and not only because of the war in China."

Laughton looked round the table and wondered if anyone was actually interested. Major Harland puffed on the stub of his cigar and focussed his piggy, bloodshot eyes on a point just above Rodmell's head; Margaret Rodmell looked on adoringly; his own wife, Mary, was studying the intricate cross-stitching on her serviette; the Fosters (Laughton did not know them, but had been told that they were in rubber somewhere) nodded in unison; and Miss Dekyvere smiled in a way which saved her from committing herself to anything. Mrs. Harland, in the meantime, had long since gone to the bathroom and failed to come back. Nobody, it seemed, was overly concerned by her prolonged absence. No, no one was interested, Laughton decided, stifling a second yawn.

"You see," said Rodmell, "just look at the facts. The Hong Kong dollar was a silver dollar. It had, therefore, to fluctuate as the value of silver fluctuated. In the twenties, one Hong Kong dollar was worth something like six shillings and yet, during the slump of 1931, it couldn't even drag itself up to much more than one shilling. The problems for commerce are self-evident, I would've thought?" He looked swiftly round the table, but not for confirmation. Major Harland withdrew the stub of his cigar and waved it once or twice before his face, although he would venture to say nothing. "The only reason they continued to respect the silver dollar," Rodmell went on, nodding towards Major Harland perhaps in gratitude for his continued attention, "is because it was then tied to the ups and downs of the Chinese economy." He paused but more to take a mouthful of brandy than to draw breath. He swallowed quickly and raised an ominous finger. "But," he continued, "by freeing the economy from these restrictions, by ridding it of its ties to China and to the silver market, we opened a door on trade with the rest of the world! Only the other afternoon, Sir Vandeleur Grayburn assured me that in less than a year..." And he stopped, though whether it was because he had let slip a snippet of confidential information or because he had quite simply nothing else to say, Laughton could not decide.

"What about the Triads?" Major Harland was saying. He should have known better than to mention such a thing in Rodmell's presence. "What do they think of all this?"

But Eliot Rodmell was in too good a mood tonight to let Harland's indiscretion upset him. He waved the huge bowl of his brandy glass once or twice beneath his nose before saying, "The Triads are too busy pumping their money into supporting anti-Communist forces. Most of Chiang Kai Shek's generals belong to the Triads, everybody knows that, Major. The only thing they are worried about right now is this alliance. They would much rather keep Mao Zedong and his Communists out of the way. They'd even prefer the Japs to win than Mao."

Alfred Laughton closed his eyes. It was not that he didn't care about the political situation across the border, or in Europe, for that matter, where Hitler and his National Socialists had been monopolising the recent news (the swastika had been ceremoniously hoisted outside the German Legation only the other day, much to the indignation of Major

Harland) it was just that it still seemed to be such a long way away. And his thoughts turned to Tung Nien. He had seen her a few days ago in the back of the white Bentley driving past the end of his drive on her way home. Laughton had taken a glass of whisky out into his garden so as to be able to drink without his wife making a snide comment which would ruin it for him. As he had stood by the gate looking out over the city, the car had crawled slowly up the hill towards him. She was sitting there looking back towards him and for a moment their eyes had met. Laughton, caught staring, had raised his glass awkwardly and his heart had missed a beat. She had smiled at his clumsy gesture before looking away again. Yes, thought Laughton, Tung Nien, unlike the war, was here. She was tangible. She was real. And she was beautiful. So beautiful, thought Laughton, that no one would blame you for turning your back on the rest of life, for your being blinded to anything else that was not her.

"Still with us, darling?" It was his wife reminding him not to be objectionable. Laughton smiled across the table and would have spoken, but Rodmell was still speaking.

"You see the dilemma? Whilst Britain has certain treaty rights which it must, at least, try to defend in China, it knows that the strongest power here and now is Japan. At the same time as we are supporting China, we have to be polite to the Japanese." Eliot Rodmell fixed each of them in turn with his cold dove-grey eyes. Laughton feigned interest and nodded. "As the Japanese advanced through China, they began cutting off what was, quite simply, one of the most significant networks of trading routes in the world, where all kinds of things imaginable were traded. China then suddenly found it could no longer use Shanghai, Tianjin or Qindao. The only major sea-lane remaining for trade with the rest of the world was through Guangzhou and Hong Kong!" Rodmell's eyes were shining and their colour had become a more piercing blue. "Our trade with that part of China not overrun by the Japanese had increased ten-fold! And then our government, in its wisdom, prohibits all imports from Japan or from areas under Japanese control. Coastal trade with the mainland is, at this moment in time, at a virtual standstill! It is disastrous!"

"You mean," asked Laughton, awaking from his lethargy, "That, even after the invasion of Manchuria, even after the bombing of Shanghai, you continued to trade with the Japanese?"

"What else were we to do, Laughton? Be sensible!"

Laughton shrugged. Having made his objection, he found that he was uninterested in taking things any further and so, making a point of turning away from Rodmell, he looked across the table. "How's that young girl getting on, Ruth?" he asked. Nobody could see the relevance, but Miss Dekyvere, for one, was pleased to change the subject of conversation.

"Wonderfully well, considering," she said, ignoring Eliot Rodmell's frown of annoyance at control being taken from his capable hands. "She's even found a friend. I sneak him in to see her from my garden when there's no one else about. You see, it would not do for them to be seen together."

"Why ever not?" asked Mary Laughton in astonishment.

"It is a long story," said Miss Dekyvere, "And one which I fear would bore you all terribly."

"Do tell!" suggested Mary Laughton, sensing gossip.

"I mustn't," said Miss Dekyvere, and she smiled across the table at Laughton as though she thought that he, at least, might understand, as though she recognised a certain empathy between them which set them apart from the other diners at the table.

"Besides which," Miss Dekyvere continued, "I feel sure that Eliot would rather we ladies retired and left the gentlemen to their port and cigars."

And with that, she stood and led the other ladies away, perhaps, thought Laughton, with a wry smile, to search out and rescue the unfortunate Mrs. Harland who had still not returned from the bathroom.

Eliot Rodmell beckoned towards Major Harland, and the two men, drawing their chairs together, turned their backs slightly away from Laughton, who was left with no choice other than to suffer the conversation of Mr Stephen Foster. Whilst he listened to the rubber planter droning on about something or other to do with minimum yield and new trees, "subsidised by the Government back home, don't you know? Stocking up supplies!" Laughton found he was inadvertently eavesdropping on a conversation which was far more interesting.

"We all know it goes on, Harland, for God's sake!" Rodmell was speaking in an urgent and hoarse whisper, "Been going on, in fact, for years! What I want to know is how can I get trustworthy information on it?"

"Don't quite follow, old boy," said Harland reluctantly, drawing his rounded shoulders still nearer to Rodmell and glancing into the older man's blue eyes. "Of course, besides the regular constables and officers, most of whom are Chinese or Indian, it's true—as you know, only the senior officers are Europeans—there do exist a few scraggy, badly-equipped, badly-trained squads, but their only value to the Army is that they provide intelligence. To get information, don't you see, you need local knowledge?"

"Yes! Yes! Yes!" said Rodmell, exasperated. "But what about the District Watch Force?"

"Not at liberty to say," said Harland, reverting to the military in an attempt to avoid sounding rude.

"Look, Harland, don't be obtuse! Everybody knows the Police themselves choose the Chinese who are going to make up the District Watch Force and, by the same token, everybody knows the members of the District Watch Force are paid by private individuals, that they are not a part of the police force. We are all also constantly being told what a valuable part they play in the island's security system. Now then," said Rodmell slowly, pausing for emphasis and a sip of port, "What I want to know is this: Does Chen Liew have his thugs out in the Hok Un district?"

"Thugs?"

"Oh, damn it, Harland! All right, his Watch Force!"

"Your tobacco plant?" Major Harland whistled, suddenly appreciating the importance of the question. "You mean you have to pay protection money?"

"Not yet," said Rodmell ominously, stealing a furtive glance towards the other side of the table where Laughton and Foster were apparently deeply involved in a discussion about the Straits economy. "I don't know, something like seventy per cent is produced by small holdings, I believe," Foster was saying. "But don't quote me on that!"

"What I mean, Harland, is that before I pay up, I have to know who it is I am likely to be upsetting if I don't pay."

"Like Chen Liew, you mean?"

"No, Major Harland. It is not, shall we say, wise to upset Chen Liew. Why the hell do you think I'm asking you all this in the first place? If I knew it was Chen Liew, I'd just have to pay and cut my losses. Rumour has it, though, that it's Tang. Now that is a different kettle of fish altogether!"

"Well, I don't know, Eliot. It's all a bit beyond me, out of my field, so to speak," said Major Harland heavily. He did not even pretend to hint that he was sorry he could be of no more help. Rodmell scowled across the table towards Foster and Laughton and pushed his chair away from the table rudely.

"Let's go and find out what the damned women are up to!" he commanded and began to stride purposefully across the dining room towards a wide, sweeping staircase which led to a covered terrace on the upper deck of the floating restaurant.

(iii)

A few days later, Dr Alfred Laughton left Hong Kong to attend a conference in the small British colony of Penang, just off the north-west coast of Malaya, where he was to read a paper entitled, "Morphine: From Miracle Drug to Menace. (To what extent can we blame the Bayer Laboratories?)" He had written the paper because he had been told to "rubbish the Germans". On the long trip south and during the lonely week he spent in the Runnymede Hotel on Penang Island, Laughton had plenty of time to think, and he spent a lot of time thinking about his wife, but most of his time thinking about Tung Nien. In Penang, it was hot and sticky. Laughton enforced an unnecessary isolation, retiring early to his hotel room to lie beneath a single, crisp, white sheet where his loneliness nourished his obsession with Tung Nien. It amused him to invent a character for her, to think her into different moments with him, but the more he did so, the more he realised the attraction he felt was purely physical. When he closed his eyes, he could almost feel her lying next to him. It was a conscious dipping into physical absence and memory for, after the initial excitement of being together had worn off, sex between Laughton and his wife had at first become sporadic and then all but ceased altogether. For a time, their physical union had somehow compensated for their lack of any kind of mental affinity but then, as they both came to realise how little they had in common, they drifted apart, and sex for Mary had become an unpleasant and unwanted obligation, a succumbing to a person she had begun to detest and for Laughton it was little more than a trophy won at the end of a long and arduous battle against tremendous odds. Their desire for children had kept up the pretence long after the physical attraction had waned. There was no one point, though, where Laughton could say it all fell apart, although he could identify a long period of loss and loneliness when the smallest touch from his wife might well have brought everything back together again. But neither he nor Mary seemed willing ever to make the smallest kind gesture. They might have planned the nasty ones. And so he felt no guilt as he thought of Tung Nien and fantasised with her slender body. Alone in Penang it was more natural for him than thinking of his wife and more romantic than taking one of the cheap prostitutes who hung about around the docks in their brightly coloured, flimsy, cotton skirts where, every morning, before breakfast, he walked out to buy a two day-old copy of *The South China Morning Post* as soon as it was delivered from the British air base across the water in Butterworth. Then, sitting on the lawns behind his hotel and eating fresh papaya and durian, he would read of what was happening back in Hong Kong. Just reading about the affairs of the Colony helped him feel closer to Tung Nien. It gave him a world to place her in, a context for his imaginings. But, to judge from the articles published in *The South China Morning Post*, nothing much was happening at all. As the public found it difficult to relate to news from Europe and because they preferred to close their eyes to the cruelties of the Japanese and their inexorable progress through China, very little news of the war was being published at the time. When the Japanese blockaded the British settlement of Tianjin, some seventy miles to the east of Beijing, it warranted less newspaper space than an article celebrating the opening of the Jubilee Reservoir, which, Laughton read, had been marred only by the mortal accident of a labourer who had fallen during the opening ceremony. The Jubilee Reservoir, it was explained, as though this fact were far more important than the death of a Chinese coolie, was the highest reservoir in the British Empire.

By this time, Tung Nien's English was good enough for her to read the simplest articles in the paper but when she read of the Jubilee Reservoir she wondered why she had made such an effort to learn a language which only served to emphasise her boredom. And neither had Molly's presence been quite the positive relief she had hoped for. It was true that they enjoyed each other's company. Being with Molly allowed Tung Nien to relax into a certain immature irresponsibility which was denied her in the strict presence of her husband. They went swimming at Deep Water Bay, with Chan patrolling the headlands behind them, and sometimes they were driven down to Central where Chan would pluck an old Chinaman from his shop to tell them their fortunes in the plush leather seats in the back of the Bentley. But it was still not what Tung Nien had imagined life should be and she was still bored.

If her life on The Peak had failed to live up to her expectations, her married life was worse. Chen Liew had fulfilled his marital duties only until their first wedding anniversary. Then, one day, he had announced quite simply, between two mouthfuls of chop suey, that he would no longer be able to ejaculate. Sex, he had explained, would no longer be permitted. He was not impotent, but his sperm, he said, seeing that procreation, the reason for his marriage, had failed, must now be reserved for a different purpose. It was his vital life force and must be conserved if he were ever to find eternal life. After the age of sixty, he explained, ejaculation was not permitted. "You are a woman," he had said. "And for a woman it is not the same, for in sex you lose nothing of yourself."

Tung Nien was not sure whether or not this meant she was still permitted to have sex, but she decided, then and there, that she would, if for no other reason than to spite him. She looked at him across the table and saw, not the great, all-powerful Chen Liew who had talked her through the poetry and religion she could not understand alone, but a feeble, pompous old man who was so concerned with himself that he could not even begin to appreciate her simplest needs. He was like a neatly packed suitcase, locked and waiting in the corridor of an abandoned house, the owner living on only in the tight folds of the used and pressed linen suits which tidily concealed the fact that the case was void of souvenirs. She, on the other hand, had not yet travelled enough to even know what was worthy of becoming a souvenir, unaware of what she would stash away in a limp bag with a bundle of loosely folded clothes.

Even Molly had more of a life than she did. Whereas she was denied all contact with the outside world, Molly had been allowed to befriend Wu Tang. Tung Nien recognised the bright, arrogant face of the boy who had been the head of the dragon from the Cheung Chau bun festival. Often, when she had been left alone, she would sit in her bedroom at the back of the house and she would listen to the two teenagers whispering to each other beneath her window and then, she would try at least to luxuriate in the spaces she had surrounding her, for space was what she had always thought she had missed whilst growing up in the Walled City and the sound of voices always seemed to hem her in. But she now found that space alone could be as restricting as the flat walls of the tenement building of her childhood. Now the walls still existed but they had been pushed back and they were capped with an encrusted line of broken glass. As a child growing up, her lack of privacy had been oppressive and inhibiting, but she knew now that privacy could also be absolute and inviolate. The pleasure of just being alone had palled once she had run out of simple things to do and once she had found that she had no places left to explore.

"Why won't he let me out?" she complained to Miss Dekyvere one morning.

"He thinks you have all you need here," said Miss Dekyvere evasively, "And, besides, it is dangerous."

Tung Nien looked across the lawn at the stern, blank walls of her prison.

"I spent all my life out there," she said. "Nothing ever happened to me."

"You weren't Chen Liew's wife."

"And why is that such a big deal?"

Miss Dekyvere, too, looked towards the walls. A single hose swished and watered a flowerbed of hibiscus and frangipani plants.

"I, personally, don't think it is," she said, "But my opinions have always been notoriously misguided. And, besides, I don't really know enough of the world to be able to make that kind of judgement. I know only that he is afraid for you."

"I know how to look after myself," Tung Nien objected.

Miss Dekyvere felt the vocabulary of her experience insufficient to explain. She struggled still with a vengeful God and had had no time to forge the words or sentiment with which to express evil outside of a simple breach of the Commandments. Her intuition, though, hinted at many unspoken sins.

"You might be kidnapped," she admitted finally, as though she had read it somewhere once and, whilst not altogether believing it, had stashed the information away to be used in just such an emergency as this.

Tung Nien laughed.

"Why should anyone want to kidnap me?"

Miss Dekyvere wished she had not started.

"I don't know," she said. "It is what I have heard, that is all."

But of course it was not all. Only she had decided that if no one else had explained to Tung Nien what her husband did and why it was dangerous for her to be out in the city alone, there must be a reason for it, and she was not about to violate the unspoken trust that Chen Liew had placed in her. Miss Dekyvere is a tomb, the other women would say, almost reproachfully, for the secrets they imparted they generally wanted to be told. Why else would they offer them up so readily? But Chen Liew had said nothing, and that made all the difference. If she were a tomb for Nurse Gemmell's strident infidelities, the more reason to respect the wishes of her unsung guardian. And so she said:

"Why don't you ask him yourself?"

"I can't even ask him if he's happy," Tung Nien replied quietly and, after a moment's thought, "I think, somehow, I have failed him. I think there was something else he wanted."

In Wu's mouth everything was an adventure. Love was a mystery to discover slowly together, to be whispered about, to be unwrapped in darkness and folded away in the deepest reaches of your heart where nothing could get in to spoil it, to make it commonplace. Molly loved to hear him speak to her of love.

"Just because we have never seen the snow does not mean we cannot sense it falling, blanketing the plains and mountains away to the North."

Molly did not tell him that she had been born into a drift of snow that was deeper than a river valley and that she had spent the first five years of her life making entire cities out of ice.

Love, said Wu, was like the snow they had never seen. Something which existed on the other side of knowledge. Knowledge was the war and the Japanese. Love was the snow.

"For me it is like hunger," said Molly. "It arouses a longing."

And so they kissed eager teenage kisses and Molly's were pure and fresh as the snow and Wu's were like small, sweet, decorated buns.

Towards the end of the Autumn, just as Dr Alfred Laughton was returning from Penang with his obsession for her still intact and, if anything, even greater than before, Tung Nien approached Chan and tried to make him talk to her. If they could be friends, she thought, he might allow her to bend her husband's rules a little. But she was unprepared for the strength of Chan's loyalty. She asked him all kinds of questions about Chen Liew but it soon became obvious that he would tell her nothing. She then tried to make him talk about himself but her questions were greeted with an even more stony silence than before. Then one Saturday morning, she had been sitting in the garden with Molly and Molly had suddenly looked up and said, "Why does everybody hate the Tangs so much?"

"The Tangs are bad people!" Chan had said immediately. "They're not honest. They do not respect the unwritten law of the monks. They think only of money. They have no respect for honour," he continued. "The old principles are disappearing all around us. Only Chen Liew," he said reverently, "still respects the traditions..." At which point he stopped.

Tung Nien tried to coax some more from him but Chan, realising he had already said more than he should, remained silent. Molly complained that Chan was being unfair and that he didn't know what he was talking about but not even that could make him speak further. Later, as she lay alone in bed, Tung Nien found that she could not forget the conversation. The words "Only Chen Liew respects the old traditions" went round and round in her mind and Tung Nien realised that whatever these traditions were, they were the reason behind Chan's fierce loyalty to him. As she lay alone in bed, awake and waiting in vain for Chen Liew to come to her, she repeated the sentence to herself. "The unwritten law of the monks" she decided finally was what had brought about an end to their sex life together, and she could not help but resent it. When she tried to lead Chan back to the conversation, he became sullen and said only that he should have kept his mouth shut and that she should forget about it.

Chan's silence irritated her and because she had so little to think about, the more she thought about the monks, the more she wanted to be given an explanation as to what it meant. She asked Miss Dekyvere, but Miss Dekyvere said only that she did not trust monks as far as she could throw them. And then one morning over breakfast, she heard Chen Liew refer to the Englishman, Harry Osbourne, as "that guttersnipe who knows more than what's good for him." And it had seemed to Tung Nien the answer to her prayers. Harry Osbourne would be able tell her about the monks and explain why she was not allowed out of the grounds.

Tung Nien decided that she must arrange for Osbourne to be called to the house. Miss Dekyvere could ask him. She could suggest a gathering for Molly's father on some pretext or another. After all, from her experience of him, Willard Russell was scarcely any different from Osbourne. As far as she was concerned, they were both self-centred drunkards.

"Alfred Laughton might accept," suggested Miss Dekyvere quietly, although she failed to see why Willard Russell should not come alone. After all, it was his daughter.

"I don't want him to feel obliged or embarrassed," said Tung Nien.

Miss Dekyvere did not like to argue. And so it was arranged. There would be a social gathering the following week to which Miss Dekyvere would invite Osbourne, Russell and Laughton.

When Alfred Laughton received the invitation he felt the excitement and the anticipation of a young teenager being presented with his first date. True, no mention was made of Tung Nien in the invitation, but he felt the same driving impulses which had led him to follow her and Molly to the bun festival. He would be near her, and that was enough. He looked again at the invitation.

—Afternoon tea and Mah-jongg—

But he didn't even play mah-jongg.

Osbourne, on the other hand, was totally nonplussed. The invitation had been delivered to him at his office during the morning, but he had not even deigned to give it his attention until later in the evening when, sitting before a glass of whisky in the Glory Hole, he had rediscovered it in his jacket pocket whilst searching for a book of matches. He flipped the note open before him and sneered as he read aloud to Sergeant Fletcher.

"Mah-bloody-jongg!"

He glanced round the dim room but he was not looking for anybody.

"Mah-bloody-jongg!" he said again.

Fletcher laughed because it was expected of him and he said, with predictable simplicity: "Rather you than me, mate!"

"They wouldn't ask you, Fletch!" Osbourne replied unnecessarily. A taxi-girl had sauntered over to their table and began to flutter her dance coupons beneath Osbourne's nose, fanning them out before his face like a hand of cards.

"You want fucky-fucky?" she was saying without the slightest expression of interest. Osbourne brushed her to one side.

"It'll be a right rave up!" Fletcher added sarcastically, allowing his eyes to linger on the girl as she wandered off to another table.

"Christ, Fletch, you've got a lot to learn!" said Osbourne, replacing the invitation in its envelope and the envelope in his pocket. He took a match and twisted it between his thumb and forefinger before striking it and lighting a cigarette. He blew a cloud of smoke across the table and prodded his cigarette at Fletcher. "Nobody in Hong Kong, Fletch," he said, "but nobody, asks you out because they want your company. There's always an ulterior motive. The question you have to ask yourself is: Why me?"

Fletcher looked at his friend and wondered just how much of what he said was really true. So much of it seemed to be said for effect, as though he felt a desperate need to show off, almost as though he were constantly searching for approval or respect.

"So, why you?" Fletcher asked obligingly and he added with the hint of a snigger, "And why Miss Dekyvere?" The idea of the old spinster wanting to see Osbourne was incongruous. But Osbourne's mind, practised as it was in analysing seemingly illogical situations, had already raced over all the possible permutations.

"Stands to reason, Fletch," he said smugly. "It isn't her that's asking, is it?"

Fletcher could not see why not. The invitation had seemed perfectly innocent.

"Who is it, then?" he asked challengingly.

Osbourne ran his finger down the side of his nose and squinted across the table.

"Ay," he said removing his glasses and looking at them for a moment before replacing them on his nose, "There's the rub!" And he beckoned the taxi-girl back towards their table.

Kenji had advised Willard Russell to accept immediately, but Russell was reluctant. Miss Dekyvere had included a short note with his invitation explaining that Osbourne and Laughton would also attend.

"I can't stand that damned reporter!" Russell had objected. "And who the hell is Alfred Laughton?"

"Does it matter, Willard? After all, it is for Molly that you will go."

Russell looked at Kenji's bland Japanese features reflected before him in the barber's mirror. They were drinking camomile tea in the barbershop at the Peninsula Hotel. Kenji had run the blinds down over the door and the room was silent save for the slow ceiling fan rotating through the dusty air. Any mention of Molly always made Russell feel guilty. He had not visited her for over six months.

"I embarrass her, Kenji," he explained weakly.

"No, Willard. She embarrasses you."

"She speaks Chinese to me!"

"What do you speak to her? Do you say anything at all?"

"Should never have let her go," Russell muttered beneath his breath. He found he had nothing to say to her. It made him wonder whether they had ever spoken much to each other, although he was sure they had. They had been very close. Everybody used to comment on it.

"Take her a present," Kenji suggested.

"I'll take them both a present," said Russell. "The old woman too."

(iv)

Despite Miss Dekyvere's efforts, the atmosphere at her "mah-jongg party" was tense. Harry Osbourne had made a special effort to make himself presentable and had buttoned his recently laundered shirt right up to the neck where the small, tight knot of his tie seemed to be slowly choking him.

"Now I know how the Chinese feel!" he laughed, in a clear reference to the news that the Japanese were executing Chinese prisoners by garrotting them. Nobody had found it amusing and Osbourne felt uncomfortable as well as suspicious. He had not yet managed to fathom the reason for his invitation. It seemed as though they might actually be expected to play mah-jongg for the drinks had been placed on the four corners of a rose-wood table where the walls of ivory tiles had already been meticulously prepared and the Ming containing the four winds had been placed in the centre.

"I saw some newsreel about the war in China in a cinema whilst I was in Penang," Laughton was telling them. He thought it might ease Osbourne's embarrassment. "Open graves filled with mutilated bodies and, close by the graves, packs of wild dogs prowling..." He stopped, realising that he was not making the situation any better. He did not know the circumstances of Suyong's death and he was surprised at Willard Russell's pained expression. He broke off abruptly. "I didn't know..." he apologised. "I mean, do you have family...?"

Willard Russell waved his hand and adjusted his position in his chair. "No matter," he said gruffly. "Just don't like to listen to things like that." He glanced at Miss Dekyvere. "I don't suppose any of us do, do we?"

Miss Dekyvere smiled. "Sometimes we have no choice," she said quietly.

Alfred Laughton looked across the small table and noticed the old woman was frowning. He wished he could have felt less awkward and that he could have thought of something interesting to say. Years of leaving it up to Mary, I suppose, he thought. Years of letting your wife do the necessary communicating whilst you got quietly drunk in a dim corner of the conversations. And now you don't even know what sort of thing they might like to hear you say.

"You know," he blurted finally, interrupting Osbourne, without realising it, in mid-sentence, "I don't play mah-jongg, I'm afraid."

What the hell did you bloody come for, then? Osbourne said to himself.

"But you can learn, Alfred," Miss Dekyvere smiled at him. And then to the others she said, "Alfred is my bridge partner."

Osbourne pulled at his tie and scowled.

"Rumour has it, Willard," Miss Dekyvere had apparently decided to take the situation in hand, "That you are studying Taoist Buddhism."

Osbourne sneered across the table at the invalid. The things people do!

"Not studying so much," said Russell, "Just sort of taking a look."

Miss Dekyvere nudged the whisky decanter towards Laughton and continued, making it obvious that she was now addressing all of them: "Don't you find it rather apposite that the Taoist god of literature is called 'Man'? I mean, what better name could he have?"

Osbourne sniffed. "You mean 'man' in Chinese?"

"No, Mr Osbourne. I mean his name is 'Man'."

"Don't see the point, then," said Osbourne, whose mind, after one or two drinks, was too sluggish to follow anything but the most simple expression of truth.

Laughton watched, but did not listen to, them talking. He poured himself another drink. They have interests, he said to himself. He looked at Osbourne's weasel-like face nibbling at a prawn cracker. They are all living, they are all part of something I have never known. I go along to the Golf Club, the Cricket Club, the Chess Federation, but I go because it is expected of me, because Mary expects it of me, not because I enjoy it. It is supposed to help me along a path that I did not even choose for myself in the first place. But, then, I have nothing with which to replace it all. Except some stupid boyish infatuation with a woman I have never even met. Look at Osbourne. A slob, maybe, but look at his eyes, his expression. He is alive, at least. And Russell, there, laughing in his wheelchair. He is enjoying himself. He has relaxed and he is joining in, whilst you sit here smoking, drinking and despising everyone without even the faintest idea what they are talking about.

"Oh, yes, Willard, I agree," said Miss Dekyvere, "But the Chinese are more modest. Their Goddess, Tin Han, can only walk on the water if we mortals provide her first with a straw mat!"

And they all laughed until Miss Dekyvere stood up from the table and, motioning towards the French windows which gave onto the garden, said, "May I introduce my friend and neighbour, Tung Nien?"

Laughton snapped his eyes away from the whisky decanter through which he had been observing the refracted wall of ivory mah-jongg tiles and he felt his heart leap and begin to thump against his chest. Tung Nien smiled at each of them in turn and then treated Osbourne to an indulgent, lingering look which seemed immediately to exclude the others. Laughton felt irrationally jealous, like a child who has seen an elaborately wrapped parcel, who has already half-guessed what is inside and who is suddenly told that it is not for him, but for him to give to someone else. Laughton could not take his eyes from Tung Nien. She was so impeccably beautiful. He watched her as she placed herself on a stool beside Osbourne.

"I did not want to come before you finished your game," she said, and her voice was all the more seductive for her sing-song accent. Laughton felt he must speak to her, but Miss Dekyvere, he noticed suddenly, was speaking to him.

"Would you push Willard, Alfred?" she was saying. "Out into the garden. He must speak to Molly."

Apparently, they were to leave Tung Nien and Osbourne alone. Given the depth of his infatuation, Laughton could think of only one possible reason for two people to be left alone. As he pushed Russell from the room, he felt as though all the breath had been punched from his body.

Molly was sitting beneath a banana palm waiting for them. Beside her, Wu Tang was lying back on the grass, his eyes closed. Miss Dekyvere sighed and thought of the unnecessary complications which were certain to be caused by Wu's presence. Her guests, if only out of politeness, would want to know who he was. A Tang playing with Chen Liew's ward! It did not bear thinking about! She felt a pang of regret that she had ever been party to allowing the situation to arise in the first place. Whatever had she been thinking about? And she had done so well in keeping the friendship between the two teenagers not a secret so much as a mystery. When she saw them, Molly nudged Wu in the ribs. He sat up, saw Laughton, and ran towards him down the incline of the garden. An innocent onlooker would have been forgiven for thinking Wu and Laughton, rather than Molly and Russell, the estranged couple. At first, Laughton, whose mind was still inside the house with Tung Nien and Osbourne, did not recognise his friend from the bun festival six months ago. Molly, Miss Dekyvere and Willard Russell looked on with some surprise as Wu stopped running to walk the last few yards up to Laughton and to clasp him arrogantly by the shoulder.

"Ah, my friend, Mao Zedong!" he explained to them with a grin.

"You've met, then, Alfred?" said Miss Dekyvere, adding, perhaps for Russell's sake, for she was certainly not surprised, "Really, Alfred, you are so full of surprises!"

"The bun festival," Laughton explained. "In the Spring."

Why, he thought, did it sound like an apology?

Russell was waiting for Molly, and Wu's effusive reception of Laughton only served to emphasise the gulf that had opened up between them. He remembered the present, a porcelain doll, which he had brought with him, but seeing her so grown up and independent of him he thought better of it and forced it down between his lifeless thighs and the edge of his wheelchair. Molly remained stubbornly beneath the tree.

"Eh, Mao?" Wu was asking Laughton, "You a friend of Molly's?"

Laughton, for want of anything better, was nodding. In his suddenly confused state of mind, which had been brought on by the surprise of seeing Wu so soon after the disappointment of leaving Tung Nien with Osbourne, Laughton was none too sure who Molly was, although logic told him it was the young girl at the end of the garden. It was only when he began to push Russell across the grass that Molly stood up and Laughton recognised her as the girl he had followed with Tung Nien to Cheung Chau.

"So, Molly's your girlfriend, is she, Wu?" he asked in what he hoped might be a jocular tone of voice.

Wu nodded. "Yes, Mao," he said. "My girlfriend."

Tung Nien had no wish to waste any time with Osbourne other than that which was absolutely necessary. For his part, Osbourne was feeling pleased with himself. Hadn't he said all along that he was not being invited to play mah-jongg? He cast an appraising eye over Tung Nien. Close to she was even more beautiful than he remembered. Mind you, when he had gatecrashed the wedding party with Russell he had been three sheets to the wind and he would have had difficulty in noticing anything. Remembering anything he had managed to notice would have been impossible. No. That was not entirely true. He had not forgotten the Hakka. But then, who had? And because he was thinking of the Hakka, he did not find Tung Nien's question as strange as he might otherwise have done.

"Tell me, please, about the Tangs, Mr Osbourne," she said. "And don't just tell me they are bad people, I already know that. I want to know why they are bad people."

Osbourne held up his hands. "Woah!" he said. "Hold on a minute!" He scrabbled in his pockets for a cigarette.

Osbourne's mind began to race. His first thought was that Tung Nien should pay for the information, his second thought that she could just ask her husband and his third thought that, being who she was, the wife of a Head of the Dragon, a 489, no less, he should be very careful and do exactly what he was told. He sat forward, his elbows resting on his knees, and he lit the cigarette. "What exactly is it that you want to know?"

Before he himself was willing to say anything at all, it was important for him to discover exactly what Tung Nien knew and what she might be prepared to give him for his own knowledge.

"I want to know what connection they have with my husband."

Osbourne allowed his eyes to rest for a moment on Tung Nien's perfect complexion. She's not even wearing make-up, he said to himself in some amazement, being used, as he was, to the thick, powdery embraces of the taxi-girls. He tried to force his mind towards a sensible analysis of the situation. She would know nothing. The Chinese did not consider women sufficiently important to share in the kind of information she was asking of him. All that they expected of a woman was that she be a good and loyal wife, whore, or whatever. No thoughts, no opinions—consequently, no information. He should be careful not to say too much for his own good.

"None that I know of," he said in as casual a tone of voice as he could muster. And this, at least, was not untrue. Most of Osbourne's knowledge of the situation in Hong Kong could have been found by any competent researcher in a couple of hours in any history book in the local library. It was a mass of vague generalisations. What made him different from everyone else, and, in fact, what made him a potential danger to the likes of Chen Liew, Tang or even Eliot Rodmell, was that he was possessed of an incredible intuition, a stunning talent for guessing correctly.

Tung Nien decided to try a different approach.

"Chan spoke of monks," she said, as though revealing a secret. "Do you know why he said that?"

Osbourne sniffed and rubbed his hands along the thighs of his trousers where the material was worn and as shiny as silk. Now, this was something where he did like to consider himself a bit of an expert.

"Foo Chow, I imagine," he said.

He felt more comfortable. He could speak freely of Foo Chow because it was common knowledge.

"When the Manchus ousted the Ming Dynasty," he began, lighting a second cigarette from the stub of the first, "I don't know when it was—

I've never been much cop when it comes to dates—seventeenth century, I reckon. Anyway, when the Manchu hordes swept down from Mongolia, over the Great Wall and gave the Mings the elbow..."

He stopped talking and blinked from behind his smudgy glasses at Tung Nien. Her expression suggested that she was having some difficulty in understanding him.

"...Forced the Mings out, rather," he corrected himself, and explained with a blunt shoving movement of his hands followed by a jutting of his shoulder, "There were, naturally enough, a lot of people who were none too happy!"

Tung Nien watched Osbourne struggling with his story and thought, I cannot like him. He is so dirty. There is nothing likeable in him at all. But, then, I don't have to. He is nothing to me. I just wish there had been someone else I could have asked. Just to have him here, talking to me, is offensive. It is almost as though I were being paraded naked before him, the way he keeps turning his goggling eyes on me, all over me. He is such a filthy man. You can almost see his little mind plotting and trying to find a way of having a hold on me.

She despises me, Osbourne said to himself. And she doesn't even have the decency to hide it. It's the same with all these bleeding Chinese women. Never been properly fucked, I reckon! Osbourne hated talking to women because they always had a way of making him feel inferior. Still, this was not just any woman. He had to remember that. This was Chen Liew's wife. His respect, not for the social order, but for what he saw as the natural order of power in the Colony, was stronger than his feeling of derision, and so, he continued.

"Finally, some time later, be about twenty, thirty years later," he said. An involuntary smile crept over his lips as he thought suddenly that he would not accept payment for his information. No, he thought, I like people to be in my debt. I like people to owe me one. He went on, his voice slightly more animated now. "All the anti-Manchu feeling, as it were, found its focal point in this monastery, at Foo Chow, in the south of China. All these monks, you see? They wanted to organise the local people, form an army, what have you, and reinstate the Ming Dynasty.

Of course, the Manchus found out about it, didn't they? and they attacked the monastery."

Osbourne reached for a prawn cracker which stuck between his teeth. He continued to speak as he hooked at his teeth with a dead match stick.

"Of one hundred and twenty-eight monks, only eighteen managed to escape torture and death at the hands of the Manchus. Of these eighteen, they say only five survived. And," he flicked the crumb of prawn cracker away from his teeth with the end of his tongue and swallowed, "It's these five monks that your man Chan was talking about, I reckon."

"Why?" asked Tung Nien quietly. "What have they to do with Tang and my husband?"

But she knew the answer even before Osbourne spoke and she looked through the window only half-listening. She could see Molly and her father beneath the banana palm.

"Well," said Osbourne, "These monks, they formed the first Triad Brotherhood. You know? The Triangle—Heaven, Earth and Man—(whatever that's supposed to mean!). All the threes, everything divisible by three, 426, 489, 36—for the 36 oaths of allegiance. Of course, to be fair, in those days it wasn't a criminal society at all. It was just there to get rid of the foreign invaders."

Tung Nien stood up and walked to the window, not that the interview was over, but she wanted to think for a moment.

Osbourne watched her straight, immobile back, silhouetted against the light from the garden. He felt he had somehow disappointed her, that he had not said what she wanted to hear. But what did he care about that?

Tung Nien watched the two groups of people in the garden, Molly and Russell beneath the tree, and Miss Dekyvere, Wu and Laughton, strolling in the shade of the wall that separated her garden from Miss Dekyvere's. There was something familiar about Laughton, but she could not place it. She looked fixedly at Laughton but she had stopped seeing him. Osbourne was as good as saying openly that both Chen Liew and Tang were members of the Triads. That, in itself, was not surprising. It was said that one in twenty people in Hong Kong were connected with the Brotherhood. The rest belonged to the Police or the District Watch. It was not the existence of the Triads which bothered her. It was the fact that Tang was obviously and unscrupulously stepping on her husband's toes and that Chen Liew, despite Chan's evident desire to the contrary, was allowing it to happen. She turned back to Osbourne, catching him with a handful of prawn crackers halfway to his mouth. He looked at her from behind his glasses with startled, guilty eyes. But she smiled.

"So why did Chan say they are bad people?" she asked, not moving from the window and sensing suddenly, perhaps as a result of her new found knowledge, that Osbourne was actually, despite himself, afraid of her.

"Tang's been selling arms to Mao, or so I'm told," he said, speaking through the crackers.

"But surely the original purpose of the Triads was to rid the country of foreign invaders. So what's wrong with that?"

"Yeah, but Tang's been selling guns to Chiang Kai Shek as well." He raised a finger and pointed, not at her, but at the rosewood mah-jongg table. He had stopped looking at her, almost as though he no longer wanted to know who he was talking to. "And that's your husband's patch, you see?"

Tung Nien would have spoken, but Osbourne continued.

"And it's not only that," he said. "They do say he's also supplying the Japs. Especially up north. In they go, into Tianjin, then by train through Shanhaiguan, see? Zip! Straight up the coast, past the Great Wall, and before you know it, you're in Mukden! Or wherever."

"I thought it was opium," Tung Nien said, almost to herself.

"It's that too," said Osbourne, helping himself now to another glass of Miss Dekyvere's whisky, "But that's not such a volatile market." The word 'volatile' sounded awkward in his mouth and so he exaggerated its length before snapping the word 'market' across the end of the sentence like slamming a door shut. Then, just to assure Tung Nien that there was more locked away somewhere if she could only find the key, he muttered, "You'd be hard pressed to find something the bastards aren't involved in!"

Tung Nien had had enough. She moved away from the window and walked slowly over to the French windows. Osbourne fancied he could make out the shape of her breasts against the light, but it was just that—a fancy.

"But the British are to be blamed there," he was saying, openly ogling what he took to be the impression made by a nipple. On closer inspection he would discover it had been no more than the loose thread left behind by a missing satin button.

Tung Nien was tired of speaking English and tired of Osbourne.

"Yes," she said. "The British." And then she reverted to Cantonese. Osbourne did not need to be a linguist to know that he was being dismissed. As he stepped outside into the garden, he was greeted by the sticky humidity which always came before a tropical thunderstorm. He blew his cheeks out, expelled the air, and belched a piece of prawn cracker into his mouth. When Laughton approached him he was chewing thoughtfully on a match.

"What did she want?" Laughton asked. He did not even pretend to make the question sound disinterested. Osbourne sniffed.

"I can't tell you, mate," he said. "More than my life's worth!"

Which is not very much, Laughton said to himself.

"So!" Osbourne continued cheerfully. "Looks like I've been missing the party, eh? Willard! Willard!" Calling out over the lawn. "I said: Looks like I've been missing the party!"

"Where's Wu?" Molly asked as they arrived.

Osbourne looked round, not really understanding what they were talking about. "What?" he said, his eyes wide. "Disappeared, has he?" And to Miss Dekyvere. "Who is he?"

"Wu?" said Miss Dekyvere. "Wu Tang. A friend of Molly's."

Osbourne's mouth dropped open, but this time he was not feigning surprise.

"Bloody hell!" he said.

(v)

When the three men left the house, the thunderstorm, which had been rumbling around the summit of the Peak for over half an hour, finally broke. They were all grateful, for the rain meant that good-byes would be kept to a minimum and each of them was anxious to be alone, to mull over the recent events.

Kenji was waiting for Willard Russell in the back of a taxi. As Laughton helped the American into the car, the rain drumming onto the metal roof was loud enough to drown any comment either man might have made. They smiled at each other and Laughton closed the door. Osbourne had already left. Laughton could make him out, huddled into his brown raincoat, about fifty yards away down the hill, walking along in what shelter was provided by Chen Liew's garden wall.

Osbourne hardly noticed the rain. His mind was stealthily picking over the events of the afternoon, all of which fell into a certain logical and gratifying pattern until the appearance, or rather, the disappearance, of Wu Tang. No matter how Osbourne looked at it, it did not make sense. He was, by nature, too suspicious to accept the only solution to the problem: that they were friends. In Osbourne's world, nobody did anything for a reason as simple as friendship; nobody did anything unless it would, in some way, further their own interests. It became obvious to him, therefore, as he trudged down the road towards the tram station, that Wu had been planted there by his father, that he was, in a word, spying. He glanced into the dark sky as a crash of thunder rolled across the Peak, but he was only half-satisfied with his conclusion. It was too simple, and experience had taught him that nothing is as simple as it seems. He took out a cigarette but, before he could light it, it had disintegrated in the rain.

There was a covered gateway a little further down the road to his left, broken glass encrusted into the brick-work from a height of some six feet to the top of the wall. Osbourne ducked beneath the shelter of the archway and leaned his back up against the double doors of the gate.

He managed now to light a cigarette and, once he had drawn the smoke deep into his lungs, he wiped his hand across his face and tried to think it out again, beginning this time with his interview with Tung Nien.

A Chinese woman, he thought, would never speak to the likes of me unless...But there was no unless. Chinese women hardly even spoke, were allowed to speak, to men of their own race, let alone to a foreigner! And if they had to speak, it was not to have opinions. Maybe things were changing here, in Hong Kong, too, as they were in Britain, he thought sullenly. But it was no answer, because he knew they were not. Even Tung Nien, he smiled to himself, had been purchased. Everyone knew that, if only because it was such a common practice. He knew it for a fact, for he had investigated a little, as much as he had dared to, after the wedding and he had discovered that Tung Nien's brothers now did the She-K'ou opium run into China, under the guise of innocent fishermen. So who had sent the Chinese woman to interrogate him? And why?

By the time Osbourne finally got onto the funicular tramway, the rain had abated, but as he looked down over the lights of the city he was a very confused and worried man.

Willard Russell sat back in the seat of the taxi and thought, My life has run aground. It has foundered and been washed up against the rocks. And I have no one to blame but myself. Molly did not even want to speak to me! Why have you come here? she asked when I saw her. Not Hello, how are you, long time no see. Why have you come? she said. As though I didn't have any right to visit whenever I damned well felt like it! But that was it, of course. I forfeited that right at the moment when I said Yes. And you can't go back and start again. She has gone from me. And maybe it is better that way. I have so little to offer. I have nothing left even to offer myself. There is Kenji here beside me, smiling as he listens to the rain drumming on the roof and he is smiling because there is, for him, a reason for everything, even the rain. But he cannot give me a reason for my failure except to say, It is so that you can find yourself. I told him I didn't think I'd like what I might find. And he said, First you will be cleansed. But what for? What damned good is it to me being cleansed and purified if I have lost my daughter? And he said, Then it will not matter to you. But it will always matter to me, I said. And I hope to God it will!

Laughton watched the taxi as it drew away. Russell's head looked like a small full stop through the back of the car. Laughton watched until the taxi had gone round the nearest bend in the road and disappeared, and he watched until Osbourne too had gone. Then he pulled the brim of his Panama hat over his eyes and thought, It will be ruined in this rain and Mary will complain. He sniffed and turned to look back at the lights in Miss Dekyvere's house. Well, he thought, To hell with Mary. And to hell with the hat.

Despite the rain, he had no desire to go home. Nothing waited for him there. Mary had even tried to stop him coming to the party in the first place. Why should you go? she had said. Mah-jongg? You don't even play! I can imagine what you'd've said if I'd suggested it! So why is it so important?

And he had come for Tung Nien. He had come for her and she had not even noticed that he was there. But when she had walked in, she had been so beautiful. It had been worth going, if only to see her. It did not matter that she had not seen him. He had seen her. And she was beautiful.

Laughton stood in the rain, looking back at the house for over half an hour. He could not drag himself away although he was getting drenched. He was happy because he knew that Tung Nien was still inside. He was not even hoping to catch a glimpse of her. He was just content to be near where she was. It was as though proximity were enough to satisfy his longing for something more. And there will be more, he told himself. There must be, if only because I want it so badly. I have never before wanted anything, in all my life, as I want her.

As he stood in the road in the rain, Laughton neither thought about his wife nor about Chen Liew. Only two people existed for him in all the world. He knew little enough of Chen Liew's power, but even had he known, he would have felt the same, thinking, He has so much and I have so little. He will probably not even notice! Nor did he consider his wife for she had long since disqualified herself from such considerations. Always putting me down, he said, Always making me look ridiculous. Always wishing I were somebody else instead.

(vi)

Eliot Rodmell sat at his desk and pushed a Chinese calligrapher's pen backwards and forwards across the brown leather inlay. The pen, which had been a present from Sir Vandeleur Grayburn himself, was chewed at one end where two black Chinese figures on the bamboo stem said Good Luck.

He looked out over the harbour. From his office he could just see the Hok Un district and if he screwed his eyes half-closed he could imagine that he could see the long, red, corrugated-iron roof of his tobacco warehouse. For two months he had been paying a fixed amount into a numbered bank account, supposedly to protect his property and his raw materials (in this case, not only Indonesian tobacco leaves but also field radio components) and yet, for two months, somebody had been lifting whatever they wanted with impunity. Rodmell suspected the Tangs, but he had no proof. He sat back in his chair and looked at the sea. Two junks approached each other from opposite ends of the harbour but they were moving so slowly that they looked almost like a painted scene.

Rodmell put the soft, feathery tip of the calligrapher's pen into his mouth and sucked it into a sharp point. The thing is, he said to himself, You can't just let these things happen. At some point, you have to make a stand.

However, the problem facing Rodmell was far from simple. He could not merely tell Chen Liew that the money he was paying him was not being put to good use because it would be tantamount to telling him that Tang's organisation (he had recently been told that it was known as the Silent River) was more efficient, or perhaps, even, more powerful than his own. To compound his doubts as to what move to make next, he had heard rumours which suggested that Chen Liew was losing favour. His detractors blamed him openly for having bargained with Tang over the opium exports into China and, despite the recent Communist-Kuomintang alliance, he was being criticised behind his back for his blinkered support of Chiang Kai Shek and his refusal to even consider any agreement with the Communists or the Japanese. It was a particularly sensitive moment for Chen Liew and he would not welcome any interference from Rodmell.

No matter how he thought round the problem, Rodmell could see no way through it. Whatever direction he took ended up with a dead end. He looked across the harbour where the two junks had now met and, with one behind the other, they seemed to have momentarily fused together. It was, he thought, a visible manifestation of how reality was sometimes less real than dreams. He knew the junks were moving, but he could not see them. To his eye, they were glued together, had become one and the same thing. And yet he knew there would be metres of water separating them. He found the idea attractive—to make the obvious appear to be something different and yet, at the same time, even more convincing than the truth. It was, he thought, a wonderful conceit. If only they could never be broken apart by time, but only by perspective—because he knew that, seen from his house high up on the peak, the junks would be two already. You could control perspective, after all, whereas time, or the passing of time, was inevitable. If whatever he decided to do could always be so co-ordinated so as to give the illusion of permanence, to be unaffected by the passing of time and the changing of perspective. If whatever he decided to do could move accordingly so that it would always appear to be constant and consistent.

It was the kind of conceit that pleased Rodmell although it did nothing to alleviate his problems. He remembered an evening of bridge when he had announced, quite for what reason he no longer knew, nor cared, for that matter, "Time, when you think about it, is only distance, isn't it? I mean to say, if you could see from far enough away, you would, in effect, be looking into the past—you would be looking at something happening which had already taken place." He had been treated to raised eyebrows and an inquisitive cough and so had added reluctantly, "Like the stars, I mean."

Eliot Rodmell drew two crosses to represent the junks on a note pad and then he drew converging lines to denote where he would have to be if he always wanted to see them together. The last point he found, before he was interrupted by Michael Robinson, his personal secretary, was somewhere to the north of Papua New Guinea. Then, he mused, they would not only still be together, they would also be in the past, the reality would be doubly unreal and, for that simple reason, it would be even more wonderful.

"The Japanese are backing off from Tianjin, sir," Robinson called out from the door before entering and rubbing his hands together.

Rodmell watched the junks separate again into two distinct units.

"Yes, Robinson," he said. "I know that."

"Good news, eh, sir?" Robinson continued enthusiastically and he sat down uninvited at Rodmell's desk.

"Good news, indeed!" said Rodmell. But he could not concentrate. What did that matter now that he had two junks again out there on the water?

"And they've set up three refugee camps in Kowloon!" Robinson pronounced the sentence as though he expected Rodmell to show an interest.

"How ludicrous!" said Rodmell, almost to himself.

But Robinson, unperturbed, was continuing to reel off the most recent developments provoked by the proximity of the Japanese.

"The Tung Wah Group, sir, have opened up their hospitals to the refugees, and I believe an Immigration Department is to be set up under a cadet officer. All Chinese must apply for certificates of residence."

Robinson was not to know it, but this news, at least, pleased Rodmell. Wherever there was bureaucracy, there was an opening for corruption. He smiled sardonically as he said, "The next thing you know they'll be slamming taxes on us!"

"Sir?" said Robinson.

Rodmell leaned back in his chair. He did not want to talk about it. He was looking at the junks and thinking that the key to the whole problem with Chen Liew and Tang was, finally, his own reputation. He could not afford to sit back as though nothing were happening. He could not allow anyone to think he was weak.

"More refugees, Robinson," he said, "means more illness. Smallpox, cholera—we already have a water shortage, damn it! How the hell are they going to look after any more people?"

(vii)

The opening of the new offices of the Hong Kong and Shanghai Bank promised to be the most important social event of the year. Everybody who was anybody in the Colony had been invited. The only qualification for one to warrant an invitation was a certain elevated purchasing power and financial solvency. Of course, only the elite and the press were invited to the buffet which would follow the opening ceremony.

The biggest talking point was the ultra-modern interior of the building and the fact that the offices were going to be air-conditioned. As Major Harland commented: "In India we made do with a punkah-wallah. And then it was only for the commissioned officers, mind you. I don't hold with all this modern technology. Bound to be bad for you in the end." And his opinion was shared by most of the population.

"It's a damned waste of the shareholders' money, if you ask me," said Eliot Rodmell.

"It's bloody shameful!" Laughton told his wife over breakfast. "Air conditioning! I mean some seventy percent of the bloody population don't even have electricity yet! Most of the island will still be living in the Middle Ages and that pompous windbag is going to install air conditioning!"

"But they are only Chinese, aren't they, dear?" said his wife. "What would they do with electricity?"

The art-deco interior was another reason for heated discussion. It would include the largest contemporary mosaic in the world. Some four million glass tessarae had been used, each one of which had been specially made and shipped in from Venice. It had been described as "a pastiche of classical, modern, industrial and commercial, Oriental and Western themes."

"The Orientals used to beat themselves on the head with stones," Kenji told Russell, "to elicit sympathy and so be given alms. That must be the most fundamental form of commerce, in a way, and the most honest. However, I do not expect to see it represented in the mosaic."

"Commerce," said Eliot Rodmell one evening. "Well, of course, commerce and Hong Kong have always been inextricably related. We must never lose sight of the fact, if we are to understand Hong Kong at all, that the British acquired the island in the first place purely and simply to facilitate the selling of opium to China. The opening of the new offices is a solid manifestation of Hong Kong's increasing importance in the world's commercial markets and its progression over the past eighty years from Sun Yat Sen's barren rock which, in 4,000 years, China had done nothing with, to the labyrinth of factories and workshops, all buzzing and humming, all rolling along to the sound of money. A question of mentality," said Rodmell.

"Luck!" said Osbourne.

"Exploitation!" said Laughton.

"There are more important things than money," said Kenji. "There is honour and there is virtuous perfection."

"I can see no evidence of either honour or perfection these days," said Russell. " Only violence and progress. And you can't stop either. That is the worst thing about it."

"You step outside of it, Willard."

"Then you are lost," said Russell.

"I don't see what luck has got to do with it," said Sergeant Fletcher. "I see a lot of damned hard work and co-operation."

"Balls!" said Osbourne.

"But I still must insist that this Pharaonic manifestation of wealth and power is taking things too far," Rodmell explained to his wife.

"Well, tell him so, dear," said Margaret Rodmell, who could not care less. "Tell Sir Vandeleur. You know he respects your opinion."

Rodmell suddenly wondered what had ever attracted her to him. But he knew that. It was her almost childlike body—devoid of breasts and hips—and, apparently, brain!—which had first excited him. Making love to Margaret Rodmell in her youth had been like making love to an adolescent girl. Now, however, she had become more rounded, slightly plump, and the attraction for him had evaporated. He scowled and said, "I think I shall say nothing of the kind, darling."

For the Chinese, however, the opening of the new offices was significant only for the recognition given to the most important families. For the majority of the residents of Hong Kong, Kowloon and the New Territories, it was something they would never be privileged enough to see and, indeed, most of them knew nothing about it at all. For Chen Liew and Tang, therefore, both of whom had been invited not only to the opening ceremony but also to the buffet party, it emphasised their respect and acceptance.

"They could never have built it in the first place without our money," Chen Liew said to himself as he reluctantly dressed in a stiff white shirt and restricting black bow tie.

In the next room, Tung Nien and Molly were dressing in white—white being the traditional Chinese colour for mourning. It was Chen

Liew's little joke.

"They," he said, meaning the Westerners, "will see it as the marriage between East and West, but we shall know that it is a recognition of the grief of the Chinese people who, instead of supporting their brothers on the mainland, are finally giving themselves up to the British and their system for good."

Molly had never spoken much since she arrived and today was no exception. At first, Tung Nien had thought that it was because she had been wrenched away from her father, and that she felt lonely and shy, but she now knew that it was not that. It was as though Molly would only speak if she wanted to know something specific. She would never indulge in small talk nor would she just chat for the sake of it. She would only ever involve herself in a conversation if she could get something out of it which affected her personally.

"Do you suppose my father will be there?" she asked. "Because I do not want to see him."

"Your father?" asked Tung Nien. "I very much doubt it. Why on earth should he be there?"

"No reason. To ruin it for me?"

Tung Nien knew she should have said something reassuring, but she felt no guilt at having taken Molly from Russell and she could not defend him. He was a weak and stupid man who had earned his daughter's derision on his own merit.

"Wu will be there," Molly continued with a smile.

"But you must not speak to him," said Tung Nien seriously. "Not today."

"He loves me," said Molly, smiling at her reflection in the mirror of the dressing table.

"Don't be so silly!" Tung Nien replied shortly and turned away to look for a ribbon. "How can he love you?"

"I'm fifteen. My grandmother was married and had had a baby by the time she was fifteen."

"Your grandmother's marriage had nothing to do with love. And, anyway, tonight, you shall not speak to him."

For Tung Nien, who had decided that she herself had never loved anyone, the matter was closed. She might have been able to love Chen Liew had he let her, but it was pointless to dwell on that. Love, she had decided, even before her husband's decision to refrain from ejaculating, was a myth, something you read about in poems. She slipped the ribbon round Molly's waist and fastened it with a clip at the small of her back. She stood back a little and sighed.

"You have the body of a Chinese," she said, "And the mind of an American. Why else would you have this obsession with love?"

Molly would not allow herself to be angry. Tung Nien knew that the easiest way to hurt her was to remind her of her mixed blood and Molly knew why she had done it. She smiled and said something which she knew intuitively would hurt in turn.

"You're just jealous," she said, and as she flipped her hair away from her eyes, Tung Nien saw that they were shining and defiant. "You're just jealous because you have no one!"

"I thought I had you," Tung Nien said quietly, but she knew she did not altogether mean it. However, having embarked upon the pretence, she would have to follow it through. She sat down slowly and looked away from Molly to the window where she could see a magnolia tree in flower. She concentrated all her attention on the creamy-white flowers and shut out any feeling of emotion for she knew that Molly was right. She was jealous.

"I didn't mean it," Molly was saying. She had stood up from the dressing table and had walked across to the window from where she too looked out into the garden. Tung Nien reached up and took her hand.

"I know," she said softly and she smiled. "But don't speak to him tonight, Molly. It would not be at all convenient for anyone."

(viii)

"... and this building represents that faith, that hope for the future, which, even in these difficult times ..."

The speech seemed to be going on for ever. Harry Osbourne wrote automatically and tried to pick out the faces he knew from the crowd. As he looked round the hall, he was struggling to think of something nice to say about the mosaic for the morning's issue of the paper. It struck him that nobody was actually listening to the great Sir Vandeleur Grayburn. They're all as bloody bored as I am, he said to himself, for there was Eliot Rodmell, with his wife, yawning and not even bothering to hide the fact with his hand. The Chinese, Chen Liew and Tang, separated by a prudent smattering of other guests, surrounded by their entourage of bodyguards and concubines, looked neither bored nor stimulated by the speech. But then they never do, said Osbourne. You never know what the bloody Chinese are thinking. Their faces don't move like ours do. They just stay there, always the same. Even when they laugh they don't really look as though they're enjoying it. That's the bloody trouble with them! You can never know what makes them tick. Or if they're even bloody ticking at all! Osbourne chuckled as he remembered the broken English of the Chinese watchman down at the Police Station. I don't know what makes them tickle, he had said. It is a very supple problem, Mr Osbourne. And there was Laughton! Asleep! With his head on some poor sod's shoulder. I reckon he's probably even snoring too, the way his wife's looking!

"... and so, with great pleasure, I declare these new offices, this symbol of wealth and prosperity for the future, with great pleasure, I declare these new offices open!"

Laughton was woken by the applause and automatically began to clap. The first thing he became aware of was his wife, hissing into his ear.

"I've never been so humiliated in my life! You should be ashamed of yourself! You were lolling all over that woman! Whatever will people think?"

"I don't care so very much what they think," said Laughton, not bothering even to lower his voice beneath the volume of the clapping. Mary Laughton cringed, but said nothing. Had she spoken, she would have insulted him.

As they walked out of the huge doors of the bank and down the stone steps, Laughton felt a large hand on his shoulder. It was Eliot Rodmell.

"I thought that went off very well, considering, didn't you?" Rodmell was speaking to them because he had momentarily been left without a more worthy audience.

"I don't think Alfred would be able to say," said Mary Laughton acidly.

"Good! Good! Splendid!" said Rodmell. "So then," he went on, rubbing his hands and talking out towards the ample, tree-lined square and the jubilee memorial to Queen Victoria, "See you all in a bit at the Parisian Grill!"

"You see what you've done, don't you?" Mary Laughton continued to hiss in her husband's ear. "Publicly spurned by Eliot Rodmell!"

"Shut up, Mary!" said Laughton wearily. He did not care whether they had been spurned or not, although he could not help pointing out that they had not.

"I don't know what you'd call it, then!" said his wife. "And after I've tried so hard!"

Osbourne could see them arguing and he smiled to himself. It only went to prove what he always said. "If there is anything in this world that is incompatible, it is a man and a woman!"

(ix)

As the guests filed in for the buffet dinner at the Parisian Grill, a string quintet was already playing Beethoven, according to Mrs Harland, and Brahms, according to Eliot Rodmell. Whatever it was, Margaret Rodmell considered it, for some reason, fitting. Eliot Rodmell, taking full advantage of his unusual height, surveyed the scene. The Tangs had congregated at one end of the room and Chen Liew and his group at the other. Between them a sea of European faces.

"The Chinese have brought their children!" Margaret Rodmell tutted.

"How gauche!" agreed Mrs Harland with a condescending smile.

"For the Chinese, any celebration is principally a time for children, I believe," Laughton was about to say but, looking at Margaret Rodmell's thickly powdered cheeks and painted lips and, from there, to the Major's blustery face and Rodmell's rheumy blue eyes, he thought better of it. What on earth should he tell them that for? Why bother to say anything at all? Anyway, his wife was speaking on their behalf.

"They have no real idea of etiquette, have they?"

"I think that it is because their society is so strongly weighted in favour of the man, if you see what I mean," said Mrs Harland, offering it up as a piece of profound wisdom that she might have read somewhere. "And men are so insensitive, aren't they? To everything."

Laughton moved away from the group. He did not even bother to tell his wife he was going. She would know where to find him anyway. He began to look for somewhere to get a drink. Once he had located the bar, he stationed himself there, despite the fact that it meant he might have to converse with Harry Osbourne.

He had drunk most of his first whisky and soda before Osbourne so much as recognised his presence. Looking up at him, his mouth filled with the remains of a king prawn, Osbourne grinned.

"Could get to see some fireworks tonight if we're lucky!" he said with a wink.

"I really can't think why, Osbourne," Laughton said as coldly and indifferently as he could. But Osbourne was nothing if not thick-skinned. He motioned with his glass, first to one end of the room, and then to the other.

"Unheard of," he said.

"What is?"

"Two—count them, Laughton—two *Heads of the Dragon*. In the same room!"

"I'm sorry, Osbourne, but I really don't know what you're talking about."

"Chen Liew and Tang. Unheard of to see them together. Next thing you know, some berk'll be trying to introduce them, you know, because they're Chinese." Osbourne laughed, but it was a miserable sound, without humour. He nodded towards the counter. "Another one?"

"Why not?"

With the mention of Chen Liew, Laughton had automatically begun to scan the anonymous faces in the room in search of Tung Nien. He had stopped listening to Osbourne who, nevertheless, had begun to explain the incongruity of the situation, and the potential dangers involved.

"It's seen as a provocation, you see?" he was saying, but his voice had lost its initial edge of excitement, blunted now by the whisky he had been drinking, for he had begun long before the party, as was his custom, as soon as the sun had gone down. "My curse is that no matter how much I drink I don't get drunk."

Laughton could not be bothered to comment, and besides which, he had seen Tung Nien.

Tung Nien was standing at the far end of the room with Molly beside her. They were both looking towards the bar where he and Osbourne were the only drinkers. Laughton's heart missed a beat and he thought again of Osbourne's interview with her. He could not bring himself to believe that there was anything between her and Osbourne, but, even so, he was jealous. He was about to turn away and return to his wife—he could see her across the room enjoying herself with the Rodmells and the Harlands, the Robinsons hovering there too—when he heard the stilted English of a voice he knew but had not realised how much he liked.

"Eh, Mao! All the places I go to, you go. You following me, or what?"

When Laughton smiled, it was because he was genuinely pleased. Ridiculous as it might seem, he felt that Wu was one of the only people who accepted him for what he was.

"Wu!" he said. "What are you doing here?"

Laughton then learned what everyone else in Hong Kong already knew.

"My father!" said Wu, nodding over his shoulder towards the other end of the room.

Major Harland thought that Rodmell was particularly nervous. True, it was hot. There was a sticky, humid breeze blowing in off the harbour, but Rodmell was actually sweating. And it was not only that. He kept taking a silver snuffbox out of his pocket, tapping the top with his forefinger and replacing it again in his pocket. It was almost as though he were waiting for something momentous to happen, as though things had passed, for once, from his large and capable hands.

"And because I cannot speak to Molly," said Wu, "You will take her this paper which tells of my love."

Laughton looked at the elaborate scrawl of Chinese characters on a neatly cut square of paper. "What does it say?"

"It says," said Wu very seriously, "When you wake in the morning, my love is the dew on your breast."

Laughton looked at the boy with renewed interest. He himself had struggled with his emotions for months and yet he had never come close to such a clear expression of what he wanted to say. He was about to speak when Wu patted him on the arm and said simply, "You. Take the note. I go now."

Laughton held the paper in his hand and with his heart thumping in his chest he made his way across the room. Tung Nien smiled at him as he walked towards them. She held out her hand and he took it clumsily in his own, which held the note for Molly.

"How are you, Dr Laughton?" she said.

"I am the dew on your breast," he said, without thinking, without knowing what he was saying. Molly laughed and Laughton passed her the note. "From Wu," he said.

When Molly had read the note she laughed again and tugged Tung Nien's sleeve. She whispered something in her ear and Tung Nien smiled, first to herself, and then at Laughton. "Molly says that you are in love with me, Dr Laughton," she said simply.

Laughton's first reaction was embarrassment. He would have denied it profusely, excused himself, muttered something about his wife, about being married, but there was, he thought, something in her eyes which challenged him. He glanced quickly past her to the thickset face of Chan. Even his inscrutable features seemed to be willing him to tell the truth.

"How ridiculous!" he said, and he could hear himself saying it and it was as though his voice belonged to someone else.

"I don't see why you should find it ridiculous," she said, still smiling at him and still speaking as she might have done about the weather.

"No," said Laughton, "perhaps not." And it was hopelessly inadequate.

Molly had turned away from them and, resting the paper on a coffee table, she was crouching and writing elaborately on the back of Wu's poem. Laughton watched her, because he felt too nervous to look at Tung Nien. He felt that if their eyes met again he would be sure to ruin everything. After so long willing the occasion to arise, after so many months of following her all over the island just to be near to her, now that he had her right in front of him and he had spoken to her, he did not know what else to do. And so he looked up. She was smiling at him.

"Molly was right," she said, and her voice sang and lilted beautifully over the words. "When we saw you at the bun festival, she said were you were quite handsome for a foreigner."

Laughton felt the colour rise to his cheeks and searched desperately for something to say that would not sound awkward or stupid. He was saved from further embarrassment by Molly who pressed the paper back into his hand.

"Would you, please, give it back to Wu for me?" she asked, glancing quickly at Tung Nien, as though for permission.

"What does yours say?" asked Laughton. He actually wanted to know. He looked at Tung Nien and returned her smile. She was wearing no make up at all and yet she was more beautiful than the rest of the women in the room put together.

"It says," said Molly, without the slightest hint of self-consciousness, "I will stand on the hill in the morning where the dew is thickest."

Molly and Tung Nien watched Laughton as he crossed the room and took up his place once again beside Osbourne at the bar.

"Do you like him?" Molly asked.

"I hadn't really thought about it," said Tung Nien.

"Wu says he is a Communist."

"Does that make a difference?"

"It means that he is probably kind."

"What would I do with kindness, Molly?"

Molly shrugged. "Miss Dekyvere says it is a great virtue."

Laughton's mind was racing when he returned to the bar. He felt elated, almost drunk. He wanted to tell them all what had happened, let them all share in his happiness, but one look at Osbourne was enough to cure him of his euphoria and to bring him back to the tedious reality of the party.

"Harland's getting his ear bent by Rodmell," said Osbourne who noticed things like that. No doubt he is trained to, thought Laughton. He felt suddenly benevolent, happy to allow everyone their little quirks and failings, happy to let everyone be exactly what they were without demanding anything from them. Even Osbourne.

"That means, in my book, something's cooking."

"Could be they're just arranging this week's hunt at Fanling," suggested Laughton. "It wouldn't be the first time."

Osbourne shook his head. "No," he said. "You only have to watch their faces to see it's important. What I wouldn't give to be a fly on Rodmell's trousers!"

Laughton stole a glance at Osbourne from the corner of his eye in case it was meant to be funny, but Osbourne was speaking in deadly earnest.

"It's Chan I want to overhear it, Major," said Rodmell. "All you have to do is stand there. You don't even have to say anything. Just nod your head from time to time, you know, make out that you are listening and that you know what I am talking about."

The Major turned his tiny eyes away from the floor where they had been tracing the lines of the carpet and he looked into Rodmell's face. A vein had burst at the side of his nose and the small delta of blood beneath the skin looked to be tinged with blue in the dim light of the dining hall.

"So long as you don't put me in a spot, Eliot. Things are a bit delicate at the moment, and I know you."

"I shall respect the discretion which anyone in your position deserves. You see, the question is this..."

Major Harland shook his head vigorously. "No," he said. "I would rather know nothing about your problems with the Chinese. You forget, perhaps, but I have to work with them."

"Harold!" said Rodmell, and his voice was slightly menacing.

"Never mind Harold!" said Major Harland quickly. He felt nervous, but he could not say why. "Look, Eliot! Of late, every bloody time you see me, you pump me for information—the District Watch Force, wasn't it, last time? Well, I cannot..."

Rodmell interrupted him with an impatient twitch of his upper lip.

"All I am asking you to do is listen! Your rank will do the rest. Whatever I say to you—nod! Got it?" Rodmell looked over the heads of the dinner guests towards Chan. He was still standing behind Tung Nien and Molly. "Right!" he said, taking Major Harland by the elbow and easing him away from their wives who were still talking to the Robinsons. "Let's go!"

And then Eliot Rodmell did something which was totally out of character. He made, not so much a mistake, as a miscalculation. He positioned Major Harland over by the window, away from the rest of the guests, so that they could talk and look out over the dark reflection of the harbour, but he positioned him just a little too far to the left, and when he began to speak, it was not Chan who overheard their conversation. It was Tung Nien.

4

"His neck is fastened in the wooden cangue,
So that his ears disappear."

(i)

At the beginning of 1939, an Air Raids Precautions Officer arrived from Britain and it emphasised Hong Kong's precarious position even more than the Japanese bombing, for the second time in six months, of Lo Wu in the New Territories. This was probably because, as Osbourne had been quick to point out, the bombing of Lo Wu was more of a logistical question than a political one.

"Rather than an attack against Britain and the Colony," he explained to an unusually jumpy Sergeant Fletcher, "I reckon it was a warning to the Triads and to the likes of our friend Eliot Rodmell."

"How do you make that out?" asked Fletcher. He was not convinced.

"Stands to reason, Fletch," said Osbourne, amused at his friend's uneasiness. "Lo Wu is on the Sham Chun River, isn't it? The border between the New Territories and China, right? Well, it serves as, you know, like an outpost, a sort of last warehouse before China. It's where all the arms and stuff for Free China end up before they miraculously disappear from right beneath the Japs' noses."

"What makes you so sure, Harry? I mean, no one but you has said anything about it, as far as I know."

"It's obvious, Fletch! Even if the warehouses didn't exist, which they do, and even if they weren't being used by Chen Liew, Tang,

Rodmell and the like, which they are, we have the irrefutable fact of the Japanese bombing. Why the hell should they bomb some poky bloody Chinese village if there's nothing there but a handful of peasants?"

Sergeant Fletcher knew the official reason and would repeat it. He glanced round the smoky atmosphere of the Glory Hole and then leaned slightly forwards, his elbows on the table. "It's a show of force, Harry. That's what the C.O. told us."

Osbourne listened patiently, an ironic, disbelieving smile on his lips. He lit a cigarette and nodded patronisingly as Fletcher continued.

"You see," said Fletcher, warming now to the idea, "Hong Kong is a fortress..."

"Bollocks!" said Osbourne.

"No! Come on! Hear me out!" Fletcher protested. He took one of Osbourne's *'Craven A'*, lit it and began to turn the packet annoyingly over between his fingers. "Hong Kong is a natural fortress, right? You only have to look at it to see that! And even the Japs realise it, see? So, the thing is this: They don't want us, the Brits, to get involved. They know we have agreements with China, so..."

"So, they bomb one of our bloody villages!" Osbourne interrupted. "Come on, Fletch! Don't be so naïve, for Christ's sake! You can't swallow that, it makes no sense!"

"So," Fletcher continued patiently, "So, they do a bit of sabre rattling on the border in a place that nobody cares about."

"Why?" said Osbourne bluntly.

Fletcher blinked at him.

"Why what?"

"Why the hell would they want to do that? Why not just leave well alone, eh?"

Fletcher had not thought to ask, and the C.O. had not informed them.

"I reckon the big-wigs will've thought that one out, don't you, Harry?"

"I doubt it very much, Fletch!" Osbourne said. He was enjoying Fletcher's confusion and his nervousness. "It's like this nonsense they're pumping out in Europe," he went on, "Linking Britain's future to that of Poland." Osbourne glanced round the bar, waved towards a far corner where he thought he saw a face he knew, and continued, his voice rising angrily as he tried to get out all that he wanted to say before it occurred to Fletcher to voice the official verdict again. "To ensure peace in Europe—old Chamberlain says—we will defend Poland against any aggression from Germany. Ensure peace, my arse! You know what day they made this wonderful announcement on too, don't you? That should give you a good idea of how much they believe in it. April bloody fools day, wasn't it! It's cobblers, Fletch! Anyone can see that. They all know there's going to be a bloody war sooner or later. They just don't want you to know it, that's all. So they tell you what they know you want to hear because they don't want you to think about it."

A look of malicious amusement spread over Osbourne's face as he realised that Fletcher had finally begun to question the official, military version of events. And that, for him, was enough. He was not concerned with the truth, nor was he really concerned whether there would be a war or not. He had no further desire to speak of the matter, but as a parting shot, he added, "I might just take myself out to Lo Wu, all the same. Have a look see."

(ii)

"An Air Raids Precautions Officer, indeed!" said Eliot Rodmell theatrically, but his mind was not really on the subject. The other members of the Fanling Hunt seemed, however, intent on dragging out the conversation.

"I wonder if he plays cricket," said Rodmell.

Major Harland was indignant. "Really, Eliot!" he said a little testily while Foster smiled at Rodmell's comment.

The lounge of the Peninsula Hotel seemed to have been totally overrun by the red jackets of the members of the hunt. Rodmell watched them as they conversed about the possibility of war in Europe and the possibility of further Japanese aggression in the Far East. He realised that he would have no choice but to join in, much as it bored him to do so. What did he care about England, anyway? He had only ever been there when he had been sent away to boarding school. All he could remember now were short, damp days when the sun never shone and where it was already dark by 4:30 in the afternoon. He could feel nothing for the place. It was not his home. He had no friends there. There were one or two relatives, it was true, but he could not remember ever having met them more than once or twice. He had been sent one Easter holiday to an uncle's house, but all he could remember about that was treacle pudding and custard and waking up with a hot-water-bottle gone cold against his feet. Of course, Major Harland and the others would, one day, have to go back. It was, then, comprehensible, he decided, that they should be concerned. But not on account of some damned ARP officer!

"It shows the precarious situation they must be living in back home," Robinson was suggesting, "If they think that we, who are living, after all, atop a natural fortress, might need the assistance of ..."

Rodmell had had enough. They have no idea, he said to himself. He reached lazily for his glass of gin and bitters and began to declaim in such a way that no one there would have dared not to listen to him, and once having listened, to contradict, although there was a sad, resigned tone to his voice.

"I have an idea," he began, "that there is not going to be a war. I think," he went on, having quickly surveyed the satisfied expressions on the red, smiling faces before him, "that after a lot more talk, they are bound to reach a more rational solution."

"Quite so!" said a fat face Rodmell did not recognise but smiled at all the same.

Robinson, too, was happy to accept Rodmell's conclusion. After so many years of the British and French Governments preferring to turn their backs on all awkward situations, of following, in their own words, a policy of "detachment and appeasement" with regard to Germany, the recent declaration by the Chamberlain Cabinet that they would defend Poland had come as quite a shock.

"They didn't defend Austria, though, did they?" said Robinson.

"We have to accept that things have changed," said Major Harland ominously. "You see, one thing was to allow Hitler to advance toward the East. It's quite another thing for him to move into Poland!"

Rodmell grunted. He could see that Major Harland was going to thrash out the whole damned question. The military mind, he said to himself, always in step. And he sat down and glared grumpily out through the window of the lounge at a junk in the harbour. There was a line of coolies tottering unsteadily down the gangplank and onto the quay unloading bales of what looked like sugar.

Rodmell grunted and glowered at Major Harland, but, despite Rodmell's sour, warning glances, Major Harland, it seemed, would have his say.

"If, and let us all pray to God that Rodmell is right, but if nothing can be done and we find ourselves involved..."

He is speaking as though he still lived there, said Rodmell. The damned fool! What he and nobody else here seems to realise is that, if anything happens in Europe, if the worst comes to the worst, we'll be damned well isolated out here, fortress or no bloody fortress! No one is going to worry about us out here, are they, all these thousands of miles away? That is the point. Never mind the free world, for God's sake! Never mind the rise of fascism—what about my bloody warehouse? Adolf Hitler! What about that Japanese bastard Sakai bombing my property with complete and utter impunity? They don't care about that, do they?

Willard Russell was peering through the slats of the drawn blind in the barber's shop. He could hear the raised voices of the members of the Fanling Hunt and he could make out the gist of their conversation. To him, it seemed quite simply that the world had gone mad. Problems whichever way you looked, the future a black wall into which they were all going to crash. It was only a question of time. If it wasn't the Germans, it was the Japanese, and if it wasn't the Japanese, it was the Russians. Who could blame him, then, if he had begun to find solace, comfort, a kind of peace even, in Kenji's teachings? Who was to say that he was any madder than the rest of them? Only that morning, he had thought he had made his first important step forwards. He had been meditating, rolling his eyes, forcing them round and together, nine times in each of the four phases, as Kenji had taught him, and then six times in each of the phases.

"What do you see, Willard?" Kenji had asked him.

Russell had been surprised to see a dim, circular light, hovering like the impression left by staring at the full moon. Despite himself, he had felt a certain stirring of anticipation.

"A light!" he had said, unable to hide his satisfaction. Kenji had told him long before that if, in meditation, he ever managed to unite the dragon and the tiger, the sun and the moon, a light would be produced. "A mysterious pearl," Kenji had called it. "The gate for returning to the source."

"What colour is it?" Kenji had asked him quietly.

"White!" he had said, his eyes still closed, all his energy forced into maintaining the light before him.

"Open your eyes, Willard," Kenji had said. "Now what do you see?"

"You," Russell had said, looking into Kenji's flat, Japanese face.

And Kenji had sighed heavily.

"What you have seen, Willard, is the negative spirit. It is absolutely useless. It is the emptiness of the void. It can only lead to death."

Russell had felt frustrated.

Looking out now at the members of the hunt, Russell made a gesture as though perhaps to give them his blessing, but he said, "The emptiness of the void, which can only lead to death" as he moved his hand and made the sign of the cross.

"You heard them out there, Kenji?" he asked over his shoulder. Kenji walked over to the window and moved the blind slightly to one side. "All of a sudden they're all neurotic."

"It will pass," said Kenji, "so long as nothing else happens. It is human nature. You mustn't blame them for it. Besides, they have to complain about something, don't they?"

Russell turned his chair away from the window. "Do you think there will be a war, Kenji?" he asked.

The Japanese walked across the room to a small china basin which was set into the wall beside the barber's chair and he began to wash his hands. When he had finished, he took a yellow hand-towel and proceeded to dry them thoroughly, rubbing them round and through the towel. He replaced the yellow towel beside the basin in a neatly folded square and then looked up seriously.

"I am sure of it," he said.

Russell was shocked. He had expected Kenji to give him some non-committal answer, some meandering, philosophical truism. And then he remembered the ominous phrase, 'The Greater East Asia Co-prosperity Sphere.' He looked carefully at the Japanese, trying to detect even the smallest flicker of emotion in his face. But there was none.

"Here, too?" he asked finally, his voice heavy with resignation, for he knew what Kenji would say.

"Oh, yes, Willard," the Japanese replied. "Here, too. But not quite yet."

Russell found it difficult to equate Kenji's certainty with his generally vague attitude to the material side of life. Kenji had made a concerted effort over the years to convince everyone, not only Russell, that he had embarked upon a spiritual journey of discovery which nobody but he himself could ever hope to understand, with the result that no one took him altogether seriously; they thought of him, in fact, as a bit of a fool, a dreamer, someone who was totally out of touch with reality. And yet, here he was, proclaiming with utter certainty, when even Major Harland doubted, that there would be a war.

Russell would not question how Kenji could be so sure. He believed him because he could see no reason not to. And it worried him vaguely that he had put his trust so completely in the Japanese. But, once he had lost Molly, he had needed someone to hold him up, and Kenji had been there. Kenji had never questioned his actions, merely reprimanded him from time to time, usually for drinking too much. And he had just slowly and gently pulled him away from the edge of the abyss.

Now he has swallowed you up, Russell said to himself, turning again to look out into the lounge. You are totally dependent on him, like a damned child! What perhaps troubled Russell more than anything else was that he did not really care. No, it was worse even than that. He was happy to be led. He would have been even happier if he could have stopped thinking too.

Out in the lounge, Eliot Rodmell had stood. He seemed to be looking straight across at the drawn blind of the barber's shop as he said, with the kind of authority which only comes with knowledge, "What we should be worrying about out here is the Japanese. This damned war in China, it's crippling our economy. What should have been a golden opportunity for a quick killing, if you'll excuse the pun, Major, is turning out to be a bloody economic disaster!"

Major Harland took hold of Rodmell by the arm and pulled the taller man towards him slightly.

"Steady on, old boy!" he hissed. "They might get the wrong idea! Wouldn't do at all for a man in your position. Patriotism at all costs, Eliot! That's the key word at the moment."

"You fuss about like a bloody mother hen sometimes, Harold," said Rodmell, smiling to himself and leading the Major over to the window of the barber shop. He brushed the Major's hand away from his arm.

"You do see the problem though, Harold, don't you?" he said, sucking emphatically through his teeth. "This bombing out at Lo Wu. You know what it's all about, don't you?"

Major Harland explained the official reasons. Rodmell shook his head.

"It's quite simple," he said. "The Japs have got bogged down in a guerrilla war in China and the only way out for them is to continue to advance south until they manage to destroy all the supply lines into China." He prodded Major Harland in the chest. "That means us, Major!"

"But surely, Eliot," Major Harland protested, "Trade has stopped."

"Oh, yes," said Rodmell breezily. "Of course it has—officially."

And he smiled. He took two steps forward and then turned to face the Major. He was still smiling, but his face had a kind of inner vacancy, as though his mind were not concentrating on what he had been saying, but were far away, amongst different people and in a different conversation. Slightly unnerved by his friend's attitude, Major Harland decided to change the subject.

"Still on for golf tomorrow?" he asked, he hoped, brightly.

(iii)

Chen Liew spent the first two hours of every Friday morning at the Temple of Man Mo. Mo was, paradoxically, the patron of both police and criminals, and was, perhaps more appropriately, supposed to protect people from the deprivations of war. In the dim, hazy, incense-filled atmosphere of the temple, sitting on a tasselled silk cushion between two brass statues of deer, Chen Liew would hold court and receive visits and requests for his favour. His mentor, Liao K'ung, would stand at one shoulder, and Chan would stand at the other, as the respectful and slightly frightened were led before the great man. On this particular Friday, Chen Liew listened impassively as he was informed of the damage caused by the Japanese bombing of Lo Wu. Both his own and Rodmell's warehouses had suffered in the attack, although apparently Tang's warehouses had miraculously been spared. Chen Liew then nodded sadly as a proud young man stood squarely and defiantly before him and told him of a recent smallpox epidemic and the lack of proper drinking water in the New Territories. Chen Liew beckoned quietly to Chan and the man was led discreetly out into the back of the temple where Chan explained to him that Chen Liew did not appreciate complaints, especially about an area which was anyway not part of his jurisdiction. As politely as he could, Chan informed the man that the New Territories were under Tang's control. From the temple, Chen Liew would visit his factories painstakingly one by one. In recent weeks he had taken to stopping off at the refugee camps and hospitals where he could bolster his reputation as a kindly and caring *lo ban*. He would occasionally pluck some unsuspecting immigrant from the sickly crowd, present him with a residency certificate, and set him up in a small shop in the back streets of *Central* or *Wanchai*, another eternally grateful *foki* to add to his collection and to save for some still nebulous use in the future.

Tung Nien was too frightened of her husband to speak to him directly about Liao K'ung but still involved enough to be worried by the news she had overheard. Not knowing who else to turn to she had again asked Osbourne to visit her. As Tung Nien watched the Bentley disappear through the gates at the end of the drive, she was already wondering what exactly she was going to say to him. This time, she had made no pretence but had simply posted him a note which said:

I wish to see you. Come, please, on Friday.
—Tung Nien.

When Osbourne had received the note, he had not been surprised. One of the unwritten rules in the game he played with life was never to let anything at all surprise him. He had looked out of his kitchen window at the rows of washing hanging from the balconies of the tenement across the street and he had thought simply: Friday 13th.

As Tung Nien waited for Osbourne in the garden, she leafed through the pages of the newspapers; the English one was full of propaganda and the Chinese one had so obviously been tampered with by the Authorities that it scarcely made any sense. She did notice, however, that both newspapers conceded that there would soon be a water shortage. Too many illegal immigrants and refugees; the population had doubled over the last ten years and, at the last estimate, there had been over a million people crammed onto the island; smallpox and cholera were rife in the refugee camps; the Chinese had organised an illegal demonstration in the Hok Un district against compulsory registration which had been unceremoniously broken up by the District

Watch Force and the Police. She let her eyes wander over the paper without really taking in what she was reading.

Tung Nien tried to concentrate her thoughts and focus them on Chen Liew and Liao K'ung. She closed her eyes. She had never liked the monkey-faced Liao K'ung but was not stupid enough to think that Chen Liew would take kindly to simply being told, especially by her, that she had heard he was a traitor. Despite the fact that she also disliked Osbourne intensely and despite the evident danger in asking him to the house, there was something of an adventure about the whole affair which excited her. A Catalina sea-plane flew low over the Peak, sweeping down towards the bay at Kai Tak, and then an insect, a faint echo of the plane, began to drone in her ear so that she got up impatiently and walked back into the house.

She was arranging a vase of flowers when Osbourne arrived. He looked tired and unwashed although it was only eleven o'clock in the morning. Tung Nien allowed Ying to greet him at the door and lead him through to the lounge. There they sat opposite each other awkwardly, like the last two pieces on a chessboard.

"Mr Osbourne," Tung Nien began almost rudely, wishing to terminate the interview as quickly as possible, "You must realise that I have asked you here as a friend," (she even hated to lie about it; just having the word friend in her mouth referring to Osbourne made her feel sick), "And not as a reporter. You will not be able to print anything that I tell you..."

"So, why bother?" he interrupted, sniffing and taking his cigarettes and matches from his pocket.

"I want you to give me your opinion," Tung Nien continued, ignoring the interruption. "Normally I would ask Chan, or my husband directly, but, you see, it is a delicate question and I would rather not worry him unnecessarily."

Osbourne sat back and crossed his leg over his knee. "Fire away," he said. "I'm all ears."

Tung Nien looked at him blankly and said nothing. Osbourne

began to smoke and thought, She is trying to unnerve me. He did not realise that she had not understood him. Finally, seeing that Osbourne would say no more, Tung Nien looked for a logical place to begin.

"What do you know of Liao K'ung?" she asked suddenly. Osbourne rubbed his chin.

"Nasty piece of work," he said. "Intelligent, scheming, unscrupulous."

"Loyal?" she asked.

"Not necessarily," he said. "Who is these days?"

"What could he possibly gain by teaming up with Tang?"

Osbourne thought for a moment.

"Nothing," he said. He felt uncomfortable talking about the Triads. Like everyone else on the island, he would provide information for them, if he had it, and he would find it, if he didn't. He had occasionally even been asked to do them the odd favour, such as locating the wayward Willard Russell, but what he would never do was publicly have an opinion of his own. It was far too dangerous. Rather than look at Tung Nien, he turned his head slightly and looked nervously through the window into the garden. What most troubled him at that moment was that he was being interrogated by a woman and not by Chan or Chen Liew himself.

Tung Nien thought again how unattractive Osbourne was, and it was not because she had always been taught to believe that the epitome of manhood was a weak, intellectual figure. She had realised that that particular ideal was false soon after she had married. Osbourne was simply scruffy. He even had dandruff on the lenses of his glasses. She was, therefore, surprised to notice that he actually smelt clean. She forced herself to smile at him and then said, "I have heard that Liao K'ung is plotting with Tang to overthrow my husband."

Osbourne let out an involuntary whistle but recovered his composure quickly.

"I can't see it myself," he said, wishing at the same time that he could have said something more anonymous. The last thing that he wanted was to get involved personally. Nevertheless, his basic inquisitiveness forced him into a brief examination of the situation. If it were true, if Liao K'ung really wanted to take over, it could only be a political question, and if it were a political question, it either had to do with Mao, the Japanese or the British Authorities. But why should he bother with Tang? It didn't make sense. He didn't need Tang. There were other ways. "No," he said, shaking his head, "Can't see it myself."

Tung Nien could see that Osbourne was reluctant to speak and that he wanted to leave. She began to regret having asked him in the first place. Ying had bought them a tray of herb tea but she had not offered any to Osbourne and had taken none for herself. They both sat looking at the silver tray in silence. Tung Nien thought back to Rodmell's conversation.

"Liao K'ung has been stealing from my warehouse even though he is supposed to be protecting it," Rodmell had said, "because he knows Chen Liew will blame Tang. Chen Liew will be forced to act against Tang who, being innocent, will have every right then to attack Chen Liew. Once Chen Liew is out of the way, they put Liao K'ung in his place as a kind of puppet dictator. You see how simple it is?"

Osbourne had transferred his attention from the tray of tea to the flowers she had been arranging when he had arrived. He had pushed himself up from the sofa and he was saying in his most persuasive voice, "I'd just forget about it, Miss, if I were you. In fact, that is exactly what I am going to do. Forget about it."

As Tung Nien watched Osbourne walking away down the drive and out into the street she felt frustrated. She sat down again and poured herself a cup of the tea. As she stirred it distractedly she wondered whether she should not be better off taking Osbourne's advice and forgetting the whole thing and to look for adventure elsewhere. She still felt she ought to warn her husband, but Chen Liew did not like her to have opinions, still less put them into words.

(iv)

Molly was lying out on the grass in the moonlight with Wu. They knew they were safe because Chen Liew would be out for most of the night. He had gone to a soothsayer to have the *I Ching* read. Wu was speaking excitedly of the ease with which the Japanese were moving South through China.

"I thought you supported Mao Zedong," Molly objected, looking at the full moon through her fingers.

"We did," said Wu simply, "But my father says now the Japanese will win."

Wu thought of the empty streets and villages left behind by the advancing army, but he was distracted by Molly's scent, not an artificial scent, but the scent of her body. His inexperience made him feel tight and awkward but a clumsy longing burned for her in the pit of his stomach and blurred the sharp edges of hatred until it melted into, not love exactly, but a desire to simply hold her close to him. He slipped his arm beneath her head and tried to look with her at the moon. He wanted to see what she saw, feel what she felt.

Molly's political ideas had developed no further than the plain acceptance of good and evil. If Mao had been good not so long ago, she could not understand how he had become bad. She had even argued once with Chen Liew on Wu's behalf until the old man had angrily told her that she knew nothing. She tried to concentrate on her own feelings and to allow the world to get along without her. Wu's arm was a firm comfort beneath her head. She could sense him turning towards her and, losing sight of the moon, she moved her body slightly on the grass, turning her back to him so that, as he tucked his legs up behind hers, they lay coupled together, inseparable as words and meaning, provocative as perfume and make-up. Molly was excited by the closeness of his body and frightened vaguely by the thought of his arousal which she could feel stiffly pressing between them as Wu tried to find a recess in her body where it might pass unnoticed. He was torn between desire and embarrassment and longed sometimes to have the smooth, flat crotch of a woman, to be able to press himself still closer against her yet, at the same time, he loved the hard potency of his penis and the spasm of love which shuddered through his body when he pressed himself too close and seemed to be enveloped in the melting solidity of her back as she arched her body slightly within his arms.

Tung Nien was lying awake, fully clothed on her bed, the tedium of being alone alleviated only by the sounds of Wu and Molly talking quietly beneath her open window. "When you begin your life with the emptiness of old age," she thought bitterly, "you have nowhere left to go. I don't even have the memories of love to go back to and relive."

And so, listening to Wu and Molly's incipient lovemaking, she turned her mind to her recent, short meeting with Alfred Laughton.

"Molly says you are in love with me," she repeated to herself, conjuring up Laughton's look of shock and embarrassment. "I think if we had not been where we were I might have just reached my mouth up and kissed him," she thought. "Just to be wicked. Or to see what he would do." And she turned over on her bed and looked at the wall and then tried to sleep and then looked at the wall again. Suddenly, Molly cried out in pain from the garden. It was a reluctant, guttural yell that she took at first to be an emphatic end to virginity, but when she cried out again, still more loudly this time, Tung Nien got up from her bed and raced across to the window.

(v)

It was after dinner and Dr Alfred Laughton was trying to read by the light of a lamp by the window. He did not feel much like reading but it was preferable to talking to his wife. She talked on to him anyway, but he knew that if he held the book open before him she would not expect him to reply with anything more compromising than an occasional grunt. He was using a brown official envelope with the black letters ***O.H.M.S.*** in the top left corner as a bookmark. The letter had arrived that morning. It had contained a brief informative note which stated simply that an ordinance had been passed requiring the registration of all European males between the ages of eighteen and fifty-five. Laughton had not even mentioned the fact to his wife. He knew that had the same letter arrived even as little as six months ago he would have made some disparaging comment to her over breakfast. It was not that he no longer felt the need to speak, but that he no longer felt the interest. Their lives had drifted apart completely. Laughton had seen it happen to many couples over the years, but then, in so many cases, there were always children to hold things together. Maybe that was what you did when love faded. You put your energy and your life into your children. Maybe that was how people managed to get through the day. Alfred Laughton looked up from his book and stared at the dark night on the other side of the window.

If Mary Laughton had noticed any change in her husband, she did not mention it. She had long since accepted the fact that they had nothing to talk about and consequently, although she found it difficult, did her best to ignore his periods of silence, which might sometimes last as long as a week. The fact that he was sitting over by the window, pretending to read, his face set in a fixed grimace of incommunication, did not, therefore, either surprise or bother her. Some years ago, she might have asked him if something were wrong, thinking that perhaps he was worried, but as he had never either admitted to worry, nor accepted her offer of help, she had shut herself off from him and left him alone in his misery—or whatever it was. When she talked to him it was out of habit, or just because there was no one else there.

"Margaret Rodmell has invited us to the races," she said. "She says that Eliot is of the opinion that we should not let the recent events get on top of us. He says it will all blow over and that it is important for the Community to act, as far as possible, as though nothing has happened."

Alfred Laughton ran his finger along the edge of the brown envelope. His wife had moved onto something else. Laughton was only half-listening to her.

"Do you ever wonder why we stay here, Alfred? I mean, I'm not suggesting we live badly or anything, I just thought the other day, you know, with all this talk of war in Europe and so on, it set me thinking..."

Inertia, said Laughton to himself. Why do we do anything? I sit here looking at my reflection in the window because I can't be bothered to do anything else. Why do we stay in Hong Kong? What would we be doing anywhere else that was any better?

"It is at times like this that I understand why people turn to God," he said aloud, interrupting his wife without meaning to, but it was typical of his peculiar kind of selfishness that he automatically considered his own statements to have more importance than anyone else's. Indeed, he would have been a little surprised to learn that his opinion was, in fact, valued very little.

"What's that got to do with it?" asked his wife patiently. She would not be aggressive, not if he had been drinking.

Laughton looked up at her in some surprise. He had not meant to say it aloud.

"I just meant that you can see why old Russell, for example, has taken up with that crazy Jap and his mysticism. I mean, why not? What have you got to lose?"

"I think 'Why not?' is a poor basis for Christianity, don't you?" said Mary Laughton. "And, anyway, that Russell!" Her tone of voice dismissed Russell from further consideration.

Alfred Laughton picked up his glass of whisky and soda and a drop of condensation fell onto the open page of his book and another onto his trousers.

"It's Taoism," he said, unnecessarily. After all, what did it matter what it was?

"What's Taoism? Selling your daughter?"

"He did not sell her. And even if he did, what's it to you?"

Mary Laughton sighed heavily.

"You can have an opinion, Alfred, without having to enter into a long, philosophical discussion, you know. Things don't have to affect you personally before you begin to think about them."

And then, as though to save them from what they both knew was on the point of degenerating into an argument, the telephone rang. Alfred Laughton watched his wife's firm, straight back as she left the room to answer it. It reminded him of an exclamation mark. He blotted the smudge of whisky on the page of his book with the back of his hand, quite prepared for his wife to be away for at least twenty minutes. But she returned almost immediately.

"Talk of the devil!" she said from the door.

Laughton had already forgotten which devil they had been talking about.

"Miss Dekyvere," said his wife, still standing at the door. "Can you go? The young girl's not well."

Laughton hated to be called out at night, but no sooner had he left the house than he felt his depression lift from him. His head felt slightly fuzzy with whisky and so he decided to walk up the hill to Miss Dekyvere's bungalow. As he walked, he looked at his feet and thought, "Maybe she'll be there too." He leaned his weight into the steepness of the hill and began to count his footsteps to take his mind from Tung Nien. At first, after their brief meeting at the opening of the Hong Kong and Shanghai Bank, he had half-expected her to get in touch with him and he had looked stupidly every day for a note in his pigeon-hole at the hospital. Sometimes he had looked more than once. But, as time had passed and he had found nothing, instead of taking the initiative himself, he had tried to forget about it. But now, as he walked up the hill towards Miss Dekyvere's bungalow, all the original fire and desperate longing swept back into his blood and it seemed to pump slowly and thickly through his veins.

When he reached the high wall of Chen Liew's garden and the small, wrought iron gate of Miss Dekyvere's next door, the old woman was waiting for him.

"Sorry to call you out so late, Doctor," she was saying as she led him inside. "Normally, I would have waited till morning, but I think it's the appendix."

Laughton decided that Miss Dekyvere's original diagnosis was probably correct and, as he came out from Molly's room, she was already suggesting that Chan and the Bentley be used in preference to an ambulance.

"Chen Liew would do anything for Molly," she confided as she poured him a drink.

Laughton felt the whisky, not yet softened by the ice or the soda, sharp against his throat.

"Is that so?" he said. He willed her to ask him to sit down, not that he wanted to speak, but he would have done anything to put off the moment when he would have to go home. If she did not ask him, he decided, he would go down to the Parisian Grill and see if they would let him play the piano for a bit. They sometimes did. But as she left him to go next door he said, although it was untrue, "I'm thinking of joining the Hong Kong Voluntary Defence Corps." He wanted the kind of empty, insignificant conversation that he so despised as being now a lesser evil than loneliness.

"That's nice, dear," said Miss Dekyvere, whose thoughts were elsewhere.

Left alone in the house, Laughton felt like an intruder in the old woman's life. He could not avoid seeing things which were private and which he considered, without justification, as being signs of her loneliness: a tin of throat lozenges, an unfinished letter on an open bureau crammed with unused writing paper and pale blue air mail envelopes, a cold cup of tea and a copy of *Woman's Weekly* from six months ago. It did not cross his mind that she was perfectly happy with her life, that she sucked throat lozenges because she liked the taste of them, not because she was ill, that the letter was to her cousin, and that they had been corresponding for years, ever since Miss Dekyvere, at the age of twenty-two, had first left England to work in a mission in Szechwan, and that she had kept the copy of *Woman's Weekly* because it had a recipe in it for quail which she intended to try just as soon as she discovered a suitable small bird in the market. Laughton's sense of disillusion was such that everything he saw seemed to be impregnated with the fusty aura of his own loneliness and the inability to come to terms with the emptiness of his life.

He knew he should just have quietly finished his drink and left, but something made him sit down. He told himself that it was courtesy, that he could not leave without saying good-bye, and professional dedication, that he could not leave the girl alone in the house, but, at the same time, he knew he would be lying. It was the same sense of inertia he had felt at home earlier in the evening. Nothing seemed to be worth the effort even of doing it.

Laughton was almost asleep when Miss Dekyvere returned with Chan and Tung Nien. He was leaning on an arm of the sofa, his whisky and soda untouched and dangerously close to spilling onto the floor, and his mouth slightly open. Chan went directly into Molly's room and Miss Dekyvere and Tung Nien walked into the centre of the lounge.

"Still here, Dr Laughton?" Miss Dekyvere asked, but her tone was kind, almost as though she had expected no less.

"Didn't like to leave the patient," he said quickly. He managed to recover the glass and place it on a small camphor wood chest before he realised that Tung Nien, too, was there. He stood awkwardly, too quickly, in his embarrassment, but Tung Nien did not seem to notice.

"Dr Laughton," she said, "Thank you for coming. We were so worried."

Miss Dekyvere nodded and busied herself clearing away what Laughton had earlier defined to himself as the debris of her life. Miss Dekyvere folded away the copy of *Woman's Weekly* but said nothing. She simply set about restoring order amongst her sparse possessions.

Miss Dekyvere closed her bureau as Chan appeared at the door with Molly in his arms. A glance at Tung Nien told her that she would have to go with Molly and Chan to the hospital. She could not imagine why it should be so, but she could see Tung Nien almost physically reaching out and enveloping the hapless Laughton. Tung Nien was gazing into Laughton's eyes with a vague, dreamy look on her face and Laughton was responding as she supposed any man would have done, with a slightly concerned but self-satisfied grin. No doubt the same grin that Adam gave Eve when he took the apple, she said to herself. And she left.

As Miss Dekyvere bustled Chan into the Bentley and laid Molly out along the back seat of the car, she fancied mistakenly she could see Chen Liew staring out into the garden from the lighted window of his study and she thought, rather bitterly, It is not my job to help him keep her!

Tung Nien did not believe in providence but would gladly have used it to explain away not only Laughton's unexpected presence, for she had expected Miss Dekyvere to call a Chinese doctor, but also the nervous excitement she felt as she sat beside him on the sofa, close enough for their knees to be touching, and she looked into his eyes. She needed desperately to be loved. Laughton would have been captivated even without the gaps in his defences which had been brought on by three glasses of whisky. He reached out slowly and took one of her hands in his, turned it over and ran his fingers over her palm. He half-expected her to pull her hand away but she didn't.

It is obvious what is happening, he said to himself. Don't fight it—it's what you've been after for months! Why should you feel now that it is wrong? She leaned against him and he ran his arm behind her along the back of the sofa.

"I'm a little rusty at this kind of thing," he said aloud with a tight, self-conscious laugh.

"Don't talk," she said. "Just kiss me!"

And so he did.

It would not have been strange if, after so many months, Tung Nien had fallen short of Laughton's dreams, for he had built her up in his imagination until she formed an almost abstract perfection, far beyond any basis in reality. But, as she eased herself closer to him, he pushed towards her, still expecting, perhaps, the slightest murmur of protest. He lay back and looked at her face which was darkly silhouetted by the small chandelier in the middle of the room. Beside the light, the ceiling fan moved slowly, not even lifting enough air to ruffle her hair. Laughton reached up and pulled her face towards him. When he kissed her, it was as though he had never kissed anyone before. Her mouth moved over his lips, opening and closing and, as her tongue first recoiled from his and then sought it out with almost savage intensity, he became aware that her breathing was thick and heavy and it excited him to think that he could excite her. He pushed himself towards her and he felt her body pushing back against his. Slowly, he slipped his hand beneath her blouse and up to her breasts. She moaned and arched her back. Laughton bit into her neck and smelt the jasmine scent on her hair as she flung herself back towards him and brushed his face with her lips. Then she took his hand away gently from her breast.

"Don't you want to?" he heard himself saying, but she kissed him into silence. Laughton found he was already consciously trying to anticipate remembering every kiss and every touch of her hand, her thick breath and the musty smell of jasmine, the feel of her soft, beautiful skin. He lay back and watched the fan turning in slow, slow circles which seemed to be brushing away all the words he wanted to find to say to her.

Tung Nien pushed his hand away gently for the second time and ran her hair across his face. She would not let him do it tonight. She wanted him to hunger for her first. He was surprisingly gentle, almost docile, as he sat beside her, and she could feel the blood pulsing through his veins as he strained against her. She ran her hands across his stomach and he shuddered a little at her touch. She could feel a warmth from his body that was new to her and a potent masculinity which she knew had succumbed completely to the faintest touch from the tips of her fingers and which she could not help but compare with Chen Liew's reticent erections. But she was careful to separate a part of her mind from the passion that he was drawing from her each time he ran his hands down to the small of her back. To hold back, to not allow herself to surrender completely was like a self-imposed torture as a shiver was wrenched from her body, but she knew it was important to leave him hungry.

He watched her walk towards the bathroom. As he listened to the sound of running water from the bathroom, Laughton realised that through all their love-making she had said nothing to him and that, apart from his one clumsy sentence, he had said nothing to her.

When Miss Dekyvere returned from the hospital Laughton was

waiting for her alone.

"How is she?" he asked.

"Molly?" said Miss Dekyvere. "She's fine. They've taken her appendix out. She'll be home next week."

"I wanted..." Laughton began, but he ran out of words.

"So I see," said Miss Dekyvere walking into the kitchen. "Tea?" she called out.

Laughton could not, for the life of him, say what he was doing still sitting there. There was no explanation other than the fact that he did not want to go back to his wife. So long as he did not go home, maybe he could pretend it had not happened. No. That was precisely where the problem lay. He did not want to pretend it had not happened. Quite the reverse. He was glad it had happened and he wanted to treasure it. And that was why he would not go home. Not to Mary.

Miss Dekyvere brought in the tea and sat down in the armchair opposite him.

"It is two o'clock in the morning, Alfred," she said. "Your wife will be worried."

It annoyed him that she should think, quite rightly, that he had not thought to telephone.

"She knows I often wander down to the Parisian Grill," he said, "To play the piano."

"But you are here," she said.

"As far as she is concerned, I might just as well be there."

He was pleased with that. It put things into perspective, he thought. Miss Dekyvere was not of the same opinion.

"Don't be flippant, Alfred," she said. "You do not do it well enough."

Miss Dekyvere poured out two cups of tea and passed one of them to Laughton.

"Look, Alfred," she went on, and her voice was tired. She rubbed her hand across her forehead. "I know it is none of my business," she said, and she stopped. She looked at him as though she wanted him to take up the conversation. But he had nothing he wanted to say. "But please, Alfred, be careful! It has nothing, let me assure you," she went on, successfully preventing him from interrupting, "to do with my feelings for Chen Liew, nor do I mind unduly—after all, at my age, why should I?—whether or not people indulge themselves in whatever pleasures help to alleviate the natural tedium of life. No, Alfred, I am not taking up a moral stance here, but some things in this city can be very dangerous."

Laughton looked at the sad cup of tea before him on the table.

"Do you think I could have another whisky?" he asked.

"No, dear," she said. "I don't think you should drink any more, do you?"

(vi)

Eliot and Margaret Rodmell were getting ready to go to the races. Margaret was helping her husband with his bow tie.

"The Jockey Club was reluctant at first," Rodmell was saying, and the loose skin on his neck rippled as Margaret Rodmell pulled the two ends of the bow tie into a taut knot. "But we told them, out of season or not, there had to be a meet—for the good of morale and what have you."

"I'm sure you're right, dear," said Margaret Rodmell placing a pair of pearl earrings back into her ivory jewellery-box and taking out her rubies.

"It's especially important for the Chinese," continued Rodmell, stepping back to inspect his reflection in the mirror. "All this business of registration has put the wind up them, you see? They must be made to see that it takes more than a handful of Japanese moving down the east coast of China towards Hong Kong to disrupt the running of the Colony. Otherwise, next thing you know, they'll be throwing in their lot with the Japs." He reflected a moment before adding grumpily, "Can't trust them, you see? Bally Chinese! Don't know when they're well off!"

Margaret Rodmell did not like to be reminded of the Japanese presence across the water and, like most other Europeans on the island, she preferred to ignore the fact. She resented her husband's bringing it up and determined to change the subject. She situated the possible upheavals on the other side of the world by stating, "That funny little nurse, what was her name? Nurse Gemmell? Well, no matter! Whatever her name was, she is, or so I've been told, sailing back to England. She says she will be of more use there."

Rodmell only vaguely remembered the woman who had once been the butt of his cruelty, but he laughed as he said, "Fat lot of good she is here. Can't even play cards!"

Leaving his wife to finish dressing, Eliot Rodmell walked stiffly into the stately expanse of his lounge and poured himself a sherry. As he looked out of the window at the lights of the city and the harbour, he was pleased they had insisted on the races being held in the evening. It made it so much more of an event. He opened the window and listened to the strident noises of the insects in the garden and he sipped his sherry.

Rodmell was, however, a little concerned that, as far as he had been able to make out, nothing had come of his conversation with Major Harland. He was concerned principally because he could not understand why not. He had planned it all so meticulously and he prided himself that he understood the Chinese mind. Chan would have had no choice but to inform Chen Liew of what he had overheard, Chen Liew would have had no choice but to act against Liao K'ung and Tang, and Tang, being innocent, not of the thefts but of collaborating with Liao K'ung, would have had no choice but to act, in turn, against Chen Liew. In the resulting battle, the only person who stood to gain was he himself. And yet, nothing had happened. Rodmell frowned into the darkness. The only good news in recent weeks was a lucrative little business he had set up with the recently arrived cadet officer who controlled the immigration and refugee camps. It was symptomatic of Rodmell's behaviour that he could never resist the opportunity, however small, of increasing his wealth. The business of the registration certificates had seemed too insignificant, at first, to warrant his attention. But, then, he had told himself, if he didn't do it, someone else was bound to. "It is surprising," he mused to himself as he watched the lights of an aeroplane dipping its wings above the harbour and turning towards the airport at Kai Tak, "how much money these penniless refugees can actually get their hands on when they put their minds to it."

A little lower on the Peak, Doctor and Mary Laughton were also dressing. Mary had not expected her husband to accept the invitation to Happy Valley and she had already made excuses for his absence.

"He is so tired when he comes back from the hospital. And then hardly a night goes past when he is not called out. I blame all these refugees. Everybody is so nervous now. The slightest sign of a temperature and they all think they've got smallpox or cholera."

"Good of you to honour us with your presence this evening," Mary Laughton said as she brushed her hair. She no longer even tried to hide her feelings. Laughton nodded. He wondered whether it was his imagination or whether she had really become more objectionable recently.

"But you won't enjoy it," she was saying, "so I don't really see why you're bothering. After all, nobody expects anything of you any more. They know what you are like."

"They only think they know," he said, but he could not be bothered now to argue, so that when she said, "No, Alfred. They have seen it often enough—the rudeness, the drinking, the complete lack of even the most rudimentary etiquette!" he said nothing. And that annoyed her perhaps even more than if he had answered her accusations.

"Still," she said. She had finished brushing her hair and was now powdering her face. "If you insist on coming, do try to be sociable. Don't ignore Mr Rodmell and the Major. People notice that kind of thing and it offends them. Not only that," she added, and he knew that this was the important thing, "It reflects badly on me as well."

Laughton left his wife in the bedroom and walked through the house and out into the garden. The night was humid and sticky. Laughton could almost feel the sweat as it formed on his bare arms. He looked up as a 'plane flew over the Peak and he thought, Tung Nien will be hearing that too. It made him feel empty and filled at the same time. He thought, It is sad that I cannot share my happiness with anyone. For there is no one to listen to me. And what I have to share is not what they want to hear.

Near the waterfront in Wanchai, Harry Osbourne was having a quick bite to eat before catching a tram up to Garden Road and the Happy Valley racecourse. He too watched the 'plane as it circled slowly over the harbour and drifted away towards the airport, but it suggested little to him. There was not, in Osbourne, any capacity for fantasy. When he saw the 'plane, he thought only of the emptiness that induced people to try to search out some promise of life in travel. They don't realise that you take your ghosts with you, he said, but he did not even feel strongly enough about what he was thinking for it to be bitter. It was a simple observation, as he might have thought, They've been a bit heavy-handed with the soy sauce!

Osbourne was sitting at a small bamboo table, which had been pushed out for him onto the pavement at the corner of Gloucester Road and Fenwick Street. He had asked to be separated from the bar because it was full of sailors, whores and lost-looking Chinese labourers and stevedores from the Victoria Docks. Osbourne finished eating and smoked a cigarette. He felt lethargic. A Benny Goodman song crackled out into the night from a radio somewhere. Osbourne hummed along as a girl's voice took over from the clarinet.

Goodnight, my love,
The tired old moon is descending.
Goodnight, my love,
My moment with you now is ending.

Osbourne felt he recognised something in the strained nervousness of the sailors in the bar and the strangely appropriate melancholy of the music which reminded him of the pre-war tension of 1914, when everyone spent their time waiting for something concrete to happen which would define their terrible future for them. At the same time, desperate relationships seemed to flower and fade almost nightly if for no other reason, thought Osbourne, than to allow the soldiers and the whores to sing along with the popular songs.

The stars above
Have promised to meet us tomorrow.
Till then, my love,
How dreary the new day will seem!

The sailors, Osbourne noted, were from the destroyer, *HMS Thracian.* He wondered vaguely whether they knew any more about the situation than he did. Probably not, he decided. After all, the fact they were getting drunk meant nothing. They always got drunk almost as soon as they set foot on dry land. It was probably all just a product of his imagination, the fact that he was having to invent things to stave off his boredom.

"What I need is a good story," he said to himself as he stood and pushed his way back into the bar to pay for his dinner. "Something I can get my teeth into. "

As he was leaving, a raw voice called out to him. "Osbourne, you old tosser! How about buying us a drink?" But Osbourne pretended he had not heard.

Molly was excited at the thought of going to the races in the evening. As she had lain in bed in the hospital recovering from her operation she had built the event up until it had taken on the significance of a landmark. It would, she had convinced herself, be the point at which everything changed in her life, when she would cross the threshold from adolescence into whatever came afterwards. She had had plenty of time to think whilst she had been lying there alone.

Dr Laughton had taken her some books to read, but apart from one called "Mummies," they had not interested her and, anyway, as she had told him before, she did not like reading in English. He had looked a little hurt by that but she did not feel like explaining. To please him, though, she had read the book on Egypt. When he had come to visit her again, she had given the book back and said that although it had been very interesting she thought the Great Wall more impressive than the pyramids because, on the one hand, she had seen it, and on the other, it served a purpose. Dr Laughton had muttered something about them both being signs of oppression and power before he left.

Miss Dekyvere had visited her in the hospital every day between twelve and one-thirty. The first thing she told Molly each day was that her father would be in later on. But he never went, which was a relief to Molly. She did not want to see him.

"By why not, Molly? He is your father," Miss Dekyvere tried to persuade her.

"He killed my mother," said Molly, and turned over in the bed, pulling the sheets up to her chin.

But Miss Dekyvere was kind. She brought sweets, a pack of cards, a notebook and pencils, and one day, she brought Wu. He bounded into the ward, a big grin on his face, and told her he had escaped from school by climbing through a toilet window the moment he had heard that she was in hospital. Molly was pleased although she knew Wu did not go to school. Miss Dekyvere left them alone and went off to see Nurse Gemmell.

"Because she is leaving us," she explained.

Wu told Molly that he had been out at the village of Lo Wu during the Japanese shelling. He talked in graphic detail, his eyes shining, of explosions, acrid smoke and mutilated pigs lying bloated in the river. Molly listened, fascinated despite herself, and a little frightened, and then Wu sat forwards on the bed and took her hands in his. His face grew very serious as he said, "And soon they will come here to free us from the hated British exploiters!"

Molly could not like the Japanese any more than she liked the British.

"I thought we wanted Mao to win," she said again, not wanting to contradict him.

Wu tossed his head arrogantly. "My father says the only future is with the Japanese. Mao is in league now with the British and the American pigs."

Molly could not put her fear of the Japanese into words, but she had seen the hundreds of refugees with her own eyes in the streets of Shanghai, many of them crippled, all of them starving. She remembered there had been very few children and when she had asked her father why this was, he had said, "The children rarely make it, Molly. They have to be carried. In the end they are a heavy load." And in the weeks before the bombing, as they were getting ready to leave, just the rumour that the Japanese were about to attack had sent a terrified stream of people pouring from the city—homeless out of choice, homeless in preference to a life under the Japanese. Much as she wanted now to agree with Wu, and much as her hatred of her father was pushing her in that direction, her fears were such that all she said was, "I hope they don't come. I hope nobody comes."

When Miss Dekyvere returned they were playing cards and laughing as though they did not know there was such a thing as war.

Tung Nien visited her just before she was to be released from hospital. She arrived with Dr Laughton and they presented her with a somehow mutual silence so that she had to ask, "When can I go home?"

"Tomorrow," said Dr Laughton.

"And next Tuesday evening," said Tung Nien, "I shall take you to the races."

The idea of going to the races had been thrilling enough to all but banish her thoughts of marauding Japanese soldiers. When Chan and Miss Dekyvere came in the Bentley to collect her, it was the first thing she said to them. When Dr Laughton and the red-haired Nurse Gemmell waved her off from the hospital steps, she called out, feeling very grown-up and special, "See you at Happy Valley!" The first thing she did when she arrived home was sit down with Tung Nien and Miss Dekyvere to decide what she should wear.

"Anyone would think you had never been out before," said Miss

Dekyvere.

"I've never been out like this, I've never been out *anywhere*!" said Molly, her eyes shining. And Miss Dekyvere sighed as she was forced to recognise how much you lost as you grew older.

"It is more than just the fear of what the darkness holds," she thought. "It is that we must eventually find out that it is only that. Darkness."

(vii)

It seemed that the out-of-season race meeting at Happy Valley had attracted the entire European population of Hong Kong together with those Chinese who had sufficient money to be considered almost honorary Europeans, but, even so, a certain stiff protocol was maintained and only the most important public figures were allowed inside the Members' Enclosure. The rest of the crowd managed to separate itself almost instinctively into little cliques defined either by contacts or salary. A person who had a basically insufficient financial status could find himself promoted on the weight of his social standing. And so it was that Alfred Laughton and his wife were ushered into the elegant confines of the bar above the Members' Stand. They were with the Rodmells and the Harlands, and it was said that Sir Vandeleur Grayburn would be arriving shortly with the Governor, Sir Geoffrey Northcote. A few necessary minions, including Robinson and the apparently marooned Fosters, mingled. This small group, due principally to the imposing presence of Eliot Rodmell, felt itself to be the nucleus around which various satellite groups rotated. There was Hughes, Manager of the Union Insurance Society of Hong Kong, with a handful of acolytes—Sycophants! scoffed Rodmell—and in another corner of the room, J.P. Pitkethley. No one had ever discovered what the J.P. stood for, but it mattered little, for there he was with the entire Board of Directors of the China Light and Power Company, one of whom was a Chinese.

"Eliot!" hissed Margaret Rodmell, when she noticed. "Really!"

But Eliot Rodmell shrugged. "Move with the times, Margaret. We must face facts," he said, and his voice betrayed a certain longing for the old days. "Some of the richest and most powerful families are Chinese these days." And, as if on cue, Chen Liew entered with his entourage. Rodmell looked up quickly for some sign of nervousness or undue apprehension in Chen Liew's face, but the Chinese was a study in calm contentment. It was obvious that he did not have a care in the world and, when he saw Rodmell, he actually treated him to a smile of recognition and a slight nod of his head. Rodmell responded in kind and then turned away brusquely.

"Dashed if I understand a damned thing, Harland!" he said to the Major gruffly. But Major Harland was not listening. Like most of the other men in the Members' Bar he was looking at Tung Nien who stood at her husband's shoulder and shimmered in the lamplight like a strange and exotic flower. Laughton felt a rush of love and pride coupled with a certain incredulous wonder as she floated towards them across the thick pile of the carpet.

Chan was leading Chen Liew over to their group, one hand opening a passage through the crowd and the other at Chen Liew's elbow. It was clear that he was going to speak to Rodmell. Major Harland nudged the Taipan in the ribs and Rodmell turned in time to take Chen Liew's small, pale hands in his own puffed, beetroot-coloured fingers. He glanced quickly past Chen Liew to the small monkey-face of Liao K'ung in search of a clue as to how he should behave. After all, it was always possible that they had talked over his rumour, decided it was untrue and even discovered its source from Chan. Rodmell was not by nature a nervous man but the cold, inscrutable stare which Liao K'ung presented him with made him fear the worst. He was hardly listening when Chen Liew said, "Mr Rodmell! Such a good idea, these races! I have always thought it unnecessary to restrict the season."

Rodmell was so relieved that he actually placed his arm around the smaller man's shoulder and smiling, replied, "Quite so! Quite so! Although it was the Jockey Club, you know. I merely suggested..."

As Chen Liew and Rodmell exchanged a few polite comments about horses, Tung Nien approached Laughton and placed her hand in his, but in greeting, not in love.

"I wanted to thank you," she said, and not even her eyes betrayed any feeling for him, "For all you did for Molly."

"It was nothing," said Laughton and, as he released her hand, she pushed a small square of paper into his. He slipped it into his jacket pocket as he moved to kiss Molly on the cheek.

Molly smiled at him and decided he was definitely the only Englishman she liked, if only because it was so obvious that all the others disapproved of him. When he had spoken to Tung Nien, she had noticed that Major and Mrs Harland had turned away to complain quietly to Mrs Laughton.

"I mean, Eliot *has* to speak to them," said Major Harland in a stage whisper. "But there is absolutely *no* need for the rest of us to lower the tone."

And so she would annoy them still more by speaking to him further.

"I am going to bet on 'Catinat'," she said and she smiled. Laughton realised it was a confidential tip and taking a pen from his pocket, he wrote the name of the horse on the back of Tung Nien's note.

Molly and Tung Nien moved away to the back of their group and were hidden by the broad expanse of Chan and the monkey-face of Liao K'ung. Laughton was left holding the small square of paper. He looked at it for a moment where he had written the name 'Catinat' and then turned it over. There was a single line of unsteady handwriting which said simply:

"In the Tiger Balm Gardens by the statue of the
Unpredictable Ghost after the third race."

He was still looking at it when Miss Dekyvere spoke to him. He registered a voice but did not hear the words. When he looked up he noticed that she was staring down at the note in his hands. Quickly he screwed the paper into his fist and said with a forced laugh, "Molly gave me a tip."

"Don't do it, Alfred," said Miss Dekyvere seriously. But Laughton was already drunk with anticipation and hungry with desire.

"Oh, don't worry, Ruth," he said casually. "I never bet more than I can afford to lose."

She gave him a meaningful look and said, "I hope that is true, Alfred."

There was a lot of laughter, cheering and clapping during the races, even in the usually restrained Members' Stand. Major Harland had brought his hip flask along and he and Rodmell imbibed freely after winning on the first horse.

"I told you to bet on an Aussie rider, Foster," said Rodmell happily to the plantation owner who had not shared their good fortune. Major Harland snorted into the hip flask.

"They were all Aussies, Eliot!" he laughed, mentally counting his winnings.

"Were they now?" said Rodmell seriously, hiding a nasty grin, for, of course, he knew they were.

Major Harland relaxed into his drinking. It was always a tense moment for him, the beginning of an evening out with Rodmell. You never knew who he would decide to pick on, to make the butt of his jokes and his vicious sarcasm. The Major had escaped for so long that he could not help thinking that the law of averages meant that it would soon be his turn. It was with a surge of relief that he realised that the unfortunate Foster was to be baited this evening. Rodmell was like a fighting bull in his jocular aggressions: once he had chosen his victim, nothing would distract him from his goal—which was quite simply the humiliation of his opponent. For it was, thought Harland, an opponent. Mrs Harland had dared once to suggest that Rodmell was basically an insecure person and these unwarranted attacks were his way of proving his superiority. Major Harland had said that he had not stopped to think about it. And it was true. Knowing why it was would not make it go away. And anyway, he had to recognise that, as soon as it was clear that he himself had not been singled out, he joined in with a vengeance, not only laughing, sometimes even offering up his own particularly biting witticism. They all did. It was the animal instinct, to band together behind the strong and to ostracise the weak.

Dr Laughton was sitting in the row behind the others. Although there had been plenty of room for them all to sit together, Laughton could think of nothing worse than forming a part of Rodmell's adoring circle. Mary had flashed him a warning glance but he had just smiled back at her, knowing she would do no more than that in public. He had been slightly taken aback then by the look of utter hatred in her eyes. She despised him thoroughly, he knew, but he had not been prepared for such a complete absence of any affection at all. As a kind of childish assertion of his individuality he sat back and put his feet up on Rodmell's chair. He looked along the row of heads before him and shot each one of them with his fingers pointing like a gun. Like metal ducks at a fairground, he thought, exploding another bullet in his cheek.

Rodmell turned heavily in his seat and brushed Laughton's feet away. "I say, old man!" he grunted, frowning at Laughton and Laughton looked away across the hundreds of heads in the stand to the bright, green, empty turf. He could feel again his wife's disapproving eyes boring into him. Ignoring her, he put his hand into his jacket pocket and closed his fist around Tung Nien's note. In the row in front of him, everyone but Foster and his wife were laughing again. Then suddenly all the heads turned and they looked off to the far end of the track where the bright colours of the jockeys' shirts could just be seen emerging from the paddock. Although it was only the second race, Laughton decided he had had enough and he got up to leave.

"Alfred!" Mary leaned towards him, her expression this time appealing to him to behave himself.

"I've had enough, Mary," he said, "I think I'll take myself off."

"You know we've been invited to dinner," she reminded him. And he had forgotten.

"I've got a bit of a headache, Mary," he said. "Maybe some fresh air will help to clear it."

He pushed his way along the row of seats to the aisle and began the long climb up the steps and out of the stand. Finally, he had felt sorry for Mary. He knew how much all this meant to her, this social climbing and rubbing elbows with the rich and powerful, and so, as he climbed the steps to the bar, he turned, caught her eye, and waved, he hoped, reassuringly.

Poor Mary, he thought. I wonder what it is she hopes to find when she finally arrives.

From his press box Harry Osbourne had a sweeping, panoramic view of the home straight and the Members' Stand. Looking through his binoculars he followed Laughton's upright back until it disappeared into the bar.

"Now where's he going?" he mused to himself, panning back down to Rodmell's group. Mary Laughton was laughing, primly taking the perspiration from her forehead with a handkerchief and speaking energetically to Margaret Rodmell. Rodmell and Harland were drinking and looking away off in the direction of the paddock. Osbourne focussed his binoculars on the Chinese who were sitting some ten rows below and to the left of Rodmell's group.

The three wise monkeys, said Osbourne to himself.

Chen Liew, with Molly sitting beside him, leaning her chin on the rail, Liao K'ung and Chang. Next to them, Tung Nien looked distracted and Miss Dekyvere out of place. Osbourne put his binoculars on a small writing desk before him and lit a cigarette. He noticed a low, silver cloud of smoke hung over the stand reflecting the harsh white of the spotlights and he blew a mouthful of smoke out to join it.

"Well," he said. "When I get a moment, I'll nip out to Lo Wu and nose around a bit. There is obviously nothing for me here. Despite what the woman says, you can tell just by looking at them that Liao K'ung and Chen Liew are still the best of friends."

Molly had been allowed one bet in the third race and she held the receipt Chan had brought her by one corner so as not to crease it. She looked round the crowded stand and tried to find things to remember so that she could tell Wu the next time they met.

"We do not go to the races," Wu had told her. "It's a bourgeois invention. My father says it is just another way of subjecting the masses—giving them the illusion that by betting the little money they've got, they might, through a stroke of good fortune, rise out of the misery of poverty."

"What is wrong with that?" Molly had asked him.

Wu had not yet quite thought things out for himself. "My father says that there is no shame in poverty."

"That is easy for us to say," Molly had thought, for she had seen it first hand. But she said nothing. Now, however, amongst the obvious opulence of the Members' Stand, the same thought occurred to her but, this time, it was not conditioned by any feeling of pity. She was happy to be privileged and she felt a sudden warm feeling of gratitude towards Chen Liew and Tung Nien for, not only had they rescued her from a life of misery, they had also rescued her from a life as a European. She was smiling, happy and excited, as she turned and kissed Chen Liew on his leathery cheek. The old man smiled and accepted her affection without offering anything in return other than an almost imperceptible squeeze of her hand, but for Molly it was more than enough. She felt protected, privileged and proud as she looked out across the bobbing heads in the stand below and then past them to the horses.

Laughton walked straight through the bar, where one or two straggling groups were still drinking, and out into Leighton Road. Pushing his hat to the back of his head, he strolled slowly down to Tai Hang Road and into the Tiger Balm Gardens. He could not forget how both he and Mary had reacted to the cruel, plaster, painted figures of the gardens when they had first arrived in Hong Kong. Mary had seen nothing but blood and guts and violence, but what had caught his attention more than anything else had been the garish combinations of colours. As for the scenes depicted by the statues, they had reminded Laughton of the paintings of Heronymous Bosch and he had felt a little annoyed when Mary had begun to criticise all things Chinese as barbarian merely on the strength of their visit to the gardens. Everybody was always so quick to see the bad in things they did not want to understand. When he had mentioned Bosch, she had just said, "I don't like him either. Flemish, wasn't he? Or Dutch?" As if that might have been reason enough. "Anyway," she had continued, "We don't need all this fire and brimstone, Alfred. What about nice things?"

Now, in the darkness, the figures were even weirder, even more evil and even more difficult to comprehend. Laughton half-expected them to come to life as he walked down the looping lanes and up the small hills in search of the *Unpredictable Ghost.* He found it without difficulty as each scene was carefully labelled with its corresponding gods and demi-gods together with a little explanatory paragraph in English and Chinese.

"The Unpredictable Ghost is the demi-god which leads men's souls to the underworld.
He is often depicted, as he is here, carrying gold and silver coins. The bridge on which he is standing..."

Laughton looked at the leering painted face. The teeth looked to be too big for the mouth and from the mouth there pointed a snaking tongue. The eyes were extraordinarily wide for a Chinese and Laughton took its expression to be one of mock fear. To his left, smaller figures were being disembowelled, roasted alive and buried face down in a solid, concrete expanse of bubbling mud. Laughton turned away, lit a cigarette and sat on the raised green concrete wall which separated the figures from the path.

Paddy White on 'Catinat' won by more than three lengths in the third race but because it had been odds-on favourite, relatively little money changed hands. Molly did not notice. The excitement of winning had caused her to jump and scream and shout in a way which Chen Liew evidently found quite unbecoming, so that Tung Nien could hardly believe her luck when he turned gruffly towards her and Miss Dekyvere and said, "Take Molly out. Buy her a soft drink or something."

Miss Dekyvere knew what was happening but she would rather not have known. When Tung Nien left her in the bar with Molly, Miss Dekyvere thought, "It is not fair of them to do this to me. Nothing would have made me be a party willingly to this deception and now, merely by not revealing what I know, I will have become involved." That they had not intended her to be involved she did not doubt but, she said, "That you are not aware of what you are doing does not free you from the responsibility, nor from blame for the results."

Miss Dekyvere sat down and wished to God that life could be more simple. Of course, for Molly it was. Just approaching sixteen, she had yet to progress from the solid and honest emotions of adolescence, which Miss Dekyvere visualised in her mind as unbroken blocks of primary colours, to the more nebulous misunderstandings, longings and deceits of maturity when, in Miss Dekyvere's mind, the colours ran together forming new tones that could no longer be separated into their pure elements.

"I just hope she gets a move on," she said to herself. She made an effort to set her mind to more practical considerations, but before she could completely relax she had to say something and so, drawing Molly close to her she said, "Remember, Molly, when you are older, that everything you do, no matter how small and insignificant it seems to you, will always, somehow, affect someone else too."

Molly smiled at her and nodded. "Can't we go back?" she asked.

"Not just yet awhile," said Miss Dekyvere. "All the noise out there has given me a bit of a headache."

And there is the first lie, she thought sadly. Now you have become actively as well as passively involved. Now you have made a step of your own volition and you have lied for them. No matter what happens now, you will have no one to blame but yourself. She looked at Molly's bright, excited eyes and thought it would not be long now before all her colours ran together.

Tung Nien saw Laughton leaning against the wall and smoking. He had pushed his hat to the back of his head and was gazing out across the gardens in the direction of the Jewish cemetery. Not for the first time, she felt strongly attracted to him although now he reminded her more of the confused child she had seen at the Bun Festival than the passionate man of their recent lovemaking.

Laughton suddenly heard the clicking of her heels on the concrete path. He turned and she ran towards him smiling. Laughton put his arms round her waist and they kissed.

"I've missed you," he said. She pressed herself against him so that he had to move his hand round to her back and she kissed him again. She sat on the low concrete wall. Laughton wanted only to touch her, to feel her body pressed against his, to kiss her. He desperately wanted something to be passionate about. He did not particularly want reason to interfere and he did not want an intellectual companion. He had had enough of the intellect. All he wanted at that moment, he admitted a little guiltily to himself, was something which would satisfy his most basic instincts. He wanted sex. Not sex with just anyone. After all, there were plenty of places where he could buy it. He wanted sex with her. Now, though, she was separating herself from his unthinking vision of her and she was becoming a person, a person with thoughts and feelings. He found himself unwillingly recoiling into the silences he had so painstakingly built up between himself and anything he did not understand. So far, their relationship had not transcended those barriers; it had remained within the secret confines of his imagination; real as the fondling, kissing and loving had been, it had not separated itself and become a mingling of anything more than bodily juices. Now she seemed to be infiltrating her self beneath his defences and he knew that before long he would no longer be just a lover, he would be a person. He was not sure that he felt brave enough to accept that responsibility. Why couldn't it have just stayed as a dream, he thought to himself. Just the two of us. Alone. Together. Away from all things commonplace.

Tung Nien wanted to forget her problems and lose herself in his embrace, only he seemed in some way to have distanced himself from her.

"What's the matter, Alfred?" she asked finally, resting her head against his shoulder.

"I don't know," he said.

She kissed him again longingly on the mouth and he could sense the promise of abandon that so excited him. He would, he knew, do anything she asked, because the force of his passion was greater than his reasoning. Tung Nien felt him relax into her arms and they kissed.

5

"For a moment when you held me close in your arms
I thought the river stood still and did not flow."

(i)

"For crying out loud, Eliot! Of course there is a military strategy for defending the Colony from a Japanese attack!"

Major Harland's face was red due to a combination of the Napoleon brandy he had been drinking and the offence he felt at Rodmell's insinuation that the army did not know what it was doing. Major Harland's attention was drawn towards an open copy of *Punch*. A cartoon showed the figure of Europe awakening from a dream and through an open window the nightmare of war was disappearing. It was late afternoon and Major Harland and Eliot Rodmell were in the lounge of The Pen having a gin after their twice-weekly round of golf and Eliot Rodmell had had the nerve to suggest to Major Harland that the Colony was in the hands of a bunch of soldiers who had no real understanding of the actual situation.

"Conscription is being considered now!" he had scoffed. "I read it the other day. All men between the ages of eighteen and forty-one who are fit for active service—whatever that is supposed to mean—are, in the event of war, to be allocated to the Hong Kong Volunteer Defence Corps or the Hong Kong Naval Defence Force. It is hardly going to impress the Japs, is it?"

"European nationals have volunteered in considerable numbers," Harland had countered. "And you know yourself that the HKVDC is under professional soldiers and regular army discipline."

And then he had said it. "But there is no defence strategy, Major, is there? Even if these soldiers are worth anything, which, personally, I doubt, what are they going to do?"

Pride dictated that Harland would have to explain. He did not notice that Kenji and Willard Russell had just moved across towards them. They had sat down at the next table and would, inadvertently, hear every word he said. Had he noticed, it would probably not have changed things. Rodmell had insulted him and he was determined to set the record straight.

"And," Rodmell was saying to him, "they want me, and people of my age, the over fifty-fives, I think they said, to put ourselves under the orders of that nincompoop Hughes. Even started calling themselves the 'Hughesiliers', for Christ's sake! It's pathetic, Major!"

Major Harland swallowed a mouthful of cognac. "We are, as it happens, ready to repel either a sea-borne attack or a land offensive," he stated confidently.

"At least you have begun to admit the possibility that the Japs may not be altogether friendly. That's a step in the right direction," said Rodmell with a hint of sarcasm in his voice. Major Harland blinked at his friend, not altogether sure that the interruption had been as complimentary as it sounded. "Artillery on the southern coast of Hong Kong Island," he said, "And a line of pill-boxes has been built in the New Territories which runs right the way from Gindrinkers Bay in the west to Tide Cove and then, from there, over the hills and down to Port Shelter."

"All well and good, Major," said Rodmell, "But who is there to man these pill-boxes. Myself and the other 'Hughesiliers' perhaps?"

"Don't be silly, Eliot. Heavy machine-guns," said Harland, "The Middlesex Regiment!"

"And?" said Rodmell.

"Light infantry and mobile artillery are to be sent out from home," Major Harland added a little sulkily.

"So," Rodmell continued. "We have a military strategy that relies on soldiers being sent out from home in the event that we need them, by which time, I mean, by the time they arrive here, the Japs will be sitting in the Parisian Grill having dinner and listening to that chump Laughton banging out those awful songs of his on the piano!"

Major Harland thought for a moment and his eyes rested on the smooth face of the Japanese at the next table. Kenji was looking at him, for all the world, thought Harland, as though he too were waiting to hear how he would respond. Willard Russell was slumped back in his wheelchair, his eyes closed, but Kenji was looking at him. It was disconcerting, but prompted by Rodmell's clear blue eyes and slightly mocking smile, Harland had to continue.

"We have agreements, Eliot. The British have promised to take no action prejudicial to the Japanese in China. I hardly think the Japanese are likely to turn round and invade us after that!"

Rodmell was beginning to lose interest in the conversation. "For goodness sake, Major! Be sensible!"

"They won't invade," stated Harland finally. "The threat will blow over here as it has done in Europe. You'll see that I'm right."

Eliot Rodmell yawned and decided to change the subject. "Blow over or not, Major, it's an ill wind, as they say. The Chinese are so stuck now for even the most basic commodities that they are willing to pay any price for them and, let me tell you, they are not so particular where they get them from any more."

"What do you mean?" asked Major Harland, still a little concerned by Kenji's expressionless eyes looking over at him. But Eliot Rodmell merely tapped the side of his nose and closed one of his gull-blue eyes as though he thought the Major might understand.

As Kenji listened to Major Harland's explanations he wondered if any of them actually realised how vulnerable they really were. Probably not, he decided, for nothing had yet managed to ruffle even the surface of harmony of the ordered society of Hong Kong. The Rodmells and Harlands were unaffected by the water shortage, the cholera and the smallpox epidemics struck down only the poor Chinese, and the refugee camps, whilst an eyesore, were far enough away to pass unnoticed for most of the population.

The official stance, thought Kenji as he watched the red-faced Major trying to impress his pompous friend, was perhaps even more blinkered than that of the civilians. They had steadfastly refused to build public shelters but, at the same time, by commissioning their ARP Officer, they had admitted that an air-borne attack was a possibility. To fight off such an attack, an eventuality conveniently skirted in Harland's defence plan, they had three obsolete Vildebeeste torpedo bombers down at Kai Tak. And now, for the land attack, this belated building of pillboxes! It was rumoured too that a bunker was being dug out in Central, an underground HQ, the 'battle-box', Kenji had heard it called, fifty feet below the Victoria Barracks. And yet everything seemed to have been designed to preserve the harmony of society at all costs, as though the preservation of harmony alone might be sufficient to prevent not only an invasion but also the outbreak of evil and disintegration symbolised by the Japanese forces across the border. Kenji felt justified in despising the British, for they deserved no less.

Rodmell and Harland were about to be joined by Rodmell's secretary, Robinson, and so Kenji turned his attention to the other guests in the Lounge. They all laugh at me, he said to himself, but it is they, not I, who are out of touch with reality. They are stuck out here, alone and undefended, on the far side of the world. Europeans who are effectively cut off from Europe which, anyway, is itself plunging towards its own war. They are perched here on the brink of the abyss and, not only are they not concerned, they can't even see the gap opening up before them. They all act as though nothing were happening and as though there were all the time in the world.

(ii)

Osbourne drove out to Lo Wu on the border with China in his old Vauxhall. As the moon came up it reflected in the seemingly endless paddy fields which stretched away on either side of the road. The car rattled over the uneven surface of the tarmac and Osbourne wondered what he hoped to find when he arrived at the village. "Still," he said to himself as he peered through the mud-spattered windscreen into the semi-darkness, "Better than sitting on your arse and waiting for a story to fall into your lap. Sometimes just the illusion of work is important." For Osbourne had suffered from the same feeling of tired suspense as everyone else. They had all been waiting for war to break out and the present reprieve, rather than allowing them to relax back into their normal lives, had left them all wondering whether their normal lives were worth finding again. Instead, they went through the motions, but with less conviction than before, and the continued pretence that everything was quite as it should be had almost convinced them that, in fact, it was. "Of course," Osbourne admitted readily, "We all want to be convinced, don't we?"

Osbourne scarcely noticed the walled village of Kat Him Wai, although it loomed solidly through the darkness away to the left of the road. He was looking at the bloated carcass of a dead water buffalo, intrigued by the light of the moon on its horns. Fortunately, he was driving slowly, for it was only at the last moment that he noticed, standing in the middle of the road, the shadowy figure of Tang's 'red pole', Dong Feng. Osbourne braked quickly and wound down his window. From his expression, Osbourne could tell that Dong Feng had been expecting someone else. He walked slowly round to the side of the car and looked in, as though perhaps his expected visitor might have been skulking in the back seat. Osbourne did his best to smile but he could feel his cheeks resisting.

"Jóu Táu," said Dong Feng.

Osbourne nodded. He had not understood but he had learnt that nodding was always politic with the Dong Fengs and Chans of this world. Although he knew Dong Feng's English was as rudimentary as his own Chinese was he said, "Just going out to look at the pill-boxes!" Osbourne sensed that he was going to be asked to step out of the car when another set of headlights appeared from over the rise in the road some two miles behind him. Dong Feng stepped back and waved him on. Osbourne waved politely and finally managed to produce the smile he had been searching for.

"Bastards!" he hissed as he drove off. "Damned Chinese! Don't know when they're bloody well off. They'd soon learn what was good for them if we upped and left and let the Japs take over. There'd be a bit more respect then, I reckon."

When he drove into Lo Wu, the village was in total darkness. Osbourne turned off the lights of the car and pulled it over towards the side of the road, hiding it beneath the sloping roof of a makeshift barn. It was almost invisible in the darkness. Since the last Japanese bombing, the villagers had imposed their own curfew and blackout which, considering they had no electricity, had been quite simple. Tang's and Chen Liew's guards made sure it was not violated as the black-out conveniently protected the warehouses. Osbourne felt nervous in the darkness and the unnatural silence of the village.

Osbourne had always erroneously thought of himself as a kind of Everyman. Now, though, suddenly alone in what appeared to be a deserted village on the edge of nowhere, the insignificance and pointlessness of what he was doing came home to him, and he realised, almost with a sense of satisfaction after all the cheating, that, rather than Everyman, he was No One. He represented nothing, unless it was the kind of empty despair that most people shied away from, but which he embraced. It was symbolised, he thought, by his drinking and his whoring with Fletcher. He rarely really wanted to drink, almost never wanted to be with Fletcher and, apart from a momentary spasm of pleasure, got nothing out of going with the girls in the Glory Hole. But now, in the overwhelming immensity of the silent, claustrophobic, walled streets of Lo Wu, he realised that what he feared more than anything else was not his own insignificance in itself, but that that insignificance would lead to his dying alone and lonely. The living alone and lonely he could manage, but the idea of dying in a damp, rented flat in Kowloon, all alone was—the only word that occurred to him—repugnant. Or would it be worse, he thought suddenly, to die out here? In search of a non-existent story, which would be censored anyway if I found it? Where not even my body would be found, never mind my soul!

Osbourne glanced quickly down a dark, narrow street. Two rats scurried across a muddy, stone step and disappeared inside a lean-to with a corrugated-iron roof which, on closer inspection, he found to be a storeroom for sorghum. He thought he saw a figure move in the shadows at the far end of the street, but it might have been the wind. He began to regret ever having left the bright lights and empty lives of Victoria and Kowloon. He turned very slowly, because it might not have been the wind, and he began to retrace his steps towards his car. When he was close enough to make out the shape of the Vauxhall through the darkness, the same headlights, or so it seemed to Osbourne, in his nervous state of mind, that had saved him from Dong Feng at Kat Him Wai, appeared again at the end of the road. He ran quickly and stealthily to his left and scrambled down into the dank and stinking sanctuary of a stagnant monsoon drain. From there he could watch the car and its occupants as they passed his own without seeing it hidden beneath the lean-to and parked not more than twelve feet away from him. The driver of the car, Dong Feng, switched on a small green light beneath the dashboard and Osbourne could see the face of the second person in the front of the car. It was the Japanese barber, Kenji.

Osbourne lay low in the monsoon drain until he heard Dong Feng and Kenji drive away again. He knew he should have been more careful when he ran from his hiding place towards his car but his actions had ceased to follow the logical thoughts of his mind. His body seemed to be functioning automatically, without him, as it did when he was drunk. He stumbled across to his car and leaned breathlessly against the windscreen. A torn piece of paper was plastered against the glass, held there by the heavy fall of dew that was building up as the dawn approached. He took the paper without thinking and stuffed it into his pocket and then, without looking again at the village, he started the car and headed back towards what was, although he had never before thought of it as such, civilisation.

(iii)

It was Chen Liew who first suggested that Molly should perhaps go back to her father. He said it in the cool, empty room he called his study but which he used almost exclusively to prepare himself for death. It was a long room which had no natural light and which was illuminated by a small cluster of candles at one end. Molly and Tung Nien had been called into Chen Liew's study and they sat on two silk cushions at one end of the room whilst he, from his cushion at the far end by the candles, had said it as though Molly herself had not been there.

"I think perhaps the girl should see her father."

There was a silence, during which Molly willed Tung Nien to say no. But Tung Nien said nothing.

It is to stop me from seeing Wu, thought Molly, but Chen Liew continued to speak slowly.

"When the time comes," he said, "the European women will be evacuated. If she were with her father and if she dressed differently, she could pass for one of them. They would have to let her leave."

Tung Nien put her hand over Molly's to stop her from speaking. They had not been asked there to give an opinion, but to listen, and to act accordingly. Chen Liew shifted his position slightly on the cushion.

"I have backed the Chinese. It was patriotism rather than common sense. But now no matter. It was a gamble. Like any other. But the Chinese cannot win. And when the Japanese have control of China, where will they go then? Tang has paved the way for them to come here—at a price of course. The Japanese, in return, have promised to burn the police records on the Triads."

Chen Liew had finished speaking to them and they left.

Later that night, Molly stood in front of her dressing table and, looking hard at her reflection, she narrowed her eyes into little slits. She thought about her father and hated him for giving her the memory, however faint, of America in her blood.

"Chen Liew says we must make Molly see the convenience of getting back together with her father," Tung Nien was saying to Miss Dekyvere.

"But neither of them, it seems to me, wants it," she objected. "And I don't think we have any cause to believe the worst of the Japanese simply because we don't understand them, do we?" And she was thinking that God does not cease to exist just because Man has ceased to believe in Him.

"Evil is a better judge of reality than Good," said Tung Nien. "If Chen Liew says they will come, they will come—not to please him, but because he knows."

Miss Dekyvere was beginning to tire of her involvement in the lives of others but, because she had no reason not to, she said she would speak to Willard Russell.

"I knew you would," said Tung Nien and she smiled. But it was not a smile of triumph; it was resigned and sad.

(iv)

Osbourne waited patiently in the Sergeants' Mess at Victoria Barracks for Fletcher to come off duty. He drank a sickly sweet cup of tea and thumbed through the '*Morning Post*' listlessly, bored. Lloyd George was bellyaching in Parliament back in England, he noticed. Something about putting Hitler into a position which made war inevitable. Osbourne sniffed and tossed the newspaper to one side as he saw Sergeant Fletcher, already in mufti, loping towards the Mess across the parade ground. Osbourne walked out to meet him. He wanted to avoid eavesdroppers. Taking Fletcher by the arm, Osbourne steered him away towards the open, empty expanse of the parade ground.

"Look, Fletch," he began, dispensing with the formality of a greeting, "You remember what I was telling you about the bombing of Lo Wu?"

Fletcher remembered only vaguely for it had not really interested him. "Refresh my memory, Harry," he said, "And then how about a game of crib, eh?"

"Never mind crib, Fletch!" said Osbourne, stopping in the middle of the parade ground and turning the soldier to face him. He placed his hands on Fletcher's shoulders and looked him in the eyes. "I told you the Japs had bombed the warehouses, right? To cut off supplies to the Chinese?"

Fletcher nodded. Perhaps he had not been listening, for he remembered very little.

"Well, I was right!" said Osbourne smugly.

"How do you know?"

"I've been there. I was out there last night. And what do you think I found?"

Fletcher did not know.

"Chen Liew's warehouse still showed signs of damage from the bombing. Rodmell's warehouse had obviously been bombed, too. But Tang's warehouse?"

Fletcher shook his head. He did not know the answer to that one either.

"Tang's warehouse had not so much as been scratched!"

"Perhaps they missed it?" suggested Fletcher.

"Bloody right they missed it, Fletch!"

"So, what does that prove?" asked Fletcher, beginning to walk again towards the guard post and a temporary escape into civilian life. But Osbourne pulled him back.

"It means, sunshine, what I've been saying all along. Tang is in league with the Japs!"

Fletcher laughed. "Pull the other one, Harry!" he said. "It's virtually common knowledge that he's helping Mao!"

Osbourne did not mention the presence of Kenji in Lo Wu, but he did pull the scrap of paper he had found on his windscreen from his pocket and he pushed it into Fletcher's hands. "Have a butcher's," he said.

Fletcher smoothed out the paper and looked at it.

"Chinese?" he said.

"Japanese!" said Osbourne triumphantly. And he went on, "Now, look, Fletch, can you give it to your bods, you know, your experts, and let me know what it means, eh? You know, where it comes from?"

Fletcher held the grubby paper between his fingers and turned it over twice.

"Okay, will do," he said finally. "I'll give it to Colonel Dutton, see what he can make of it." Then, taking Osbourne by the arm, he pulled him away from the parade ground. "Now let's get down to the Glory Hole and have a good stiff drink and a hand of cards!"

The Glory Hole! Drink and cards! said Osbourne to himself and not for the first time in his life, he reflected how sad it was that what was important for one person so often proved to be utterly insignificant for another.

(v)

Alfred Laughton stood on the veranda of the Rodmells' mansion and watched the Indian houseboys carrying rattan armchairs out onto the lawn. They placed the chairs facing west and between each pair of chairs they put a small, round wicker table. Watching the sun go down at the Rodmells' on Saturday evenings was one of the most important social events of the week. You would be forgiven, thought Laughton to himself dryly, for believing that, for the rest of the week, when the Rodmells weren't watching, the sun didn't bother to set, or if it did, it did so opaquely with none of the glorious colours, ranging from salmon pink and turquoise to orange and indigo, with which it gave its valediction every Saturday.

On this particular Saturday, September 2nd, 1939, the sunset had taken on a particular significance. Although, at the time, it was not seen as necessarily tragic, it did seem to represent the passing of an era, and nobody who sat in the Rodmells' garden on that humid night to witness the going down of the sun would ever quite be able to forget it. As

Major Harland had ceremoniously announced before even the placing of the chairs, "This is it, lads! Yesterday, Hitler invaded Poland. It is now only a matter of time!"

Laughton thought sadly that he could detect the smallest note of pleasure in the Major's voice. It was the old bulldog spirit, the up-men-and-at-'em, the blind determination of the public school which he had found so alien as a boy and so distasteful as a man. Certainly there was a glint in the Major's eye when he added, with no thought of the problems a war in Europe would inevitably bring to the precarious situation in Hong Kong, "Our boys, I'll wager, will give Hitler a bloody nose!"

Laughton could not share the euphoric patriotism of the event. Where the others saw the melancholy passing of an age in the sunset, they also imagined a new dawn for tomorrow, a dawn which would, apparently, be built on the swift and complete destruction of the hated Third Reich. Laughton, however, saw only the tremendous agony of some great, once powerful animal which was on the point of extinction.

"And it's about bloody time!" he even heard Major Harland confiding to Robinson. "I was, I can tell you, getting bloody fed up with all this hanging around. At least now we know the worst!"

"Have we declared war?" asked Mary Laughton. It sounded as though it had nothing to do with her.

"Not yet," said Harland, and then to Rodmell, who had appeared suddenly, thus allowing the sun to begin its descent, "How long, Eliot, do you suppose?"

"Been speaking to Sir Geoffrey," he said. "Matter of hours, I shouldn't wonder."

"There is no chance, then, of them calling it off?" Mary Laughton continued to speak of the invasion of Poland as though it might have been a game of cricket. Laughton felt embarrassed on her behalf and would have spoken, but Major Harland was already speaking to her in that patronising way adults generally reserve for speaking to young children.

"Come, come, Mary!" he said. "We gave our word to the Polish people that we would protect them!"

Laughton wandered down from the veranda to take up the chair which had been allotted to him, apparently beside the tiresome, unimaginative Stephen Foster.

"The sun looks like a drop of blood, don't you think, Foster?" he said, trying to be polite, at least.

Foster looked obediently towards the west but he shook his head.

"I think I might have tried to find a less offensive image," he said. "Under the circumstances."

"I think it looks like a drop of blood," Laughton insisted. He had never felt comfortable with these people and he realised now that he positively disliked being with them. He could not understand them. He did not know what they thought, nor what they felt, nor what they wanted. He only knew that he did not think it, feel it or want it.

They watched the sun in silence and the greens on the island of Lantau turned first to blue and then to black. Behind the island, the sky was awash with colours.

"Like one of those awful American cocktails," Laughton suggested to Foster, but the rubber planter found this simile equally inadequate.

"I see God there, Laughton!" he announced suddenly. "That's what I see. Never mind blood and alcohol!"

But it was more than just God which separated them. Laughton stopped trying to be sociable and allowed his thoughts to drift and stray towards Tung Nien. He raised his glass and looked through his whisky at the sunset. The drop of blood was about to be obscured by Lantau's most southern point and the oranges and pinks and blues were at their most magnificent. As with the others, the reality and significance of a war in Europe had yet to force itself into Laughton's private world and so he was able to think still of a future which was related directly to his own personal present. His life had yet to become inextricably tied to, and conditioned by, the fate of the rest of the world. So, looking at the sunset through his whisky, he thought, "I wonder if she'll call me tonight."

(vi)

From slightly lower on the Peak, Tung Nien was looking in the opposite direction, watching a sliver of silver moon as it came up from behind the clouds over Hok Un. She could hear Chen Liew moving slowly from one room to another in his section of the house. She turned and looked at the house. The lights went on and then snapped off as he shuffled around looking for something. He seemed to have given up trying to sleep. Instead, he spent the nights in meditation locked away in his candlelit study, locked away in some illuminated corner of his mind.

The other day at breakfast, one of the rare moments of the day they still spent together, she had asked him why he didn't sleep, had asked him whether something was bothering him, transferring her own fears of the future onto him, and he had said, "You would not be able to understand even if I knew what it was. Just as writing cannot express words completely, so words cannot express thoughts completely." He had stopped then, to think, before adding a little reluctantly, "Yet, silent fulfilment needs no words."

And Tung Nien was thinking as he spoke, "You are no more fulfilled than I who am close to being so when I am abandoned by my sense of what is right and I allow Alfred to know every fold and every corner of my body, my sense heightened by his touch and by my own fear of being discovered, when I can feel him trying to identify his own smell on my body, leaving it, he says, invisible like the stamp of a watermark on a sheet of paper, seen only when held up to the light, his smell mingling with my own and becoming something new, neither his nor mine, nor yet ours, but rather an independent and potentially treacherous piece of evidence, the unique fingerprint of our love.

Tung Nien watched now as night fell across the city and lights began to come on, first along the coast where the darkness came more quickly, then on up the mountain as though part of a single fuse that was slowly burning up and past them, all the way up to the radio mast on the summit where it petered out in a flashing red warning light that seemed almost to be rotating in mid-air. It was a sticky, humid night and Tung

Nien felt the perspiration beneath the cool silk of her *cheongsam* as it sidled along her spine. She was looking up at the stars when she heard footsteps behind her on the veranda.

"I have argued with Wu."

It was not a voice she had been expecting. Molly rarely left her bedroom in the evenings. Tung Nien turned slowly to face Molly, as though reluctant to take her eyes from the stars' slow emergence as the sky darkened, the image of a photograph seeping through the negative as it develops.

"What about?" She could think of nothing kinder to say.

Molly walked across the lawn and took her by the hand. They sat beside Chen Liew's ornamental goldfish pond. Molly looked at the reflection of the stars in the water. She could not explain it. Something had happened for they had argued, but she no longer knew exactly what it had been, unless it was simply that they had not agreed. She began to cry, knowing it was more the product of frustration than sadness. Tung Nien placed her arm round Molly's shoulder because touch was all she could offer. As she tried to think of something positive to say, she realised that she was not thinking of Molly but of Laughton, imagining the yawning emptiness there would be in her life if he left. The idea that she might be in love with him both enthralled and frightened her. But Molly was speaking again.

"I told him that Chen Liew wanted me to go back to my father—I thought that he, at least, would be on my side—but all he said was 'Good'."

"Good?" said Tung Nien absently.

"He said that Chen Liew was right, that the Japanese will invade."

Tung Nien looked at the darkness above the city. And because we helped the Chinese, they will kill us as well, she thought, and it was a fact and not an emotion and, as such, it was hard and real and cold, and unlike the nebulous warmth she felt when she thought of Laughton. And it was the idea of her life being made so patently finite which led her to saying, "There are so many minutes of my life that I have wasted. It happens to all of us. It seems the only thing we have too much of is time. And yet there is never enough, is there?"

Molly would agree because she was thinking of something else. So Tung Nien continued to speak her thoughts aloud, to articulate a vacancy in her life which had been made solid by the thought of her death at the hands of the Japanese. She had a sudden blind desire to be rescued by Laughton, for him to erase her features with the tips of his fingers, to blow through the debris of her past like the monsoon leaving the streets clean and shining in the sun, leaving her ready to learn to live again somewhere where the world was not at war. She wanted badly to invent a present which was different from the one she had, one which would lead inevitably to a different future. And so she said, "Going back to your father is not the worst thing that could happen to you." Although she was thinking, From the moment you admit to being in love you can already sense the enormous burden of loss, the weight of leaving.

Molly looked up at her.

"I won't go back," she said.

"Maybe you'll have no choice," Tung Nien replied, thinking We were both of us plucked away from our original destiny and it would be foolish to think it might happen again.

"I'll run away," Molly said.

"It is easy to find things to run away from," said Tung Nien, "But not so easy to find somewhere to run to."

"Wu would have me."

"He might not be allowed to."

"I will never go back to my father," said Molly firmly. "He killed my mother, he got rid of me as soon as he could. He doesn't deserve me, and, besides which, I hate him."

Tung Nien had no argument with which to contradict her but still she had to say something.

"It would be for your own good, that is all," she said finally. "I don't believe there is anything worth dying for. Not even love."

"I'd rather die than be without Wu," said Molly stubbornly.

"No, you wouldn't," said Tung Nien. "You only think you would."

She hated saying it, because it sounded like a typical adult response to the freer emotions of adolescence. And then suddenly, more brightly, the moon slipping out from behind the storm clouds that had blown in from beyond Lantau, "Let's get Chan to take us to the fortune teller tomorrow and then out to Deep Water Bay for a swim. See if we can forget for a while." Although she was thinking that maybe that way she might get a message to Laughton, if not see him.

That night Molly lay in bed awake for a long time. A storm raged outside, thunder crashing down from the mountain and out over the harbour. She was afraid they wouldn't be able to go swimming. As the thunder exploded high above the house and rolled out across the New Territories, she thought of Wu and imagined him listening to the same thunder, a miraculous union across the miles that separated them, like looking at a map, the stiff corners of the paper held down by small china cups of *sake*, when she felt warm just to read the name *Kat Him Wai*. She went to sleep finally to the overwhelming sound of the rain falling heavily onto the gravel driveway and running off into the street like a memory of the rapids that had brought down the bridge near Nanking and temporarily stopped their flight South, now so long ago it seemed it might have happened to someone else. She had been satisfied then by more simple things, like looking at the clouds through the latticed web of her fingers. She felt that life was now unnecessarily difficult and she folded her complicated love into her arms to protect it, and herself, from the stingy mediocrity of day, when she would turn aside from those realities that did not please her, for they were, anyway, she thought, false.

But that night for Wu the lightening was no more than an impediment to remaining hidden. He was in Hok Un with Dong Feng and a handful of other men. They had broken into Rodmell's warehouse and were stealing radios and flashlights to pass on to the most advanced of the Japanese forces who were now no more than twenty kilometres away. Wu rested beneath the shelter of a rusted corrugated iron roof where the rain blistered and collected in the troughs. A continuous stream of water fell into a muddy puddle at his feet and he looked through the sheeting rain to see that he was not alone. He held the stolen radio close to his chest and could almost sense the hum of the valves and the dim glow of light as the power seeped in, the vibrations as a message was crackled over the air and out through the brittle cardboard of the speaker which was the size and shape of a large saucer. He felt he was doing something worthy, brave even, but he remembered again his father saying, "The memory of a brave man disappears before even his bones have crumbled away beneath the earth." And he pushed himself further back into the recess of the door.

Tung Nien sat at the window of her bedroom and looked at the rain falling beyond. She had left Chen Liew eating alone. She felt shabby when she was with him because he did not notice her presence. She found it hard now to remember the timid old man who had been fascinated by her nudity and made shy by her absurd and open rejoicing in sex. They had always slept apart, she thought. Even when they were together, there was a solid sheet of rationality between them. He would not recognise me, not even if I told him who I was, not even if he could see past his selfishness to the place where I am still imprisoned by his fear of me becoming a separate being. Only now I know there is something else. There is something inside of me which is struggling to show me that I have the right to be alive, to live.

(vii)

As night fell over the garden, Rodmell's Indian houseboys began rapidly and efficiently to remove the rattan chairs and wicker tables and those not fortunate enough to have been invited for a second drink within the house began to take their leave. Foster extended his hand to Laughton and frowned.

"Well, Doctor, when next we meet we shall doubtless be at war," he predicted grumpily, slightly resentful of the fact that Rodmell had preferred Laughton's company to his own. Laughton smiled politely, but he was not listening. "A sad thing," Foster insisted, "But inevitable." He shook his head and made his way slowly across the lawn to his wife who was conversing with Mary Laughton and Margaret Rodmell. Laughton watched the rubber planter's hunched shoulders and bowed head for a few moments before turning his attention back to the sky, but with the sunset gone, whatever magic might have existed before had disappeared. There was nothing there but the night.

Mary Laughton said good-bye to the Fosters and looked across at her husband. He looked lonely and out of place. "But that is his own fault," she said, and she could no longer feel sorry for him. She now had more important things in her life which occupied her thoughts, although the coming war was not yet one of them. First of all, there was bridge tomorrow. And then the WVS, which, significantly, her husband was not even aware that she had joined. "But then that is his own fault," she said again.

"You can almost feel the tension, can't you, Eliot?" Major Harland suggested. Eliot Rodmell felt nothing, but he agreed. He was, in fact, wondering how a war in Europe might affect business in the Far East, and his business in particular. The drug trade, based on the solid foundations laid down over fifty years ago, would always thrive. Recently, he had once again begun to move significant quantities of both licit and illicit merchandise into China, and his little agreement with the Immigrations Officer and the selling of Residency Certificates was bringing in enough ready cash to keep the whisky flowing at his bridge parties. What worried him more than anything else was a rumour he had heard that, in the event of a war, a corporation profits tax and, of all things, income tax would be imposed on the Colony as its way of helping the war effort. "There'll be an outcry!" Rodmell muttered, thinking aloud. Major Harland nodded politely, although he thought it a strange thing to say, and when Rodmell continued with, "All that it will bring about is a flight of capital! Don't they see that?", he suspected that they were talking at crossed purposes and so they walked in silence back towards the house.

Left alone in the garden, Laughton relaxed. He had decided he would not join the others for another drink, but that he would wait until they had all gathered in Rodmell's lounge and then he would sneak round the side of the house and make his way down to Central and the Parisian Grill. He felt like playing the piano.

(viii)

"My love for you is too big for me to keep hidden. If I try, it will burst out and betray me. So, I have found a place where we can meet."

Tung Nien was thinking of the note she had written to Laughton as she dived beneath the clear, salty water at Deep Water Bay. As she felt the cool water wash over her body she would have liked to have been naked, but she was not alone. Not only was Chan patrolling the headlands, there were some Europeans swimming a little way down the coast and, to Tung Nien's surprise, Liao K'ung, neither paddling nor swimming, but rather wading up and down the shallower part of the bay, a long, white gown billowing full of water and then sticking to his leathery skin. Tung Nien dived beneath the water and, as the sounds of the outside world were replaced by the thick, chugging noises of her body, the blood humming in her ears, the soft explosion of air in her mouth, her eyes smarting as she opened them against the water, it was easy for her to think that it was all possible. She would meet Laughton as she had suggested in her note, in the upstairs part of the geomancer's shop, and, there, they would create their unreal pocket of existence. They would no longer have to rely on Miss Dekyvere's discretion to keep their secret, snatching at their moments of love nervously and greedily before the old woman tired, as she always did too soon, and told them yet again that it was a dangerous game. In the geomancer's, she thought, they would indulge their love and watch it grow vast and all encompassing and the whole world would shrink to the four corners of the shop.

As she turned in the water, a hand grabbed at her foot and pulled her back. She and Molly came to the surface together and waited, treading water for a moment before speaking. They could see Liao K'ung, the water washing about his waist, half way between them and the shore, and, behind him, on a rock overlooking the bay, Chan squatting on his heels.

"He looks ridiculous," said Molly, looking back at Liao K'ung.

"Like he doesn't really want to be here," said Tung Nien.

"When we were in China," said Molly, "We used to swim while the ice was still frozen in the lake, the snow like white sand washed away in the waves. That would've made his face pucker," she said, nodding towards Liao K'ung for, even from that distance, they could see the lines drawn painfully across his face. Tung Nien, who had never seen ice, tried to imagine it. Molly said it cracked like thunder when it thawed and lay adrift in the middle of the lake like a white prayer dissolving slowly."

"A prayer!" said Tung Nien, swimming a little until she could rest her toes on the sand.

"I couldn't think of anything else white enough," said Molly, swimming up beside her.

"A prayer's not white," Tung Nien objected.

"It is to me," Molly smiled. "Prayers and hopes are white. Love is orange."

At that momet, Liao K'ung fell forwards in the water in a flat dive. Tung Nien and Molly laughed at the clumsy splash and at the awkward shape swimming face down in the water, his white frock fanning out behind him like the wake from a ship.

"Love is too solid to be a colour," said Tung Nien, looking distractedly across at the lumped shape of Liao K'ung in the water.

"I have colours for everything except my father," said Molly. "You're blue and Miss Dekyvere's pink."

"He hasn't moved," said Tung Nien.

"What?"

"Liao K'ung—he hasn't moved."

The white shape bobbed on the water as a wave rolled in towards the shore. They could see Chan racing down the rocks towards the sea and, without speaking, they both began to swim back towards the body. Molly was a stronger swimmer than Tung Nien and she reached Liao K'ung first. She grabbed hold of the folds of the white frock and wrenched the body onto its back. Liao K'ungs lips were pursed tightly shut and were blue around the edges. His eyes were wide open and vacant like the eyes of a fish. Molly threw herself backwards as though death might have been catching. Tung Nien and Chan reached the body at almost the same time but neither of them touched it. Chan looked around quickly. There was no one in sight except the handful of European swimmers who were too busy acting out some farce with a beach ball to notice them.

"Go back to the shore quietly," said Chan. "I'll deal with this."

Sitting huddled in towels and shaking, but not from the cold, Tung Nien and Molly watched as Chan pushed the lifeless body out to sea. He gave it a final push and, first rising a little over the waves and then dipping, with the white frock filling with water, Liao K'ung sunk slowly beneath the surface.

They were silent in the Bentley for most of the way home. It was Tung Nien who finally spoke. She was looking through the window of the car at the passing trees.

"Couldn't we have done anything to save him?"

"He was dead before we got to him," said Chan. "What could we do?"

"We could have brought his body back with us," said Molly.

"This way he'll just disappear," said Chan. "It's often easier that way."

Molly shuddered. She could see the fish picking the bones clean. Chan seemed to be reading her thoughts.

"Fish or worms, what difference does it make anyway?" he said. Although always reluctant to talk, it seemed that for Chan too death had unlocked some secret door onto the loneliness of living, for he continued, "A death requires the presence of the Police and the Police are a nuisance. If they don't find what they are looking for, they are likely to find something else. Disappearances happen all the time and are not given the same care and attention. Chen Liew doesn't like the Police," he added unnecessarily, for both he and Tung Nien knew that Chen Liew would barely notice were the Police to arrive and overturn the entire contents of the house. He seemed to be fading like an old watercolour, all definition gone. He could still go through the motions of certain acts, his visits to the Man Mao temple, as though habit was formed by a different impulse than memory or thinking, but he would take on nothing new, an overloaded boat set adrift and taking on water, sinking slowly and listing heavily. Most decision taking had already passed to Liao K'ung and this was Chan's only concern with the old man's death. Almost instinctively, he knew that he was going to ask Tung Nien to take over. For her part, Tung Nien sensed nothing, although when the time came she would exchange her agreement for Chan's collusion in her affair with Laughton.

(ix)

The news that the British Government had declared war on Germany reached Hong Kong with some delay but it was welcomed, when it did arrive, with cheers and a general feeling of relief that the waiting and the uncertainty was finally at an end. Queues of young men formed outside the offices of the Hong Kong Volunteer Defence Corps and these queues included even the occasional Chinese. All foreigners, however, were looked on with more suspicion than pleasure by the other would-be soldiers.

"Use them as drivers, as orderlies," suggested Major Harland. "It would be sheer folly to arm the little blighters. Got to admire their spirit, though," he added a little reluctantly.

Sergeant John Fletcher agreed but his opinion was not required. He stood by the door of Major Harland's office and looked through the window at the baking tarmac of the parade ground. Major Harland was reading from an official list.

"Priorities, Fletcher," he said, and he adjusted the cap of his fountain pen. "Make a note. We have been ordered to set up temporary war departments." He looked at Fletcher from behind the sheet of paper and then continued. "A Controller of Enemy Property." Fletcher thought you could almost hear the capital letters falling into place. "A Controller of Trade, a Controller of Food, a Censor and a Detaining Officer."

"Enemy Property, sir?" said Fletcher. "Is that Japanese property?"

"No!" growled Harland, "It's German property, man!"

Fletcher had not yet identified Germany as the enemy for it all seemed to be happening so far away. Major Harland stood up from his desk and walked across to the window that gave onto the parade ground.

"Supplies, Sergeant!" he grunted, tapping one hand against the other behind his back. "That is the greatest headache these days. Modern warfare depends one hundred percent on the availability of raw materials." He turned to face Sergeant Fletcher. "And that is where the Empire comes in!" he said.

"Yes, sir," said Fletcher obediently. He sensed that a lecture would follow and tried to rest less heavily on his feet. Major Harland returned to his desk.

"Twenty things, Fletcher, are needed to create today's fighting machine. Know what they are?"

Fletcher shook his head. The Major was already counting on his fingers.

"Ammunition and explosives: nitric acid, sulphur, mica, asbestos, mercury, glycerine, cellulose, copper, nickel, lead and cotton. Transport: petroleum and rubber. Coal, wood, iron. Aluminium for aircraft. Platinum, antimony and manganese. Twenty!" he announced triumphantly. "So, Fletcher, you see how important we are. The far flung reaches of the Empire may not yet be involved directly in the fighting," it was clear from the tone of his voice that Major Harland would have rather been fighting than talking to him, "but we have a vital rôle to play in this war!" Fletcher did not think that Hong Kong produced any of the Major's twenty commodities but he knew better than to comment.

It was dark before Fletcher managed to escape from Major Harland's patriotic frenzy and he took a rickshaw down to the Glory Hole where he had previously arranged to meet Osbourne. When he arrived, Osbourne was already waiting for him, an empty glass and six cigarette stubs in an ashtray before him on the table. He had placed a languid, disinterested hand on the buttocks of a taxi-girl and he was talking up to her, blinking through the smudgy lenses of his glasses, so that he did not notice Fletcher until he had sat down at the table. Then he turned his face away from the girl and scowled bad-temperedly across at Fletcher.

"You're late!" he said, taking a Craven A from the table and lighting it. "Well?" he said, through the smoke. Fletcher grinned both at Osbourne and at the taxi-girl.

"Old Harland," he explained. "Been telling me about the techniques of modern warfare. Couldn't get away."

Osbourne smoked and was annoyed to notice that Fletcher had a smug, self-satisfied grin on his face.

"You were wrong!" Fletcher said finally, and began to fish through his pockets. He took out Osbourne's Japanese script and put it on the table between them. "That's not Tang's," he said. "It's Rodmell's!"

Osbourne picked up the paper and dismissed the girl with a smack on the bottom. He leant his elbows on the table.

"Rodmell's?"

Fletcher nodded and turned to order two whiskies.

"That's right, Harry. You see, Rodmell has been importing Japanese goods into Hong Kong. He then relabels the lot and exports them to the Chinese. You know, because they won't touch anything from the Japs' sphere of influence." The words "Japs' sphere of influence" sounded as though he were repeating something he had read. "What you found, Harry, old horse, is one of the original labels in Japanese!"

"And Tang?" said Osbourne.

"Tang is as clean as the proverbial whistle, Harry, I told you!"

"My Aunt Fanny he is!" said Osbourne, thinking: Rodmell! The cunning old fox! Wherever you bloody well turn that bastard's got his finger in the pie somewhere! And what was wrong with cheating the Chinese? There was no story in that!

Fletcher was still grinning at him across the table. He thinks he has caught me out, said Osbourne to himself, so that when their drinks arrived, he said: "I saw the Jap barber out there with Tang's men!" And it was his turn to be smug.

(x)

It was all unreal for Laughton, both the declaration of war and his increasing dependence on Tung Nien. He scarcely noticed that his wife was spending less and less time in the house, that she often left him to dine alone, and that she no longer seemed to care or worry about his irrational and irresponsible behaviour (her words). She had said nothing when he had preferred the piano at the Parisian Grill to an evening with the Rodmells, and when, the other night, he had spent until the small hours wandering aimlessly through the bars in Wanchai, he had returned home to find her sleeping and not waiting up for him, sour-faced and belligerent. But his mind was so completely taken up with thoughts of Tung Nien that he did not even notice.

He had begun to read poetry again, something he had not done for perhaps fifteen years when, as an under-graduate and upon meeting Mary, he had discovered the somewhat cloying melancholy of Swinburne. Now, though, it was Byron. As he sat in his surgery at Queen Mary Hospital, he looked out at the peaceful, virtually uninhabited tranquility of the island of Lantau and he said:

"If I should meet thee
After long years
How should I greet thee?
With silence and tears."

It pleased him to tinge his love with sadness, with its inevitable conclusion. Somehow, it helped to bring it into perspective if he could see it ending. And yet all he seemed to do was spend the hours away from her in waiting to see her again. Whilst other members of the Colony were concerned with the progress of Hitler's tanks through Poland and the ineffectual, even pathetic resistance of the Polish cavalry—"Cavalry went out with the American Civil War!" Major Harland had said indignantly, as though taking its use as a personal affront—Laughton dreamed of holding Tung Nien in his arms. There was nothing like it on earth. Time and feelings stood still. All the world was reduced to the working of her fingers over his body and the beautiful submission he felt as she opened her legs to him and he looked on in boyish wonder, amazed that anything so immaculate could have subjected itself to his perversity. Because his conscious drive towards self-destruction and his total surrender to an inordinate and consuming passion which he knew could only end with Byron's silence and tears was perverse. But what drove him forwards was the fact that he also knew that never before had he felt such passion, never before had he felt the pulse of life so close. Whatever the outcome, the way through would, he thought, make it worthwhile.

Mary Laughton, on the other hand, having freed herself from any concern for her husband, had found a new lease of life. She was actually, and for the first time that she could remember, enjoying herself. Her work at the WVS satisfied her need to feel wanted and her friendship with Margaret Rodmell had progressed to such an extent that they now even occasionally took an informal afternoon tea together at the Peninsular Hotel. And it was during one such tea that it first became clear that Willard Russell was, as Margaret Rodmell put it, "not all there!"

The two women could not help watching him. Kenji had wheeled Russell across to one of the plate-glass windows of the Hotel lounge and left him there with the sun streaming into his face. For no other reason than the fact that her upbringing obliged her to do so, Mary Laughton had walked over to Willard Russell with the intention of saying Good Afternoon, but before she had been able even to construct a suitable expression, Russell had started to roll his eyes from side to side, his head lolling back in the chair and his hands clasped tightly in his lap. Caught between formality and embarrassment, Mary Laughton had turned to Margaret Rodmell for assistance, but the Taipan's wife had only shrugged. Russell had continued to roll his eyes like a man demented for over half an hour, successfully ruining the ladies' tea.

(xi)

News travels quickly in a closed society and it was not long before Miss Dekyvere was told of Willard Russell's mental instability.

"Mad as a March hare, Miss Dekyvere!" Mary Laughton had proclaimed at bridge the other night. "As a fruit-cake!" Margaret Rodmell had added. And the great man himself had concluded, "You could see it coming, of course." Although no one was quite sure how. Only Alfred Laughton had failed to give an opinion and so Miss Dekyvere had asked him. "Don't know the man, really," Laughton had said dreamily. "But, if you want my opinion, we've all gone mad!"

And because Miss Dekyvere had been asked to, she had invited Willard Russell to her house for a sherry. She had been made to see the convenience, in the event, of a possible reconciliation between Molly and her father.

"Just in case," Tung Nien had said. "If war breaks out finally over here too, it will be her only chance of getting off the island."

Willard Russell sat before her like a man in a trance. He seemed to speak as though he were reading, as though he no longer had any thoughts of his own. When Miss Dekyvere had asked him why he always had to wait to be invited to visit his daughter, when she had asked him why he never came of his own accord, he had said, "If a man carries a burden on his back and nonetheless rides in a carriage, he thereby encourages robbers to draw near."

"What carriage are you riding in, Willard?" she would have asked, had she been more unkind. Instead, she said, "What are you doing,

Willard, these days?" as she poured him a sherry. "People have begun to talk."

Willard Russell held the thin stem of the sherry glass between what seemed to him brutish fingers and said, "I think I have reached the seventh or eighth stage; the silent meditation and the quieting of the mind. Together these lead to the destruction of the mortal heart and the resurrection of the immortal heart."

Miss Dekyvere sighed. It reminded her of her days as a novice, when they had had to study, and enact, Saint Ignatius of Loyola's Spiritual Exercises. Aloud, but not necessarily for Russell's sake, she gave the full title: "Spiritual exercises for overcoming oneself and regulating one's life without being swayed by any inordinate attachment." Russell recognised a kindred spirit and nodded, but Miss Dekyvere remembered to add, "I know all about meditation, Willard." She would not say, though, whether she thought it served a purpose or not.

Russell began to shake his head vigourously. He rested his hands on the arm-rests of his wheel-chair and squeezed them tightly until his knuckles pressed white against his skin.

"You cannot know all about it, Miss Dekyvere," he said, "For that is a contradiction in terms."

When she looked at him, she knew he meant what he was saying. He was totally convinced and sure of himself when he said, "Did Saint Ignatius tell you that the perfect man is he who is free from dreams?"

"What would we do without dreams, Willard?" she countered, but he was not listening to her.

"The dust of passions obscures the moonlight of essential nature," he said. "We must drive our mind into the field of concentration; we must stop the mind wandering outside, so that consciousness will melt away and spirit and vitality will gather within and no longer be scattered without."

I cannot criticize something I don't understand, Miss Dekyvere thought. And how much more humane it sounded than the penance and flagellation of Saint Ignatius which she had been forced to go through. Man is created to serve and to praise God. To do that, as Russell in different words was repeating to her so many years later, they had had to acquire detachment from all created things. The only difference, as far as she could see now, was the process. Where Russell talked of dust and moonlight, Saint Ignatius had spoken of hell and penance. "When we take away superfluity," she remembered, "it is temperance, it is not penance. Penance means that we take away things which everybody has a right to have." No sleep. No food. And pain through all our waking hours—hair shirts, cords and chains against the flesh. Never to think of agreeable thoughts, never to laugh nor to say anything to provoke laughter, but to grieve over our sins. The meditation of the invisible to see, not as Russell suggested, spirit and vitality, but the soul imprisoned in this corruptible body and the whole compound self placed in the world as though in banishment among brute animals. No, she was not the person to preach to Willard Russell. But she would ask one question.

"Where is Molly in all this, Willard? Does Molly have a place in your search for—what is it? Immortality?" She wished it had not sounded so patronising.

"The 'I-Ching' will tell me that," he said simply.

"The 'I-Ching'? Whatever are you talking about now, Willard?"

"The Chinese Book of Changes," said Russell seriously. "It tells me what I should do." He waited a moment before adding, "And what I should not do."

"And Molly?"

"The leg of the bed is split."

"Oh, stop being so obtuse, Willard! At least speak to me in a language I can understand! We are talking now about your daughter's future."

"Those who persevere are destroyed."

"All right, Willard," said Miss Dekyvere quietly. She noticed she was talking to him in her nun's voice and coughed quickly. "You are still Molly's father." She was about to continue when the thought struck her that Willard Russell was probably not even aware that a war had broken out, never mind what might happen in Hong Kong as a result. "Willard," she said again, "What on earth are we to do now?"

Willard Russell looked at her but it was from a long, long way away.

When Kenji arrived later to take Russell home, Miss Dekyvere invited him in. At first, the Japanese resisted, but it soon became obvious to him that he was not being given a choice.

"I blame you for this!" Miss Dekyvere began, pointing at Russell, and having sat the Japanese at a lower height than herself. She might even have wagged a finger. Kenji shrugged. There were more important things on his mind than Willard Russell's precarious mental state.

"I just gave him what he wanted," he said. "Which was more than the rest of you could do. You can only give people the truth. You can't control what they do with it."

Miss Dekyvere was too tired to argue, but she did say, half to herself, "Whatever happened to the simple truths, like love?"

(xii)

Laughton and Tung Nien made love regularly. The pact between Chan and Tung Nien had given her a little, but previously unthinkable, freedom. Instead of being driven down to the Fortune Teller's shop in Central with Molly, Chan took her alone, and it was there that she met up with Laughton. Whilst they made love in the upstairs room, Chan would either patrol the streets outside or sit with the Fortune Teller and watch him smoke a pipe of opium, all the time listening to the sounds of love and sometimes argument that came down quite clearly from the room above.

On one particular night, however, Chan had driven her to the geomancer's in the Bentley as usual and then, without waiting for Laughton to arrive, he had said quite simply, "Make sure you've finished in an hour." And he had left.

Walking up the steep steps of the street outside the Fortune Teller's shop, Chan had passed Laughton who was walking down. Laughton did not seem to recognize him. He had a lost, absent expression on his face and he was looking up between the buildings at the stars. As with most of the other Europeans in Hong Kong, Laughton was confused by the circumstances of the war in Europe. They, the British, had declared war on Germany and then promptly done nothing at all, it seemed. It was as though everything were exactly the same as it had been before. They had been told it would only be a matter of time before Hitler advanced through France and prepared to invade the British Isles, but Hitler had done nothing either. Laughton began to wonder what they had all been so worried about. He had conveniently forgotten that no one in Hong Kong had really shown more than a passing interest anyway in the fate of Europe.

Chan continued on up the hill and then turned left and made his way towards the terminus of the Peak Tramway.

When Laughton arrived at the Fortune Teller's, he climbed the narrow stairs to the upstairs room and found Tung Nien lying in darkness. She had not lit the small oil lamp. She had not even taken it across to the round wooden table beside the bed. Laughton stood at the top of the stairs and looked into the room. Tung Nien was lying on the bed already naked. She looked steadily at Laughton for a moment, as though she might have been expecting someone else to arrive and then she beckoned him across to the hard bed. Laughton watched her as he undressed, but she did not move. She lay on her back in silence in the darkness just waiting for him to go to her. Downstairs, the Fortune Teller sang a strident song and clanged the metal instruments of his trade. Laughton placed one knee on the bed and the wooden boards creaked. He pulled up Tung Nien's knees until her legs formed the shape of an "M" and he buried his face in the musty smells of her body. Tung Nien pushed herself towards him and he moved his hands up and round to the small of her back. He ran his tongue over her skin and into the hollow of soft flesh at the top of her thighs. He smelt her excitement, a thick, stuffy smell, and he pushed himself over and on top of her.

Chan got out of the tram one stop before he needed to and walked the rest of the way to Liao K'ung's mansion. He was thinking of a simple comment he had overheard in the Temple of Man Mo. Liao K'ung had been sitting with his back up against the shining flank of a brass deer and he had talked directly to Chan. He had expressed a certain preference for the Japanese over the British and had even mentioned Tang. "Tang has the right idea," he had said. "After all, we owe nothing to the British. True, we owe nothing to the Japanese, either." Liao K'ung had been trying to point out the convenience of sitting on the fence, of not taking sides in the imminent hostilities, of waiting to see which of the warring factions would best serve them later. "It is rumoured," he had said, "that Tang has already made certain agreements with the Japanese. You scratch my back and I'll scratch yours, that kind of thing." He reached behind him and ran his fingers up to the pointed horns of the brass deer. "Chen Liew must learn to move with the times."

Chan thought how convenient Liao K'ung's disappearance had been as he carefully broke the seal on one of the back windows of Liao K'ung's mansion

"You have to go now," said Tung Nien. It was the first thing she had said to him since he had arrived and he needed more than that.

"Why?"

"Because Chan will be back early."

Laughton looked at the dark, smoke-stained ceiling. "Chan will be back early," he repeated. He pushed himself up on one elbow and the bed creaked. He leaned across and kissed her on the mouth. "In that case I'll go down to the Grill and play the piano a bit. Maybe even have a drink or two." Laughton was still sufficiently infatuated with Tung Nien that he would not yet allow his emotions to degenerate into bickering, even when he was disappointed. He had, he knew, to be thankful that he could be with her at all. What did it matter how long? He would go for a drink.

As he pushed himself out of the bed, she ran her fingers along his spine. "It is like trying to polish a brick and turn it into a mirror," she said.

"What is?" he asked without turning round.

"Understanding you," she said.

"There's very little to understand. That's probably where you're going wrong."

"You have no secrets?"

"One or two, maybe. Nothing important." Laughton lit a cigarette and bent slightly to look beneath the rattan blind and into the street. "My wife's always been the one for secrets," he said.

There was an ambulance backed on to the end of the street and Laughton recognised two orderlies from the hospital. He turned back into the room. "To have secrets," he said, "You need to have someone to hide something from. Who do I have?"

Tung Nien was not really interested but she would say it anyway. "Chen Liew," she said, and he could not work out whether it was a question or a threat.

As he walked down the steep steps of the street and past the waiting ambulance, picking his feet over the falling stream of sewage, Laughton became conscious, perhaps for the first time, of the danger of what he was doing. Previously he had always managed to separate Chen Liew from Tung Nien in the same easy way as he had forced Mary out of his own life. He walked out into Wellington Street where the light came more from the illuminated reds and yellows of the Chinese characters advertising the shops than from the street lamps. The street was filled with bustling, pushing Chinese. Almost all the men wore white, short-sleeved shirts, open at the collar, and black trousers, except the older men who still dressed in traditional peasant clothes. They all looked at him, but none of them seemed to notice him, to register his presence among them, and yet, suddenly, he felt that they were all working for Chen Liew, all watching him, all of them would later report back his every move. He quickened his step and it was with a sigh of relief that he walked across the brightly lit foyer of the Parisian Grill and out to the bar where he took up his place at the piano. Before beginning to play, he had time to notice Eliot Rodmell sitting alone in a far corner of the room, apparently reading a copy of the morning's *Post.*

Chan felt nothing as his soft shoes padded along the empty corridor of Liao K'ung's house, the smoke from the joss sticks on a camphor wood chest prickling in his nose. He could hear voices coming from a room at the far end of the corridor, but they were women's voices. When he left the house again he held something round and shiny behind his back. It was Liao K'ung's *pat kwa* mirror.

(xiii)

"They won't even allow us to investigate the death!" Major Harland complained later.

"I wouldn't worry your head about it, Major," said Rodmell. "It's obviously an internal affair. A question of gang warfare, I shouldn't wonder."

"But you know what they're saying, don't you?"

"I can imagine, Major, but tell me anyway."

"Damned superstition! They say the poor old sod had to die because he lost his lucky mirror! Bloody poppycock, of course!"

"Of course," smiled Rodmell, and sipped his gin. "But then, correct me if I'm wrong, with no body you have no crime."

"Oh, Liao K'ung was murdered, Eliot, make no mistake about that. What I fail to understand is this damned, blind acceptance that a piece of polished glass might be the cause of his death. Can you think of anything quite so—," he searched for a word, and then found it, "—primitive?"

"Or convenient," said Rodmell.

6

"A lifetime is just a dream,
And today does not ensure tomorrow."

(i)

The geomancer looked at the hexagram and muttered "Six at the top" to himself. To Tung Nien he said, "It is the wounding of the light. The sun has sunk below the earth."

Tung Nien sniffed and stifled a yawn. She already knew what her immediate future entailed. She had discovered that she was pregnant. Her feelings towards the unborn child were mixed. She knew it was stupid to think that Chen Liew would permit her to have the baby and yet she could not accept the idea of killing it. She had, so far, managed to hide the fact of her pregnancy from both Laughton, the father, and Chen Liew, her husband, but she knew that time was running out and that soon she would be forced to take a decision. Although she hated to admit it, she also knew what the decision would be and she had to find a way of convincing herself that it was the right one.

"You must not let yourself," the Fortune Teller continued, "be swept along by unfavourable circumstances, nor permit your courage to be shaken." She knew this would be followed by a laborious interpretation based on the trials and tribulations of the twelfth century King Wên of Chou and she did her best to shut out the Fortune Teller's thin voice.

Tung Nien sat back and looked past the geomancer's head towards the door of the shop. The bright square of light where the top half of the door was open darkened from time to time as Chan walked up and down the street.

"In adversity," said the Fortune Teller, "It furthers one to be persevering."

"I shall persevere," said Tung Nien to herself as Chan again moved away and the bright square of light returned.

"And here, the six in the fourth place," the Fortune Teller went on, warming to his commentary to such an extent that Tung Nien could have got up and left him alone and he would probably not have noticed, "depicts the situation of Prince Wei Tzû, who was able to save himself only by timely flight abroad."

"Molly," said Tung Nien to herself.

"Whose attributes are beauty and clarity," said the Fortune Teller seriously.

If she had been a peasant, she thought absently, although tradition would have forced her to have the child, once it were born, it would then have been quite permissible for her to abandon it somewhere to die. But her own situation was more complicated than that. She and Chen Liew had not had sex for over a year and he would know he was not the father. If she looked at the situation in that way it was obvious that she could not go through with the pregnancy. It was as simple as that.

"King Wu had no intention of acquiring personal power," the Fortune Teller said and looked into her eyes. "It fell to him because of his character."

Tung Nien smiled back at the old man automatically.

The Fortune Teller rocked back on his heels, leaning away from the table between them. He placed one hand on each corner of the table and let out a long, opium-filled sigh of resignation. It was evident that he was coming to the end of his discourse. Tung Nien leaned slightly towards him and listened with an expression of polite interest on her face.

"The line stands at the top," he said very slowly, pointing at the hexagram. "This is where the earth veils the sun most heavily." He raised a finger, thought better of it, and replaced his hand on the table. "But it is also the first to be unmasked in its sinister character when the sun reappears."

Tung Nien stood up and turned away towards the door.

"I'll wait upstairs," she said to Chan.

The geomancer's upstairs room was stuffy and heavy with the sticky smell of opium. There were three hard wooden boards on the floor with wooden stools for pillows where the old man smoked with his friends. Beside one of the bunks were the remains of a recent pipe, the pellet of opium charred black. Tung Nien walked across to a small window which was set high in the wall and pushed the rattan curtain slightly away from the sill. She looked down into the street. It was not a road, but merely a long line of steep steps climbing away to her right. A thin waterfall of sewage fell from the top of the street, washing down over the steps until it settled in a grimy puddle at the edge of the main road to her left. There was no sign of Laughton and so she turned away and sat down on one of the wooden boards. After a while, she lay back and rested her head against the hard wooden stool and closed her eyes.

As Laughton walked along the waterfront, he looked absently towards what was, although he did not know it, one of Rodmell's ships, laden down with Japanese rice and radio equipment. All Laughton saw was a ship steaming towards the harbour with half-a-dozen coolies, the size of matchsticks, up on deck.

He could already feel Tung Nien's breast beneath his hand, her small, hard nipples and the softness of the skin at the top of her thighs. When he thought of her, his heart quickened and an emptiness opened up before him. He seemed to spend all his waking hours thinking of her, talking to her and reliving the moments they had spent together. Whenever anyone spoke to him he automatically associated their conversation with her.

When, the other afternoon, before leaving finally for England, Nurse Gemmell had said, "Doctor, I think I ought to tell you...", he had immediately thought, "She knows! And now she is going to give me a lecture on infidelity! A dangerous game!" But Nurse Gemmell had only said, "One of the Chinese orderlies has been found stealing."

"Right!" Laughton had said in some relief, although a part of him wanted everyone to know about Tung Nien. His mind still raced through a defence of his relationship—without her he felt only as though he were treading water, he was not going anywhere, the only thing in his life was the hope of his next meeting—and Nurse Gemmell wanted him to worry about petty theft!

And yet Laughton lingered restlessly on the wharf, watching Rodmell's ship, as though the pain of not seeing her and the anticipation of an end to his pain were almost as satisfying as their time together. He thought of her fingers in his hand, her head against his cheek, the little intimacies that sprung up after they had made love when they seemed to be content just to be close together, touching, and the whole world lay with them, or else it disappeared. He turned away from the harbour back towards the bustling city. In his mind, he was not middle-aged, but an intrepid youth embarking on what would be the love affair of his life.

Upstairs at the geomancer's, the light was tawdry, as though it had been used before, thought Laughton to himself, and the air was foetid and stale. Even the wooden beams and bunks seemed to be impregnated with the smell of smoke and opium. Laughton's romantic ardour would have been dashed had it not been for the presence of Tung Nien, apparently asleep on one of the bunks. She was lying in the darkened room, her hands folded across her breast, like the statues on the tombs in the village churches of his childhood. He walked slowly across to her, bent beside the bunk and rested his hand on her shoulder, slipping it down then near enough to feel the rising of her breast. But Tung Nien was not asleep. She pushed his hand away and sat up. Laughton sat beside her on the bunk. When he sat down, she stood up. He watched her walk across the room to a tall, thin walnut cupboard, the door of which was stained almost black with use. Inside was a bottle of whisky. Usher's Green Stripe.

"Chen Liew requisitioned it," she told him over her shoulder. "I have brought you a bottle."

Laughton wanted only to stand behind her, press his body up against hers and pass his hands beneath her arms and up to her breasts, but any mention of her husband had always put a stop to physical contact. Tung Nien used it as other women might have slapped. The effect was the same. Frustrated, his desire itching to find an outlet, Laughton clasped his hands behind his head and lay back on the bunk.

"Thank you," he said. "I think I'll try some now. No time like the present, after all." There were so many other things he would have said, but she had mentioned Chen Liew. That meant there would be no sex, at least not until they had spoken.

"I am pregnant," she announced suddenly, and she uncorked the bottle of whisky. Laughton watched her back. She required no answer from him and he did not have one to give. When she turned to face him, he thought he could see the faint remains of tears at the corners of her eyes which disconcerted him.

"I've always wanted children," he replied absently, looking away from her to the rattan blind which covered the window. He was not talking about her child, he knew, nor Mary's child. It was a selfish longing and it was his alone. It was his child he wanted and had always wanted for as long as he could remember. Tung Nien's pregnancy did not seem to have anything to do with him.

Tung Nien passed him the glass of whisky and tried to weigh the importance of what he had said, but he was not referring to them. She could see that he was talking out to some empty, irretrievable part of his life when, perhaps, it had all, all of it, been possible.

"I can't have it," she said.

Laughton continued to look at the rattan blind but the expression on his face changed. He tried very hard to allow her words to sink in slowly and he tried not to rush towards a reply, because whatever he said, if he said it now, would be insulting. He glanced towards Tung Nien and saw, not her magnificent breasts and perfect, almost sculptured, face, but simply a woman who had said, "I can't have it." The moment passed but the damage had been done. Laughton's mind raced over all the excuses he could think of to forgive her but all he could think of to say was, "Why not?"

He willed her to give him a medical reason, a tangible impediment for her not having the child. But she said simply, not because it was the truth, but because she had decided she needed to distance him from her and the unborn child, "I don't want it."

Laughton did not want to look at her. He turned his face back to the rattan blind which had begun to slap against the window frame in a breeze which had suddenly blown up from the harbour.

"Does your husband know?" he asked, but he was not thinking that.

"No," she said.

"What would he say if he did?"

Laughton mistakenly imagined that Chen Liew was the father because he was the husband.

"It is my body and my life," she said, and sat down beside him. She realised she had underestimated the strength of his feelings and she wished she could have started the conversation again. She took his hand and leant her head against his shoulder.

"You don't understand, do you?" she said.

"No," he said. "I don't understand."

They were silent for a moment.

"How can you even think about it?" Laughton said, but it was almost as though he were speaking to himself and not to her. He seemed to notice suddenly that he was holding the glass of whisky and he drank it off in a single, vicious gulp. "Christ Almighty!" he said and stood up.

Tung Nien was confused by the violence of his reaction. Although she knew it would have been better to say nothing at all, something, either her love for him, a sense of pride or the need to justify herself, made her speak. But her voice lacked all its normal self-assurance and confidence when she said, "With so much violence in the world, who is going to notice one more brutal act?"

She felt angry with herself that she had used his vocabulary, his terms. Exasperated, she stood up. Laughton was pouring himself another glass of whisky from the bottle of Usher's Green Stripe.

"It's true," he said, finally. "It's not my life either. Who am I to interfere?"

Tung Nien looked at him with all the manifest tenderness she could muster, passed her hands around his waist and put her lips close to his ear.

"Oh, Alfred," she said. "If you could only know what I know; feel what I feel. You would understand. I know you would."

But she knew he would not and so she would not tell him. That a baby would ruin her. Now that she was finally doing something—living, maybe—Maybe it was as simple as that. She felt alive for the first time in years. She had an aim and a purpose to her life. She was no longer drifting from day to day.

"All my life," he was saying. "The only thing I ever wanted was a child."

And it was then that she decided to let him make love to her. He caressed her with unusual violence as though he really meant to hurt her. When he held her breasts, he squeezed them tightly and tugged viciously at her nipples. He bit her and scratched his nails along her thighs and across her back. He turned her onto her stomach, pulled her up onto her knees and forced himself into her from behind with one hand pulling her head back by the hair. She could feel him banging against her buttocks and she tried to push herself up to meet him, but he tugged her head back by the hair again until she had to collapse the top of her body down onto the sticky wood of the bunk and let him thrash out his anger and his passion, if that was his way of fighting it. And it was. Laughton was crying out against all the injustice in the world. But, more than that, he was trying to dash himself against his own inability to change, to be, for once, strong and resolute. For he should have left. He should not have been there, making love to her, as though nothing had happened, as though nothing had come between them. And so he turned her away from him so as not to see her face, so as not to see how much he loved and wanted her, and he tried to channel his anger and frustration into a raw, animal lust which would hurt.

When it was over and they lay together on the bunk, Laughton waited for Tung Nien to speak, mostly about his lovemaking but maybe about the baby, but she lay beside him, breathing heavily and looking at the dark beams of the ceiling. He listened to her breath as it came in thick gasps, to finally subside in a long, slow sigh as she said, "I'm going to have a pipe."

Laughton was shocked. He pushed himself up on one elbow and looked at her naked body as she walked across the narrow room to an ivory box where the opium was kept.

"But you don't smoke!" he said.

"You have no idea what I do," she said, without even deigning to look at him.

(ii)

Osbourne had spent the last week tailing Kenji for every minute of the day. It was a thankless task. The Japanese seemed to be living a life which bordered on conventional tedium. He opened the barber's shop at the Peninsula Hotel at half past nine every morning, and did not leave again until half past five every evening. His only visitor, other than customers, was Willard Russell, who was wheeled into the hotel by his rickshaw boy at midday and who remained the rest of the afternoon with Kenji until they had tea and left together after the barber's work was over. On some evenings, Kenji and Willard Russell stayed together until late at a bar in the railway station and on other nights Kenji deposited Willard Russell in his tenement flat before returning home alone. And then, suddenly, late on a Friday evening at the end of October, Kenji, having left Russell as usual, took a rickshaw and headed, not towards the Star Ferry terminal and home, but in the opposite direction, towards the Floating City.

"This is it," thought Osbourne to himself, already imagining the headline in tomorrow's '*Post*': "British Reporter uncovers Kempei/Triad Connection in Kowloon and Hong Kong."

It was a sticky night and Osbourne could feel the sweat gathering at the small of his back, beneath his arms and under his chin. Twice he removed his glasses and wiped the bridge of his nose with his handkerchief before Kenji's rickshaw stopped just past the Floating City.

Osbourne looked with distaste at the mass of bobbing lights attached to long, bamboo poles on the sampans and waited in his rickshaw for Kenji to do something, but the Japanese just stood on the edge of the wharf looking out to sea.

"They'll probably arrive by boat," Osbourne thought to himself, and he looked past the interminable rows of sampans in search of a ship's light. He could see nothing but the blackness of the night and, when Kenji gave no suggestion that he intended to move, Osbourne dismissed his rickshaw, thinking it too conspicuous, and crossed the road to where he would be hidden in the shadows of the buildings.

"I could be at home," he said to himself bitterly, lighting a cigarette. "With a nice glass of cold beer. What the hell am I doing here? No one will thank me for it. I'll not get any more money for putting in overtime. My life will be exactly the same tomorrow as it was yesterday, regardless of what happens tonight." But Osbourne knew that he stayed because *this* was his life. He did not have anything else. And because he did not demand that other existence, he was able to pretend that it really did exist somewhere, waiting for him, full of lazy hours that would somehow be taken up with things he never did—the latest novel, a crossword puzzle, idle conversation with a group of friends he could feel comfortable with. If he had stopped to think, he would have realised what a ridiculous notion it was, but it was important to him to preserve his dream so as to keep from being laid open to the fact that he was one of those thousands of people for whom life consisted of the mere passing of days in which they did nothing well.

"What the hell does he think he's doing?" Osbourne grunted to himself, and he squashed the stub of his cigarette out on the pavement with the toe of his shoe.

Kenji was waiting, not for any of Tang's henchmen, as Osbourne suspected, but for a message from the Japanese forces in occupied China. He wondered how much the recent turn of events in Europe might affect the Great East Asia Co-Prosperity Sphere. There had been some talk that Hitler looked to the Japanese to distract the Russians from the crisis in Europe, but now the Russians and Germans were allies. As he looked out across the greasy surface of the water, Kenji thought of his colleagues still fighting not so very far away now to the North and, whilst he could not say that he longed to be with them, he did feel an intense loneliness, as though he had been left behind. He was missing out on the forced friendships and camaraderie that seemed always to be formed in critical moments. When all he had was Russell and his religion, both of which were difficult to sustain in the nights when he felt even the bungling Major Harland must suspect him and he lay listening for the sound of footsteps on the stairs. But the lonely, silent nights always passed to give way to uneventful days.

As he mulled over his thoughts Kenji kept an eye on one particular lamp on one particular sampan some hundred metres out into the Floating City. He was waiting for the light to change almost imperceptibly from white to yellow. It made him think of his studies in Taoist Buddhism and he gave a wry smile. "When a golden light appears in the eyes, the dragon's hum and the tiger's roar are heard in the ears." There were times when Kenji fervently wished he could actually believe in it all. Sometimes, he would have believed in anything, just to have something to believe in, because it was hard when you were certain that the only life that existed after death was the mutation of cells inside the stomachs of an army of worms. But Kenji could never be melancholic for long. There was something practical in his character which shied away from self-indulgence and it was relatively easy for him to present the stoic face to the world that the world expected.

(iii)

Laughton was angry with himself for loving Tung Nien so much. When they had said good-bye he had tried to present her with no expression at all on his face, to show how much he disapproved of what she planned to do, but as she stood at the door of the upstairs room she looked so beautiful and she spoke so gaily that he would have forgiven her anything. He was just grateful that she allowed him to be with her and he smiled despite himself.

With Tung Nien gone, the room was oppressive and empty. A sticky, damp heat seemed to seep in from beneath the rattan curtain and settle along his body. He could hear raised voices from the street outside and the splutter and cough of a badly-tuned car passing slowly along Wellington Street. When he stood up his whole body ached. He felt as though he might have dozed for a while for there was a stale, sour taste in his mouth. Slowly he walked across to the walnut cupboard and took out the bottle of Usher's Green Stripe. He poured himself a large measure and then drank it off in a single, stinging swallow before returning the bottle and making his way downstairs and out into the night.

Laughton blinked into the bright lights of the shops. His shirt felt tight and sweaty under the armpits and damp at the small of his back. He pushed his hat onto the back of his head and put his hands in his pockets. He did not know what to do with himself. It was still early evening and if he went home his wife would be out. She almost always seemed to be out nowadays. The other day she had said, "I gave you your choice and now it's too late. I can't go back and if you don't want to come forward with me then that's your own lookout." He had been a little shocked. He could not remember what the choice had been.

Laughton sighed. There had been talk behind his back at the hospital, too. He knew it as surely as he knew that his wife would not be at home. "Spends all his time drinking and playing that damned piano!" he had heard one of them saying the other day. "And what the hell do they expect me to do?" he said aloud, and the blank face of a Chinese looked at him. Laughton nodded and walked on. "The whole world is falling apart around our ears. What would they have me do?" He thought of Tung Nien and her warm body when he rolled against her after they had made love when she would groan and push him away saying, "Hot! Too Hot!" And now she was pregnant. "Wouldn't think old Chen Liew had it in him!" Laughton smiled to himself, and turned away almost automatically towards the Star Ferry wharf. "She can't really want to do away with it," he said as he joined a straggling queue and watched the yellow lights of the ferry approaching. "In the end, she will come to her senses." It seemed to him such an unnatural thought that he could not reconcile it with her who was so beautiful. For some reason, Laughton still equated beauty with kindness, ugliness with sin. It was a childish concept, he knew, but when he looked at the inky sky above the harbour and he remembered Foster, the rubber planter, telling him he saw God in the sky, he thought sulkily, "They say God cannot feel pain or disappointment. In that case, how can he be the God of love? Pain and disappointment are almost all you get from love, in the end."

He stepped onto the ferry and it smelt of fish and oil. "Given time," he said, "She will see that she wants the child." He leaned on the rail at the back of ferry and watched the lights of the city of Victoria reflecting in the murky water of the sea. Up on the Peak, the lights seemed to twinkle more richly. It seemed impossible that they should have declared war on Germany. Everything looked the same as it always had.

(iv)

Kenji stood slightly to one side of the yellow light on the prow of the sampan and informed General Sakai's aide of the state of Hong Kong's defences. He told him of the artillery on the south coast of the island, of the Gindrinkers line of pillboxes and of the almost non-existent Air Force. The aide smiled as if he had expected no less and then he said, "Can we trust Tang?"

"I don't think you can trust anyone," said Kenji. Neither of them noticed the change in pronoun from we to you. Anyway, for Kenji it was merely an expression of his sense of isolation. He reached up to touch one of the circular metal rungs that supported the green awning of the sampan and he turned his eyes away from the aide's face as the sampan to their left knocked against the side of their own, pushed up by the wake of a ferry making for Tai Kok Tsui.

The aide picked at his teeth with his little finger nail and rocked with the movement of the sampan. "Tang says that when the time comes, there will be many Chinese who will be only too willing to help us to overthrow the British oppressors. What do you think?"

Kenji could not help disliking the aide's distant superiority. "My work is with the Europeans," he said. "Not with the Chinese."

"But you will have an opinion."

"The Chinese are notorious for somehow always backing the winning side."

"So, we can expect them to help us?"

"I didn't say that."

"But surely," the aide began to pick at his teeth again, "You are helping Tang to set up a Fifth Column here in Kowloon and Hong Kong?"

"I was not aware that that was part of my responsibilities."

"I would have thought it obvious."

Kenji sighed. "I was told," he said, "To provide information on defence strategy and the general attitude of the European civilian population." He willed the aide to locate whatever was stuck between his teeth and bothering him. "I was told that others would be infiltrated for more specific military tasks."

The aide shrugged, suggesting that an answer to this was superfluous. Instead, he said, "Tang has informed us that he already controls the District Watch Force in Hok Un. Is this true?"

"Quite possibly," said Kenji. "Although Chen Liew is there too."

"And?"

"Strange things have been happening. Many thefts from the warehouses. There and at Lo Wu on the border, too. Chen Liew is being called into question by members of his own organisation. They suggest Tang is slowly pushing him out."

The aide smiled. Kenji was telling him nothing he did not already know. "Go on," he said.

"Chen Liew is old. He lacks ambition. Now that Liao K'ung has disappeared, there are rumours that there could be a struggle for power."

"I suppose that would be all to the good," the aide admitted grudgingly. He seems, thought Kenji, to find the whole affair tedious and boring. He had the air of a man who was being kept from a prior and far more important engagement. The sampan rocked slowly on the water again. The sound of a woman's voice carried to them suddenly through the night and the aide grinned lewdly. You did not need to understand the language to know that what the girl had said had been a prelude to love-making. "A whole city out here on the water," the aide observed, but to no one. "A whole city that does not even know the British are just across the harbour."

"Nor that the Japanese are about to replace one kind of repression with another," thought Kenji. He stood shakily and without acknowledging the aide's casual wave he stepped out of the green awning and into the slightly raised bows of the sampan. He put his hands on his hips and breathed deeply. The tangy salt air prickled in his nose and he looked across the identical curved green canvas awnings of the sampans as though he might have been trying to locate which one contained the girl and her lover. Then with a sigh of resignation he began to hop from one boat to another and he made his way back to dry land.

(v)

Osbourne had waited on the wharf until Kenji had reappeared and left. Then he had walked slowly and pensively back towards the Star Ferry pier. He felt that he had all the pieces which made up the puzzle of his story, but he could not for the life of him put them together. As he walked past the entrance to a bar on Canton Road by the bus station he saw a face that he recognised and, although it belonged to a person he despised, his desire for company after his lonely vigil and his need for conversation after his enforced silence overcame his dislike of the man.

"Dr Laughton!" he called out from the doorway and he pushed his way through the long, narrow room.

Laughton's heart sank. "Oh, Christ!" he said to himself. He had come across to Kowloon precisely because he had wanted to be alone and now here was that tiresome reporter grinning towards him, for all the world as though they were the best of friends. Despite the heat, Osbourne was wearing a dirty beige raincoat, the belt of which was dragging on the floor behind him. As he walked over to Laughton he kept treading on the dragging belt. "Osbourne!" said Laughton coldly. "What are you doing out here?"

Osbourne grinned and heaved himself up onto a stool at the bar. "On a job," he said. "And you?"

"I came to get drunk," said Laughton, "And to get a bit of peace and quiet."

Miserable sod, thought Osbourne to himself but he desperately needed to talk, not about Kenji, but about anything else, and so he said, hoping to touch on something that might interest the doctor, "Precious little going on back home, eh? You know the Yanks have already begun to call this a 'phoney war'? Bloody typical of them, mind you."

Laughton grunted and saw that he was going to have to offer the man a drink.

"Mine's a beer," Osbourne grinned.

Laughton ordered another whisky and soda for himself. The fifth. Seeing that the war in Europe had failed to stir any response in Laughton, Osbourne tried a different approach, that of shared experience. "Bloody funny business, eh? that, up at the old woman's house? I never did get to the bottom of it."

For Laughton, the mah-jongg party arranged by Miss Dekyvere seemed to belong to a different life—his life before Tung Nien. But he said, "It was to get the Russell man out to see his daughter, I believe."

Osbourne snorted. "Don't you believe it, Alfie, mate!" he said.

Laughton winced. Alfie? "Do I look to you like an Alfie, Mr Osbourne?"

Osbourne shrugged. What did it matter? "It's your name, ain't it?"

Laughton sipped his drink and decided to drop the subject.

"Alfred. Alfie. Alf." Osbourne tried all the permutations. "Doc!" he said with a grin. He knew he was annoying Laughton, but sometimes he could not resist. "I'll settle for Doc, I reckon," he said.

"Settle for whatever you want," said Laughton, looking pointedly past Osbourne's head towards the door. Osbourne shuffled forwards on his stool.

"So, how come you know the Tangs, Doc?"

"What?" said Laughton absently.

"The Tangs," said Osbourne. "Wu Tang. He was at the mah-jongg party, remember? Called you Mao, if I'm not very much mistaken." And he laughed.

"Yes," said Laughton. "Wu." And then, "I don't really know him. Haven't seen him again since then, as a matter of fact." He regretted that he was not aggressive enough to tell the reporter to go away and leave him alone.

"Yeah! Pull the other one!" said Osbourne. "Still, none of my business, as they say. Mind if I have another beer?"

Laughton shrugged. Apparently he was paying. Osbourne decided to return to his original line of attack.

"They are saying now that the war in Europe is spurious."

Laughton felt that the word spurious was not an habitual part of Osbourne's vocabulary. It sounded awkward, as though, perhaps, he was unaware of its meaning. And then, as if he needed to confirm the contrary, he went on, "They say that neither the British nor the French are really serious about it. You know, they don't really want to become involved."

"I don't believe it," said Laughton, although the truth was that he had not thought about it before.

"Well, anyway, we've got enough on our plate here, haven't we, Doc, without worrying about the other side of the world?"

"Yes, I suppose so," said Laughton, but he had managed to channel his thoughts away from violence and back to Tung Nien. It was something he did well—think of one thing whilst allowing conversation to pass him by. He had done it for years in the company of his wife. He smiled blandly as Osbourne spoke on, and he thought of Tung Nien and the baby.

"Yeah," said Osbourne, "They're saying that they're just waiting for a chance to negotiate peace, that there's not actually going to be any real fighting at all." He looked at Laughton but the doctor was drinking. He was forced, then, to continue. "Either that, or they're being cunning about it. They have a plan to trap Hitler as soon as he makes his move. What do you reckon, Doc?"

"I really don't know, Mr Osbourne," said Laughton wearily, thinking: You should know! You should, at least, have given it some thought!

"I like that, though, don't you? Phoney war! It's good that!" Osbourne continued to talk on. "And I suppose you're one of these who thinks the Japs are going to make for Burma once they've stitched up the Chinese?"

Laughton sighed. He realised he had not really thought about that either. "I see no reason to doubt it," he said.

"Don't you?" Osbourne shook his head. "Don't you? I reckon they'll go for the lot at the same time. Burma, the Philippines, Malaya, Singapore and Hong Kong. What's to stop them? You just pick up a map, Doc, and you'll see we're already effectively surrounded."

And it was true. Laughton drew a mental picture of the area and saw that, in the event of Japanese aggression, they were indeed isolated. Having no opinion of his own, he quoted something he had read: "But the Japanese have a moderate government, I don't see..."

"What's your moderate government doing in China, Doc?" Osbourne interrupted rudely. He was enjoying making Laughton feel uncomfortable. He did not like him and he did not like what he thought he stood for. Osbourne saw in Laughton a representative of all that he detested—the relaxed, moneyed, leisure classes of the Peak. All pink gin and bloody cricket, Osbourne grunted to himself. Need a good war to shake the bastards out of their complacent lethargy. Aloud he said, "But then, it is a well known fact that Japan has always been a nation of soldiers."

"I suppose it has," said Laughton, who did not know. He sipped at his whisky and held it in his mouth until the bubbles of the soda died on his tongue and then he swallowed. He thought again of Tung Nien and both the Japanese and Osbourne receded. The reporter continued to talk, but Laughton was not listening. He was trying to envisage how a baby might affect their relationship but, for him, a child was such an unknown quantity that he was incapable of placing it in their future. When he looked ahead he saw only himself and Tung Nien, seemingly sleeping off an eternal surfeit of sex on the dry, stained, wooden boards at the Fortune Teller's shop. Laughton's obsession was such that he had never even questioned what event had caused Chen Liew to grant his wife the freedom she needed to be with him. He had accepted it as he accepted everything in his life. Whatever the reason, it was out of his hands.

A sudden movement made him look to his left. Osbourne had removed his glasses and was rubbing them vigorously against the lining of his raincoat. He was still speaking, but it was no longer the war. "Best be making tracks, I reckon, Doc," he was saying. "The last ferry back leaves at eleven and it's already twenty to."

They left the bar together once Laughton had settled the bill and they walked slowly down to the harbour.

"Can't stand Kowloon!" said Osbourne with a derisive sniff and he spat a flake of tobacco towards the side of the road where the carcass of a water melon rotted slowly.

(vi)

Whereas previously Chen Liew had spoken to Tung Nien only as and when it was necessary, he now spoke to her hardly at all. But neither did he speak to anyone else. He would spend long, silent hours, sitting cross-legged on a rush mat, looking across the harbour to the hills of the New Territories, occasionally turning his eyes to stare at the faintly corrugated surface of the sea away to the West. And yet he was not in mourning for his friend. Mourning was an alien concept for a man who had directly brought about the deaths of more than a score of people, and indirectly many more. He felt quite simply exhausted by life and, if anything, he envied Liao K'ung for having become a part of the great void before him.

Chen Liew was even tired of his spiritual exercises. All he wanted to do was roll over and die. "I am too old," he told himself, "for yet another internal struggle within the Brotherhood. Let them do what they will. Of course, Liao K'ung was right when he told me we had to take a fresh look at our position here but, for myself, I cannot be bothered. I no more want to fight amongst ourselves than I want to fight the British or the Japanese. Liao K'ung, of course, would have held it together. He had a special talent for that. And now it will all fall apart."

Tung Nien stood with Molly and watched him sitting cross-legged and immobile on the rush matting.

"He's so quiet always," said Molly, as though it were more a cause for wonder than concern. "He just sits there."

Tung Nien sniffed and turned away. She had been promised so much and now she felt she had been let down. She could almost sense the embryo growing inside her and it was just another barrier between herself and her future. The only positive outcome in the whole affair was the fact that Chan, in the absence of his master, had gradually become more and more devoted to her. He came out of the house as they turned to go in.

"Take him some soup, Chan, at least," she said, and walked on into the house. She would have a smoke, relax and forget about it all for a while.

(vii)

Eliot Rodmell held the bright, sticky cocktail that had been prepared for him at arm's length and he looked through the glass and the blood-orange coloured liquid at Major Harland. "'Planter's Punch', you say?" he grunted. "Well, it's too sweet and too fizzy by half, if you want my opinion."

"That's the grenadine," Major Harland informed him. "And the soda water." The unfortunate cocktail had been his idea and he felt somehow responsible.

"Grenadine, is it?" said Rodmell with a frown.

"Well, not only grenadine. There are fresh fruit juices," admitted Major Harland. "And a dash of white rum."

"Give me a gin every time," said Rodmell, and Major Harland made a mental note not to be so modern in the future.

"Getting to the dry season, at least," Rodmell grunted again, dismissing any further reference to the drink.

Major Harland nodded. "And Christmas. There'll be water rationing again, I suppose," he warned. He chose to ignore the ceaselessly swinging hoses which were watering Rodmell's garden and the slow bubbling of the purification plant for his swimming pool.

"They've done it, you know, don't you?" Rodmell barked suddenly. Major Harland did not know who they were or what they had done, but he had had sufficient experience of the Taipan's unpredictable behaviour to know he was about to be given the reason for the great man's bad mood.

"Have they, indeed?" he said, innocently, sipping his cocktail. He, at least, found it refreshing. He, at least, did not care that it was American in origin.

"Set up their War Revenue Committee!" said Rodmell, and he turned in his chair to fix his blue eyes on the Major. "Despite warnings that it would only bring about a flight of capital. And I told Sir Vandeleur Grayburn, himself. You can't, I told him, introduce income tax in Hong Kong. Thought he'd taken the point, but what do they decide to do instead? They capitulate on the income tax. They withdraw the proposal. Only to reintroduce it under a different name. You know what this War Revenue Committee intends to do, don't you?"

Major Harland knew only too well, but he knew better than to ruin the pleasure Rodmell would get in telling him.

"They're only talking of introducing a property tax. Five per cent of the rateable value on the first five thousand dollars and ten per cent thereafter. And a corporation profits tax of five per cent on profits from ten thousand to a hundred thousand. Ten per cent, then, for any more than that!"

"Lucky for you, then, that most of your money is, shall we say, opaque," said Harland to himself, who had never seen ten thousand dollars. But Rodmell had not finished.

"And where is this money going to go? To finance their phoney bloody war!"

Rodmell was obviously unaware of the origin of the phrase. Had he known it had been coined by the American press he would have been devastated, for he would sooner have paid the tax than associate himself with them. Major Harland smiled, but discreetly. "The invasion of France, Eliot, is only a question of time. Your money will be put to good use, let me assure you."

Eliot Rodmell felt a light tickling on his forearm and looked down. A silk-worm had fallen from one of the trees and was making its way up his arm. Rodmell prodded the tiny worm with the end of his finger and watched as it pulled its four back legs towards its four front legs and arched its back into a Ω shape. Then it pushed the front legs forwards and stretched out before arching its back again. Ω. Rodmell flicked the silk-worm from his arm and turned to Major Harland. "Only fed on mulberry leaves, you know?" he said. "For the best quality silk, I mean."

Harland, who had not seen the silk-worm, was again at a loss. Fortunately, Rodmell did not require him to reply. He stood up and tipped his 'Planter's Punch' into a flower bed and said, "I'm going to get a serious drink, Harland. Something that looks like a drink and tastes like a drink."

As Rodmell passed his wife and Mrs Harland, he heard one of them saying, "A lovely production of 'The Mikado'. Doreen was one of the Three Little Maids. Quite exquisite!" He watched them as they walked on out and into the garden and he felt that none of them realised the gravity of the situation. There was Major Harland with his soppy drink and his invasion of France, and his wife with Gilbert and Sullivan. He, on the other hand, was going to have to relinquish more than fifteen per cent of his income to the British Government!

Rodmell watched the amah putting two ice-cubes and two fingers of gin into a squat glass and his thoughts turned to the Chinese. "They're not going to like it," he said, "Any more than I do." The amah passed him his gin and instead of returning to the garden, he sat down with his drink at the kitchen table. He looked blankly at a long Chinese print of a bamboo plant, a copy of a thirteenth century ink drawing, his wife's choice, which hung on one side of the fridge, and then to the other side where there was a more elaborate print, his choice, of the staked-out body of a sacrificed bear. "The bamboo," he thought to himself, dragging up from the past a vaguely remembered conversation with his father, "the fastest growing plant in the world."

Rodmell was slightly concerned by the fact that he should be thinking of his father. As far as he could remember, he had not done so since his wedding to Margaret. Perhaps it had been prompted by this taxation business. Poor old Ernest Rodmell would be turning in his grave. Eliot Rodmell sipped at his gin and turned on the wireless. He tuned in to the BBC Empire Service for the news and listened distractedly:

"It is estimated that more than eighty thousand Poles have passed over neutral frontiers to escape from the German advance. Despite the official surrender to Germany on October 5th, guerrilla resistance continues both in Warsaw itself and the outlying areas."

Rodmell stood up and, leaving the wireless on, walked slowly back through the house to the garden and his guests. He had decided, as spontaneously as he could, that he should visit Chen Liew and sound out the Chinese reaction to the news of taxation. "After all," he told himself, "It will not, anyway, come into full force and effect until the Spring. Who knows, if we put up a common front, there may still be a way round it."

(viii)

Eliot Rodmell did not like to visit anyone, let alone the Chinese. He liked to be surrounded by familiarity, by his own things. He liked everything to be done in accordance with his wishes. He liked dinner to be eaten when he was hungry, gin or whisky to be offered when he felt like a drink, things to be said because he was interested in them and people to leave when he became bored. As soon as you stepped into someone else's house, you handed that initiative over to them and they were automatically in control of the situation. Rodmell did not willingly allow any situation even to exist unless it was entirely of his own making. And so when Ying answered the door he spoke to him gruffly.

"I am expected!" he said, although it was not entirely true. Ying left him at the door and Rodmell turned to inspect the grounds. It was his first visit to Chen Liew's house—nobody had, in fact, been invited since the wedding with the exception of Willard Russell—and Rodmell smiled in appreciation at the immaculate lawns and tidy flower-beds. The view over the harbour, whilst seen from lower on the Peak than his own, was, if anything, even more spectacular.

"You may come in," a voice said behind him. Rodmell turned and was faced by the enormous figure of Chan.

Chan led him along a seemingly endless corridor which ran along the front of the house, past the red and green *pat kwa* mirror, and then left into a large, open room decorated in silk screen prints and black, lacquered furniture.

"Wait here," said Chan, and closed the door.

Rodmell decided he would not sit. Instead, he walked across the room to a thin, glass-fronted cabinet which was filled with small copulating ivory figures. He was still looking at the little figures with some distaste when Tung Nien came into the room.

"Well, Mr Rodmell!" she said, smiling at him but not offering him her hand or making any other sign of welcome.

"I have come to see Chen Liew," Rodmell said shortly.

"I am afraid that will not be possible. My husband is busy. Anything you wish to say to him, you may say to me."

It was a situation Rodmell could never have anticipated and he felt uncomfortable. He would not even speak to English women if he could help it. To be faced with a Chinese one was unthinkable.

"I hardly think," he began, "that you are really in a position to..." And then he stopped because Chan had returned and taken up an obviously protective stance at Tung Nien's shoulder. She sat down seeing that he would not. Her stockings hissed as she crossed her legs. "In a position," Rodmell continued, regretting now the spontaneity of his visit, "to answer my queries, my questions."

Tung Nien smiled at the Taipan and recrossed her legs. She was only just beginning to comprehend the extent of her husband's influence and the power that she might, at least momentarily, be able to wield. "I don't see why not," she said simply.

When Eliot Rodmell avoided the steady stare of her eyes, his own seemed to alight on the cabinet of fornicating figures. Still, he would do his best to be polite, at least. He would not say that it was because she was a woman.

"Chan," he said instead, "How about letting me speak to Liao K'ung's replacement?"

"This is Liao K'ung's replacement," said Chan quietly.

Rodmell looked from the impassive face of the bodyguard to the beautiful woman sitting before him and then back to the bodyguard, but he had no words.

"And, now, Mr Rodmell," said Tung Nien slowly, "If you would begin?"

Rodmell thought quickly. There was no point throwing his lot in with a woman. The other Chinese would soon get her out of the way anyway. His only alternative, much as he disliked the idea, was Tang. He would have to fob Tung Nien off with any old nonsense and then high tail it out of there. There was no future in speaking of common fronts with a woman, still less in doing business. And he still refused to address her directly.

"Chan," he said, "Tell Chen Liew I shall return at a more suitable moment." And he bowed respectfully in preparation for his departure. "How humiliating!" he said to himself as he bowed and looked at his shoes. "It would be like letting one of them talk to Margaret!" He reversed from the room, feeling now more angry than anything else. As he strode rigidly down the drive towards the hibiscus at the gate his eyes rested, like the yellow eyes of a snake, on Molly, and his heart missed a beat. "Now that," he muttered, as he got into his car, "is what I call pretty!" It almost made up for the humiliation of his interview with Tung Nien.

"Bald with a beer-belly, Miss Dekyvere," Molly said with a laugh as she watched the distinguished upright form of Eliot Rodmell making his way down the drive. "That's what my father used to say was the ultimate destiny of all men."

"Well, my dear," said Miss Dekyvere quietly, "It only goes to show."

"In a way," said Molly, referring to Eliot Rodmell, "He's more like a Chinese. Instead of fat, he's wizened, instead of bald, he's got a full head of hair."

"But taller than a Chinese," said Miss Dekyvere, for that was the main difference.

"And distinguished," said Molly.

"But," said Miss Dekyvere, "He is not a nice man."

"Are there any nice men?" asked Molly, picking at a blade of grass.

"I've never met one," Miss Dekyvere was tempted to say, not because it was true, but because it would have ended the conversation. Instead, she said, "In his way, Chen Liew is a good man. Your father," she added doubtfully, "And Wu." She had given her Wu because she knew Molly needed him to be included.

"Wu is too good," said Molly.

"Yes, he is." Miss Dekyvere would agree because it could do no harm.

"He sent me a letter, a note," said Molly. "He wants to know when my father and I are leaving. He says if we go now, we'd be in Singapore in a couple of weeks and, from there, we could go on to Australia."

"Your father will not leave," said Miss Dekyvere. "He is not in a fit state. And anyway, why should he?" Although she knew perfectly well.

"That's what I said," said Molly confidently, sure that she was right.

Tung Nien watched Eliot Rodmell's retreat from a window in the long corridor of the house. "Why did he come, Chan?" she asked. "What, do you suppose, were his questions?" Chan shrugged. Tung Nien turned away from the window. "There is one thing I am sure of, Chan," she said. "We cannot afford to let anyone know, at least, not yet, of my husband's mood, his apathy. Everything must be seen to be perfectly normal. Everything must be seen to be going on exactly as it should, as it always has. I may need your help for that."

Chan was willing to see the logic in maintaining a semblance of order and he was sure Chen Liew would soon come to his senses. He owed it to his *lo ban* to keep the house in order until such a time as Chen Liew might once again take the reins. "No one need know anything," he said, and turned away from the window.

Tung Nien walked into the garden. Molly stood up as she approached. "Can Chan take us out to Deep Water Bay for a swim? It's so sticky and humid here. At least out there we might get a breeze in off the sea."

"I have other things I must do, Molly. You will spend the evening with Miss Dekyvere."

Miss Dekyvere would do it for Molly, but she looked up at Tung Nien. "Please," she said, "Do not take me for granted."

Tung Nien smiled, but it was a smile of impatience. "Oh," she said, "I wouldn't do that."

(ix)

Osbourne sat at his desk in the offices of the South China Morning Post and he began to jot down some sketchy notes for the story as he saw it. The Japanese barber was helping Tang to smuggle arms across the border to the Imperial Japanese Army. Eliot Rodmell was importing goods illegally from Japan, relabelling them and then selling them to the Chinese in unoccupied China. Chen Liew, for some reason, was allowing Tang, in turn, to steal from Rodmell's warehouses and, for all Osbourne knew, from his own, too. One thing was obvious: Tang was on the way up and Chen Liew on the way down. But that had always been on the cards from the moment they had allowed him a foothold in the opium trade.

Osbourne sighed and sat back in his chair. "Let's face it," he said. "Bugger all!" Had Osbourne been possessed of a different temperament, he would have felt frustrated. As it was, he felt merely that providence was against him, was preventing him from finding the key to his story, and he felt bitter. It was not fair that he had discovered so much and that it should serve for so little. And so it was mostly bitterness which made him write an article which would effectively discredit the immigration cadet officer and end in his being sent back to Britain in disgrace. It was virtually common knowledge to anyone who cared that irregularities were being committed with regard to the issue of Residency Permits to the Chinese, but it required Osbourne's vindictive need, being hurt himself, to hurt someone else and to bring it to light. And because once the article was written it could not be ignored, the cadet officer was forced to resign from the Immigration Department and was sent packing. Osbourne, partly because he was not stupid and partly because the only purpose of the article had been to inflict pain, had deliberately underplayed Rodmell's rôle in the affair, presenting him as a slightly gullible and innocent party.

And so it was that Rodmell approached Osbourne one lunch-time in the Parisian Grill to say, "A fine article, Osbourne. Drink?"

"Beer," said Osbourne.

"Yes," said Rodmell guardedly, for he was not comfortable imparting praise, "Fine work. We can do without his sort, what?"

"There are many 'sorts' we can do without, Mr Rodmell."

"What? Oh, quite so, Osbourne. Quite so. Many sorts." Eliot Rodmell looked at his gin. He wished Osbourne would hurry up with his beer so that he could leave him, but because Osbourne knew that

Rodmell would not leave until he had finished, he left it untouched upon the bar.

"No more problems at the warehouses?" Osbourne asked suddenly, hoping to catch Rodmell off his guard, but Rodmell was not the kind of person ever to lower his defences.

"Oh, no, Osbourne. The Japanese had to do a bit of bombing. Largely for political reasons, you know? But we knew beforehand that it would happen so the buildings were empty. It's all a bit like an elaborate game. You just have to know the rules, that's all."

"Or when to bend them," said Osbourne.

Rodmell looked grumpily at the reporter's glass of beer, still insolently full on the counter of the bar. "What are rules for, Osbourne, if not to be broken from time to time?"

"I was under the impression that they were meant to be kept," said Osbourne, although that was not strictly true. He knew, as did Rodmell, which rules you could break.

"Come, come, Osbourne!" said Rodmell, unable to prevent a slightly patronising tone from creeping into his voice.

"Just look at our friend the cadet officer, Mr Rodmell."

"He was a fool," said Rodmell.

Osbourne finally sipped at his beer. "How do you make that out?"

"He was caught, Osbourne," said Rodmell, relaxing as the beer progressed from Osbourne's glass into his stomach. "He was caught."

"Yeah, he was caught all right!" said Osbourne, pushing the empty glass towards the barman. "Fancy another?" It was perhaps the first time Osbourne had ever offered to buy anyone a drink in his life, but he knew Rodmell would refuse. "Another beer, Charlie!" he called out to the Chinese barman, whose name was Lee, and he looked expectantly at Rodmell.

Eliot Rodmell breathed deeply before demurring. He turned to leave. "The nasty little man has forced me out!" he grumbled to himself. "Can hardly stay having refused a drink. But he knew that, of course. Did it on purpose, to put me on the spot. Should have damned his eyes! Instead of which, I must leave, with nowhere to go but back to the office or home to Margaret!" Neither of these options appealed to Rodmell in the slightest. He had been looking forward to a quiet drink and perhaps a game of chess in the Lounge Bar, watching the sun go down and just passing the time until dinner. Now his evening had been turned upside down, and he did not like it. He stood at the entrance to the hotel, absently watching the pedestrians and the traffic in the street, a scowl of anger creasing his forehead. A hand suddenly clasped his shoulder and he turned to be greeted by Osbourne's grinning face.

"See you around, cock!" said Osbourne happily. "Thanks for the beer!"

Eliot Rodmell felt the hairs rise at the back of his neck, but he said nothing. At least he would get his game of chess.

(x)

"If you don't do it for me, Alfred, somebody else will."

Laughton had nearly finished the bottle of Usher's Green Stripe. He could not understand how she could ask him to do it. It was not even as though the baby would endanger her life if she went through with it. Quite simply, she had said as much herself, she did not want it. But Tung Nien had managed to convince herself that it was not a baby, as it was for Laughton. It was a problem that she had to rid herself of and she made sure that she thought of it as she would a cancerous cell. It was not alive any more than her liver was alive, part of her though it was. And like a cancerous cell, for her to keep living, it would have to be cut out. She would have been more receptive to Laughton's obstinacy and his objections if they had had some basis in religious faith. As it was, all he had said was, "I could never kill anyone. Still less a child. Not a child, Tung Nien. You don't seem to understand just what you are asking me to do."

She was going to say, "But, Alfred, if you loved me!" Only she knew him well enough to know that that would not be a reason and so she said, "If you don't do it, someone else will. I'd just rather it were you."

Laughton drank his whisky and then emptied the last of the bottle into his glass. He was trying very hard to hate her so that he could just stand up and walk away, but even then he knew that he wanted her, that he would always be jealous of her kisses and her body. Love was not something he could turn on and off at will, nor was hate a natural part of his character. It was something he would have to cultivate and as yet in his life he had had no cause. He felt that he had only just discovered what it was to love. Somehow, he had managed always to avoid strong emotions until he had met her. But, as he drank his whisky, he tried very hard to hate her for what she was asking him to do. So that then he could leave. He even managed to stand up, but she placed a soft hand on his arm.

"The Chinese," she said, "do it with a tube of bamboo. I'm not sure how. They shove it in and blow, I think. Many people do not survive. You surely don't want me to put myself at risk when for you it would be so simple."

He pushed her hand away and walked across the room to an alcove by the stairs where the Fortune Teller kept his store of opium. For the first time in his life he could see the attraction of the drug. If he could smoke a pipe and just forget everything, at least for a while. For he felt that something was tearing at his insides and sucking his heart down into his stomach to be smothered.

"Go on!" said Tung Nien gently in his ear and picking up the carved box with the opium. "If that's what you want." She pushed the box into his hands and he looked at it. The carving on the lid depicted a tiger and a dragon entwined within a kind of casket. Laughton ran his fingers over the raised ivory figures and handed the box back to Tung Nien. "No," he said. "I think I'll just lie down for a bit."

Tung Nien shrugged and watched him lower himself onto the hard wooden boards of the bed. "It's an escape like any other, Alfred," she said softly as she picked the pipe from the stool beside the bed. "I think sometimes we cannot take too much of the world as it is. That is when we smoke. It doesn't change the world, but it makes it go away for a while."

"But it comes back," said Laughton dully.

"Of course it comes back!" said Tung Nien. "Only religion can make it go away for good."

Laughton had no way of knowing that she was speaking of her husband and he thought it an odd thing to say. But it was not odd enough to save him from the pipe.

"I don't even like the smell of it," he protested as she began to prepare the pellet. She smiled and spoke to him as though he were a child. "It doesn't taste like it smells," she said, and she ran her cold fingers along the tenseness of his forehead.

The drug seeped slowly not across, but into, his brain. It seemed, he thought, to ooze, as though the smoke became viscous as he inhaled, but it numbed him and he was grateful. He felt his muscles unknitting and the tight dread which had gripped his stomach relaxed its hold on him. Beside him, Tung Nien lay on her side on the bed, her head resting on a wooden stool, and the opium crackled and glowed like a bonfire as she breathed the smoke deep into her lungs. Her eyes were already glazed and unseeing, but Laughton could see her. He could almost see into her, he thought for a moment and, although his throat was parched and dry, he reached out for the pipe. She groaned a slight protest but passed him the thin, stained bamboo tube and kissed him gently on his eyelids. Her breath so close to him smelt sweet and clammy and a part of him wanted to reach out and hold her, only his muscles seemed now to be filled with water and he could not move. There was a moment when he thought she had left him and he cried out until he felt her warmness once again lying out beside his own sticky body.

They smoked four pipes each. Laughton was surprised that the pipe only lasted about thirty seconds before it was burnt out. He had thought, for some reason, that smoking opium would be more like sitting down before a roaring fire during a winter in England and smoking a traditional pipe of tobacco, making it last, dragging out the sensation to its limits but, after his first pipe, he watched Tung Nien pierce the gummy mass with the sharp needle before kneading it into the bowl and he tried to empty his second pipe in one go, as he had seen her do, breathing the smoke in time after time, without breathing out, until the opium had consumed itself and became charred and deformed. When he lay back and closed his eyes, he felt relaxed and at peace with the world. He could hear Tung Nien talking to him but, rather than hear the words, he saw them. As she spoke, the words were printed on a long scroll inside his head which unravelled too quickly for him to be able to read what it was she had said. He watched the words rolling away from him and he went to sleep.

That night would be the first of what he later discovered was known as a white night. He slept deeply and untroubled, and when he woke, he found he was alone in the geomancer's room. Tung Nien had gone. He sat up on the hard bunk feeling totally refreshed and he reached for his watch. It lay face down beside the oil lamp they had used for preparing the opium for the pipe. He looked at the time. 12:45. He had been asleep for, at most, forty minutes and yet he felt rejuvenated, relaxed and alive. He had the sudden strange thought that he must have slept, not for forty minutes, but for twenty-four hours and forty minutes. But that was impossible. He lay on the bunk, looking at the smoke-stained rafters and he felt calm. It did not seem to him at all strange that he should be alone and, whilst he knew that he should have tried to move to go home, there was something which prevented him from sitting up. After about an hour, an hour which passed almost without him noticing, he began to feel drowsy again and he drifted into another deep, dreamless sleep of about thirty minutes.

This sleeping and waking continued throughout the night and each time he woke he thought it would be morning, but it never was and he lay calmly on the bed waiting for the drowsiness to return and come upon him again. When it was finally morning, he drank a cup of cold, unsweetened, green tea that they had made the night before, he washed in hard, cold water, and he caught a tram over to the Queen Mary Hospital. He felt no need of breakfast and he felt as though he had slept all the worries and nervous tension out of his body. He felt refreshed, relaxed, calm and at peace with the world.

(xi)

Kenji was becoming more and more wearied by his pretence with Willard Russell. The longer it took for the Japanese to surround Hong Kong, the more disillusioned Kenji became with the life he was being forced to lead. And the worst thing was that he had found he had actually started to think of Russell as a friend. Kenji knew the potential danger of allowing emotion a foothold in his life and in order to distance himself from the American he increased the rhythm of their religious training.

Kenji had learned the ancient teachings so thoroughly that he was able to feed Russell with the necessary profound thoughts while thinking himself of something completely different.

"Think of your body as a country, Willard," he said, "and remember that the vital breath can only increase the country's prosperity and provide security for its population—the generative force."

For some reason, tonight, Kenji found Russell's physical presence imposing on his thoughts. As he looked at the crippled American in his wheelchair, he knew that he had virtually destroyed his powers of reason. The American relied on his friendship almost as much as he now relied on his daily dose of faith. That was, perhaps, what Kenji found so strange. Russell actually seemed to believe what he repeated to him. And there was no question but that it was a perfect front for him. When they had started out together on their search, Kenji could never have imagined it would have all worked out so well. The Japanese barber and the American invalid, united in their crazy search for immortality! "But you have destroyed him," Kenji told himself again. Until a second voice said, "He was destroyed long before he met you."

"We each have seven emotions, Willard," he said aloud. Willard Russell nodded, almost as though he already knew what they were.

"Pleasure," said Kenji, "anger, sorrow, joy, love, hate and desire. And these emotions are upset by the five thieves: the eyes, the ears, the nose, the tongue and the body."

Willard Russell smiled. When he heard the words he felt, somehow, close again to Suyong. When he focussed on Kenji's eyes, he could almost make them melt and form the expression of his dead wife, looking back at him, as she had always looked when he had come home late and tired from work, somewhere between pity and understanding, for the utter uselessness of his efforts. If he thought of Molly at all, which was rarely, she was still a baby, her eyes wide and, Suyong said, ugly, like a peasant's from the south western provinces. But he was not only living with his memories. He was certain that Kenji's great emptiness existed and he was determined to find it. For there he would be once again united with Suyong.

Kenji looked at Willard Russell's blank stare which seemed to recognise and register nothing and he thought, "If he was destroyed when you met him, you could have saved him instead of pushing him under." But he knew it was a futile discussion. There could be no room in his life for friendship, for, although nobody as yet seemed to be aware of the fact, the war had already effectively started in Hong Kong, and war was not concerned with building. It was about destruction.

"This is the state of deep serenity," he said to Willard Russell and he stood up, stretching his legs. He kicked away the small, cloth-covered, bun-shaped stool he had been sitting on. He left Russell lolling in his chair and he stepped out onto the balcony in Russell's tenement flat. He could see a cloud of mosquitoes, silver in the light of a gas lamp on another balcony opposite. "The state of deep serenity," he said, this time to himself.

(xii)

When Laughton saw the broken and dismembered foetus with its perfect hands and fingers at the end of the severed and tiny arms no bigger than his thumb, the foetus placed neatly on a towel in six pieces which formed a shattered but almost perfect embryo, with the white of the towel stained red in places but showing brightly below the pink of the flesh which had not even bruised with the violence of his cutting, he broke down and cried bitterly, as much for himself and the children he could never have as for the child before him that would never be.

And when, because he had to know, he had asked her again why she had gone through with it, why she had insisted, she had looked at him dreamily through the fading anaesthetic and had said simply, as though she had expected him to understand, "Because it was yours."

7

'First he climbed to the heaven,
Then he plunged to the depths of the earth."

(i)

Laughton was haunted by the image of the mutilated foetus. He seemed to carry it with him throughout the day, not at the back of his mind, but as a constant presence. A red Chinese character painted on the window of a grocer's shop opposite the hospital gates seemed to him to be an exact copy of the blooded shape he had left on the towel. When he had a break for coffee in the mornings, there was a poster of a newly born baby on the wall of the hospital canteen to remind him of what he had done. The clicking of the metal wheels of the trams passing by in the street outside his office were like the sharp cracks of breaking bone. His only escape from the nightmare of the abortion was through opium, and Tung Nien was unhappy enough following the operation to share in his slow drifting towards addiction.

They met up at the geomancer's every other evening but, although Laughton scarcely noticed, they now hardly spoke to each other. Tung Nien would prepare a small china cup of green tea and several pipes. Laughton did not even see enough of the world any more to realise that they spoke so little. All he wanted was oblivion, to blot out the awful memory of the foetus and to assuage the guilt he felt.

"It is a wonderful drug," said Tung Nien, "which changes form into nothingness."

Laughton lay back on the wooden bed and felt childishly proud of the fact that he had managed finally to empty a pipe, his fourth, in a single draw of breath. He screwed his eyes together and then opened them, but she continued to drift away from him. He tried vainly to register what it was she had just said and wondered whether she was waiting for him to give her an answer. "What?" he said finally.

Tung Nien smiled at him. "It changes form into nothingness," she repeated. Chen Liew had used the sentence that morning to explain to her the essential qualities of the Golden Light. She had thought then of opium and had even envisaged herself repeating it to Laughton. It gave her a certain satisfaction to know that sometimes things could still work out as she wanted them to. She yawned and waited for Laughton to drift away from her, as she knew he would.

Although he was not yet aware of the fact, over the last few months, his continual absences, his detachment and his rudeness to those she considered her friends had hardened his wife, Mary, against him. And now, again without his realising it, his total dependence on the drug as his only means of escape from the desperate reality he imagined he could see all around him was hardening Tung Nien and pushing her too away from him. But Laughton, locked away, as he was, in his isolation and selfishness was unaware of everything other than the small wad of putty-like opium in the end of the pipe. He groaned a little and turned onto his side. Tung Nien waited until he had drifted into sleep and then stood up. She could hear him snoring behind her as she walked across to the small window to look out into the street.

Chan no longer patrolled the steep steps outside the geomancer's store, although he would come for her later in the white Bentley. Tung Nien looked at the rotted rattan of the blinds in the shop across the street and at the rusted corrugated iron of the roof. Where the nails had been crudely banged into the wood of the beams, there was a brown, dripping stain on the tile-shaped curve of the iron. When she breathed in, the sickly, prickly smell of Durian caught in her throat and made her want to vomit. She looked down into the open sewer of the street. An old man was shovelling rice into his mouth from a bowl tipped at his chin. He was squatted, resting on his heels. She felt totally emptied of emotion. She looked back at Laughton stretched out on the bunk and she knew that something had come between them. She felt sorry for him and did not like it. She wanted to love him but she seemed to have moved on to somewhere he could not follow. Her love, it seemed, was not sufficient to fight against his despair.

At first, because he still loved her at least, Laughton had tried to find some justification which could excuse Tung Nien, but because her crime had been neither sexual nor emotional—he would, he realised sadly, have forgiven her any infidelity so long as she eventually returned to him—because her crime had violated something within him that was rooted beyond the kind of petty jealousy that could be cured with a kiss or a promise to change, however obviously empty, as all kisses and promises seemed to him to be, because she had destroyed, or more truthfully, forced him to destroy an essential, elemental part of himself, to disregard his own carefully conceived code of ethics or belief, he could think no further than his own individual involvement in the killing of the only son, for it had been a boy, he was ever likely to have. Of course, he knew that had she had the baby he would never have been allowed to see it, but it would have been alive and would have taken a part of him with it off into the world. Instead, a part of him had died.

Laughton looked up at the ceiling. Let's hope the Japanese come soon with their 'planes and bombs and blow us all to Kingdom Come. Life is a luxury we have lost the right to enjoy.

When Tung Nien had left Laughton alone in the geomancer's shop, she had told Chan to drive her down to Wanchai instead of home. She felt relieved now when she was out of Laughton's presence. He was an unwelcome reminder of a part of her life she would rather not have happened. As she sat in the back of the Bentley she thought of him lying back in the shop with his opium and his despair and there was something inside her which willed him to be stronger, to be the kind of man who might still take her away from the misery her world had become. Because she herself would refuse to accept it. If Tang and Rodmell were, at present, to be far more important to her than Laughton, then Laughton, she knew, would have to become a part of her past, despite her love for him. She could try to convince herself that there had never been any way that he could ever have been anything else. And they had both known that anyway. She had nothing to feel guilty about. She had read, in one of the strange books that Miss Dekyvere forced onto her, that once you had had a lover you always moved on to another one, that you never went back to your spouse, and she smiled to think of Laughton doing that. Trying to kill her memory in the arms of another woman. For her part, she knew the memories she would have to kill if she were to move on and she knew she did not want to kill them.

The car stopped at a set of traffic lights and Chan turned to face her. "I'll get out and walk for a while," she said. Although there had recently been various blackout exercises, tonight the city was a mass of lights and as Tung Nien looked into the eyes of the people who were passing in the street it was difficult to believe that the Japanese were little more than an hour's march away across the harbour. She had not wanted to think of Laughton again but there was something in the empty expressions on the faces of the people which took her back to the moment that afternoon when she had arrived at the geomancer's. Laughton had been looking from the room out into the street and as she had opened the door he had turned to her and said, "They're right, you know. Did you read it this morning in the paper? The editorial? The Hong Kong outlook, it said, is compounded of reaction, faith, determination, nervous anticipation, evasion and simple fatalism. You can see it all out there if you look. But most of all the simple fatalism of the Chinese." Now, as she made her way down towards the harbour she could see it too. They were all walking along as though only half awake. It was almost as though elementary emotions like reason and passion had disappeared to be replaced by a stoic acceptance. It was only by making a tremendous effort that she could free herself from this wave of apathy and concentrate on the fact that there were things that she had to do. If the Japanese were going to win, and only a fool or an Englishman would think otherwise, she had somehow to get herself on their side, or rather, them on her side. But before that she would have to see to Rodmell and Tang.

(ii)

Major Harland was worried. He was worried by the fact that he had been ordered to arrange for the future evacuation from Hong Kong of all the European women and children. But he was also worried by the news that was arriving from Britain. All of it bad. He knew that, by not including the Chinese and the Indians in the evacuation, he (although acting merely as the mouthpiece for his Government) would, quite rightly, be accused of racial discrimination and he knew that when the civilian population heard that the British Expeditionary Force had been isolated at Dunkirk, faith in the army's ability to defend Hong Kong from an eventual Japanese attack would be severely diminished. "Everyone with any sense will want out," he said aloud, thinking at the same time, "But where shall we send them? There is no safe haven anymore."

Major Harland made a jerking effort to move his mind on to more pleasant things. Only there weren't any. Even Rodmell had let him down recently. Twice during the last week they had arranged to meet for a sun-downer at The Pen and on both occasions Rodmell had failed to show up. It was not like Rodmell not even to 'phone to apologise and this small overthrowing of the harmony in his normally ordered life only served to add to his uneasiness. And yet he was supposed to present a confident front to the civilian population, they expected him to act as though nothing were happening. What was it Governor Northcote had said the other day when opening that new power station in Kowloon? "What is it," he had said, "that the vision of the China Light and Power Company foresees? Obviously, it is to a great manufacturing future for this town of Kowloon that the company is looking, and I readily take my stand beside them in that confidence."

Major Harland stood up from his desk and walked across to the window of his office. He looked over the parade ground where the 2nd Royal Scots were drilling. "A great manufacturing future!" he repeated, as though trying to convince himself that it was possible. He was still absently watching the movement of the soldiers when the telephone rang. It was Eliot Rodmell telling him to get down to the bar of the Parisian Grill.

"You have to understand, Harland, my whole life's here," Rodmell had begun. No word of their other two meetings when Harland had waited in vain for his friend for over two hours. "It's not the same for you, is it? For the others, it's not the same."

Harland sipped his beer. He looked slowly over at Eliot Rodmell. Even he has been changed, he thought. Instead of the powerful, confident, pompous, overbearing man of a few weeks ago, here was Rodmell, submissive and insecure, and, by the looks of it, he was going to ask Harland for his advice. This further upsetting of the normal order made Harland more concerned than ever.

"What's not the same, Eliot?"

Rodmell grunted, partly in annoyance at not having been understood and partly because he felt uncomfortable having to speak to Harland at all, let alone having the man cross examine him. Rodmell decided to try to order his thoughts.

"The Japanese are going to close the border, Harland," he said.

Harland did not deliberately mean to misunderstand the fact that Rodmell, as always, was principally concerned with the effect this would have on commerce.

"They won't attack, Eliot," he said. "Not yet. They are still more concerned by the Chinese than by us. Mark my words, their next focus for attack will not be here. It will be the supply lines on the Hanoi-Kunning railway. Or else the Burma Road."

Eliot Rodmell's reason for speaking to Harland was basically to justify himself. He thought that by saying aloud what it was he intended to do, it might serve to relieve himself of some of the guilt he felt in doing it. Whilst Rodmell fumbled towards the suitable words to explain, Harland looked at him from over the rim of his beer glass. He has aged these last few months, thought Harland. His skin now seems to hang loosely. More loosely than before. Rodmell drank from his gin and tonic and Harland sensed, rather than saw, the liquid filling the thin folds of skin on his neck.

"The Japanese have the upper hand, then, Harland," said Rodmell finally, "And when they choose to, they will come for us. It is only a matter of time."

Harland shook his head. Despite the fact that he didn't believe it, he had to believe it or his work would become unbearable.

"Nonsense!" he said. "Hong Kong is a fortress, Eliot. Everybody knows that. A natural fortress!"

"Do you deny that you have started building air-raid shelters again?"

Harland shook his head, but he said, "It is partly psychological. We must keep the troops occupied."

Rodmell sighed.

"The fact is, Harland, if we were to place bets on an eventual Japanese victory, we'd end up with odds of something like ten to one."

"Oh, I don't know about that. Hong Kong is a fortress." Harland did not like to repeat himself but he found that he had no other argument to offer. Rodmell placed his gin and tonic carefully onto a cardboard coaster and turned the glass round twice. Then he leaned back and clasped his hands behind his head.

"I have to think of the future, Harland. My future. Remember, this is all I've got."

"I don't know that I see what you're driving at, Eliot. What else does any of us have, if not the here and now?"

So, Rodmell thought. He is going to force me to speak plainly. I had thought a little hint might have been sufficient. But he is too self-centred. His world is restricted to the slow moving of troops upon a map, to the giving and obeying of orders. Doubtless, a Japanese invasion can mean only one of two things to him: death or imprisonment. For even he cannot be foolish enough to believe in victory. Rodmell took a deep breath and then a long drink of gin and tonic.

"So," he said, "I don't see that I have much of a choice, when all's said and done. Not if we leave patriotism on one side, of course."

Rodmell was speaking quickly in an effort to ensure that Major Harland would not interrupt, but not quickly enough, for there was the absurd little man saying, "What will our chaps in Dunkirk do without patriotism, Eliot, eh?"

"Oh, fuck Dunkirk, Harland! We're talking about me!"

And Major Harland really had not realised until then what should have been patently obvious. They were talking about Eliot Rodmell. They were not talking about the war at all, but about how the war would affect Eliot Rodmell.

"When—and I said when, not if, Harland—when the Japanese win, what do you suppose will happen to the likes of me? I have to make provisions now. Look," he said, and he leaned forwards and breathed gin into Harland's face, "A meeting has been set up—me, Tang and that Tung Nien woman; Chen Liew, you see, he's out of it now. Mainly because, like you, he thinks the British will win." And here he paused. Although he had no need to scoff, the scoffing tone had been present in his voice from the moment he had said Chen Liew. "We are all, I think, agreed. We are going to throw in our lot with the Japanese."

Harland withdrew from Rodmell's intense leaning towards him. It was not only that as an Englishman and as a British soldier he was shocked by what Rodmell was saying, it was also that he needed to know why he was being told. He looked at Rodmell from the distance provided by the small, round table between them. Rodmell's face revealed nothing. He did not even blink, but rather lowered his eyelids slowly over his grey eyes and raised them again. He has aged, thought Harland again, wishing he could have thought of something more constructive. The two men sat in silence. Harland because he could think of nothing to say and Rodmell because he had, unless Harland forced him to speak, nothing more to say. Harland, therefore, found the silence more uncomfortable than Rodmell did. Rodmell could roll the bubbles of the tonic over his tongue, he could pick the lemon from his glass and, holding it between thumb and forefinger, suck the gin from between the small, leaf-like pieces of fruit, and he could run his tongue around the sour inside of his mouth before saying again, for no other reason than because he had enjoyed the look of disgust on Harland's face, "with the Japanese."

Harland frowned. "Why are you telling me this, Eliot?"

The directness of his question surprised both of them, but Rodmell was nothing if not practised in the art of hiding his true feelings. Although the question was not one that he had been expecting, he managed to fabricate a smile which conveyed to Major Harland his patience and his contempt, this latter feeling being one which Rodmell would have preferred, at least for the time being, not to have revealed.

"I would have thought that was obvious, Major."

"Well, it's not," said Harland. "It's not obvious at all. You can see what a spot it puts me into. I can't know things like this and keep quiet about them, can I? So why have you told me? What is it that you want from me now?"

Had he had more time to reflect, Rodmell might have learnt something of human nature from Harland's insolent outburst, how people under pressure can find a previously hidden courage, but there was no time. On the other hand, he could not just blurt out, To justify myself to myself, Harland, why do you think? Rodmell shook his head.

"Always thinking of number one, aren't you, Harland? Why am I telling you? I would have thought, as I said before, that it were self evident. We all know, don't we, that there is a Japanese Fifth Column here in Hong Kong, and we all know, don't we, that Tang has been using this Fifth Column to sell supplies to the Japanese? So far so good?" And he raised his eyebrows awaiting a response. Harland nodded and wiped a tired hand over his eyes. His brain seemed sluggish and he was still unable to see what Rodmell was getting at. He didn't even know that he cared anymore. Rodmell, exasperated, ordered more drinks and some vestige of their friendship made Harland guzzle down his still half full glass of beer.

"Tell it to me straight, for once, Eliot. Don't play with me. Don't try to make me guess because we both know I'll only get it wrong, all right?"

"Okay, Harland, this is it. You scratch my back and I'll scratch yours."

"How?"

"Quite simple, Harland. Quite simple."

A Chinese waiter brought their drinks to the table and there was a moment's pause. Rodmell watched the Chinese as he poured Harland's beer and then, just before his gin was poured, he wagged a finger.

"Not that one," he said crossly. "Bombay gin." He looked across at Harland and said, before the Chinese had left, "Been drinking here for years. Never drunk Gordon's in my life!"

Harland grunted. Rodmell looked grumpily at the broad, expressionless face of the waiter. The problem was not quite simple at all. Harland had called his bluff and Rodmell was none too sure how to go on.

"If I join the Japanese, I'll find out who's organising the Fifth Column," he blurted out, but it was quite unsatisfactory for both of them. "And turn him over to you and your bods," he added needlessly, for Harland was no longer listening. He was wondering how he was going to tell his wife that Rodmell had cracked up and he was wondering whether he was not just a little pleased that it had happened.

(iii)

Osbourne had been told to write something stirring about the Allied retreat from Dunkirk and had visited Major Harland in the hope that some of the Major's empty jingoism might rub off on him, but Harland had merely puffed out his red cheeks and said, "A miracle, Mr Osbourne. This will be known down the years as the miracle of Dunkirk."

"But why didn't the Germans attack, Major?"

Harland had looked at him emptily and had said, "A good headline, that, for your article: 'The Miracle of Dunkirk'."

In his office, Osbourne copied out the official figures listlessly. "By 4th June," he wrote, "almost 340,000 troops had been landed in England, including some 95,000 allied soldiers. There were only 2,000 losses." Osbourne looked through the window and then back to his notes. "And only 6 days later, Italy entered the war," he wrote. "In North Africa, there are 18,000 British troops as opposed to 300,000

Italians." He stopped writing. "Should've evacuated our boys from Dunkirk and dumped them straight into Libya," he said. "To even things up a bit." But nobody was listening to him. He looked around the office. It was hot, crowded and dirty. A pall of cigarette smoke hung thickly in the middle of the room above the bent and industrious heads of his colleagues. It was depressing. They all seemed to have something to say, something to write about. Maybe, he thought, some of them might even care. Osbourne could not remember the last time he had really cared very much about anything. He decided to go out. He was bored and he was getting nowhere with the 'Miracle of Dunkirk'. As he left, he said good-bye to no one and told no one where he was going. Nobody so much as looked up when he closed the door.

Osbourne walked down Harbour Road and out to the end of Fenwick Pier. He looked in vain for the Colony's four destroyers, although two, he knew, had left for Singapore the other day. Two Naval motor boats bobbed innocently on the wash that was rolling in from a big freighter out in the harbour. "They call them torpedo boats," said Osbourne with a smile. "Supposed to be some gunboats somewhere, too. God knows where they are! And that, it would seem, is the sum total of our sea defences." He brooded pessimistically that in fact they were worse off in Hong Kong than either the soldiers in Dunkirk had been or the soldiers in the North African desert were. "We don't stand a chance," he grunted, "Fortress or no bleeding fortress." And despite his orders he decided he would not write anything about the war. He would do what he always did on the occasions when he did not have a story. He would go down to the Police Station.

Osbourne walked into the main guard room where a single Chinese sat in the middle of the room at a large desk. Behind him a door led off to the cells.

"Who've you got, Chong?" asked Osbourne, nodding towards the cells. "Anything interesting?"

Chong pretended to be writing in a big, leather-bound ledger. He did not like Osbourne, nor did he like the way he referred to the Chinese in his articles. For Osbourne, if they were women they were whores, if they were men they were petty criminals.

"The usual," said Chong without looking up.

Osbourne stared at a poster on the wall to the right of Chong's desk. It was a call, from more than six months ago, for the Chinese to join the Volunteer Defence Corps as drivers and orderlies.

"Rape, armed robbery," said Chong, "And one of your lot—drunk and disorderly."

Osbourne looked away from the poster. "Soldier?" he said. "Should've called the Military Police by now, Chong."

"No," said Chong. "Not a soldier. A civvie. A Doctor Laughton."

Osbourne grinned to himself. There was no story in it, but it gave him a certain pleasure to think of Laughton locked away in one of the stuffy cells of the Police Station.

"He's sleeping it off," said Chong, returning his attention to the ledger.

"Can I see him?" asked Osbourne, adding unnecessarily and untruthfully, "He's a friend."

Chong shrugged.

"Door's not locked."

As he walked along the corridor, curiosity made Osbourne look in turn into each of the cells through the spy-hole in the door. The Chinese prisoners all sat in the corners of the cells hunched down on their heels and looking patiently into the empty middles of the cells. Laughton, on the other hand, was sprawled across the floor on his back, his mouth open, snoring thickly, not through his nose, but in the back of his throat. He looked as though he had not changed his clothes in weeks. Osbourne leaned against the door frame, took off his glasses and began to clean them. He put his glasses back on and lit a cigarette. It gave him a certain satisfaction to see a member of the "Peak-set" brought so ignominiously down to earth. "Serves him right," he said to himself. It was a vindictive thought. There was no reasoning behind his hatred, merely a vague jealousy and a feeling that the world was basically unfair. "Snobs," he grunted, and would have left had Laughton not chosen that moment to come round.

If he was surprised to wake up in a cell of the Police Station, Laughton did not show it. Nor did he show any surprise at the fact that Osbourne was standing in the doorway. He merely pushed himself to his feet, tucked his shirt into his trousers and ran his fingers through his hair.

"Bit of a bender, last night, I fear, Osbourne. And, I think, the night before that, too, come to that. Do you suppose they'll rustle me up a coffee in this place."

"I'll take you over the road for a coffee, Doc," said Osbourne, surprised into generosity by Laughton's unexpected lack of embarrassment. As they walked through the guard room, he actually put an arm around Laughton's shoulder. "Been locked up myself a few times," he confessed. Laughton nodded, but he was not listening.

They had been in the bar for over an hour before Osbourne realised that, other than to request black rather than white coffee, Laughton had said nothing. For his part, Osbourne had been moaning on about his life as a reporter.

"A dog's life, Doc. You're the lowest of the low. You know the saying, 'There's always someone worse off than you are'? Well, you can bet your bottom dollar that that someone is a bleeding reporter."

He had mistaken Laughton's silence for interest until, some time through their second cup of coffee, Laughton had rubbed his hand over his eyes and looked at Osbourne.

"Damnedest thing, you know, Osbourne?" he said.

Osbourne was quickly digesting the fact that his personal tragedies meant absolutely nothing to Laughton and he was wondering how he was going to make good his escape without finding Laughton tagging along behind him for, now that he looked at Laughton a little more closely, he could see that he had the confused and unprotected expression of all drunkards who are surprised by the terrible realisation that they have been suddenly returned to the reality of being sober.

"I swear the place was full of Japanese," said Laughton emptily.

"What place was this, Doc?"

"The Floating City," said Laughton. "I could swear it was full of Japanese."

Osbourne whistled, but not because of the Japanese.

"You been out in the Floating City, Doc? You must be off your trolley. You're bloody lucky to be here to tell me about it. White men aren't looked on kindly there, you should know that. I mean, we don't go. It's not done. Ninety percent of all the casualties of this war have happened out there. Soldiers disappear. It happens all the time. They go off—whoring, gambling, looking for drugs—and they don't come back. It's that simple, Doc. What the hell did you want to go out there for anyway?"

Laughton was wondering whether it was too early in the day to ask for a whisky. Too early not because of what Osbourne, or anyone else, might think of him, but because he didn't want to get himself drunk again until it was dark.

"What?" he said quietly, looking at the rows of different whiskies along the back of the bar. There was also a bottle of yellow liquid with a couple of lizards suspended in it that struck him as being sadly familiar, but he could not remember exactly when he might have drunk it.

"The Floating City, Doc. What the hell were you doing?"

"I don't remember exactly, Osbourne, I must confess. I just seemed to find myself there. I started off down here in The Wanch, I had intended to go to the Parisian Grill and play the piano a bit, but somehow, I don't know, something must have happened. I guess someone took me there."

Osbourne was still shaking his head.

"Anyway, there were Japanese, Osbourne. That barber chap, Kenji, he was there too."

Osbourne shook his head now more vigorously.

"Not Japanese, Doc. That'll have been Tang's men. It's been known for a long time now. Tang is in with the Japs. This Kenji, he's their contact." He puffed himself up a little proudly and sniffed. "Been on the case myself, actually. Even tailed the Nip out there one night. But nothing happened."

Laughton decided finally to have the whisky. He waited until he had taken his first sip before turning to Osbourne.

"They were in uniform, for God's sake, Osbourne! How else do you think I'd have known the difference between them and the Chinese?"

(iv)

Kenji knew that he had begun to behave with less care than he should. There were various reasons for this, all of which he was well aware of. He had grown tired of the whole business of subterfuge. What had started out as an elaborate game, with him pitting his wits against both the British and the Chinese, had been for him such an easy victory that he no longer considered it worth even a minimum of effort. They accepted him for what they thought he was now no matter how he behaved. With the additional help of Willard Russell, he had become, to all intents and purposes, invisible. And then Russell was another cause for his apathy. At the start, he had looked upon Russell as a challenge. The whole Taoism adventure had struck him as a brilliant way of creating the alter ego he so badly needed. With Russell's arrival he had seen the opportunity of making his false mysticism public, just so long as he could manage to convince Russell to go along with him. Only it had all been so easy and now Russell was well on his way either to total madness or to immortality. Only the other day Russell had confided to him that he felt he was "gathering the macrocosmic alchemical agent for the final breakthrough." Then there was the waiting for him and the fighting for his fellow soldiers. It was, perhaps, this aspect that Kenji found hardest to bear. Although they kept informing him of the importance of his job in Hong Kong, there were no visible results. Nothing happened. A small section of the Imperial Army remained across the water whilst the bulk of the troops had pushed their way south into Burma. It was like being posted to some lone outpost on the edge of the Empire, forgotten about and mostly ignored. Whatever he had to say was always going to be overshadowed by some more momentous event. For a while, Kenji had fought against these feelings of inadequacy by being over-zealous in everything he did, thus effectively making himself far more conspicuous than he had been to date, but when he realised that the only person who had taken even the slightest interest in his movements had been that chump of a reporter, Osbourne, he had felt almost offended. Now he was going out to Aberdeen and South Bay to follow up a rumour that artillery had been moved to the south coast of the island as protection against a Japanese sea-borne attack. Again it was a pointless thing to do and more a product of his current mood than a desire for information. He knew the Japanese would not attack from the sea anyway, so it made precious little difference to General Sakai whether or not there were troops there in the first place. He went because, if anyone had been watching him, they would have found it a strange thing for him to be doing. It was with more than a little frustration that he looked at the Pok Fu Lam coast road stretching out emptily behind him in his wing mirror as he drove along.

Willard Russell was studying the 'I-Ching' when Chan arrived. "It says," Russell informed him, "that we should do well to stick with the lowly as that is the only possibility of renewal. Who do you suppose are the lowly in this war, Chan?"

Chan, rather than answer, explained the reason for his visit.

"The Japanese barber has gone."

"What do you mean, he's gone?"

"He's not in the hotel."

"So?"

"We thought you'd know where to find him."

"He'll be back. He's always going off alone these days, but he always comes back."

"Do you know where he is?"

Russell shook his head. There was something about the I-Ching hexagram before him on the table that was bothering him.

"This here, this could mean danger, of course," he said softly, pointing at the first horizontal line.

"There is a meeting," said Chan. "He is supposed to be there."

"If he's supposed to be there, he'll be there," said Russell, and then he added sadly, "He never comes here. Nobody comes here. People say they like me, but they never come, they never visit."

Chan glanced quickly around the dirty apartment. He could hear Ah Chien rattling some plates somewhere in a back room. A sink in the corner was crawling with light brown cockroaches and there was a stain, a long, rusty line down to the plug where the tap was dripping. Russell sat in his wheelchair and looked at the hexagram before him on the table. "It's confusing, isn't it?" he said. Then a flash of light came into his eyes and he looked Chan in the face. "Well, go on, then," he said. "What do you want?"

"The barber," said Chan.

Willard Russell rubbed the palms of his hands together annoyingly slowly. "The barber?" he repeated and waited. Chan could not help noticing that his voice was soft and very kind. "A goat drawing a cart uphill, Chan," he went on, and then he rolled his eyes slowly once and pressed his tongue against the roof of his mouth, sucking breath in through his nose. He stretched the small of his back forwards in the chair and then relaxed back again as though exhausted by the effort. "I can't do it. Not yet. I am not ready." He looked disappointed for a moment and then, "The barber?" he said. "He's a spy."

(v)

Wu's commitments to the Brotherhood and the activities he was forced to carry out for his father had meant that he had to abandon Molly for long periods of time. She had not taken his advice and had made no effort to renew her contact with her father. It was not through stubbornness. It was because she felt, and she wanted to feel, Chinese. She wanted nothing to do with the Westerners and she certainly did not want to be included in an eventual evacuation of the island. Molly had tried to be angry with Wu for not coming to see her, but she just felt hollow and lonely when she thought of him.

For some time now the only person she had seen or spoken to had been Miss Dekyvere. Tung Nien seemed always to be busy or out and Chen Liew rarely left his rooms. They all had their meals separately, Molly alone on the veranda, and there were enough rooms inside the house for all personal contact to be avoided. Molly was lonely and completely isolated. She knew little of the war's progress, only what Miss Dekyvere chose to tell her, which was carefully censored and generally optimistic. However, Miss Dekyvere occasionally forgot that Molly's war was not in Europe.

"The Germans have entered Paris, Molly," she told her, shaking her head at the gravity of the statement. "The Germans have entered Paris."

Molly ran her hand along the top of the gate which separated the gardens.

"If I could just see him, speak to him, it would make me feel better," she said.

Miss Dekyvere was used to the fact that Molly did not always listen. In the end, she felt, it did not matter all that much. They were basically only foils to each other's depression because, although she did not like to admit it, Miss Dekyvere was depressed. The world, as she knew it, was changing and would, she realised, never be the same again. Not that it was, by any stretch of the imagination, a perfect world—it had its faults, and many of them—but she was comfortable in it. She could not, however, see a place for herself in the new world, whatever the outcome of the wars in Europe and across the water. She looked at Molly, sad and desperate in her loneliness, and said the only thing that came into her head, ignoring the fact that it was totally inadequate.

"I would have thought that seeing Wu would make you feel worse, not better."

"That is because you have probably forgotten what it's like."

"I know perfectly well what it's like to miss someone."

"To be in love, I meant."

"Maybe you are right. I am not sure that I have ever been in love."

"You'd know," said Molly confidently. "It fills your whole life. The missing, I mean. When he's not there. It's a huge, aching nervousness that doesn't let you think of anything that isn't him."

Molly leaned on the gate. Miss Dekyvere continued to weed her flower beds.

"Love," said Molly, "if it doesn't die, will kill you in the end. That's why it turns into something else. You wouldn't be able to go on living if you were always in love because it eats you up and gets in the way of everything else. You can't even think of anything that's not him."

Miss Dekyvere looked up from her weeding.

"That sounds to me like what we used to call infatuation. Surely love must be a less selfish and more noble emotion than that?"

"Why should you think that?"

"I suppose I was brought up to think that," Miss Dekyvere admitted. "As I said before, I do not believe that I have had the experience at first hand. Certainly I have felt nothing like you have described."

"Well, I think that is very sad."

Miss Dekyvere stood up and removed her gardening gloves.

"Oh, I don't know about that, dear. From what you have told me, it doesn't sound like an altogether pleasant experience."

Molly swung on the gate.

"It's not all bad," she said. "It's bad because he's not here. If he were here, instead of the emptiness, I'd be filled. The whole world would disappear because we would have no need of it."

Miss Dekyvere shook her head.

"I still say that love should be more generous, Molly. Don't you think it should include, rather than exclude, the world?"

Molly smiled and stepped off the gate. She moved away from the dividing wall and looked down towards the city and the harbour.

"I don't want this world," she said.

Miss Dekyvere would have liked to offer Molly something positive, but she couldn't. "No," she said. "I don't think I want it either."

"But what can we do?" asked Molly, still looking out over the city. "Because we can't change it, can we?"

Miss Dekyvere tried to think how she might have coped had she been Molly, until she realised that she wouldn't. That was why she had turned to God. She had escaped from the senseless destruction of previous wars by sacrificing her own feelings to a conscious exercising of the teachings of God. There had been something a little self-destructive, she realised, in this negation of her self and perhaps, she thought, Molly was right to be selfish.

"No, we can't change it," she said. "And I am sure you are not alone in not wanting it to be as it is. It is, after all, not a particularly nice place at present."

"You haven't answered me," said Molly, turning to look at Miss Dekyvere. "I said: What can we do? We don't want the world, but we can't change it. What can we do? We surely shouldn't just accept things without a fight. I know my mother, and Ah Chien, would tell me that things change only when it is time for them to change, only I don't think I want to believe that anymore. I don't want to be that helpless."

Miss Dekyvere sighed and wished that she had an answer. She could not even think of a reasonable Christian platitude, for the ones that came to mind were nebulous and insubstantial. She would not, for example, tell Molly that God moved in mysterious ways or that all things came to those who waited because she no longer believed that they were true. She knew, from experience, that nothing came if you waited for it.

"We are often helpless, though, unfortunately," she said finally, more to gain time than for any other reason. "But you must understand that you are asking me to have an opinion on a subject for which I am not qualified. You want me to speak of your relationship with Wu." Molly was about to interrupt but Miss Dekyvere raised her hands. "And not only that, but, like all people, you only want me to say what it is you want to hear. You want me to tell you to go and find him; you want me to tell you that everything will be all right. But I can't do that because I believe that when Wu told you that you should go back to your father, when he told you that you should make sure you got evacuated, he was right. It would be highly irresponsible of me to suggest that you do anything which might endanger your life."

Molly shrugged. "What kind of a life am I going to have without him?"

Miss Dekyvere was getting tired. "The same sort of life as the rest of us," she said.

(vi)

The sky was overcast and the evening had a pale, unreal light. Eliot Rodmell adjusted his tie and stepped out onto his veranda with a gin and bitters. He had just finished listening to the translation of a speech by Hitler which had been widely discussed on the BBC *Empire Service*. Hitler had spoken of the British Empire. He had said that it was necessary for the British Empire to exist. The British Empire and the Catholic Church, Hitler had said, were both essential elements for maintaining stability in the world. That was all very well, thought Rodmell, but then Hitler had spoken of the Colonies. They were, in Hitler's opinion, mainly a question of prestige. They could never be held in a war.

"Never be held in a war," Rodmell repeated to himself. "He's right, of course," he said over his shoulder. Margaret Rodmell came out of the house to stand beside her husband. Rodmell turned to face her. He took her hands in his and looked down at them, vaguely surprised by his own gesture of affection. "You'll have to go, you know?" he said quietly. "When they evacuate, you'll have to go."

"Where do you suppose they'll send us?" asked Margaret Rodmell, although she found it difficult to believe that it might really happen. Rodmell shrugged and released the embarrassment of her hands.

"I don't know. Singapore? Nearest safe place I'd've thought. If things get really sticky, Australia."

"But they won't, dear, will they?"

"They might still manage to patch it up in Europe," Rodmell admitted, "but not here. This," he said, waving his glass over the lights of the city, "this has finished. It stands to reason. The Japanese can't very well leave us here, can they? No matter what Mr Hitler might think of the qualities of the British Empire. I mean, we're in the way, Margaret. Quite simply, we're in the way."

"I'd like to see them try to shift us," said Margaret Rodmell, who had to have something in which to believe.

"Don't tell me Hong Kong is a fortress, Margaret, because it isn't true. It's a rock, nothing more, stuck out in the middle of the sea. But it is not being defended. Half a dozen decrepit aircraft, a handful of boats—you can't even call them ships—a line of poorly manned pill boxes and a small army cut off from its supply lines before it even starts fighting. It would be ludicrous to even think of defending the island. It would be a massacre. Hitler is right, you see, Margaret. The Colonies can never be held. In the event of an all out war, I doubt very much that London would even bother to try."

Rodmell's pessimism helped to strengthen his resolve as to the rightness of his decision both with regard to sending his wife away and with regard to, at least superficially, supporting the Japanese. The meeting with his rivals, Tung Nien and Tang, had been scheduled for that evening. It was the third time he had been summoned. The first two meetings had come to nothing due to the fact that, on each occasion, Kenji had failed to show up. The meetings with the Chinese had been a new experience for Rodmell because he had realised from the outset that they had no respect for him whatsoever. The Chinese had neither said nor shown anything. Tang had spent the whole time fiddling with a thong on his sandals and emitting little grunts and Tung Nien had placed herself behind the Red Pole, Chan, and looked down her nose at them both as though she did not consider them even worthy of her attention. Being, as he was, used to the undivided attention of everyone in his presence, it had been disconcerting for Rodmell. It had been an experience that he had not liked and would not, if he could avoid it, repeat.

"I don't think you'll find Winston Churchill such a ... such a dope as Chamberlain, Eliot. Churchill won't abandon us to our fate."

"Oh, shut up, Margaret!" Rodmell snapped.

Margaret Rodmell felt an unusual impatience with her husband's attitude. "Well, he won't, Eliot," she insisted, then almost pleading, "He can't!"

Eliot Rodmell sipped his gin. It would sometimes have been more comfortable, he thought, if his wife could have been slightly less dependent upon him. Sometimes he had enough with his own thoughts.

"Let's face it, Margaret," he said softly, not wanting now an argument, "Neither you nor I have the remotest idea what Churchill may or may not do. We can only presume. And there's no point in arguing over presumptions."

He turned away from her. He would have preferred to have told her to quite simply shut up. In fact, it was with some concern that he realised that he had done precisely that and she had persisted in her ridiculous affirmation that Churchill was going to somehow defend them. When the shit hits the fan, Margaret, he would have liked to have said, Guess who, for one, is not going to get spattered? And that, too, disturbed him. The fact that his nerves were such that he would actually have liked to upset his wife's still carefully ordered world, would have liked to see it come crashing down about her ears. But she was talking to him. He watched her thin lips moving as she spoke.

"Because we're not cattle, Eliot," she was saying.

So he had to say it.

"In a war, Margaret, much as you might like to think otherwise, that's about the best thing you can hope to be. Better than, for example, a number. A list. A statistic."

Seeing that she had every intention of continuing, Eliot Rodmell thrust his empty glass towards her.

"Another, I think," he said.

Margaret Rodmell looked at the empty glass and struggled with a feeling of frustration which was new to her. She squeezed her fingers round the glass but could formulate no words to voice the frustration she felt. So she looked at her fingers and she looked at the glass.

"I think that, while you're out, Mary might drop in."

It was the nastiest thing she could think of to say for Eliot Rodmell could not approve of the Laughtons. And before he had a chance to reply, she went to the kitchen for his drink.

(vii)

It was with a rare admission that beneath his passive exterior there existed a sense of humour that Kenji had chosen Possession Street as the site for their third attempt at a meeting. Possession Street was said to be the place, as far as it was possible to judge with any certainty, where the British had formally annexed Hong Kong in 1841. Kenji arrived for the meeting early and, instead of going to the bar he had picked out for their rendezvous—he had chosen the kind of place none of his three guests would ever have dreamed of visiting under normal circumstances because he wanted them to know how much he despised them—he ducked into a street perpendicular and a little to the north of Possession Street. The fact that he despised Rodmell, Tung Nien and Tang, and the fact that he wanted them to know it, had been the principal reason behind his failure to show up for the previous meetings. He was reminding them that he didn't need them, it was they who required something of him. But it was not only that. It was also the fact that everything was too easy for him. He did not know the precise substance of what he was to be offered, but he knew why. And when he later reported back to General Sakai that he had obtained the co-operation of two of the most important Triad gangs in Hong Kong he would be praised although he had done nothing. Rodmell's presence had no more significance for Kenji than to enforce his belief that the English were an inferior and cowardly race. He could not see what Rodmell could offer that they would not eventually take from him anyway.

Kenji walked slowly along Wing Hok Street, looking into the shops which sold dried herbs and tea, and he walked past a man who sat out in the street carving Mah-jongg tiles. He breathed in the prickly smells of snake musk, powdered lizards and ginseng and he watched the man skilfully working over the block of ivory. All along the street, people were going about their lives as they had always done, either unaware, or refusing to recognise, that a terrible future lay just around the corner. With the Germans' advance through France and then the Armistice, the British had finally realised that they were not invincible and that their world was crumbling, but the Chinese seemed to behave as though it were all happening to someone else. Which, of course, it is, said Kenji to himself. At that moment, even so, he could not reconcile himself to the apparent normality of the street before him. He felt that they, the Japanese, deserved more respect, more fear even.

Kenji looked at his watch. He still had over half an hour to kill before the meeting and so he turned, instead of to his right, to his left and down to the Macao Ferry Terminal. Looking at the mainland had become, he realised, the only way he had of feeling a part of the fighting. He spent long hours of every day looking across the harbour towards Kowloon, the New Territories and an imagined China trying to think himself into uniform. Trying, too, to imagine what it was like to be hacking a path through the thick, mosquito-infested forests and jungles of Burma. Two British soldiers walked down to the waterfront to his right. They had been drinking and they were slightly unsteady on their feet.

With no regard for where he was or for who might have been watching, one of the soldiers undid his fly and began to urinate against the back wall of the ferry terminal. As he did so, the other one spat between his feet and sniffed.

"Fucking French!" said the urinating soldier.

"Fucking right!" said the other.

"Fucking bastards!" said the first, and he hitched his trousers back into place. Seeing Kenji watching him, he turned and called out loudly, "What you looking at, Chink?"

Kenji turned his eyes back to the water. He could still hear the soldiers as they staggered back towards the city.

"Forty fucking days! 'S'all it took, you know, once the Krauts got stuck in. Forty fucking days!"

"Fucking Frogs!"

Kenji had arranged for a table and four chairs to be placed behind a carved walnut screen at the back of the bar. He was sitting at the table before any of the others had arrived. That morning, in the barber's shop, Willard Russell had come along with his morning's I-Ching pronouncement: "The superior man keeps the inferior man at a distance, not angrily but with reserve." And now, as Kenji sat waiting, the sentence came back to him. "The superior man keeps the inferior man at a distance by being as reserved and as inaccessible as heaven." Kenji smiled to himself and ordered a pot of tea. To think that Willard Russell was, from his madness, in a position to give him advice; albeit unknowingly. Russell had, in fact, been providing his own explanation for the retreat from Dunkirk. "A timely retreat, Kenji, chosen by the strong, not forced by the weak." Kenji had decided not to point out that this was not entirely true, that the retreat had certainly been forced by the Germans. "As reserved and inaccessible as heaven," he repeated to himself as he poured a cup of green tea.

Kenji was not surprised that Eliot Rodmell was the first to arrive. He would have been disappointed had anything happened to upset the notion of British punctuality and punctiliousness. Kenji watched him through the slats in the carving of the walnut blind. Rodmell looked with disbelief into the dim, dusty bar, the expression on his face a mixture of disgust and puzzlement. He raised a long, knobbly finger in an effort to attract the bar-tender's attention and having failed, he turned and looked back into the street.

"He's frightened, too," said Kenji realising, and the thought gave him no pleasure, nor did it provoke any feeling of sympathy. "I have only to hate them," he said to himself.

Rodmell wondered for a moment whether he had come to the right place, although he knew he had. He wondered, however, whether he should not step back out into the street to double-check. An old shop-keeper, who was carefully weighing out a yellow powder in a set of brass, hand-held scales, grinned at him with toothless gums. Rodmell scowled and looked the other way to see the unmistakable, boxed shape of Chen Liew's Bentley nosing its way along the narrow street. On a sudden impulse, Rodmell moved away from the doorway of the bar. He pushed past the man weighing out the yellow powder and stepped into the shop selling herbs and spices. He realised his hands were sweating.

Tung Nien's entrance to the bar could not have been more different than Rodmell's. Ignoring the bar-tender, she walked directly towards the walnut screen, Chan one pace behind her at her shoulder. As he watched her approach, Kenji enjoyed her beauty despite himself, as he might have enjoyed a magnificent view. You might be forgiven for thinking, he said to himself, that her sole purpose in life is to be admired. But then she spoke, and her voice was cold and lacking in emotion.

"So, finally, you have come," she said, aborting Kenji's attempt at a welcome.

Kenji smiled.

"I've had better things to do," he said indifferently. "Tea?"

Tung Nien looked at the small china pot and empty cup on the table. A shallow green puddle had been sloshed into the saucer. She shook her head, but the movement was almost imperceptible.

"You have come a long way from the walled city," Kenji said, timing the comment with Rodmell's arrival, not for Rodmell's benefit, but to prevent her from answering. It was not a comment to which he required an answer.

"Well," Rodmell was saying, "I found it! Not, I might say, without a little difficulty!" And he placed a small, strong-smelling, brown paper bag before him on the table. "Spices," he felt the need to explain, "For Margaret." He was immediately annoyed with himself and sat back heavily in his chair, clasped his hands behind his head, and smiled at each of them in turn. Kenji returned his smile, but Tung Nien looked at him as though he wasn't there.

"Tea?" asked Kenji, nodding towards the pot.

Rodmell laughed through his nose, a snort more than a laugh.

"I think a gin!"

When Tang arrived, they were sitting in silence, Kenji sipping his tea, Rodmell sipping his gin, and Tung Nien sipping at a deep-rooted hatred for both the British and the Japanese which gave to her expression the smallest of sneers although it was not quite sufficient to mar her beauty.

Tang was a fat man. Somehow, thought Eliot Rodmell, the fact that he was Chinese seemed to make his face even wider and fatter. We, he thought, tend, first, to expand in other places. And, ignoring the slight spreading of his stomach, he raised two fingers gingerly to the loose folds of his double chin. Whereas they ... And he allowed the thought to sputter and die. He could not afford to bother himself with trivialities.

Tang lowered himself into one of the chairs and, refusing Kenji's offer of tea, ordered his Red Pole to get him his own individual pot.

Should've brought my own bodyguard, thought Rodmell, smiling at the thought of Michael Robinson at his shoulder. "Robinson! Another gin!" He grinned. It was all too theatrical. But dangerous, too.

Kenji leaned his elbows onto the table and looked at each one of them slowly.

"There is no need for us to introduce ourselves. There is no need for us even to be pleasant. We all know why we are here. Each of you wishes to offer something to the Imperial Japanese Army. All I have to offer in return is a vague promise. That you will not be killed. But I cannot guarantee even that."

He looked at his hands, moved his fingers slightly, then clasped them together. He did not mind hating them but he did not like the feeling of power it gave him to be on the winning side.

"Tang," he said, "I know well. We have been doing business successfully for some two years or more. I know he can be trusted to keep his word; but only until it no longer interests him to do so. I know, too, that some of the merchandise sold to us came from Rodmell's, Mr Rodmell's," he corrected himself, "warehouses, but I am sure you will easily be able to understand that I, we, cared little about the origin of the material. Indeed, a little internal confusion would never be out of place. Tang, of course, was unaware of the fact that I knew he was using our sporadic bombing attacks to raid Mr Rodmell's warehouses." And he sat back and sighed. "Despite the fact that I made sure that he should know the exact time and place of each attack."

He looked at the table for a long time before he raised his eyes to look at Tang.

"As you can all see, I owe the Tangs nothing. Quite the reverse. I am anxious to know what it is he has to offer me."

Tang looked inscrutably and fatly back across the table. He did not even blink.

"And Rodmell," said Kenji, and his voice was tired. "What of Rodmell?"

Eliot Rodmell did not want to, but he shifted uneasily in his chair. Kenji raised the palms of his hands to them.

"Eliot Rodmell," he said slowly, then again corrected himself, although this time he managed to make it sound more sarcastic than the first time, "Mr Eliot Rodmell has spent the war supplying the Communist Chinese with supplies, with arms and food bought, if you please, from the Japanese!"

He swallowed slowly, raised his hand and asked for another pot of tea. "Then bring the chicken and rice," Kenji said. He paused for a moment before continuing. "Of course, Mr Rodmell is British! We cannot blame him for his actions. Quite the contrary, he should be praised. But," and he rubbed his eyes, although Rodmell could not help thinking it was too much of a gesture to be real, "What does Mr Rodmell possibly imagine he has to offer the Imperial Japanese Army in return for his life?"

The phrase "in return for his life" made the hairs on Rodmell's neck stand on end. It was suddenly no longer a game. This was the real thing. Gone were the times when he could gesture away the life of some coolie or other as if of no worth. The life at stake was his. So many times in the past, he had dispensed with other peoples' futures and he had not given it a second thought, but he had never been on the receiving end. Not even at school, when, although a typical bully, he had seen enough cruelty to last him a lifetime. His mind began to race. In return for his life.

And Kenji looked at Tung Nien. Tung Nien looked at Kenji without blinking.

"So," said Kenji, "We come to our little whore."

Chan stepped forwards but Tung Nien raised her hand.

"Let him speak first, Chan," she said, "There will always be time later."

Kenji smiled.

"You don't understand, do you? None of you. There is no time anymore. There will be no time for anything."

Eliot Rodmell suddenly prodded his finger at the Japanese.

"I'll tell Harland," he said. "You are finished. Coming here like this! Threatening!"

Kenji raised his hands again.

"You do not seem to understand, Mr Rodmell. This Hong Kong, the Hong Kong as you know it, is finished, with or without me. I am insignificant. You get rid of me and you get rid of your only chance of getting out of all this alive. I am many things, but I am not stupid."

Rodmell saw that he was the only one of them that was reacting at all to the Japanese and he decided to bite his tongue, although a nerve at the corner of his eye continued to twitch uncontrollably.

"Whore," said Tung Nien flatly, and it was more of a recognition than a question.

"I know," said Kenji. "Prostitution can take on many guises. It is not only physical. I, too, have been guilty of selling myself. We all know this. But you can only get away with it, you see, if you win. That makes all the difference. So long as you win, the way in which you do so is unimportant."

"I won," said Tung Nien coldly.

"The game has not finished," said Kenji.

"It is a different game," said Tung Nien.

Kenji nodded, but he said, "What is this different game? Surely that is why we are here tonight?"

The bar-tender shuffled towards them with a steaming clay dish of chicken and then returned with a second dish of rice. Kenji picked up a pair of chop sticks and began to pick over the chicken, placing the small, succulent, round pieces of breast on one side, and pushing the more bony meat to the edge of the dish. Only Eliot Rodmell failed to notice the care Kenji was taking with the chicken, because only Eliot Rodmell was unaware of its significance. When Kenji picked out the chicken breast for him, he smiled. But so did Tung Nien and Tang. He looked at the rounded pieces of flesh and his mouth watered. Eliot Rodmell was also given the speciality, chicken's feet, for which he could not feel so grateful. Watching Kenji serving the food, both Tung Nien and Tang were aware that Kenji was telling them that Eliot Rodmell was effectively being dismissed and was not going to form part of any eventual agreement, for they both knew that if a *lo ban*, a boss, offered his *foki*, or assistant, the most succulent pieces of food it meant that he was being treated as a guest and not as a member of the family, and that he would soon be out of a job. For whatever reason, Kenji had already decided to do without Rodmell, who, unaware of this fact, had already begun to eat greedily.

Kenji, by contrast, picked disinterestedly at his food, turning the small pieces of chicken over and over in the sticky brown sauce before abandoning them at the side of his plate in favour of rice.

Neither Tang nor Tung Nien seemed likely to speak and Eliot Rodmell was too engrossed in the business of feeding, so, finally, Kenji sat back a little from the table and said, "We are interested to know what it is you think you have to offer that might interest the Imperial Japanese Army."

The Chinese did not consult. They did not need to for they had done so already.

"Information," said Tang.

"And infrastructure," said Tung Nien.

Rodmell, his mouth full, said nothing, although he had thought of neither of these things. His consideration had been more economically based. In his pompous belief in his own importance, he had vaguely imagined that by just being Eliot Rodmell it would be sufficient. He had expected to be given a task or two with which to curry favour, but he had quite honestly not thought the matter through.

"And in return?" Kenji was saying, though he had not said that he was interested.

"The smallest of favours," said Tung Nien. "One which is, for you, the Japanese, basically insignificant. But which could be very important for us."

"You make the British files, the Police records, on the Triad Brotherhoods in Hong Kong disappear," said Tang.

"Bomb them. Burn them. Whatever," said Tung Nien.

Kenji glanced at Rodmell, but the Taipan must already have sensed that he was superfluous, for he had stopped eating and was looking emptily at the centre of the table.

(viii)

It annoyed Rodmell that, under the circumstances, his wife could be painting a water colour and it annoyed him, if anything, still more, that she was doing it so badly. For the umpteenth time, she was painting the view from their veranda, the long drop down to the harbour and the boats on the water. Rather than see a fresh simplicity in his wife's painting, Rodmell saw only that the colours and the perspective were wrong. He could not accept that what she painted looked nothing like what he could see, and so he said, a gruff rebuke for the sake of it, "Why do you bother, Margaret?"

Rodmell's mood had been such since his meeting with the Chinese and Kenji that his wife knew better than to respond. Not knowing the cause of her husband's bad temper, Margaret Rodmell put it down to the war, although she suspected it was something more personal. She waited, then, for him to say something else, because she knew he would. Rodmell allowed himself to be disgusted a while longer by his wife's frivolous painting and then he walked away, moving a little closer towards the offending scene. There were very few ships in the harbour and none of them were his. And what was worse, none were expected to arrive in the near future. He still felt grossly insulted by the way in which the Chinese had left him out, although he could see the logic in it. They would share out his businesses and interests between the two of them once the Japanese had arrived. He had to admit that if the shoe had been on the other foot he would have done the same, but that did not help to make matters any more palatable. His only hope, then, was for the British, the Allies, to win.

"They've bombed London, Margaret," he said finally turning back to face his wife. "Harland told me this morning."

Margaret Rodmell looked up at him from the concentration of her painting.

"What was that, dear?"

"I said, Margaret, that they've bombed London. The Germans," he added, in case there should be any doubt. "Three hundred civilians killed, over a thousand seriously injured. They bombed during the day, and then they used the flaming buildings as beacons for a night attack. From eight o'clock in the evening until five in the morning, Margaret."

She noticed that he sounded enormously tired and she got up and put her hand on his arm.

"What did they say on the wireless, Eliot"

"I beg your pardon?"

"The wireless, Eliot. Have they said anything on the wireless?"

"How the hell should I know, Margaret? I haven't listened to the damned wireless for days!" And he shrugged her hand away. He did not want her comfort, or anyone else's, for that matter. His whole world was disappearing, going up in the smoke of London's burning buildings, and she painted water colours and asked him if he'd listened to the wireless. Of course he hadn't listened to the damned wireless!

Margaret was speaking to him, but Eliot Rodmell was not listening. He was craning his neck in an effort to see the long, low, red roof of Tung Nien's mansion a little below his garden on the Peak. He did not even notice that he no longer thought of it as belonging to Chen Liew. The mere fact that he lived just a little higher up the mountainside than she did gave him a momentary twinge of satisfaction. "The bitch!" he hissed to himself. All he could think of was the way she had looked at him in the bar. As though he were nothing. Come to that, they all had. But she was a woman. That was what hurt him more than anything else.

The Chinese, he could stomach—just! But that a woman should have treated him with such derision, with such a lack of consideration for his position in Hong Kong society! But, at least, for the time being, he still lived a hundred feet higher up than she did.

"I'm going to see Harland," he said suddenly, without looking at her or expecting her to respond, so that when she said, "But we have the Harlands, the Fosters, the Laughtons, Ruth Dekyvere, too, for dinner." He could say freely, without listening to what she had said, but hearing only the Fosters and the Laughtons, "Damn them!"

(ix)

"You're not coming, then, Alfred?" Mary asked with a sigh of resignation.

"No, Mary, I'm not coming. I don't like any of them. Can't you get that into your head? Rodmell is a prig, Foster a poor old fool and Harland's a soldier who actually believes that by being a soldier he is doing the rest of us a service. Of course I'm not coming. I have nothing to say to them."

"I sometimes wonder if you have anything to say to anybody, Alfred."

Laughton was silent, hurt more by the truth of the remark than by the fact that his wife had realised.

"That's not entirely fair, Mary, is it?" he defended himself, because he had always done so, not because he cared.

"I don't see how you can say that. If you do come out with me, which is rarely, you sit about sulking. You never say anything, unless it is to make fun of someone, usually me. Nobody laughs, you know that, don't you? They think, as I do, that it is pathetic, pitiful."

"Thank you, Mary."

Laughton reached for a bottle of whisky and a clean glass.

"And why you have to drink, now, when you know I dislike it, I can't think, especially because, as soon as my back is turned, both you and I know that you'll skulk off to wherever it is you go in the evening and you'll get yourself completely inebriated."

"The word is drunk, Mary. Get myself drunk, you mean. What the hell do you expect me to do?"

"I expect you to be civil, Alfred, at least. Although I realise that it is well nigh impossible."

"Boring, you mean."

"Oh, Alfred! Stop being childish!"

"Anyway, what does it matter? You'll be gone before long. I hear Harland's pushing through this evacuation business. You won't have to put up with me for very much longer."

Mary Laughton would have loved to say "Good riddance!" But there was still a part of her that loved him, a very small part, it is true, but, for all that, a part of her. "Do try to be less objectionable, Alfred. I don't ask anything else of you." I wouldn't dare, she thought to herself, turning away.

"I sometimes think," said Alfred Laughton, pouring himself a glass of whisky anyway, "That you only ask anything of me at all so that you can complain about it when I do it badly."

When she had gone, Alfred Laughton sat for some time with his glass of whisky without drinking. He could not help but think that he had never been nasty to Mary until he had met Tung Nien. He found he resented everything about Mary which was unlike Tung Nien. Tung Nien had freed herself of clothing almost as soon as she had seen him, whereas Mary held to it as though she were still trying to shield something from him. With Tung Nien, he had talked. Of nothing and everything. With Mary, he seldom crossed a word unless it was in anger. And yet he had forced Tung Nien out of his life. "I cannot make love to a murderer," he had said, wanting more than anything else to do just that. But he had managed to feel almost happy in his self-inflicted misery because he was still able to cherish the illusion that even if he told her to go, she wouldn't. Until pushed up into a sudden sunny glare of reality, in a paralysis of alcohol induced inertia, Laughton realised that he seemed always to be only one step away from Hell, and because she was hurt, she needed to hurt him too and so she had said, "I didn't kill it. You did." And the distance between them was suddenly greater than the space between their bodies.

Laughton had watched her leave, unable to believe that their love would not survive the deep silence which had invaded the room and separated his life off from hers as surely as if she had died. She had looked back at him for a moment before the door had closed, and her eyes had pleaded with him one last time, but his need to be angry persisted and turned him away and closed him like a book that has already been read. And Tung Nien knew as she left that to try to forget him, to leave the book where it was to gather dust, she would have to sink into another story, one that would fill those hours she used to use to think about him. And now, with Tung Nien gone, Laughton made unreasonable demands on his wife which she had no chance of fulfilling. And even now as he realised, with his whisky, that it was unfair, he still disliked her for going, or perhaps, for preferring to go, rather than wanting to stay with him and his misery. And yet he no longer had anything to offer her, he knew that. And this, too, he resented. After all, if she had stayed, all they would have done would have been go to bed in silence, each with a book to read and a separate bedside table lamp to turn out when they had had enough. There would have been no communication anyway, so she might just as well be with the Rodmells, Harlands, and Fosters. At least she felt at home there. He wondered whether he ever had. And hoped fervently that he had not.

Sitting with Osbourne in a bar in the Wanch later in the evening, he looked up from his third whisky and said, "You ever been married, Osbourne?"

Osbourne was waiting patiently for Laughton to get himself drunk, for Laughton had promised to take him out to the Floating City to where he had seen the Japanese soldiers and Laughton had sworn that if he was sober he would not know which way to go. "It's a sort of memory loss, Osbourne," he had said. "I can't remember what I do when I'm drunk, until I'm drunk again. When I'm sober, it's all a blank. If I don't get a skinful, there's no way I'll find my way back through those bloody sampans."

"No," said Osbourne, "I've never been married."

"Good boy!" said Laughton. "Best keep it that way!"

Osbourne blinked at him from behind his smudgy glasses. "You what?" he said.

"Keep it that way, Osbourne. What you want to get married for?"

"So as I can get a fuck every night, Laughton, why do you think?"

"Ah, yes," said Laughton. "Why else?"

"Look, Laughton, we don't have to speak to each other, you know? We don't have to like each other. The only reason I am here is for you to take me out to where you saw them Japs, alright? There isn't anything else. No friendship. No nothing, okay? For me, it's a job, nothing else."

Christ! thought Laughton, with a bleary grin, snubbed even by the despicable Harry Osbourne!

"All right, Harold," he said. "Have it your own way. I do not need to speak to anyone. I find my own company, anyway, preferable to that of most people. Although, I understand that you might find that hard to believe."

"Bloody right!" said Osbourne, but beneath his breath.

"I have sometimes wanted to be able to enjoy the mundane, Harold, but I have just not ever managed to be able to. It has always been, you see, mundane. Like my marriage, and every marriage I have ever seen. I could even say every relationship."

"You're just a miserable sod, Laughton, that's all. It's got fuck all to do with the mundane or any other bloody thing. You're just the most miserable fucker I've ever had the misfortune to meet. Myself included. And that's saying something."

Osbourne looked grumpily through the dirty windows of the bar. The sunset was beginning to colour the tops of the buildings on the other side of the road and the shopkeepers began to move their wares further into the street to make the most of the remaining rays of sunlight. Their side of the street, he noticed, was caught in darkness already. There was a damp, pungent smell in the air, like bleach. Laughton said it was a fruit and named it, but Osbourne was not listening to him. He was thinking how strange he had found the smells when he had first arrived. There were so many different smells and none of them were pleasant. Osbourne sniffed thickly, thankful that his nose was almost always full of cold. Even so the pungent, bleachy smell prickled in his nostrils.

"What is that smell, Laughton?" he grunted.

"I told you."

"No, it's not a fruit. It's a chemical. I'm sure it's a chemical of some kind. You should know, being a doctor, and all that."

"It's a fruit, Osbourne. It just smells like a chemical."

Osbourne continued to look into the street. There were more people now, most of them Chinese and all of them shopping. A small group of uniformed Punjabi soldiers had gathered outside the bar and they were peering into the room towards Osbourne through the dusty window.

"That smell," said Osbourne, watching the Indian soldiers, "Given as how we're so far away from anywhere, I wouldn't be surprised if they haven't started trying to make explosives or something." He looked away from the window and across the table at Laughton. "I mean, you need chemicals for explosives, don't you?"

"But you don't need fruit, Osbourne."

"Fuck you!" said Osbourne. And he took off his glasses and began to polish them on the ragged cuff of his shirt. "Fuck you, Doctor fucking Laughton!"

Alfred Laughton drained the whisky from his glass but made no sign of moving. Osbourne waited, watching him. He moved the ashtray a little on the table and rubbed his fingers down the side of his chair. "Well," he said, pushing slightly away from the table, "We going, then, or what?"

Laughton shook his head.

"All in good time, Osbourne," said Laughton quietly. He did not want to go. He was not even sure if he knew where to go. He did not want to be with Osbourne. He did not want to be in Hong Kong. Or anywhere else, for that matter. He felt completely emptied of emotions and yet, at the same time, all his emotions seemed to be about to erupt at the slightest provocation. He looked blankly across the table at Osbourne, at his smudgy glasses and weasel face, and he said, "It's a fucking circus, isn't it, Osbourne?"

Osbourne grunted. "Are we going or not, Laughton? If we're not going, I've got better things to do than to sit here watching you get yourself pissed. I can go and get pissed myself for a start. Not only that, I can do it with someone I like being with."

Laughton raised his hands. "I'm only going back as a favour to you, Osbourne, so don't get on your high horse with me, all right? I have no interest in the fucking Japanese. They could come waltzing down Queensway right now, for all I care. So, we'll go, when I'm ready, not just because you're bored, just because you've got better things to do. And," he added quietly, "I'm not getting pissed. Not yet, anyway."

"Bully for you!" said Osbourne to himself.

It was almost half past ten when they finally left the bar. As they walked along beside the harbour, Laughton stopped to rest every few minutes. Each time he stopped, he lit a cigarette and then, seeming to think better of it, flicked it after a few drags towards the murky water of the sea. Then he would glance behind them up towards the heights and lights of The Peak with a lost, empty expression on his face before pushing himself once more into motion. Although he showed many of the symptoms, Osbourne decided that he was not drunk. He was, he realised, just very, very unhappy. "Still," he thought to himself, so as to dismiss any stirrings of sympathy, "Who's not been unhappy at some time or another? We all get over it."

As Osbourne tagged along at Laughton's shoulder, the realisation came to him quite suddenly that it was not that there was no danger in going to the Floating City, it was that Laughton didn't care any more. About anything. He would have walked into a regiment of Japanese or German soldiers with the same ease and nonchalance with which he was about to take him into the Floating City. It wasn't that there was no danger in what they were doing, it was simply that Laughton didn't care.

This thought began to worry Osbourne as they boarded the Star

Ferry to cross the bay to Kowloon and Yau Ma Tai. Osbourne looked at the ferry, *The Night Star*, chucking against the quay and Laughton walked slowly over to the small ticket office. "It's still not too late," he said to himself. "You must be out of your mind. Going out into the Floating City with a complete nutcase! In search of a bunch of imagined Japanese soldiers! Just turn around and go home!"

But Laughton was returning, a dreamy smile upon his face.

"He says we'll not get a ferry back if we spend too long there, so I told him we'd walk." And he smiled. "Never mind," he said. "The ticket seller didn't see the joke either."

Osbourne hated Kowloon at the best of times. To spend the whole night there with Laughton was almost more than he could stomach. He was just about to step forward, to put his hand in as friendly a way as he could manage on Laughton's shoulder and say, "I think I'll call it a day, Doc," when Laughton pushed him gently in the back and said, "Let's go, then."

For Osbourne, the seven minute crossing seemed to last hours. He spent the whole time looking at the back of Laughton's head where the parting in his hair stopped in a tight whorl. Laughton spent the crossing smoking and looking into the water. Neither of them spoke. There were, Osbourne noticed, only half a dozen other people on the ferry and all of them seemed to be on the lower deck in second class. He had had no chance of checking their nationality but automatically made them Chinese. Nobody else, he thought, would be stupid enough to be out at that time of night. As they approached the other side of the harbour, Osbourne could see the shape of the Victorian clock tower at the railway station dark against the night sky. "Damn it!" he hissed to himself.

Laughton gave Osbourne a gentle prod on the arm and said, "I know a great little place just down here. Full of caged birds and old men. Ever felt like a caged bird, Osbourne? Can't say I have, but I just wondered. It sounds like it should be the title for a book, don't you think?"

"It sounds like what?"

"Nothing, Osbourne. It doesn't sound like anything. But it's a great place for a tipple."

Several drinks later, with the Floating City of Yau Ma Tai spread out across the water before them, thick and impenetrable, the sampans moored tightly together and darker than the water and the night, Laughton and Osbourne stood on the quay and waited, Osbourne for Laughton to make a move, and Laughton for no other reason than the fact that he enjoyed listening to the sucking noise of the water against the sides of the boats and because the moon was caught behind a thin tissue of cloud and looked, he thought, much as the earth might if seen from outer space. Bright, clean and free from sin.

Way out on the water a dog was barking as Osbourne and Laughton picked their way across the sampans. It was, thought Osbourne, like stepping along the window sill of someone's front room. If you looked anywhere but straight ahead, your eyes fell upon some intimacy or another, a mother breast feeding her child, an old woman squatting over a wok frying rice, a man urinating into the water. The sampans were jammed so tightly together that they formed a floating causeway over which Osbourne and Laughton continued slowly to pick their way.

"You got any idea where you're going?" Osbourne called out after they had been walking for about five minutes. Laughton stopped and leaned against the green awning which formed the roof of the sampan to his right. He pointed past the boats and out to sea.

"Out there," he said. "I remember I'd nearly got to the end."

Osbourne peered into the darkness beyond Laughton's pointing finger. He knew he did not want to go on, but he did not know how to say it. Since they had stepped out onto the Floating City they had come face to face with no one and Osbourne was certain that they were being followed by men on either side a couple of rows of sampans away. He pulled a packet of cigarettes from his pocket, took one, and offered Laughton the crushed box.

"You reckon we're being followed, Doc?" he asked, smoking intently. He turned the cigarette in his hand and looked at the lighted end, blowing on it to make it glow more brightly, and then he glanced nervously across the boats behind him.

"Sure to be, Osbourne. I was the last time. All the way out."

"What'd they do to you? They say anything?"

"I don't remember, Osbourne."

"Why did you come? What the hell did you want to come out here for?"

Osbourne smoked the cigarette until the butt had almost burned down to his fingers.

"I came for a smoke. Opium, Osbourne. And I think I might also have had a little cuddle with a prostitute. You see, there comes a time when you need a little extra stimulus, when the life you are living has become so damned pointless that you will do anything just to give it some direction."

"What, like downwards?" said Osbourne, surprising himself with the witticism. Laughton lit a second cigarette from the butt of the first.

"Sometimes it's better to be going anywhere at all rather than to be stagnating."

Osbourne knew a lot about stagnation. He sometimes felt he had done nothing but stagnate since he had arrived in the Far East. Laughton had begun to move off again and Osbourne sensed a shadow move away to their left.

"Laughton!" he called out, his voice faltering slightly. "I reckon I might just be heading back."

Laughton turned to face him and Osbourne laughed, a short nervous snort.

"Fuck the Japs, eh, Doc? Be seeing plenty of them soon enough anyway, eh?"

Laughton raised his hand and waved vaguely.

"Suit yourself, Osbourne."

And he turned back towards the sea.

"Aren't you coming with me?" Osbourne called out more loudly than he had intended and a face poked out of one of the sampans up ahead and scowled at him.

"I might as well go on now that I'm here, Osbourne."

"What for, Doc? Come on back and I'll stand you a beer at The

Pen. Come on!" Osbourne was almost whining. Laughton waved his hand again and continued picking his way through the sampans.

"Need something a bit stronger than beer, Osbourne."

As Osbourne watched Laughton's tall shadow moving away, three smaller shadows closed in behind him and followed him out across the water. Osbourne turned unsteadily as the sampans rocked and he looked back towards the lights of Kowloon. It looked much further away than he had imagined. Something moved behind him and some hot fat cracked in a pan. Osbourne bunched his hands into fists and felt his heart pumping thickly, the blood chugging through his wrists. There were shadows wherever he looked.

"God get me out of here in one piece!" he hissed, and the sampan to his right began rocking rhythmically on the water. Osbourne could see the quay and the street lamps, lighted despite the official blackout. He could see a small group of soldiers hunched together and smoking. He could even read the illuminated shop signs, but none of them seemed to be getting any nearer. Something was still moving behind him and, not wanting to, Osbourne turned to look. He needed to know whether or not he was being followed. The only movement was the rocking sampan where Osbourne could now make out knees and naked buttocks in the moonlight. He scabbed his shin against a piece of metal and rubbed a splinter into the palm of his hand before he managed to struggle back onto dry land.

Breathing heavily, Osbourne stood on the quay and looked back out over the dark mass of boats. Although nothing had actually happened, Osbourne had the feeling that he had been released, that at any moment he could have been swallowed up and would have disappeared without trace. All the stories he had heard about the Floating City took on a new, more vivid and believable meaning. Soldiers going off with whores and never coming back, the stories of the mafias and crime squads, the doctors, the alchemists, the schools, some even said there was a Buddhist temple and a brotherhood of monks, the betting shops and opium dens all out there bobbing interminably on the greasy water. Osbourne, having been there, albeit briefly, could now believe it. He stood on the quay looking out over the dull grey of the tarpaulin roofs of the sampans, mile after mile of them, so many that it was almost impossible to see where they finished and the sea began. He breathed deeply, for once forgetting to complain about the foetid smells of the city of Kowloon.

"That Laughton," he said to himself, "wants his fucking head examined. He's got a bloody death-wish, he has."

He could hear a dog barking far out across the water, maybe the same one as before, and closer to the quay, the clacking of mah-jongg tiles.

"Well, fuck him!" he said. "I've got better things to do with my time. I don't need to get myself scared shitless to get my kicks." And he looked at his watch, wondering whether he could get back to the Glory Hole in time for a beer.

(x)

"And he just walked off, Fletch, happy as you like, into the depths of the Floating City. The man's a lunatic." Osbourne looked round the other crowded tables in the Glory Hole. He sipped slowly at a bottle of Tiger beer. "Been gone now nigh on two days."

Fletcher whistled. "You want to think yourself lucky, then, Harry."

Osbourne shook his head. "Luck's got nowt to do with it, Fletch. I was so shit-scared I wouldn't have gone on if you'd paid me."

"And you let Laughton go?" Fletcher asked a little accusingly. "Why didn't you do something to stop him?"

Osbourne shrugged. "What do you think I was going to do? Bring him back by force? Anyway, the man's old enough to do what the hell he likes. After all, it's not my fault if has problems at home, or whatever, is it?"

"The wife knows, of course?" Fletcher asked, his voice changing accusation for sympathy.

"Does she care, more like!" snorted Osbourne through his beer.

"Ah, don't be like that, Harry. Bound to be worried, isn't she?"

"I've heard say she's asked old Rodmell to help out. Pull a few strings. Use his contacts. You know the kind of thing."

"Well, I guess that's better than doing nothing," Sergeant Fletcher nodded slowly, but Osbourne jabbed his finger at him from across the table.

"You want to know what I think, Fletch? I think the poor sod's dead. Probably been dead these last two days. Not much Rodmell's going to do about that. I doubt if they'll even find the body." He shook his head slowly and looked for a moment at the table as if collecting his thoughts. "No, Fletch," he said. "That Laughton, the sharks'll've had him by now, you mark my words."

Osbourne sat back in his chair and clasped his hands behind his head. A thick, spicy smell of cooking wafted out to them from one of the back rooms together with the spitting of hot fat. The Glory Hole was stuffy and hot and full of soldiers. All around the square wooden balustrade of the first floor, the soldiers leaned, their bare arms around the tiny waists of the taxi-girls. The girls tried not to, but looked bored. The bright colours of their scanty clothes stood out against the dull khaki of the soldiers' uniforms. Osbourne looked slowly round the faces gawping down at them from the interior balcony, the white painted, China-doll faces of the taxi-girls and the ruddy, unshaven roughness of the soldiers. Osbourne and Fletcher sat smoking in silence. It seemed as though they had nothing left to say to each other. Fletcher stared across the table at Osbourne and Osbourne stared up at the balcony of soldiers and taxi-girls until finally, peering at Osbourne through the smoky, yellow light, Fletcher made the only offer he had.

"How about a game of crib, Harry?"

Osbourne was still looking beerily at the balcony, then he snapped his eyes away and focussed them on Fletcher's sallow face. He shook his head and thumped his fist on the table as though he had taken a momentous decision.

"Bugger crib, Fletch!" he said, grinning now and removing and stowing his glasses in the breast pocket of his creased linen jacket. "I'm going to see if I can't get one of them young girls yonder to tickle my fancy a bit. Christ! It's months since I've been laid!"

And he stood up, scraping his chair across the floor.

(xi)

"Are you sure there's nothing you can do to help, Eliot? Mary is beside herself with worry. I know you don't think much of poor old Alfred,"—Rodmell grunted his agreement—"but he is going through a difficult time at the moment."

Rodmell bent slightly to sniff at a frangipani flower. "He knew what he was letting himself in for when he went out there, Margaret. And besides which, it's very much a Chinese stronghold, the Floating City. I doubt very much that I could do anything even if I wanted to."

"Which you obviously don't."

"I didn't say that, Margaret."

"No, you didn't say that, Eliot, but I know the way your mind works. As there is nothing in it for you, what's the point in even trying?"

And so, against his better judgement, Eliot Rodmell was walking down from his office to the Victoria Barracks to see Major Harland. Everything is unreal with this damned war, he said to himself. Life used to be something you could count on to run its course. There was an order and a way of doing things. Nobody overstepped the mark. They all knew their individual limitations and they abided by the unspoken rules of their little closed society. But now everything had suddenly been turned on its head. The Chinese were gradually pushing him out of business, an upstart Japanese barber was telling him how he should live his life and, here he was, walking down Connaught Street, a bloody messenger boy!

Eliot Rodmell scowled and pushed his way along the crowded street. He neither heard nor saw anything as he strode along. He did not hear the hard tapping of the craftsmen's metal hammers nor did he hear the soft moaning of the monks drifting out from the temples. His pale grey eyes registered nothing but were looking towards somewhere in the future where everything would fall back into place again.

At the barracks he marched straight past the taut sentry and strode diagonally across the parade ground in the direction of Major Harland's office. Fortunately there were no soldiers drilling, for it would have meant nothing to Eliot Rodmell in his present mood and he would have barged straight through them regardless. When he knocked on the door he was hot and flustered and the sweat had plastered his shirt to the small of his back. Harland was less than welcoming.

"I'm pretty busy, Eliot, right now."

Rodmell glanced towards the disordered papers on Harland's desk where a fountain pen with the top off was serving as a paper weight.

"There've been all sorts of rumours," Harland explained vaguely.

Rodmell pulled out a chair and sat down anyway.

"Look, Harland," he said, "Don't go running away with the idea that I want to be here. Mary asked me to come. Seems there's this bod's got himself into queer street. You know Laughton? Seems he was last seen walking out into the Floating City."

"The doctor?" said Harland, unable to think of a more appropriate comment.

"The same," snapped Rodmell.

Harland stifled a yawn.

"And what do you think I can do about it, Eliot?"

"I don't know. It's Margaret. She's made it plain that she thinks I don't care about old Laughton. Which is, of course, basically true. But she's asked me. Practically begged me to do something." Rodmell felt uncomfortable, but he had to go on. "I just thought, you know, if we knew who was in control there, we might just be able to speak to them."

Harland raised his eyebrows doubtfully, so Rodmell had to continue.

"I might, I mean, be able to speak to them. At least find out what's happened."

A bugle rang out from the other side of the empty parade ground and Harland pushed himself bad-temperedly to his feet.

"What the hell are they doing now?" he moaned and walked across to the window. Troops were forming up in squads, their boots scuffling noisily on the tarmac. "We get this all bloody morning," said Harland looking across at Rodmell as though he might have been somehow to blame. "All bloody morning," he said again, settling himself once more behind the defences of the papers on his desk. He leaned forwards and put the top onto his fountain pen and the fountain pen into his breast pocket. He shook his head slowly as he squeezed the brass button through the tight button-hole. "Not even the District Watch Force hold any sway out there, Eliot. It's the jungle. No! It's worse even than that!" Major Harland could not find the words to explain. "I don't know that anyone really controls things, as such. Maybe Tang? It's the sort of place he'd feel at home."

The rhythmic tramping of the soldiers' boots caught their attention and both men looked towards the window.

"It's hell, this waiting for something to happen, isn't it, Eliot?" Major Harland puffed out his cheeks and raised his eyebrows again. He began to tap his fingers on the desktop and to fidget slightly within the confines of his tight uniform. We seem to have drifted apart, thought Harland a little reluctantly. That is, if we were ever really close. We did use to speak, to converse, at least, to talk. Now, the paradox is that, although nothing is happening, everything seems to be changing, to be moving too quickly, slipping from our hands and our control. And we have drifted apart.

Rodmell sat on in Harland's office, listening as the tramping of boots faded to be replaced by the moaning grumble of the city, the trams and cars and human sounds, the hum of dehumanised activity, mingled with the strident noises of the insects. Harland was looking vacantly at his papers.

"Tang!" said Rodmell suddenly. "And so, what the hell am I going to say to Mary? I can't ask Tang for favours, damn it!"

Harland actually felt sorry for the great man as he watched him leave, this time skirting the parade ground, his hands in his pockets and his head hanging slightly.

(xii)

Laughton lay back in a pool of mud coloured water in the bottom of a sampan. He was trying to enjoy the soft rocking motion of the boat on the water, but it was impossible. His head was thick. It felt like it had been packed with cotton wool. Although he had eaten nothing for two days, he realised that he did not feel hungry. He knew that if he ate anything, he would throw it straight back up again. He lay, trying to pick out the constellations from the stars and he wondered vaguely why he was alone. There had been two girls with him the last time he had been awake, before his last pipe of opium. But then they had given him something foul to drink and that was when he had passed out. It had been that bloody stuff with the salamanders in it that had done for him again. He tried to lift his head but it thumped back against the wooden side of the sampan.

Laughton looked at the stars and tried to collect his thoughts. Then he looked away from the stars and down towards his feet. At the end of the sampan, two rats were feeding on a small pile of leaves that looked like cabbage. Laughton kicked out one of his feet, but the rats hardly moved. They stopped eating for a moment, looked at him with their cranberry eyes, and then continued to tear at the cabbage leaves, which Laughton saw now was, in fact, the tattered sleeve of a green jacket. He closed his eyes, and tried to imagine what it might be like to be an animal where everything you did was governed by instinct and stimuli. No planning ahead, no regrets. No enormous sense of loss such as he felt now that Tung Nien had gone. Just to go through life responding to some inner law, with no need to make excuses when you failed. Of course, he had known from the start that he would never have a future with Tung Nien, but that had not stopped him loving her and it did not make it any the less painful now that it was over. All he wanted now, he realised, was just some more time with her. Not to say or do anything new, but to repeat all the things he had said and done one more time. Just to think of her sat naked astride him, her hair falling over her face, her small gasps of pleasure when he moved, the intake of breath which caught in the back of her throat, the way her legs had trembled and shivered, made his whole body ache with a longing to do it all again.

Laughton finally found the co-ordination necessary to push himself into a semi-seated position. He realised then that at his back the waters spread out into the harbour and from there to the open sea. The Floating City was not yet awake. It was a dark mass of curved tarpaulin roofs of different heights and sizes rocking on the gentle wash of the soft waves. There were no lights on and no movement anywhere. The only sound was the chucking of the waves against the sampans and the sampans against the sampans. The rats continued to gnaw through the green sleeve. Laughton closed his eyes and drifted off to sleep, pushing himself onto his side and gently up and between Tung Nien's welcoming thighs.

He was woken by the sound of talking. Opening his eyes, for a moment he was lost. Then it all came back to him and he glanced down towards his feet and the end of the sampan. Instead of the rats, three shadows occupied the end of the boat. Laughton could not make out their features, he could see only that one was smaller than the others. They were speaking together in Chinese. Laughton raised his hands in what he thought might be interpreted as an international sign of submission when the smallest of the shadows spoke to him.

"Mao!" the voice was one which Laughton had not heard for some time but still recognised. "You get yourself in pretty deep waters. These men want to kill you. I told them it was not a good idea."

"Wu," said Laughton thickly. "What are you doing here?"

Wu stepped forward and offered Laughton his hand.

"I came to find you," said Wu Tang simply. "Tung Nien, she asked my father for you to be saved."

8

"Be not sad. Be as the sun at midday"

(i)

Most of the European women and children had been evacuated and the evacuation had been accompanied by the expected protests from the Chinese and Indian population. Eliot Rodmell had felt an obligatory pang of regret as he had watched his wife packing, had felt slightly sorry for himself as he had stood with Harland and the others on the quay to wave their white handkerchiefs at the grey anonymity of the ship as it steamed and pulled at its moorings like a huge animal anxious to be away, and then, when he arrived home and poured himself a drink, he had felt quite relieved to find himself alone after so many years. At first, he had missed the space that had, until recently, been filled by his wife but, before long, it had become filled by other things: at dinner time, music, usually Elgar, and usually the Cello Concerto, on an old phonograph that had belonged to his father and, at night, by a selfish delight in having the bed to himself and in being able to stretch his long legs out without her telling him to move. The times of day when he most missed her were breakfast, when there was no one to share the news in *The Post*, and when he arrived home from work and opened the door and the house was empty, when there was no one to talk to and no one to fetch him a drink. Then he would sit grumpily on the veranda listening to the news on the Empire Service and wish there was somebody there, not necessarily Margaret, to listen to his opinions on how the war was going. And so, given that they were both alone, it seemed natural, even though they had hardly spoken for some time, for him to invite Major Harland up for a sundowner.

When he arrived, Harland was flushed and sweating, his face pink and shining. He was led out to the veranda by Rodmell's amah, Ah Ping, and he already had a pewter tankard of shandy in his hand.

"You've heard of course," said Rodmell, without turning around, without a word of greeting and without taking his eyes from the illuminated dial of the wireless.

"What's that, Eliot?" asked Harland, gulping the froth from his shandy and blinking.

"The Germans, under Rommel, have pushed us out of Cyrenaica. Ten days! That's all it took them. Ten bloody days! I mean, what is going on, Harland? Are we so outnumbered down there, or what? Is it incompetence?"

"I hardly think incompetence, Eliot." Major Harland was quite shocked at the idea. "General Wavell, whilst admittedly a little eccentric,"—Harland was thinking of a dispatch from Wavell which had spoken only about the beauty of the Spring flowers in the desert—"is one of our best Generals." But Rodmell had not finished.

"They push us out of Greece in under three weeks," he grumbled, "and then this! Ten days! I mean, Harland, what are we supposed to think? If it's not incompetence, be so good as to tell me what the hell it is!"

Major Harland was, unlike Rodmell, missing the company of his wife dreadfully. The war was depressing him and he was beginning to feel too small for his responsibilities in Hong Kong. He did not like being hated, and he knew now that he was. He had even received several unpleasant letters from various influential Indian families that he had previously counted amongst his friends. And now Rodmell was adding to his depression by his bombastic condemnation of their army.

"Just remember," he said sadly, "There are people dying out there. It's all very well to moan on using figures like 'ten days' and 'three weeks', but what about 'two thousand'" he swallowed, and then added, "casualties?"

"Oh, Christ, Harland!" Rodmell sipped his gin. "Of course there will be casualties. It's a damned war, isn't it?"

Major Harland placed his pewter tankard down on the flat surface of the stone veranda wall. "You know what really bothers me about all this, Eliot?" he said slowly and he turned to rest his back and his hands on the veranda, looking past Rodmell and into the empty house. Rodmell shook his head but said nothing. Harland recovered his tankard and finished his shandy before speaking.

"Well," he said slowly, "The way I see it, by pumping troops into North Africa, Churchill is neglecting the Far East. Nobody seems to be concerned about the Japanese at all. And yet there is an acute danger here, Eliot. Nobody thinks any more that the Japanese are going to stop at Burma. I mean, they've virtually taken over the whole of Indo-China already. And yet we have only a pitiful number of soldiers out here in the Far East. When the time comes, we are not going to be able to put up much of a show at all, I'm afraid. And when they do send troops it'll probably be too late."

Rodmell had never before heard the Major criticise, or doubt, the wisdom of his superiors. It was, therefore, a significant step, although whether forwards or backwards, it was difficult to say. The evidence was now so heavily weighted against them that not even the Major, despite his blind faith in the accuracy and the rightness of the information he received, could ignore it. Rodmell stepped towards the Major and placed his hand on his shoulder. He would have squeezed it, exerted some friendly and reassuring pressure, but such closeness, such an expression of affection, was beyond him. Major Harland felt the weight of Rodmell's hand on his shoulder but felt no comfort and no warmth. He brushed it away.

"I think I'll have another of these," he said quietly, looking into the empty tankard and through its glass bottom spattered with the spent froth of his beer at the stone floor of the veranda.

"You should have something stronger, Harland," said Rodmell, although he realised he did not care very much what the Major had. There was a gap between them, an inability to understand each other's needs, despite the necessity of being together that had been brought about by their individual loneliness. There was nothing they could say to each other, nothing they could do, to breach the emptiness that was both between and around them. They would continue on, as separate and as untouchable as they would have been if they had never met, never even known each other. For I do know him, thought Rodmell, I know exactly what he thinks and feels. I am just not interested any more in knowing it.

(ii)

Dr Alfred Laughton was enjoying being alone. He was enjoying the freedom it gave him to be utterly selfish, to do exactly as he pleased, to come home when he wanted, eat when, where and what he wanted, drink what and how much he wanted and go to bed, not with who he wanted, but with whoever he could find and afford. Sometimes, there was an Australian nurse, too. He was still smoking opium when he could get it, although it had become more difficult to find. And when he couldn't get opium, he would drink, not to forget but because he couldn't forget, because it made the abandoned landscape of his life more bearable, allowed him to embrace his fluid sadness with something akin to pleasure. It was a sadness which fed on emptiness and alcohol and it surrounded him as completely as a warehouse. When Tung Nien had had him rescued from the Floating City, an irrational hope had surged up within him that he might still be allowed to enjoy that time he yearned for. He had stupidly even tried to visit her, to, just to say thank you at least, but he had been turned away at the gate and he had been forced to accept that he did not mean to her what she unfortunately still meant to him. That night, when he had been turned away from her house, he had gone to the geomancer's, thinking maybe she had been unable to see him, but that she would know where he had gone and that she would go to see him there. But he had waited in vain, pacing backwards and forwards across the room, until he had found the empty bottle of Usher's Green Stripe on the floor beneath the bed. He had taken the bottle and smashed it against the wall before lying on the hard bunk and smoking himself into oblivion. But even then, even when he was virtually unconscious, he could not hate her. She just grew more and more beautiful in his mind, more and more exactly what he needed to drag himself back into some semblance of life.

Driven on by a desire to numb his mind, to keep it as much as possible away from Tung Nien, Laughton had begun to wander down to the Parisian Grill most nights to play the piano and he had become something of a celebrity. Unlike drink and opium, which seemed to him to somehow heighten his sensibilities and feeling of despair, the piano lulled him into a blank and unfeeling apathy. People actually went there to hear him play. It was the first time in his life that he had been anything like the centre of attention and he did not like it. He found it embarrassing because he did not deserve it. He was merely playing for himself, to keep himself, momentarily, from slipping away. As he looked out at the people from behind the lid of the piano, he felt more isolated than ever. He could not understand any of them. He could not understand why they were there.

Until one evening Miss Dekyvere stepped up onto the small raised stage and spoke to him.

"I had to come, Alfred," she said, "Because they told me you played so beautifully. But stop now and have a drink with me."

Alfred Laughton stopped playing and rubbed the fingers of one hand with the other.

"When I'm playing, I don't drink," he said, although it was not true.

"To keep me company, at least," suggested Miss Dekyvere. "Besides which, you look so sad sat up here alone."

"You haven't come to save me, have you?" he asked, "Again?"

Miss Dekyvere smiled. "I have never, Alfred, I hope, done anything with an ulterior motive. I came because I wanted to hear you play. And now I have. I would certainly never dream of trying to save you. From what, mind you, I cannot imagine. That you could not save yourself from, that is."

They stepped down together from the stage and walked slowly to a small, round table in a shadowed corner of the bar. On the table there were already two glasses. A whisky and soda and a sweet sherry.

"Because I don't think I want to be saved this time," said Laughton.

"Then don't be, dear," said Miss Dekyvere. She sipped her sherry. "Did you learn at school?"

"What? The piano? Yes."

Laughton was not sure that he wanted to be sociable. He glanced around the room, at the blank faces of the other drinkers. Or maybe he just thought they were blank, for now that he looked closer he saw that they were smiling and laughing and enjoying themselves.

"How come you're still here?" he asked, turning back to face Miss Dekyvere. "I mean, how did you escape the evacuation?"

Miss Dekyvere laughed. "Escape!" she said. "Tung Nien. She spoke to someone. You see, I didn't want to go. I have no reason to go and nowhere to go to."

"Who has?" said Laughton morosely.

"What's that, dear?"

"Who has got anywhere to go to?"

"Quite so, Alfred. Although, if you want my opinion that's rather a stupid thing to say."

Alfred Laughton thought for a moment before replying. And when he did reply, because Miss Dekyvere was right and because he wanted to know, he spoke of something else.

"How is she?" he asked.

Miss Dekyvere smiled a little sadly.

"She's fine," she said. "But you should never have become involved, Alfred."

"I know that."

Some men were dancing with a few Chinese girls on the dance floor, a thing unheard of in the past. But a lot of things have changed since the evacuation of the women and children, thought Laughton. "And Molly?" he asked. "Did she go or stay?"

"What do you think, Alfred?"

Laughton nodded and finished his drink so as to be able to leave but "Another?" Miss Dekyvere asked. Laughton nodded. He had never managed to refuse a free drink.

"Why not?" he said. "I've got nothing else I have to do."

Miss Dekyvere twirled the stem of her sherry glass between her fingers and watched the dark liquid until it settled again.

"Why do you try to be so objectionable, Alfred? I'm sure there's no need for it. In fact, I'm sure you don't really want to be so."

"It's not something I think an awful lot about, Miss Dekyvere."

"Well, Alfred," she said. "I think perhaps you should."

"It's all such a mess, though, isn't it?"

"You're not going to be like the others, surely, and blame the war, are you?"

Laughton took his second whisky and soda from the waiter's tray and looked again at the men and the Chinese girls dancing.

"It's as good an excuse as any," he said.

Miss Dekyvere sighed. "Whatever you say, Alfred," she said. "However, how many of the people who are being bombed in London, night after night, are doing what you're doing?"

Laughton put his glass back on the table.

"Have you come here to lecture me?"

"No. I came here to hear you play the piano. And I must say that it is quite extraordinary that such a bitter person can produce such beautiful sounds."

"I didn't write the music. I just played it."

Miss Dekyvere wondered whether or not to leave and Dr Laughton stared emptily at the dance floor giving her no reason to stay. Miss Dekyvere stood up.

"I'm sorry, Alfred," she said.

Laughton looked at her as though noticing her presence for the first time, but he had already drunk too much and could not make the effort to be sociable. He tipped the edge of his glass towards her.

"Don't be sorry for me, Miss Dekyvere," he said. "I'm not worth it."

She nodded. "I believe you're right at that."

It was not what Laughton had expected to hear and he found suddenly that he was laughing. But it was a hollow sound without humour. A kind of hopeless misery relieved only by the sound itself. Miss Dekyvere looked again at Laughton. It was, she thought, as though he was outside it, outside of life, unable to join in, forever on the edge and watching. She wondered whether he even wanted to be a part of it. Probably not, she decided.

"I think I shall go home now," Miss Dekyvere said quietly, and she walked away without turning back to wave.

Laughton watched her leave, a small, frail, old woman pushing her way through the strong arms of soldiers who ignored her passing. "And she came to help you, you know," he said to himself. "Possibly the only person in Hong Kong that you know and could still call a friend, and you sent her away." He glanced back over towards the piano, shining black and grand on its raised platform, but he could no longer summon the energy to even dredge up a tune, let alone play.

When he left the hotel he saw that half the island had observed the black-out whilst the other half, notably the houses up on The Peak and the tight streets of Wanchai where the soldiers would still be drinking, was lit up like an advertisement, almost like a last futile attempt to show the Japanese across the water that the British Empire was not only alive and well but was living it up and having one last, long party. He could hear the soft groaning propellers of an aeroplane flying somewhere out over Kowloon and he looked back across the harbour to see if he could locate its lights in the dark expanse of the sky. Following the sound of throbbing engines he finally spotted the blinking red tail-lights way out over the sea off the coast of Stonecutters Island.

Standing at the terminus waiting for a tram to take him back up to the cold isolation of his bungalow he tried to convince himself that there would be something he could do when he got there, other than to drink until he fell asleep, curled up uncomfortably in one of the rattan armchairs of the front room. He lit a cigarette and looked blankly along the street. It was late but there were still a lot of people about. The number of people made him feel more tethered to his loneliness than before. He had a kind of lunging urge to take the tram past his bungalow and further up The Peak a couple of stops, to walk then down the steep road to Tung Nien's villa. But he knew there was nothing there for him except for the glorious memory of Tung Nien's kisses and naked, welcoming body which he knew so well but would never see again.

Once on the tram, he was pleased to find that he was the only passenger. As he looked from the window over the dark, blacked-out section of the city, where the paper the colour and texture of bats' wings had been pinned over the window panes, it seemed to him a faithful reflection of the emptiness of his life. Where, just beyond and out of reach, everything was happening. The necklace of lights lining the harbour along the waterfront at The Wanch. As the tram was pulled up the steep hillside past the rich villas where some of the houses were doused into a papery dullness and some of them were blazing, Laughton gazed down at the lights of Wanchai. "There's nothing there for you, either," he grunted to himself, but he could not pull his eyes away from the imagined excitement and living. "Going home, then, to an empty house. An empty bed. Nothing to do, no one to speak to." Although smoking was not allowed on the tram, he lit another cigarette.

He wondered whether he had always been so out of things. Self-sufficiency, he would have called it, although he knew it was not that. But we are all alone, he said aloud as he got off the tram, the cliché pleasing him. He looked around the station, for a moment lost. Too high on The Peak, and without realising.

Laughton stood in the street beneath the dark, shiny leaves of a magnolia tree and he stood there quietly smoking. He realised that whilst he wasn't drunk, neither was he exactly sober. He was talking aloud to himself, conversing, providing the two sides of a banal conversation, a sure sign that he had crossed over the invisible line which changed his behaviour, made him feel reckless and irresponsible, happy, as far as he ever felt happy these days, and, most importantly, free. His feet scuffed a little on the tarmac as he began to walk down the hill in the direction of his bungalow, but also towards Tung Nien's villa. He continued to talk to himself as he turned a tight corner in the road and left the lights of the funicular station behind him.

—Which way would you have me go?

—She won't want to see you so there's no point filling your head with empty illusions.

—I'm not even going to look, still less stop.

—I bet you do.

—You can bet what you like, I'm not stopping.

He was silent for a moment until a thought struck him. It filled him with a feeling which was very close to panic. He could not remember whether he had anything left to drink in the house.

—You could stop off and ask her to lend you a bottle.

—I don't need it.

—I should think not. You've had too much already. Still, it would be a good excuse.

—Miss Dekyvere might, though.

—Might have, had you not been so rude to her.

—Anyway, she'd only have sherry and I don't need it.

Laughton looked at the end of his cigarette and then flicked it away to the side of the path. And then suddenly, as he walked off, he was singing.

Eliot Rodmell heard the singing before he saw him. He was standing in the street outside the gates to his long, looping drive because he had just that minute dispatched a very drunk Major Harland, sent him back to the Victoria Barracks, to mull over what Harland himself had termed: what was left of their future. Rodmell, too, had had too much to drink and his evening with Major Harland, far from being the relief from boredom he had hoped for, had left him depressed. Eliot Rodmell, to stave off the moment of being alone, would probably have invited anyone into his house for a night-cap. The fact that the singer turned out to be someone he knew, despite the fact that it was someone he did not like, made his invitation sound even more heartfelt.

"What a surprise, Doctor!" he said, gripping Laughton's shoulders between his two strong but puffy hands. Had it not been for the lingering doubt as to the state of his drinks cabinet, and more especially, his decanter of whisky, Laughton would have shuffled off the older man's false enthusiasm. As it was, he smiled, nodded, and said, "Yes, I suppose so."

"And what brings you out so late and so high up on The Peak?"

It was the lack of respect, the complete lack of interest which Laughton could sense in Rodmell's voice which made him say it.

"My lover."

"Well!" Rodmell blew out his cheeks and struggled to find a response. He stepped back a little from Laughton, began to look him up and down, thought better of it and looked once at the wall before looking back at Laughton and saying, "Well, indeed! When the cat's away, and all that, what, Alfred?"

Laughton shook his head.

"The mice have been playing for quite some time, Eliot. The cat, you see, has long been blind. Well, not blind exactly. Rather, it has had better things to do. Than to bother itself with this particular mouse."

As he looked at Rodmell's red, blotchy face, Laughton wondered what made him do it. Why did he say such stupid things? He always regretted it afterwards. Sometimes immediately, and sometimes when it came back to him later through a haze of disjointed memories.

"Things to do, eh?" said Rodmell without interest. Then he hurried on. "Look, Laughton, I know it's late, and all that, but why not come in for a night-cap?" He looked at Laughton expectantly before admitting, "I get so damned lonely without Margaret, you know?"

Laughton would never, under normal circumstances, have agreed, but his head was already half-filled with drink and at home his decanter was empty.

"Civil of you, Eliot," he said. "Don't mind if I do. After all, what else is there for us to do at the moment?" And he wobbled forwards slightly, crashing an elbow into the old man's bony chest. Rodmell winced and pushed Laughton away from him brusquely.

Both men were uncomfortable as they walked back up to the house. Rodmell because, despite the yawning emptiness of the night which lay before them, he regretted having made the invitation and Laughton because, despite his lack of whisky, he regretted having accepted. Habit forced Rodmell to point out his wife's flower beds with a wide sweep of his hand through the darkness.

"Still flowering despite her absence, Laughton."

Laughton could see that the Great Man himself was not faring quite so well as the flower beds and had indeed begun to wither and to dry up in the absence of his wife's care and attention. Even his shirt cuffs and collar were grubby and his tie had been released at some earlier time in the evening and re-tied into a ridiculously tight knot at the height of his left nipple. A shabbiness unheard of in the past.

"It's all falling to bits," said Laughton beneath his breath.

"It's whisky, isn't it?" asked Rodmell as they sat down. Laughton nodded. Rodmell opened a walnut cabinet and brought two cut glass tumblers across to the elaborate set of four interlocking tables that he had placed between them. Each table was slightly smaller than the next and slipped neatly beneath it. The tops of the tables were inlaid with ivory.

"How're things down at the hospital?" asked Rodmell sitting and crossing his long legs. Before Laughton could answer, he unfolded his legs again and sat forwards, rubbing his hand across his eyes and pressing his thumbs at the same time into his temples. "Damn it, Laughton! Don't answer that. I'm not, as it were, in the slightest bit interested. Bloody Harland's been here all night, belly-aching about the war. It's got me a bit on edge, that's all. He says the rest of the world's forgotten about us."

Laughton sighed, but Rodmell scarcely noticed.

"And then the Chinese are ruining me, Laughton. This goes on much longer and I'll have nothing left."

"They've ruined me already, Eliot," grunted Laughton, pleased with the way it sounded.

"Quite so, Laughton."

Rodmell reached for his gin and splashed a couple of drops of Angostura's Bitters into the glass. He swirled the mixture together, turning the glass between his two hands.

"Do you like Elgar?" he asked suddenly and, without waiting for a reply, stood up, cranked his phonograph into movement, put a record on and sat again opposite Laughton.

"The Cello Concerto," he informed him as the first depressing notes struggled over the crackling of the stylus. "Been playing it all the time of late. Can't think why. Margaret, you see, hates it."

"Just different ways of escape, Eliot."

"What's that?"

"Different ways of escape. Drink, women, drugs. Music."

Rodmell began to wave his head from side to side in time with the music and he closed his eyes as the orchestra joined in with the cello and then stopped.

"Ruining me," he said again, and the cello played a long low note as if to give a sinister importance to the statement. "You know what they've done, don't you?"

Laughton shook his head and looked round the room. It was strange that it was already obvious that a man lived there alone. Newspapers had been left untidily about the floor near a big, comfortable armchair. There were two empty glasses, probably the remains of Rodmell's earlier binge with Harland, on the table where the newspapers should have been put. And in a corner of the room, over by the veranda, two pairs of shoes and a shooting stick.

"They've made an agreement with the Japanese and they've pushed me out. Pushed me out of my own business!"

"What? Smuggling?" Laughton could not resist saying it, but he could have said anything, for Rodmell was not listening.

"I've got nothing left, Laughton. All gone. It's all at a standstill. Still selling a few bits and pieces to the British Army, thanks mainly to Harland. But not enough to keep body and soul together. They've banned the entrance of all merchant ships into the harbour. Can't get any new supplies in, you see? Much needed stuff, come to that, and not only for the Army, for us too."

There was a long silence during which Rodmell seemed to be debating with himself as to the wisdom of continuing, debating with himself between his need just to talk and the fact that the person he was talking to was Laughton. But it was Laughton's voice which brought him back to the present and decided for him.

"Who has made an agreement with the Japanese?"

"The Chinese, Laughton. I told you."

"Yes, I know. Which Chinese?"

"The Hong Kong Chinese. The Triads," said Rodmell gravely. "Tang and Tung Nien, to be more precise."

Laughton leaned back on the sofa and looked at the fan in the centre of the ceiling. The Triads. He did not really know whether or not he was surprised, because had he been more observant, he would have realised before. But to have it now spelt out for him made him feel both frightened and exhilarated. It was, he knew, a childish feeling, but the impossibility of the affair, the fact that it should never have been allowed to happen, added to Tung Nien's beauty and his desire to speak of it. He also felt childishly grateful, now, to Tung Nien that, rather than have him killed, she had had him rescued. "So, she must feel something," he murmured to himself.

Rodmell looked at Laughton, his mouth hanging slightly open, and he wished he hadn't said anything. But Laughton looked back at him, his eyebrows raised questioningly. It seemed to Rodmell that the ponderous silence was in danger of becoming awkward and his pale eyes sought to embrace a sign of simple friendship in Laughton which would allow him to change the subject away from his recent humiliation. But Laughton's stare was as unmoving and insolent as a schoolboy's. Rodmell sighed heavily and looked at the nasty red blotches on the backs of his hands. "They spurned me, you know?" he said. He was seemingly unaware that his previous statement had had any affect on Laughton and he realised suddenly that in fact he needed desperately just to speak about it to someone. "Them and that upstart of a barber! And what can you offer in return for your life? That's what he asked me. In return for your life! Can you imagine, Laughton?"

Laughton could not, but was suddenly trying very hard to. If he had known of Tung Nien's connection with the Triads, he knew he would never have touched her. It was far too dangerous. Nor was he out of danger now, he realised.

"In return for your life, eh, Eliot?" he tried to make light of it. "A bit melodramatic, don't you think?" But his mind was racing over images of the victims he had treated in the hospital, hundreds of violent deaths, seemingly pointless, but always the Triads. He was thinking of the stories he had heard of indiscriminate killings, blackmail, drugs and torture. Life which not more than an hour previously had seemed little more than a tribulation to be seen through to the end was suddenly very, very precious and as fragile as the glass he was holding tightly in his hands.

Rodmell had ignored his comment. He was speaking more to himself than he was to Laughton. Laughton was necessary only in as much as he was a focal point for his thoughts. He neither expected, nor wanted, a response. Laughton, whilst unable to protect him from the violence of the Triads or the Kempei, would shield him from the immense emptiness of being alone and of having to lie in bed, his head swimming and his ears straining for the crunch of gravel as footsteps came for him in the night.

"But of course it won't come to that," said Rodmell bringing the gin and whisky across to the tables, "Because, damn it! I capitulated!" He swallowed and his Adam's apple was a hard obstruction in his throat. He forced it to bob a little and release the trapped air from the tightness of his lungs. When he spoke again, it was with a gush of emotion and harsh, taut breath. "I couldn't do anything else. I had nothing to offer them. And I was frightened. What else could I do?"

Laughton realised that Rodmell now needed a contribution from him; he needed his support. He had suddenly begun to flounder in the new-found knowledge that, once stripped of the protection of power and money, he was a coward. Laughton willingly offered him the straw he so badly needed, for he had his own ghosts to lay and understood the sufferings of contrived bravado.

"What else indeed, Eliot?" he said quietly.

But Rodmell needed more than Laughton's agreement. He needed Laughton to help him re-establish his hope, his faith in the rightness of things. Laughton felt that perhaps even Margaret Rodmell herself might have had difficulty in talking her husband through his gloominess tonight and it was obvious that his empty offering was not going to be enough.

"I don't suppose we," he said, "I mean, the British, are in much of a position for bargaining, are we, right now?"

"Never have been, if truth be known. Not for years," grunted Rodmell. He was slightly appalled by the fact that he had heard himself whining. He could not afford to bare his soul to the likes of Laughton, no matter how lonely and scared he felt, and so it was as a form of defence that he changed the subject quickly and brought back on to centre stage the Rodmell he wanted people to recognise—the strong, powerful Taipan.

"Did my damnedest, you know, to get you out of the Floating City. Even spoke to Harland."

Thinking of Tung Nien had made Laughton greedy for her love again, had brought back to him the nights of tortured, biting loneliness when he had been without her, the mornings swelling with anticipated warmth when they had arranged to meet at the geomacer's, the white nights when he could not sleep and could not remember her face. He forced himself back to the solidity of words.

"I know," he said. "Mary told me all you did to get me out. I should like to thank you. Although I'm surprised the event was so important."

Rodmell laughed, pleased to be able to criticise, to attack, to divert their attention away from his own weaknesses.

"Oh, your wife made it important, Laughton. It wasn't you."

Laughton looked at him.

"As such," Rodmell added.

Laughton was slow to respond. The drinks had severely undermined his ability to be nasty in return. He could think of nothing to say.

"A fine woman," Rodmell announced, in obvious and emphatic approval. Rodmell had found a brown scab on one of the round knobs of his knuckles and he raised a hand to his mouth to bite. The scab tasted of iron. "Moved Hell and high water. Wouldn't take no for an answer." He looked across at Laughton slumped on the sofa and added unnecessarily, "You don't deserve her, of course."

"That is true," said Laughton, but somehow he did not actually feel it was.

He sat back and became aware that what he had, until then, imagined to be the annoying whistle of insects was, in fact, Rodmell's wireless set reaching out into the night and finding no transmitter. He was fascinated by the luminous orange dial which was confidently set to the wavelength of the Empire Service and yet which was emitting no more than an empty crackling whistle. And so, without really thinking, he said, "Have you never stopped to think, Eliot, how there are so many people in the world, all reaching out for each other, and yet hardly any of us actually ever manage to touch."

Rodmell winced as the scab came away from his finger leaving a raw, pink mark, not yet cured and with a little spot of blood already staining the centre. He raised his eyebrows. "Can't say I have, Laughton. No."

"And how cruel it is when you have actually found someone to have them taken away."

There was a silence during which Laughton watched the ceiling fan and listened to the crackling of the wireless, and Rodmell looked at his hands. They drank without speaking until Rodmell erupted suddenly.

"So how did you get out?" he asked. "From the Floating City?"

Laughton smiled. Even before he spoke, he realised he had been waiting to share her with someone else ever since she had first kissed him. He felt a certain pride and satisfaction that he was able to say: "Tung Nien."

"Why would she do that?" Rodmell snorted and it was obvious that he didn't believe. It made Laughton even more determined to speak.

"She sent Wu Tang to get me."

Rodmell snorted again. He stood up and walked across the room to the open doors of the French windows. Laughton watched his straight back and slightly rounded shoulders and hated him. He hated him because he did not believe it and he hated all that Rodmell stood for and all that had moulded him into this insensitive, pompous, selfish old man who stood now at his French windows looking down over the city he had, until recently, virtually owned and who was still unable to accept that he had nothing left.

Laughton felt a tremendous desire to prove to Rodmell that he was not the only one who had influence, that he was not the only one who was important. Rodmell's constant belittling of him, not only tonight, but over the years, coupled with the irrational desire he felt to speak of his relationship with Tung Nien pushed him forwards towards a place he would never have gone when sober.

"I don't see why you should find it funny, Eliot?" he said. Some momentary and undeserved respect for her memory, or perhaps respect for himself and Mary, made him change his tack. "I have known Wu Tang. On and Off. For years. He calls me Mao."

"Mao, is it?" scoffed Rodmell, still standing at the window. "That, at least, does not surprise me!"

Laughton rubbed the condensation from the bottom of his glass. He desperately wanted Rodmell to offer him another drink for he felt his spirits, his temporary euphoria, flagging.

Rodmell pointed out into the darkness over the harbour.

"Used to watch my ships come in from up here," he said.

He's going to change the subject again, Laughton said. He is interested in nothing that does not actually touch on Eliot Rodmell himself. So he decided to provoke.

"Don't tell me you have never been unfaithful, Eliot!"

And he did his best to produce a Rodmell snort. Rodmell was torn between the need to be respectable and the need to be one of the boys.

"I don't see what that has to do with anything."

"I thought that was what we were talking about."

An affair was, Laughton realised then, something a Rodmell took for granted, never talked about and was not impressed by. But that was because it was not Tung Nien. There was no one, he decided, in all of Hong Kong who had not mentally already gone to bed with her. The important difference was that she had chosen him. And here was Rodmell, treating him as though he were nothing. He was already speaking before Rodmell realised he needed another drink.

"It was Tung Nien," Laughton said. "It wasn't Wu that got me out. I told you before. We are lovers." He would never know why he had used the present tense, unless it was because he still thought of her as the present, found it impossible to relegate her to the past.

"I don't know why you are telling me this, Laughton."

"I'm telling you because you asked."

Rodmell seemed to have run out of snorts. Something there was in Laughton's expression which suggested that he might be telling the truth. He walked slowly back across the room and sat down next to Laughton. He realised intuitively that saying nothing would be more productive than giving an opinion. He could see that Laughton wanted to talk. He pushed the whisky towards Laughton and sat back.

Laughton was by now drunk enough to be almost unaware that he had company. Not that it would have made much difference. He wanted to speak of Tung Nien because it brought her alive for him. He was no longer trying to impress Rodmell, for Rodmell had all but disappeared. He was luxuriating in the mixture of pain and warmth that he found in bringing his memories to life once again as conscious thoughts rather than as unwelcome intrusions. He could see her walking towards him over the hard wooden floor at the geomancer's, naked, smiling, her arms raised behind her head to undo the tight bun of her hair; and then they were kissing, not touching each other, just kissing and it seemed to go on for ever. Until she rolled him over and sat astride him, her hair falling into his face and he pushed his hands up to her breasts and said, "You're so beautiful." She had looked at him without understanding and had said, "It's only anatomy, Alfred. It's not beauty."

"You see, we look for different things, don't we, Eliot?"

Rodmell grunted, but it was not exactly in agreement.

"And I don't mean the English and the Chinese, although that is certainly true also. I mean men and women. We look for different things."

"Does she love you?" asked Rodmell with a sudden tenderness which was totally out of character. Laughton failed to notice.

"She said she did. And then, I was in a rut. I was ready to love anybody. That it was her made it that much easier."

Rodmell nodded slowly, for all the world as though he understood. He had not even been listening enough to realise that Laughton had changed to the past tense. He was watching Laughton stumbling across the battlefield of his memories, picking his way through the corpses, and he did not even realise there had been a battle.

"Have you seen the fireflies, Laughton?" he asked, deliberately pointing past the French windows.

"Fireflies," said Laughton, but not to answer. He was thinking suddenly of all the things which had failed to come up to his expectations and of all the times when he himself had failed. There seemed to be so many of them. "I think I'll go now," he said, and he stood up. At the door, he turned and looked back at Rodmell sitting hunched in the pale light of the room and still looking out into the dark of the garden.

"I don't think I understand anything," he said. "I don't think I ever have."

Rodmell didn't move.

(iii)

Molly was on the ferry. She had been to visit her father on Miss Dekyvere's insistence. Miss Dekyvere was still convinced that Molly might be evacuated and escape the invasion if she went back with her father, although, for all the notice he had taken of her, she might just as well not have bothered visiting him at all. He had not recognised her and he had not seemed to want to. He was obsessed with the idea of snow.

When she had arrived, Ah Chien had spoken to her distantly as though they had never had secrets to share together, never argued nor agreed, never been close in any way. Molly had been slightly offended by the old amah's dismissive reaction to the one question which was on everyone's mind and recently seemed to always open conversation.

"It doesn't matter so very much when the Japanese arrive," Ah Chien had said. "The only thing that matters is that they will kill us all. That is their way."

"That doesn't worry you?" Molly had asked, realising at the same time that she was not really waiting for an answer. Ah Chien already belonged to a part of Molly's life that was dead, that had died a long time ago.

"What is there to worry about? I am looking forward to it. It cannot be worse than my life. Besides which, I feel it is time. If it is not the Japanese, it will be something else."

Ah Chien grunted and turned away into the scullery. She lit a candle and began to sift through the dirty washing.

"Why don't you put on the light?" Molly asked.

Ah Chien did not look up from Willard Russell's soiled shirts, vests and underpants.

"You can always trust a candle," she said. "The China Light and Power Company cannot put out a candle."

And so she left her there and went off to find her father.

When Molly saw him, he looked exactly as she remembered him. She would even have sworn he was wearing the same clothes: a red and black checked shirt and khaki trousers with a button missing at the waist. As she walked into the stuffy, cramped living-room, her father adjusted himself in his wheelchair and, looking through the square window at the tenements opposite and their rows on rows of bamboo washing poles, said, as though revealing the product of long and careful consideration on the subject, "Leave things to nature and then every process will be interfered with by chance. Even human nature. There is no empirical reality. No two flakes of snow are identical but they are always recognisable for what they are." He did not expect a reply, in fact Molly was in some doubt as to whether he had even registered the presence of another person in the room for he sat back and closed his eyes.

She felt awkward standing there at the door before someone she could only recognise physically. She did not know him and had only vague recollections of when he had been her father. The thing she could most clearly remember were his little bottles of coloured inks and the feathery bamboo pens. She could not but feel a sense of relief that she had escaped from having to share in his degradation. There was a stale smell of alcohol and urine in the room and, lying open on the table he had used to use for his calligraphy jobs, a copy of "The I Ching". "Simple grace. No blame," she read. And she did not blame him, she realised. She did not blame him any more for the death of her mother, for she rarely thought about her, and if she did it was as though she had belonged to someone else's life; she didn't blame him for having abandoned her, for she had grown up in luxury as a rich Chinese; and she didn't blame him for his squalor and apparent madness because she did not care enough about him to feel anything that strong. She felt instead the same kind of disgust she felt when she saw anything dirty. So when he said suddenly, "Who's there?", she said nothing. What would be the point of reminding him? she thought, perhaps to justify her silence. She cursed Miss Dekyvere for having made her come. It would have been better for her not to have known what had become of him. Willard Russell was looking emptily again towards the square of the window. "He veils his light, yet still shines," Russell muttered to himself.

It was only after Molly had left him there sitting alone in the dim, filthy light of the room that she began to feel any kind of compassion for him. Not because he had been her father, but because he had seemed so pitiful. On the ferry, she tried to bury him again. He had been dead to her for so long that she could not understand why he refused, now, to disappear. It was as though she had witnessed something dreadful. She tried to think of the worst thing she could remember seeing: a dog knocked down by a car, still alive but with its back broken, turning in uncomprehending circles, not understanding why it could no longer stand straight, not yet feeling the pain but yelping in frustration. And that something had become lodged in her mind to keep her from sleeping. Her father in a wheelchair, urine-stained khaki trousers covering his flimsy legs, his stale, alcohol-laced breath mumbling some nonsense about snow. Who had not even seen her standing at the door.

Molly tried to concentrate on the other passengers on the ferry to giver her something else to think about. She had deliberately gone down to the lower deck with the Chinese, leaving the Europeans above in the false comfort of their confidence and seeming self-assurance that just because they were, for the most part, English, they were safe. If the Chinese thought anything about the war, she decided, it was as she herself had been taught to think about it. The Japanese were just one more part of the originality of the moment, a part of the immensity of the present, which included both the past and the future, as important to the unfolding of life as the fly that had just settled on a banister away to her right, as important as her denial of her father's blood and her desire to rid her mind of his pathetic obsession with the snow.

A coolie sat opposite her, picking at his cane hat with long yellow nails. He was holding the hat before him between his open knees. The only sound other than the muffled throb of the ferry's engines was the clicking of the man's yellow nails against the canes of his hat. Until the exhaust of an aeroplane roared out above the ferry. It was a Japanese observation 'plane. Molly could see the shapes of the pilot and the observer dark against the orange sunset of the night sky. They looked too real to be dangerous. The man opposite her had neither looked up nor broken the tedious rhythm of his picking. The aeroplane had passed because it had to and it was not worthy of note.

Suddenly, the cold acceptance of the Chinese seemed to Molly to be just as oppressive as the overconfident ignorance of the Europeans. She realised she did not want to be a part of either of them. She went up on to the empty deck of the ferry and looked at the sea.

(iv)

When the two ferries collided, Harry Osbourne was sitting in a bar near the "battle-box", the underground HQ of the allied forces, which had been built some years previously fifty feet below the Victoria Barracks in Central. He had recently heard that both the beaches and the harbour had been mined, but the waiting had been going on for so long now that news of the war effort didn't seem to be really relevant any more. Nobody seemed to really care what was happening. His story of Japanese soldiers out on the Floating City had not been printed because it was pointed out, quite rightly, that he had no proof. His story of the strange relationship which he was sure existed between Kenji and Tang had suffered the same fate. So, when, the other day, the Chinese had reported on Japanese troop movements across the water, Osbourne's note book and pencil had remained firmly in his jacket pocket. The last thing he had written in his note book had been the beginning of a letter to an old girlfriend he had had in Clapham, some ten years ago. He didn't know where she was now but had begun to write all the same. It was almost as though, in the absence of a significant present, he were trying to reinvent a more acceptable past. He would have liked to have had something more tangible to remember her by than the inadequacy of his memory. A song, perhaps, or a sentence. Something she might have said that was unique to her. But so far as he could remember now she had never said or done anything of note. As he sat on in the bar he wondered whether the absence of women in the city, European women, for there were still numerous Chinese and Indian women, had prompted him into thinking of this girl. "Only spent five months with her," he said to himself. "Who'd've thought she'd come back to haunt me now?"

Osbourne was still struggling towards the flickering, dusty memory of her face when the random yet orderly wandering of the people in the street became the lunging, jerking and pushing of hysteria. Osbourne's immediate thought was that the invasion had begun. Far from feeling frightened, he felt at once exhilarated. He noticed that his heart was beating heavily with excitement. "Shit!" he hissed through his teeth. "This is it!" And he stood up and moved across to the window of the bar. Some of the people in the street were running towards the harbour whilst others were pushing against the crowd and buffeting their way towards Central and past the door of Osbourne's bar.

It was not a sense of duty, the idea of getting a story, which made Osbourne leave the bar, but the irrational fear of being separated, of being left alone and having to face the Japanese with no one to support him. He stepped out into the crowd and was carried off in the direction of the harbour, hands pushing frantically in his back and jagged elbows crushing his ribs. He craned his neck to see down the street before him but was lurched forwards and fell from the pavement into the street. He lost his footing and rolled heavily onto the ground to be trampled by the feet of the people behind him. With a curse he pushed himself back up and was again carried forward, against his will now. He turned and tried to force his way back in the direction of the bar, but it was impossible. The solid stream of people bundled him backwards down the street. He pulled his glasses off and jammed them into the pocket of his jacket along with his notebook and pencil. And then, as suddenly as it had started, the stampede abated and he found himself spewed out onto the edge of the harbour along with a handful of other men. He turned quickly to look behind him and saw that the people that had previously been a torrent of frenzied pushing and shoving had calmed to an aimless, almost embarrassed, drifting. It was not the Japanese at all. It was the ferries. Two ferries had collided. Osbourne grinned as he replaced his glasses and peered through the smudgy lenses towards the harbour. Who would have thought that fear was so close to the surface? he muttered to himself. To look at them you wouldn't think they had it in them. Inscrutable bastards, he added, using his favourite adjective and noun for describing the Chinese. He was angry because his own reaction had embarrassed him too. He had wanted to be safe.

(v)

Molly had still been standing on the aft deck when the ferries collided. With the first impact, she had been thrown to the floor. She lay with her cheek resting in the cool, dirty water of a greasy puddle. Blood from a cut on her forehead was warm and sticky like oil. She thought of the 'plane they had seen earlier and wondered vaguely if they had been bombed, when the ferry lurched forward again with a strident grinding of metal. She pushed herself up slightly and saw that they must almost be at the pier because she could see the coastline clearly and even make out the shapes of figures waiting and waving. She was at the back of the ferry and could not yet see the lozenge-like shape of the *Night Star* encrusted in their bows. Still thinking it was oil, she wiped the blood from her forehead and tried to stand up. She could hear the shouts from the passengers on the lower deck and was surprised that there were so many. She could only remember seeing the old coolie with the cane hat but now she could make out at least a dozen different voices. In fact, there were more than forty.

There was a pungent smell of gasoline all around her and it was the fear of fire that made her hobble forwards despite the throbbing stiffness of her hip and onto the first class passenger deck. As she went through the swinging wooden doors the lights inside flickered once and went out. It was then that she could see, as though through the end of a tunnel, the bright, oblong windows of the other ferry listing and horizontal across their bows. Beyond the lighted windows she could see the scurrying panic of the passengers on the other boat and from below the desperate cries of the passengers who still did not know what had happened. Their ignorance made their plight seem immediately worse than it was for, as far as Molly could tell, their own ferry had settled after the collision and was now stable and high upon the water.

A man in uniform called out to her from the other end of the passenger deck which, she realised now, was empty. Through the dull pulsing of blood at her temple and the stiffness of her hip she felt detached from all that was going on around her, as though she might have been watching it happening far away on a cinema screen, but she was not too distanced from the world to be annoyed when the man spoke to her in English. But for some reason, despite her annoyance, she too replied in English. "Don't just stand there waving your arms about. Come and help me!" The man ran towards her and placed his hands beneath her arms. He pushed her along the gangway between the seats and explained as quickly as he could that whilst the *Meridian Star*, the ferry they were on, had escaped with a minimum of damage, the only way to dry land was through the other ferry and that the *Night Star* was in danger of sinking at any moment. She could still hear the cries of the passengers on the lower deck. "I was told to get the Europeans off first," the man said, pushing her a little harder towards the open doors and out onto the fore-deck of the ferry. Molly realised that she had been saved by the vestige of her father's features and by the fact that the lights had fused. She was not sure whether to be grateful or not.

The man lifted her across the gap between the two ferries and another man took her hands and helped her to stand on the listing, slippery deck. She was looking down into the dark, churning waters of the harbour and it was only when the other person spoke her name that she looked up. She longed to be able to stand alone so that she could put her arms around his neck and not let him go away from her again. "Wu?" she said quietly. He smiled and, as though unsurprised to see her, said simply, "Let's get you off."

He left her standing on the pier and went back onto the ferry. She tried to follow his movements but soon lost sight of him amongst the thronging passengers pushing their way towards the shore. Somebody had placed a blanket around her shoulders and, although she was not cold, she tugged the corners together beneath her chin. It was comforting to feel the rasping material against her, but she felt tender all over her body and when the blanket grated against her skin she winced. She desperately wanted Wu to come back. She felt that the pain in her hip would go away if only he were with her. If he were with her she felt that even the Japanese might go away.

Osbourne was standing not more than four yards away from Molly, but he was not looking at her and he had not seen her. He was looking at the ferries with a distracted smile on his face. He had jotted down the names of the two craft in his notebook. The *Meridian Star* and the *Night Star* he had written below his abortive attempt at a letter. Satisfied with that, he had stuffed his notebook back into his jacket pocket. He would write it up later. It made a better contribution to the newspaper than the pathetic article he had half-heartedly scribbled down before embarking on his letter, the fact that the Fanling Hunt was still being celebrated despite the imminent invasion because it seemed that the English refused to believe it could happen. Or else, Osbourne had observed, it was necessary for them to keep up the appearance of normality. When nothing is normal any more, he grunted. And the crash before him was proof of that. Apart from piracy, the ferries had suffered no accidents since they had started the crossing back in 1870. A point they were very proud to advertise, otherwise Osbourne would have been unaware of the fact.

"Nothing is normal," he said, this time aloud, and he shuffled forwards a little to watch as someone was carried off the "Night Star" on a stretcher. He took out his notebook and pencil again and wrote "Casualties:-" neatly beneath the names of the ferries. At least it made it more of a story. If no one was hurt, no one would want to read about it. He had learnt years ago that a disaster could be measured by the number of deaths it caused. And failing that, casualties was a word that intrigued. Before he put his notebook away, he underlined it twice and wrote, for the moment: ":- 1".

Molly was growing impatient and the stiffness in her hip was becoming a dull, throbbing ache. The side of her head hurt. She peered towards the ferries trying to make out the shape of Wu, but could only see old peasants being helped ashore by men in uniform. It seemed the Military Police had arrived and were helping too. The engine of the ferry she had been on, the *Meridian Star*, was churning up the oily water of the harbour and was pulling away from the listing *Night Star*. The *Night Star*'s engines were started up and the crippled ferry began to edge very slowly towards the pier away to Molly's left where a single round white light marked the end of the covered gangway. Molly decided she would close her eyes until Wu came back to her, but she opened them almost immediately, not because he was there, but because the pain was somehow thicker without sight. She focussed her attention instead on the round light at the end of the pier, but when she looked at the light she felt dizzy. She looked away from the light and focussed on its reflection in the water. A slick of oil made the reflection of the white light change colour and turn a beautiful reddish, golden yellow. The two lights were, she thought, like the two full halves of a single whole.

Herself and Wu. The tiger and the dragon. Spirit and vitality. The union of the two producing the immortal seed.

A hand pressed her shoulder lightly and she turned with a smile.

"Don't suppose you remember me," said Osbourne, not even bothering to make it a question. Molly looked at the shattered reflection of the light in the reporter's glasses.

"What?" she said, coming back from a long way away, the smile gone.

"Harry Osbourne," said Osbourne extending a hand for her to take. "I was invited once to your house." Osbourne felt the need to explain the brusqueness of his intrusion. He was strangely disconcerted by the fact that she looked straight through him. "To play Mah-jongg." He broke off and laughed, but without humour. "Never have been able to play, come to that. Not then. Not now, either."

"What do you want, Mr Osbourne?" she asked, looking now away from him and back to the listing ferry and the shadowy shapes of the figures still on board moving like ghosts along the passenger deck.

"Want?" said Osbourne, and he laughed again. "That's a good one. What do I want?"

"I mean, what do you want with me?"

"Just being friendly. I don't want anything. At least, nothing you can give me. You don't look too hot, that's all. I just thought that as I'd carried your father years ago up to Miss Dekyvere's to...," and he stopped because he could not really remember now why he had done so, and then he hurried on, "It'd be a shame not to do the same for you, who are his daughter. If you needed me to, like."

"Thank you, but I am fine. I don't need you to do anything for me," she said, a little surprised at how cold it sounded. But, in the last few minutes, she felt she had moved on and away from the world inhabited by people like Harry Osbourne. She had, she felt, become a part of something grander. She was floating, drifting, enveloped in a misty, warm, glowing scent which smelt, she thought, of peaches, but of the flower, not the fruit. She remembered the blossom feathery on the snow-capped mountains to the north of Nanking where they had been taken out to visit a ruined temple laced with mists and moss, the blossom pink and feathery stretching away below them down the mountainside and out across the valley. She seemed now to be drifting back there, floating, gliding away over the dark waters of the harbour, over the silent grey lines of Japanese troops in the New Territories, past the grazing officers' horses, the tanks and the supply lorries, further north and backwards in time to be reunited with her mother, who was smiling and alive, and her father, who was clean and healthy and was her father, when she fainted and fell heavily into Osbourne's surprised arms and clammy hands.

(vi)

Tung Nien could not tell at first whether it had been Chen Liew's decision or Tang's, but Tang it was who told her she could not see Laughton again.

"Eventually someone will talk," he said.

Tung Nien looked at him emptily, wishing she had the energy—although it might have been interest she lacked—to tell him that Laughton had already beaten them to it, had already told her to leave, that she couldn't see him now even if she wanted to. For she did want to. Desperately. At first, she had embraced the rôle Chan had mapped out for her eagerly, imagining in its madness a frenetic activity which would bustle her mind away from Laughton. But the activity had been pedestrian rather than frenetic, although it was madness for all that. Maybe it was to provoke Chan that she said, "I don't care if anyone talks."

"Chen Liew would not like it. Nor would the others."

The nameless hordes.

"We could always shut them up."

"It doesn't work like that. Violence is not a whim."

And so she lost her patience.

"I'm not seeing him, Chan. But you know that, anyway."

She looked at him with eyes like wet beads.

"You know everything I do. You know I can't leave unless you take me."

Chan said nothing.

"He just wants me to know that he knows. That's it, isn't it? He's sent you here to tell me to stop seeing Alfred just to show me that he knows about it—has known, maybe, all along."

Chan did not move so much as an eyelid, until he said quietly, "I do not think that he is well."

"Do you think I care?"

"I think you should. You are his wife. You have a duty."

"Ha!"

"He thinks a lot of you and thinks of you a lot."

Chan had not, she noticed, used the word love.

"Let him tell me that himself."

"He is in The Room of the Eight Immortals."

Tung Nien turned from the window where she had been looking out into the night and the rain illuminated by the moonlight and she walked towards the room which Chen Liew used to consult the oracles and have his fortune told. She went into the room without knocking and saw her husband sitting on a mat in the middle of the room, his back to her. He looked smaller than she remembered. The tools of the soothsayer's trade, a wooden canister and a handful of bamboo sticks, stood now abandoned on an inlaid table by the window and Tung Nien looked past the sticks at the rain.

"Come in," said Chen Liew without turning, knowing she was already in the room.

Tung Nien felt she was intruding on his indifference. Something about the proud way he held his thin back and kept it turned away from her emphasised how little she meant to him.

"I am disappointed," he said finally. "Not surprised, of course. But disappointed."

Tung Nien moved a little closer to him and then stopped because he was speaking again.

"I could have had him killed," he said, pushing himself now to his feet and turning to face her. "But what would have been the point." He shrugged. "Soon the Japanese will kill him anyway."

She decided to say none of the feelings that were welling up inside her. She knew they were elusive and would fall apart before they became words. Neither did she want to make them base by parading them before someone who would not be able to understand. And so she said, "You pushed me into it. It was not what I would have chosen."

Chen Liew raised his hands wearily. She looked at him as he walked towards her. His skin seemed to have been worn away and replaced by a loosely fitting brown parchment that sagged where it had not been pulled tight enough.

"I did nothing," said Chen Liew quietly.

"Exactly."

He shook his head.

"It was too simple for it to work. I should have realised that."

Tung Nien had no desire to speak of failure nor to apportion blame. And then as though reading her thoughts, Chen Liew said, "You will not try to find him again. At least you will do that for me."

A knock at the door prevented any further attempt at communication. Miss Dekyvere stepped into the room and stood dripping rain at the doorway.

"It's Molly," she said simply. "There has been an accident but she is not badly hurt."

"Where is she?" Tung Nien asked quickly, turning away from her husband.

"She is with Wu Tang," said Miss Dekyvere. "He has, I believe, taken her home."

"Home?" Chen Liew's voice was brittle as firewood.

"I mean, *his* home," said Miss Dekyvere apologetically.

Tung Nien listened to the sound of the falling rain as it bounced on the hard round cobbles by the flower beds in the garden. It was the first storm and it marked the beginning of the Monsoon Season. She smiled to think how easily Molly had escaped and she returned to the window where the discarded bamboo sticks lay at random in their canister.

9

'It is only after snow and falling flowers
have been seen that the spirit emerges
to become immortal"

(i)

When the Royal Rifles and the Winnipeg Grenadiers arrived from Canada no equipment arrived with them. The reinforcements were greeted on the side of the harbour by crowds of grateful civilians as the answer to everyone's prayers regardless of their religion. Buddhists, Christians, Taoists and Confucians all turned out to see the soldiers ashore. The agnostics were represented by Osbourne who would rather have been somewhere else but who had a job to do.

Osbourne looked at the soldiers leaning on the ship's balustrade and said to himself, seeing their fresh, happy faces, "They don't know what they're letting themselves in for, the poor sods!"

"A fine sight, eh, Harry?" said an exuberant Sergeant Fletcher at his shoulder.

"Fine sight, my arse!" said Osbourne. "Pathetic, that's what I call it."

"How can you say that, Harry? Look at the people."

"People have nothing to do with reality, Fletch. We're no better off with this shower arriving than we were before they came. We might just as well have sent all the other soldiers off with our handful of ships to defend somewhere more important, like Singapore, for all the Japs care. They've left us one ship, Fletch! H.M.S. Thracian. Saw it myself last night. One ship!"

Although it was a Monday morning, Laughton was there because he had nowhere else to be. He went to the hospital now only when it was absolutely necessary. Nobody seemed to notice whether he was there or not. He was not in the slightest bit interested in watching the soldiers disembarking. He felt vaguely and inexplicably hostile to everyone who was waiting on the pier and to everyone who was not. An off-duty Sikh policeman stood beside him wearing a white turban and a white *dhoti*. Laughton found the Indian's clothing of more interest than the arriving soldiers. It surprised him slightly that he had not taken more of an interest before. Soon after their arrival in the Far East he had bought Mary the obligatory *cheong sam* and she had returned the gesture by presenting him one Christmas with a brightly coloured Malay *sarong* which he wore for a while instead of pyjamas. But, for some reason, the *dhoti* had escaped his notice, probably because most of the Indians, males, at least, dressed like the Europeans. "Looks like a bloody big nappy," he said to himself. "Only cool too."

Rodmell had watched the ship sail into the harbour early in the morning from his privileged vantagepoint on the Peak. "Of course," he had said. "They know where the harbour is mined, don't they?" Rodmell had then turned grumpily away from the view over the harbour and returned to the kitchen to make a pot of coffee.

Tung Nien did not bother to watch the arrival of the Canadians. She was doing something else. Chan had, the night before, brought her a detailed description of the British defences on the Gin Drinkers Line, which were, according to the paper she held before her on the table, manned by the Royal Scots. She played absently with one of Chen Liew's bamboo fortune-telling sticks. Her husband had told her to pass on all the information to Kenji and his Fifth Column, having agreed that the British were a lost cause, but Tung Nien hesitated. It was not only that she did not trust the Japanese to keep their word, she also felt she should at least try to give Laughton a chance of survival. She could not bear to think that she might be in any way involved in his death. Each fortified pillbox had been carefully drawn on a roughly sketched map, forming a wavy line, which cut from one side of the New Territories to the other. There was a brief footnote in Chan's clumsy handwriting suggesting Tide

Cove as the weakest point in the line and the best place for launching the first attack.

"He will know anyway without my telling him," she said finally to herself. "Tang will have told him that and more already."

And she folded the hastily drawn map and hid it away between the covers of an old book, one of Miss Dekyvere's Jane Austen novels. She looked through the window into the garden and thought of Laughton. She desperately wanted to see him again, to see in his eyes that he had forgiven her even if he would not take her back. She did not want to die knowing that she was hated.

Kenji could see the ship at its mooring from across the harbour. He was leaning his back up against one of the majestic stone lions outside the Peninsula Hotel. Beside him, an Indian doorman made an occasional comment, but Kenji was not listening. The recent changes in the Japanese Government—Prince Konoye had been replaced by General Hideki Tojo—effectively ruled out any possibility of peace. In fact, he knew that ships were already steaming towards the South Pacific, Malaya and the Philippines. It was now only a question of days before it all blew up and he had been told to remind the Hong Kong population of the supremacy of the Japanese by mobilising his Fifth Column. The target for their aggression would be the recently arrived soldiers.

(ii)

"What do you mean a rickshaw race?" Osbourne asked, cleaning his glasses on a dirty handkerchief. "What the hell is that?"

Fletcher nodded. He seemed excited at the idea. "That's right, Harry. The Canadians have organised it. Be a lot of money on it, I reckon. It's going to start at The Pen. You just have to hire your rickshaw boy and get your arse down there for two o' clock." And he looked eagerly around The Glory Hole where the newly arrived soldiers had quickly taken over half of the bar. They lounged in the hard rattan chairs in spruce uniforms with sharply pressed creases despite the heat and humidity. Fletcher looked down at his own khaki shorts a little wistfully. He could not remember the last time he had been bothered to make sure there were even creases, let alone whether they were straight or not. "It's a great idea, eh, Harry?" he said. "Certainly liven up the old place a bit until we get a chance to chase off the Nips."

Osbourne felt exasperated. Liven up the place? Chase off the Nips? He too looked across the room through a pall of cigarette smoke at the Canadian soldiers. "Our saviours," he said bitterly. "Don't look much older than sixteen, most of them. The poor sods!" But Fletcher was leaning towards him expectantly so that Osbourne said, "Don't reckon I'll be going, Fletch."

Sergeant Fletcher nodded again.

"I don't know what's up with you lately, Harry. You're not an awful lot of fun to be with, you know? I'd go so far as to say you're becoming a bit of a bore, mate."

"So what?"

"So nothing. It was just an observation."

Osbourne felt imprisoned, closed in by the bleakness of the world he could see all around him and of which Fletcher was no more than the closest tangible example. It was ironic that he should notice the outer world for perhaps the first time in his life when it was so unworthy of note, with nothing beautiful in it, nothing to make you want to live it through.

"Rickshaw races!" he grunted and stood up to leave.

"It'll be fun," said Fletcher hopefully, "At least take our minds off this." And he waved a hand vaguely, none too sure how to put 'this' into words. But Osbourne was not looking. He was already walking towards the door, pushing his way past the uniformed Canadians and other soldiers.

(iii)

Baffled by the number of soldiers and the long line of waiting rickshaws, Laughton pushed his way into the restaurant of the Peninsula Hotel and sat down at a table in a window, which gave him a sweeping view of the harbour and Hong Kong Island. Laughton looked around the tables. The austerities of war were evident wherever you looked these days. The normally abundant plates of food had been reduced to a poor smattering of thin, stringy birds, as though even the wildlife were suffering from the Japanese siege. Laughton looked at his hands so as not to look at the sad spectacle of the diners. He thought of Tung Nien with an empty sigh. It was becoming difficult for him to keep his hope alive, although hope for what he was not sure. It somehow eased the empty feeling that sat at the base of his stomach like hunger. Hope for something was better than just the ache of missing. And then, for the first time in weeks, he thought of his wife. She had written miserable letters from Singapore complaining of mosquitoes and the bedding which, she said, was always damp, but her last letter had come from Australia where she had, it seemed, set up a temporary home with Margaret Rodmell, in a suburb of Darwin, and where she was, on her own admission, relatively happy. Laughton had not written to her since the evacuation, using the excuse that he could never be sure where she was. Now, that excuse had evaporated and he looked emptily at his hands, wondering what he could say to her, for he had decided to write. It was a way of reaching out for something that might serve him as a comfort of a kind in the absence of Tung Nien, in the absence of a future and in the absence of God. He looked again into the street where the rickshaws were now bustling into a kind of wavery straight line across the street, in places up to four deep.

"A rickshaw race," said a voice from the next table, answering his unformed question. It was Osbourne, a piece of stringy pigeon between the mottled stumps of his fingers. He waved a bone towards the window and spoke with his mouth full. "The Canadians, bless 'em."

"What?" said Laughton. Although he had understood, he was still looking for God—now in the washed-out, hungry faces of the rickshaw boys. No point explaining to Osbourne, he said to himself. Never listens to you anyway. And what was there to explain? I am getting old, Osbourne. When I wake up in the morning, all there is before me is a precipice, a gorge, waiting to swallow me up. When I open my eyes, Osbourne, all I see is darkness. For Osbourne would not understand. He would think of the Japanese.

"A rickshaw race?" said Laughton then. Osbourne nodded, still gesticulating with the denuded pigeon bone and, miraculously, still with his mouth full. "That's right, Doc!" he said.

Laughton watched him for a while, but he was tired. Osbourne somehow managed to convert the meagre pigeon into a banquet. He was licking his fingers and carefully, almost meticulously, placing the bones around the edge of his plate, all of them picked clean. He made a small pyramid with the few last grains of rice and patted them into shape with the side of his knife. Swallowing, he looked across at Laughton. "They're running a book," he said.

Laughton glanced again into the street. "The camaraderie of war," he grunted. He thought back to his own brief experience of active service. The shared cigarette before dawn beneath a full moon, waiting for the signal to advance across no-man's land. Shared secrets and shared girls in small villages where the church towers had been bombed out. Only then it had been bicycle races along the steep, cobbled streets of a town in the Marne. And so, he thought, there was nothing new. A rickshaw race.

Osbourne was preparing to leave. He pushed his chair away from the table and stood for a while looking at Laughton as though searching for something to say. Laughton looked blankly back at him, knowing that he had nothing to say. Suddenly, a gunshot rang out from the street.

"They're off!" said Osbourne nodding towards the window and because Laughton's table had a good view of the street, he sat down beside him. He caught a glimpse of Sergeant Fletcher's flushed and excited face looking back at him from one of the rickshaws closest to the hotel. The line of rickshaws broke into a slow shambling, a shuffling forwards, and Fletcher's face lolled strangely forwards as Osbourne watched. The shuffling gathered momentum as the rickshaw boys began to trot and then to run, their thin shoulders and arms straining at the weight of their grinning cargo. Only Fletcher, it seemed, was not laughing. His head snapped backwards and his mouth flopped open as he was pulled jerkily past the window of the hotel. Osbourne raised his hand to wave but Fletcher, his head pressed against the hooded backrest of the rickshaw, stared back at him with a shocked, lost expression on his face.

"Thought they were going to use a white handkerchief to start the race," he muttered.

"Does it matter much what they use?" asked Laughton wearily.

"Does it matter?" Osbourne repeated the question almost angrily. "Does it matter? Of course it doesn't matter!"

"Does anything matter?" Laughton asked, although, rather than a question, it was a sequel to his own recent thoughts and a prelude to those he was about to have.

Osbourne shrugged. "I don't know," he said. "I guess *I* matter pretty much."

Laughton fiddled with a cigarette, rolled it between his fingers, and then lit it. He pushed the packet towards Osbourne.

"I have been thinking," said Laughton, "that it is more than possible that I have managed so far in my life to understand nothing at all. And it is only now, with this stupid, unreal life we are being forced to live, that ….."

"Oh, this life is real enough, Doc. Take my word for it."

"Why must you always burst in like that, Osbourne? I was going to say something—not anything particularly interesting—but I was going to say it anyway. Maybe I needed to share it with you. Why did you have to interrupt if all you were going to do was offer up some banal platitude?"

Osbourne frowned and his face puckered into the sulky expression of a child.

"You said it first."

"I beg your pardon?" said Laughton.

"About the rickshaw race," said Osbourne. "You said: Does it matter?"

Laughton sighed and turned away. So this is what happens, he thought. Reduced to a petty discussion about who said what and when. And why should you have thought, anyway, that Osbourne might have understood, or been interested in, anything you have to say. Still, Osbourne was right. Regardless of how unreal life seemed, it was indeed real enough.. Although I, thought Laughton absently, do seem always to have had another life running concurrently inside my head. And that has been my great failing. That I am able always to escape there when the real world fails me. When the Osbournes of the world rise out of their mediocrity to question what I am doing, I can always slip insolently away into an external silence and an inner world of voices. Wind my way through countless scenes and arguments which, no matter how often they are repeated, are never the same. For to think of Tung Nien suddenly again, as I sit here, is almost to have her here again. Her blue-black hair straight as knives. Her slim hips and the hard shape of her ribs. Anticipation always followed by fulfilment. Her excitement feeding my own so that I was almost young again. Young in my jealousies and my complete abandonment to her desires, to such an extent that my life ceased to exist when she wasn't there. Even down to the opium. Laughton looked through his memory of Tung Nien to Osbourne's plate of bones on the other table. Left alone, though, he thought, with only Osbourne and a war to look forward to. Osbourne sulking still.

Osbourne watched Laughton from across the table. Outside the window, the crowd which had witnessed the start of the rickshaw race was thinning but still boisterous. The street was strewn with broken beer bottles which crunched beneath the heavy boots of the soldiers, and the soldiers sang in loud voices, for the most part drunk. Osbourne looked at Laughton and thought, Poor sod can't get used to being on his own. I should tell him: It's a state of mind, Doc, like everything else. Once you accept it, you're half way to getting over it. What did he say a minute ago? I have understood nothing at all. I should tell him: That's because there is nothing to understand, sunshine. I mean, life is not something you understand; it is something you do. You don't look for any sense in life, only in the way people live it.

Osbourne stood up, scraping his chair noisily across the tiled floor.

"Let's go down to the Blue Elephant and see them come in," he said. "Have another drink."

"Why not?" said Laughton.

(iv)

Kenji dropped his pistol into the harbour and heard it hit the water with a dull plop. He had never killed before and he felt it should have been more exhilarating. He had been told that it was like a drug, that the rush of adrenaline and the feeling of power were as addictive as opium. Yet he had felt nothing. The stupid Englishman had just sat there and watched him pull the trigger in disbelief. Even a pig cries out, he thought, senses it is going to happen before it does.

The clouds above the harbour were full of rain as Kenji walked along the wharf. Why do I feel nothing? He said. Only this enormous loneliness.

(v)

Willard Russell did not see him coming. Willard Russell did not see anything anymore. His eyes looked inwards onto a vision that shut out everything else. When Kenji spoke to him, it was, for him, no more important than grass growing in the middle of an earthquake.

Kenji took one of Russell's long-abandoned calligrapher's pens from a jar by the windowsill and rolled the soft hairs of the pen between his fingers. Then he ran the tip of the pen over the bottom of his chin. Russell's *amah* stabbed her head round the door to see who was there, looked at Kenji and sniffed. She nodded towards Russell in his wheelchair. "I don't know why you've bothered to come. He doesn't say anything anymore," she said. "Sits there like that from morning till night rolling his eyes about and lolling his head. You ask me, he'd be better off dead."

Kenji did not bother to speak, nor even to look at her. She waited a moment at the door, looking in on the two of them, Kenji looking almost polished, Russell as though smeared by a dirty finger, then she shrugged and turned back towards the kitchen, saying, "I don't even know why I bother cooking. He won't eat anyway."

A 'plane flew past overhead and Kenji looked absently from the window. It was a British observation 'plane. The sunlight caught for a moment on the wing tips and flashed brightly as the 'plane banked to the left and made off towards the New Territories. Russell moaned, almost an echo of the drone of the propellers, and shifted slightly in his chair. Kenji looked at the dark patches of sweat at his armpits, the shirt stained blue. The sweat looked thick and sticky, as though it had been coaxed out of his otherwise lifeless body. A stain of urine darkened the groin of his grey flannel trousers. Kenji began to wonder why he had come. When he had killed Fletcher, his first thought had been the need for an alibi and where better than his calculated alibi of recent years. But he saw now that Russell would hardly serve his purpose. And he had known that. Perhaps he had come to see the culmination of the journey they had set out on together, come to bear witness to Russell's final disintegration. He felt neither pity nor pleasure when looking at Russell, just a clinical interest in observing his apparent emptiness. It was like looking at a blank page, the watermark the liquid blue of the scarcely pulsing veins on the backs of his hands. Nothing would be written there now, thought Kenji; there is not even the harvest of memory to be brought in, all blighted into a tight, dark ball of nothingness. Better for him in a way, though, to miss out on the invasion. In a wheel chair you can't run and hide. In the end I'll have done him a favour.

Kenji was tired. He was tired of his loneliness, tired of waiting for the fighting to start. He looked from Willard Russell's small, square window out onto the bamboo poles filled with washing on the balconies opposite and tried to discern some movement which would give him an indication that something had finally changed, that they were finally lurching towards their inevitable destiny. A woman, her face wrinkled and brown as a walnut, squinted up at him from one of the balconies, washing dripping in her hands and she smiled and waved. They don't want to know, Kenji said to himself, that's all there is to it. They are happier believing that this fragile pretence at defence, the arrival of this shipload of troops, is going to be the deterrent they have been waiting for to prevent the assault on their island fortress. The woman was still looking up at him, squinting into the sun. She bared a line of gold teeth in a grin, pointed towards Russell's balcony, and tapped her forefinger several times against her temple.

"Mad!" she called out.

"You're all mad!" Kenji called back and turned away from her. He ran his hand over Willard Russell's unkempt hair before he left the room.

(vi)

Eliot Rodmell had exchanged Elgar for Delius, the Cello Concerto for "Summer Night on the River". It was almost as though he were trying to escape to an England he barely knew but which had made him what he was, trying to drift back to summer afternoons where the different greens of the ash and oak trees and the almost wet luminescent green of the grass were always associated in his mind with cricket and afternoon tea, bicycle rides and sweets from the corner shop, but more than anything else, with peace and order. He sat alone now on The Peak listening to the drifting music and drifting with it. He had not turned on the lights although it was dusk, not through any respect for the black-out order, but because there was nothing he wanted to look at and because the soft half-light helped him in his drifting. Coming upon him, propped stiffly by the window in a rattan armchair, eyes closed and head tilted slightly backwards, his fingers making a nave beneath his chin, you would have been forgiven for thinking him in a state of sublime fulfilment, although nothing could have been further from the truth. He was deeply disturbed and utterly defeated.

His life had been emptied of everything that had given it its form and its purpose. First his work and then Margaret had been the difference between an ordered, steady, contented existence and the dullness he felt now, and both of them had gone. Her tiresome parties had been like bookmarks which separated off the different businesses of the week. He shambled over to the phonograph to put Delius on again.

(vii)

Wu and Molly were walking through the narrow streets of the Tangs' fortress village of Kat Him Wai. After a quick, heavy storm, the sky had blazed through a twenty-minute sunset and then paled to darkness and the streets were filled with the sweet and sharp scents of spices cooking. Men sat on their heels on street corners, smoking, talking and watching groups of dirty, half-naked children as they made their noisy way home. The Japanese soldiers might have been a thousand miles away. In fact, they could be seen clearly from the gates of the village, small, illuminated points of bonfires dotted the near horizon. Molly had been concerned by their proximity when Wu had taken her to the village after the ferry accident two weeks ago, but Wu had laughed.

"Why should we be afraid of them?" he had said. "They are our allies."

Whenever they walked through the streets of the village, Molly had the impression that they were walking round in circles and yet, as happened tonight, they always ended at the steep battlements of one of the village walls. Wu helped her to climb the uneven, dusty, stone steps to a lookout tower. Hong Kong was just an insignificant, amber glow in the night sky. Molly looked towards the soft light. Wu was looking over the roofs of the village in the opposite direction. Molly looked away from the amber glow of the city and turned to face the small, bright bonfires of the Japanese. "What will happen to my father when they invade?" she asked. "He will not be able to escape."

Wu's expression, an expression of controlled impatience, didn't change.

"Just another casualty, I suppose," he said.

"Doesn't it ...," she did not want to make it too personal by saying 'he', "mean any more to you than that?"

"He's white," said Wu simply.

So am I, she thought. But she knew she wasn't. Not any more.

Wu turned earnestly towards her.

"Look!" he said. "This is all bigger than individuals now. Individuals don't matter any more." He looked into her eyes, took her face in his hands and added in a voice which suggested he had heard it somewhere else, "Men die quicker than ideals and they are easier to kill."

She pulled away from him.

"And when they're dead, our memory of them fades faster than their bodies."

"That doesn't make anything right, does it?" she said and began to go down the steps of the lookout tower to the broken wall of the battlements. "Maybe my place is really back there after all," she said, nodding towards the glow of the city, "with the rest of them."

"There's no future back there, Molly. Can't you see that? The only future now is with the Japanese."

"So you exchange one warlord for another."

Wu shrugged.

"It's always been that way," he said.

But he needed to convince her.

"If you go back, Molly, you'll almost certainly be killed. At least here you'll be safe."

"What makes you so sure of that?"

"I've seen both sides, Molly."

Molly was still looking towards the bright, flickering lights of the bonfires when a voice from the street below interrupted them. It was one of the village guards calling for Wu.

"Do you have to go?" asked Molly. "Why do they always send you out?"

Wu smiled, pleased at her concern.

"I'll be back in a minute," he said.

Molly watched him jumping down the steps and into the street as though he could hardly wait to get there. Then she listened to the same hushed whispers that she had been hearing night after night. She felt like leaving before Wu came back to tell her he had been sent to take a message to Hong Kong, Kowloon or to the Japanese front lines. But the knowledge that there were so few nights remaining before the invasion kept her standing at the battlements, hoping that, just for once, he would not leave her alone. For a split second she saw that he was looking back up at her, the light from a torch at the end of the street flashing quickly across his face, his eyes for a moment looking into hers. Then he turned back to the guard and she knew he would be going off again into the night.

(viii)

Osbourne listened as Laughton played the piano in the lounge of the Parisian Grill. Osbourne was sitting on the step of the raised platform where the grand piano was placed and, every so often, he would stop drinking to throw out a comment between the lilting notes of Laughton's miserable jazz.

"They knew it was a murder but they couldn't be bothered to do anything about it! Makes you bloody sick, doesn't it? If it had been some poncy officer instead of poor old Fletch they'd be doing something."

His head swung unsteadily from Laughton and back to his beer.

"They sent a bloody Chogue and a Punjabi Indian to look into it. From the District Watch Force. Bloody marvellous, that is! Probably was the bloody District Watch Force did it in the first place!"

Laughton finished playing, rubbed his hand across his forehead and closed the lid of the piano. He took his drink from the top of the piano, wiped the circle of damp condensation from the surface and sat down on the step beside Osbourne.

"It wasn't only Fletcher. They killed over a dozen, Osbourne."

"I didn't know the others," said Osbourne.

Osbourne peered at Laughton through his finger-smudged glasses. Laughton leaned back against the step, his elbows on the level of the stage, and he looked across at the suddenly earnest Osbourne, his unlikely companion of recent weeks.

"I went to the cinema the other day," he said, lighting a cigarette and handing Osbourne the packet. "You know what happened in the middle of the film?"

Osbourne shook his head, but he was not really paying too much attention. It did not matter.

"They only stopped the film to put up this sort of advertisement reminding us all that we have to have those stupid uniforms they dished out for the HKVDC ready to put on. You know where you have to go when it happens?"

"What?" said Osbourne quietly.

"Where you have to go when it happens?"

Osbourne shrugged.

"What do you mean, where you have to go?"

"You have to sort of clock in, don't you? Put on that soppy uniform and grab yourself a gun. Kill some Japs, eh, Osbourne?"

"What do I want to kill Japs for, Doc?"

"So they don't kill you, I guess, Osbourne."

"You're beginning to sound like Fletch."

"I hope, God rest his soul, that I'm not."

Osbourne wondered whether he should react to the insult. But Laughton saved him from having to take a decision by saying, "Of course I hardly knew the poor chap, but he did seem a little brutish."

"Simple," said Osbourne. "That's what Fletch was. Simple. Simple and happy."

"They often go together," Laughton ventured.

"You know? I never saw him sad. Not once."

"Perhaps simplicity is the secret of happiness, Osbourne. Maybe the rest of us are just too complicated to recognise it when we find it:"

Osbourne was still feeling belligerent.

"Are you trying to say you've never been happy, or what?" he said.

Laughton's thoughts turned immediately to Tung Nien.

"Oh, I've been happy all right," he admitted. "Although it's always seemed temporary. Even at its height, at its strongest, there was always the underlying and sad knowledge that it couldn't possibly last."

"They don't let it last, Doc, do they?" Osbourne did not specify who *they* were but added vaguely and a little sadly, "Like this war."

Osbourne's thoughts turned to food. He began to wonder where he would go for dinner. Laughton was still thinking about Tung Nien, but not of happiness. When he thought of her now it was with a pained longing. He imagined himself rescuing her from some unspeakable danger so that she might be grateful enough to love him again. He thought back again and again to their meeting in the Tiger Balm Gardens, but it only made him morose. And at the back of all his thoughts was his unborn child, willing him to hate.

Laughton sipped his drink and held the whisky in his mouth without swallowing it until it began to burn on his tongue. It was as though he wanted to hurt himself, to galvanise some feeling into his life by inflicting pain, albeit small, on the numbness of his existence.

"I've been thinking, Osbourne," he said suddenly. "Love can only last if you don't have time to use it up, if you finish it, in other words, prematurely, if you are left wanting more."

Osbourne thought back quickly to his girlfriend from Clapham.

"I suppose so," he said without conviction or experience. He remembered Fletcher saying once, "I know what it's like to be lonely. I was lonely once—when I had the pox." He had thought it a joke at first until he had seen that Fletcher was being deadly serious. For Fletcher, loneliness had been having no one to go to bed with. And that was possibly the extent of Osbourne's love too—taxi-girls and prostitutes, if he was lucky, in bedrooms which always smelled of mangoes and sawdust, a baby always crying somewhere in the distance, if not, in any dark corner of any nameless street. He had not had a relationship, an affair, since being in the Far East, not since Jane in Clapham. What could he possibly know of love? He had never been given the chance of finding out.

"That must be why," Laughton went on, "that people who believe can profess to love God and to love Him throughout their lives. The only culmination of that love, the only way it can ever end, is with death."

Osbourne removed his glasses and rubbed his eyes.

"What the hell has God got do with it?" he asked.

"Not God, Osbourne, so much as death. I was thinking about death as the only truly acceptable end to love. Everything else is unsatisfactory."

Osbourne was out of his depth. He groped mentally towards the dry land of logic.

"I think that's bollocks!" he said. "Death's pretty unsatisfactory too, isn't it? For love or for anything else."

Laughton was saved from having to reply by the unexpected appearance of a rather lost looking Eliot Rodmell.

Rodmell saw Osbourne and Laughton sitting on the step of the stage, and behind them the big black grand piano. Osbourne had a stupid grin on his face and Laughton was frowning. Rodmell wished he felt strong enough to just ignore them. He stopped for a moment and cast his eyes around the plush, red, velvet decor of the room, the small alcoves set apart for romantic couples—all of them empty—and the crystal chandeliers. He settled his gaze finally on a painting hanging behind the bar which depicted an English hunting scene, but his view was intermittently obscured by the bobbing head of the Chinese barman as he busied himself with cocktails. Reluctantly, Rodmell turned again to Laughton and Osbourne. The doctor was waving, beckoning him across to join them. Rodmell half-raised his hand, but could not complete the gesture, which remained as an incomplete salute and then an energetic brushing away of crumbs from his trousers. As he walked towards them he was already making his excuses.

"Harland said he'd be here!" he grumbled.

"Probably too busy," said Osbourne—insolently, thought Rodmell.

Eliot Rodmell did not sit down with them but turned to look out across the dance floor, planting his long, thin back between them and the dancers. Laughton looked at the back of Rodmell's head where a tuft of uncontrollable grey hair stood out at right angles to his scalp, inescapable evidence that Rodmell had been taking a nap and had been too lazy to tidy himself up properly before setting out into the night. Months ago, any rebellious hair would have been firmly greased and plastered into place, if not by the Great Man himself, certainly by his wife, Margaret. Laughton looked at the tuft of hair with detachment, as he might have watched an insect dying against a pane of glass or the waiter pouring a drink—for there was the waiter now saying, "*Bombay* Gin, sir?" to Rodmell, who nodded. And the tuft wagged stiffly on the back of his head.

Rodmell turned his head slightly, but not enough to look at them, and said, "Not seen him, I suppose? Major Harland? Said he'd be here." And he looked at his watch as though wanting them to think he might have made a mistake with the time.

"I said he's probably too busy," Osbourne repeated. "What with the murders and the imminent invasion."

The word "imminent" was not a comfortable part of Osbourne's vocabulary and it sounded false and longer than its three syllables.

"Murders," said Rodmell, but it was neither a question nor an affirmation. It was merely an explosion of air in his mouth and was as communicative as a belch. He took two steps away from them and then, as though thinking better of it, returned and almost leaned his elbows on the surface of the stage. At the last moment, he tucked his elbows into his sides, as though furling two bony wings, and made an effort to maintain his posture and, possibly, his dignity. But the gesture was totally inadequate for he had already lost any dignity he might have had some months ago, and the tuft of hair at right angles on the back of his head would continue to deny him any way back.

Rodmell, Osbourne and Laughton were unaware that the Volunteers had been mobilised and the return of service personnel had been demanded on the radio and on the cinema screens that evening and, the following morning, while they slept off an excess of alcohol, the Japanese invaded Pearl Harbour.

(ix)

Kenji was probably the only one in Hong Kong who knew. Wu had given him the message the night before and just past midnight, in the early morning of 8th December, he tuned his radio into the wavelength which was reserved for the members of the Kempei. It was strange to think that in Hawaii it was still only the morning of the day before. On paper, there was a difference of eighteen hours and yet it was happening at the same time. Kenji thought it strangely appropriate that circumstance should have placed him in the future. It was still barely dawn on 7th December in Pearl Harbour and yet he had already lived his own 7th December without incident. The ships were steaming South, not only towards Hawaii, but towards Malaya too. They would be some three hundred miles to the North now, the torpedo bombers loaded with fuel, revving their engines on the long decks of the aircraft carriers, the Americans sleeping. And not more than twenty miles from Hong Kong, General Sakai would be preparing his troops. It would all explode, all come into being at almost the same time. The destruction of the American fleet in Hawaii, the annihilation of this petty band of patriots in Hong Kong, and, further South, the Japanese troops landing on the North West shoulder of the Malay peninsular. And all the while, in all the cities and towns, the enemy would be sleeping.

"The oneness of things," said Kenji to himself, smiling at the aptness of the Taoist conceit he had offered up to Willard Russell so long ago now. He smiled because he knew that the Chinese mind gave immense importance to chance, and he knew now that chance had nothing to do with the reality of the moment. It was careful planning and co-ordination.

Kenji listened to the crackling of the radio as he prepared his things for the morning. He put his neatly folded Imperial Japanese Army uniform across the back of a chair by his bed and laid the leather gun-belt carefully over the shoulder of the jacket. He placed his boots beneath the window and sat down on the edge of the bed. He looked at the shiny, empty gun belt, his revolver already rusting on the harbour floor. He felt again the empty bitterness of being alone, of not being a part of the nervous anticipation of the troops and pilots across the water. And now that he was destined to become another piece in the machine, he would still be different, distinctive and deficient. When the shooting started, he would have nothing to shoot with. False and ridiculous to the end.

Kenji lay on his bed and looked at the ceiling. The radio continued emitting more interference than coded information and when a Japanese submarine was sunk some 250 miles to the North of Pearl Harbour Kenji did not hear it. Instead, the two things that were uppermost in his mind intertwined and overlapped like an intricate carving but with the fluid, continuous movement of a mountain stream. The oneness of things and the sweeping pre-emptive strike against the enemy, something he enjoyed thinking about but could not visualise in all its extension, merged with a pathetic image of himself, immaculate and clean, almost ironed into shape, standing amongst the dirty, bloodied uniforms of his comrades as they marched along Gloucester Road behind General Sakai on his black horse and into the heart of the city.

As Kenji dozed on his bed, Major General Maltby, from his underground HQ in the "battlebox", moved his troops into position and ordered the harbour defences to be manned.

(x)

Wu and Molly stood on the battlements of the walled city of Kat Him Wai before dawn on 8th December watching the Japanese lorries and troops passing along the road below and heading towards the rising sun and Kowloon where the first lights could be seen snapping on in the distance. Wu smiled and squeezed Molly's hand. A small oil lamp burned beside them at their feet. As the first rays of sunlight began to fall across the grey stones of the wall before them, Wu kneeled down and dowsed the light without letting go of Molly's hand. She felt the slight pressure of his fingers around hers and smiled at him. But he did not return her smile. There was an itching nervousness in his stomach and a surge of expectation ran through his body. He stood again and looked down on the line of troops.

"I wish I was going with them," he said.

"I'm glad you're not," Molly replied quietly, almost absently. She could not help asking herself how many of the young men marching so confidently along the road below them would be dead within no more than a couple of hours. She looked at each flat, inexpressive face as the soldiers passed but she could see no sign of the concern she felt herself. She saw only a kind of bewildered vacancy. It was as though each one of them, if they had thought of death at all, was convinced that if it were to come, it would be to someone else. Either that, or they did not care. No, she thought, It is impossible not to care. Impossible, too, not to have thought of death and dying, to have thought of the unfairness of dying for a cause. Even if the death is heroic, it cannot possibly compensate for time. For the time not lived.

Molly turned away from the line of soldiers and made to move off the battlements.

"You're not going?" said Wu, and it was more of a command than a question. Molly looked at him.

"Yes," she said. "I can't stand looking at them. I can't help thinking of the waste."

"Waste?"

"Of life," said Molly.

Whatever Wu replied was drowned beneath the roaring engine of a 'plane which came suddenly over the horizon and flew low across the village and on towards the sun. It was followed by eleven more.

"Dive bombers," said Wu, pointing. "They'll be going to the airfield and the harbour. There's no going back now."

He was excited and happy. Molly thought of her father, sitting alone and crippled in his flat, and all the other people she knew in Hong Kong. She couldn't feel glad about any of it.

(xi)

Willard Russell did not hear the 'planes fly over. He did not hear anything any more. He imagined ice forming along the metal rungs of his small balcony but the balcony wasn't his and it wasn't in Kowloon. He imagined the birds squat and fluffed with cold in the trees, the wild cats sheltering from the frost in the hollow trunks of the walnut trees on the rough path down to the river near the house in Albany where he was born but had not been back to for more than fifty years. Then, as the first bombs fell on the airfield at Kai Tak and the smoke of the five burning 'planes made a black smudge on the clear morning sky, he could smell the tar they burned to keep warm in the winters when he was starting out, working the roads from Boston up to and through Toronto, the skies stone grey and heavy, his hands tingling with the cold when he took off his thick, leather gloves and his fingers chafed against the heavy, flat paving stones. The smoke of the steamer that brought him to the Far East drifted over the water in the wake behind the ship as he stood at the stern and watched the distant mountains of the mainland fall below the horizon. Then, suddenly, he was walking through the deep snowfilled forests in the foothills of the mountains to the North of Nanking, his hands still tingling with cold and holding an empty, wicker basket. Beside him, Suyong was beautiful and simple and the fields were awash with the cold winter sunlight. They walked hand in hand beneath the cherry trees where the pink blossom was tightly knotted against the dark wood of the branches, petals drifting up into the air in a sudden gust of wind and floating out over the thick snow. Willard Russell was freed from the confines of his wheelchair and his lifeless legs were strong and young again. He threw down the wicker basket and ran through the snow with Suyong, laughing, life seething and rising inside him, lifting him up towards the slow melting ice capped mountains and away from the flowers, away from Suyong and away from the fields and rivers choked with snow.

A stray bomb from one of the dive bombers left Willard Russell's flat in Kowloon burnt and gutted at eight o'clock on the morning of 8th December. His charred body was found still propped in his wheelchair, his head was turned towards the balcony and the skin had been burnt away to leave a bright smile of teeth in the black skin of his face.

(xii)

Eliot Rodmell heard the first explosion from Kai Tak as he was lying in bed. He moved his long legs slowly and peered dreamily out from beneath his mosquito net. His mouth was dry and his tongue thick with the remains of gin. As he padded barefoot over to the window, a thick pall of smoke began to rise into the sky away to the right. He saw the 'planes curve away from the airfield and fly back across the harbour and over Kowloon. There was another explosion and another plume of black smoke billowed into the sky from one of the apartment blocks in the neighbouring city. His immediate reaction was to put on the radio and he made his way from the bedroom into the lounge quickly. The wireless hummed for a moment and then a crackling voice informed him that a signal had been received before dawn that morning bringing news of the invasion of Malaya by the Japanese. There were rumours too of a Japanese airborne attack on Pearl Harbour, which had yet to be confirmed, and heavy Japanese troop movements just over the Hong Kong border. General Maltby had given orders to blow up the frontier bridges and to make the roads impassable at half past seven that morning. Rodmell looked at his watch. It was just before nine o'clock. He looked back over the harbour towards the airport where the smoke had started to thin into wispy black clouds. The radio informed him that twelve Japanese bombers with thirty-six fighters had put the five RAF 'planes at Kai Tak out of action. The Japanese troops, the voice continued, were, at that moment, moving towards the Sham Chun River.

Rodmell sat down heavily and then got to his feet almost at once. Still in his pyjamas, he stood before the plate glass of his window, looking down over the city, and he thought of chaos and destruction. In the garden, his chairs were still lined up facing the West, abandoned, the grass and weeds growing over the metal feet and in places a blister of rust bursting through the white paint and beyond, where there had been flowers, a mass of tangled grass had invaded. His life felt as empty and abandoned as the chairs and not even the distant bombing could rouse him from his lethargy. He thought of Margaret, safe in Darwin, and tried to be pleased. But he resented her not being there with him. He wondered what he should do and whether he was supposed to go down and report in at the HKVDC HQ. He turned away from the window and walked across to the telephone. He dialled a number automatically, A sharp, military voice answered.

"Put me through to Major Harland," said Rodmell rudely. And then, "What do you mean he's busy? Tell him it's Rodmell, Eliot Rodmell." The soldier asked him something like didn't he know there was a war on and hung up. Rodmell held the buzzing receiver in his hand for a moment and then slammed it down. He walked bad-temperedly back to his bedroom and began to dress in his Volunteer Defence Corps uniform.

He met Laughton, who was not in uniform, on the tram down to the city. Laughton knew less than Rodmell about the Japanese attack and Rodmell was pleased to be able to stop thinking in order to inform him.

"It was the airfield," he proclaimed. "Wiped out our paltry air force in one fell swoop. Stray bomb fell on Kowloon, too, I believe. Panic and looting broken out across the water by all accounts."

Rodmell could have been speaking about anything but war. Laughton looked at him in his spruce uniform and would have liked to say something fatuous, only nothing occurred to him.

"So our time has come, Laughton," Rodmell continued dramatically. "Time to defend King and Country, eh?"

Laughton sighed.

"No," he said. "It'd be ridiculous to fight. We don't stand a chance."

"Can't just give in, old boy," said Rodmell, peering through the window of the tram with a frown.

"Any sensible or responsible Governor would negotiate a surrender," said Laughton. "He has to. There are too many civilian lives at stake. And the Japs know that too. Why else do you think they've only bombed the airport?"

Rodmell shook his head.

"That's not our way, though, Laughton, is it?"

"Our way?"

(xiii)

Tung Nien had watched the bombing of the airport from The Peak. The first explosion had woken Chen Liew and he had stood beside her in silence as the bombs fell. When it was over, he had turned away and begun to walk back to the house. Before he reached the door, he turned to face her, although he looked past her in the direction of the black smoke rising from the crippled 'planes.

"We cannot trust the Japanese to keep their word," he said. "We must get ready to leave the island. I have made plans."

Chan appeared beside him, a dark shadow in the dark socket of the door.

"I'm not leaving," she said. "I can't leave. This is all I've got."

10

"The mountain rests on the earth"

(i)

"We're going out to Kowloon to help with the evacuation," shouted Rodmell, above the noise of other, more official commands. They were in the crowded barracks in Victoria, the regular soldiers and the volunteers all mixed together—like a salad, Osbourne had said—the only visible difference being the discomfort shown by the volunteers on being trapped inside the hair-shirts of their uniforms. Circumstance had yet again thrown Osbourne, Laughton and Rodmell together and this time they minded less because it seemed to rid them of the anonymity of the others. They were a group, they knew each other, they almost seemed to be old friends. Other volunteers formed into clutches of threes and fours on the other side of the room.

"Got to help get the civilians out," said Rodmell.

"How?" asked Osbourne.

Rodmell looked at him.

"Shove them onto the ferries, Osbourne. They've got the Star Ferries going back and forth non stop, getting the people over to Victoria."

"Where are they going to go then?" asked Laughton.

"Goodness knows, Laughton!" Rodmell spluttered a little. "But it'll be better than being killed by the Japs, don't you think?"

The three of them looked out into the crowded room. Major Harland was bustling officially from one side to another.

"It's chaos!" he complained. "The Japs have crossed the Sham Chun River. Made temporary bridges, of course. Then they marched straight down to Shung Nun on the Gindrinkers Line. It's almost as though someone had told them the weakest spot! The Royal Scots are holding out, but they won't be able to keep it up for long—and then the way will be open to Kowloon. They'll just march straight into the city and then there'll only be the harbour between us."

"It'll've been that Kenji bloke, you mark my words," said Osbourne resentfully.

"What will?" asked Laughton, taking a cigarette and offering the packet to Osbourne. Osbourne looked at the half-empty packet, shook his head and took out his own full packet.

"Have one of mine, Doc," he said. "These are gonna be in short supply before long. That Kenji," he went on. "He's a spy, isn't he, for the Japanese? He'll've told them where to attack." He looked at his cigarette before lighting it and added as an afterthought, "I'd been tailing him, you see."

Rodmell coughed and looked the other way. Then he looked back at Osbourne and Laughton and, with the emotion bursting out in red blotches on his face, said, "If I see the little bastard, I'll shoot him!"

And although he knew they hadn't, Osbourne said, "And after we'd made him welcome here, too. That's the way he repays our hospitality!"

"You always hated him," Laughton observed quietly. "All of you. I, for one, never even spoke to the chap that I know of, and I daresay you two never did either."

"I spoke to him," said Rodmell still with the colour in his cheeks, although emotion had been replaced by half-remembered indignation. "I spoke to him all right."

"I tailed him for weeks," said Osbourne. "I knew he was a spy. I just didn't know how to prove it." And then he added a little apologetically, "No one was interested anyway."

"They never are," admitted Laughton, although he had no reason for saying it.

Major Harland marched importantly over to them. Now that he did not need to think for himself but merely had to act out what he had been ordered to do, he was in his element. He bristled with vigour and a bubble of spittle burst at the corner of his mouth as he spoke to them.

"Good to see you fellows've turned out," he said. "We're going to need every man Jack of you if we are to put up any kind of a show at all."

He seems pleased about it, Laughton thought to himself. The prig! But he said, "Why don't we just surrender?"

Major Harland looked at him in disbelief.

"Orders," he blustered. "From Churchill himself. Defend the Island, even if it comes to hand to hand street fighting."

"Why?" said Laughton. "It'll be a massacre!"

"When you are in the Army, Laughton, you do not question orders."

"Why not?"

"It would be chaos!"

"It's chaos, anyway. You said so yourself."

Harland pointed at Laughton with his baton and struggled for words. "You tell him, Eliot," he said finally.

Laughton looked at Rodmell for an answer. Rodmell shrugged. He too knew the principles but he had to admit it seemed a bit suicidal.

"We're all a bit nervous, Harland, that's all. A bit out of our depth, even."

"Bombastic old fart!" said Laughton as they were being marched down to the pier. "Typical bloody military mind. We'll all be killed, you know that, don't you? If we try to fight them off, we'll all be killed."

"No need to be so melodramatic, Laughton. They're hardly likely to let that happen, are they?" said Rodmell.

"Don't bank on it," grunted Osbourne.

They fancied they could hear the sound of guns from across the water, but it might have been thunder.

"I never really expected this to happen, you know?" Rodmell said suddenly. "Not even when they took the women. I really didn't think it would come to this."

He looked around him. The HKVDF was made up almost entirely of men like himself in their sixties and seventies. Osbourne and Laughton were the exceptions.

"I mean," nervousness forced Rodmell on in the same way that it had dried up Laughton's stock of words and reasons, "that I would actually be doing something like this."

"You get bundled into it, though, don't you?" said Osbourne. "I mean, no one's doing it out of choice."

A few cheers of encouragement rang out from a balcony high away to their left and they kept marching on down towards the waterfront. Laughton listened to the clipped sound of their boots stepping in time against the tarmac surface of the road. He's right, he thought. Although, now it is happening, it is as though it were always the only solution. It doesn't seem now as though anything else were ever possible.

And as if on cue they halted. Over to his right, Laughton could see the steep steps that led away to the fortune-teller's shop where he had spent so many afternoons with Tung Nien. Just when you had managed to turn your mind to something else, said Laughton to himself, She comes back to haunt you. He looked up the steps where it seemed the same stream of sewerage cascaded down into the monsoon drain beside the main road. He looked at the faded green blind tapping against the upstairs window where they had made love and was struck by how empty and deserted the shop looked. But it had always been like that. It was only that when they were together they had filled it with life. The enormous improbability of their love still made his heart race. But when he had told her to go, he had been so filled with anger and bitterness that there wasn't anything else he could do. Except he had thought, maybe, that the anger and bitterness would go with her, dragging with them what had remained of his love. But with her absence, it had all multiplied. The anger, the bitterness and the love. Laughton felt a sudden urge to break ranks and race over to the geomancer's shop. But he knew he would find less there than a murderer returning to the scene of a crime. The broken glass from the empty bottle of Usher's Green Stripe hidden away beneath the bed. The nut-brown stain in the bowl of the opium pipe beside the bed on a table the colour of cigar tobacco. Everything tangible, but none of it her.

"And, of course, the civilian casualties will be terrible."

Rodmell's voice brought him back abruptly from the room above the geomancer's shop. Osbourne was nodding his agreement beside him.

"You lot sound like you don't even want us to win," complained an old voice from behind them. "The fighting's not even started and you're already giving us up for lost."

"Don't take any notice of him," said Rodmell quietly to Laughton and Osbourne. "That's only Elderfield. He used to work in a bank."

(ii)

Molly had watched the Japanese soldiers marching past until there had been nothing left to watch except the reflection of the sun in a muddy puddle in the middle of the road. She had argued with Wu again and lost. She had been unable to stop him tailing off behind the last rank of soldiers and his only concession had been that. That he would bring up the rear. Only she knew he wouldn't. She knew that, as soon as he were out of sight, he would gradually move as far towards the front as they let him. He had become so obsessed with his need to be an active part of the invasion that it had pushed away his obsession with her. He couldn't not go, even when he knew that, by going, he was likely to lose her. It was something stupid and masculine that he knew she would never understand. She did not even understand that his disregard for her wishes had nothing at all to do with his love for her. His love remained, but there was something else he had to do. But, for Molly, there was only love. And desertion. And somewhere, behind it all, there were also pride and vanity. Although she would never have admitted that. Of course, she was frightened for him, too. But she could not imagine a world where he was dead. Others would be killed, but he would always come back. Even if he didn't want her any more.

Molly watched until the sun's reflection moved away from the puddle, looked once more along the road now empty of soldiers and then turned back into the village.

As Wu marched with the Japanese soldiers into the outskirts of Kowloon, he was surprised to see that the streets were empty. They marched through a deserted and abandoned part of the city where they were neither greeted, as Wu had expected, as the conquering saviours, nor repulsed by fierce pockets of resistance as unwanted invaders. He could hear gunfire in the distance and could see the smoke from the countless burning buildings that had been gutted by successive air-raids that morning, but on the outskirts of the city the silence was broken only by the occasional, spasmodic burst of conversation in the ranks.

Wu's first taste of active service was as disappointing as their initial contact with Kowloon. As they rounded an empty corner in the empty city a shot suddenly rang out away to their right and a bullet kicked up a puff of dust, ricocheted and then embedded itself in the concrete wall of a shop behind them. Half a dozen rifles were immediately trained on the spot from where the sniper had fired and the wall was peppered with bullets, followed by silence. A couple of soldiers ran stealthily to the door of the building and stood either side of the gawping entrance. There was a sudden clatter of metal, and a rifle spewed into the street, followed by a rather frightened Chinese coolie, his hands clasped above his head. He was pushed unceremoniously to the floor and kicked gratuitously in the ribs by the two soldiers at the door. The coolie whined and cried out, but more in terror than in pain, and then Wu lost sight of him as they marched on through the town. Rather than the heroic struggle he had imagined, the scene had been degrading. Wu had not been fired with an enthusiastic sense of patriotism, as he had imagined he would be, but had been embarrassed at the squalid surrender of the coolie. There had been more gratuitous violence than calculated aggression and danger, and consequently adrenaline, had been conspicuous by its absence. Wu was still thinking about the strange, frightened expression on the coolie's face when they rounded another corner and the first line of Japanese troops, about two hundred yards ahead of him down the road, seemed to crumple and the remaining soldiers, himself included, scattered and ran for whatever cover they could find. They had walked straight into a curtain of gunfire from the rearguard of the retreating Royal Scots.

Wu cowered into a doorway. Although he would have called it taking cover, it was not. It was cowering. As he heard the enemy gunfire, he covered his head with his hands, not thinking that this offered him no protection at all. His heart heaved in his chest and his legs felt weak. Slowly, he sank towards the floor and pushed his knees up to his chin. He was terrified, but desperately wanted to pull himself together. He tried to drum up some semblance of bravery by thinking himself into the rôle his father had forced him into—a future Head of the Dragon, one of the most ruthless and powerful men in Hong Kong—but he could not find it. When another burst of gunfire crashed into the wall above his head, he cowered still more closely against the bolted door and tried to make his body fuse into the shadows. When he dared to look up and across the road, he saw what he should have been doing. A soldier in the doorway diagonally opposite him on the other side of the road was firing back at the Royal Scots. He even seemed to be taking his time to aim at a specific target. Wu held tightly to the butt of his rifle and felt his hands shaking.

(iii)

Rodmell was panting, out of breath. His blood seemed thick at his temple and his saliva had dried to a paste. He moved his tongue into the corners of his mouth, his tongue which felt fat and clumsy like a toe, and he tried to make the pasty saliva liquid. As they marched, his heart thumped in time with their boots. Beside him, Dr Alfred Laughton was panting too. Rodmell could not actually hear him panting, but he knew that he was. He could see it in the awkward, tired scuffing of the Doctor's feet as they all clattered down the metal gangplank of the ferry and onto the jetty at Kowloon.

"Kow-fucking-loon!" moaned Osbourne from behind him. "Anywhere in the world would be a better place to die!"

Rodmell turned his head quickly and said stupidly, "Oh, come along, man! Pull yourself together! No one's going to die!"

Seeing Laughton's raised eyebrows, he turned back again, thinking, "Well, so what if it was stupid. Only trying to keep our spirits up."

Osbourne was laughing. "Well, if that's so, Rodmell, I reckon it'll be the first war in history, eh Doc? With no casualties? Ha ha!"

"Why does he have to include me?" said Laughton to himself. "It's as though he might lose his grip on the world if he doesn't people it, as though it is too big when he is alone. I should tell him: Even loneliness can be a comfort sometimes."

They could hear the intermittent, spasmodic firing of guns from somewhere to the North. Laughton looked quickly at his two companions and then round at the rest of the volunteers to see whether the sudden reality of bullets had affected them in the same way it had him. Rodmell, he thought, seemed to be stooping a little more, Osbourne's eyes looked a little wilder behind his smutty glasses.

They were ordered to stop and were told they were going down to defend the power station. They shuffled across to the shelter of the buildings where Laughton took a cigarette from his breast pocket and lit it. He passed the packet to Osbourne and they watched as a thick plume of black smoke rose over the roofs in front of them.

"I haven't had the chance to be happy," Osbourne said suddenly, looking first at Laughton and then at Rodmell. "I've spent so long doing other things instead."

Rodmell's eyes were lowered to concentrate on the embarrassment he felt at this sudden outburst. For perhaps the first time in his life he didn't find someone else's weakness the cause for a cynical and superior comment.

"Now this happens," Osbourne continued, "And you realise how much time you've wasted just getting through the day."

Laughton crouched on his heels and leaned up against the wall.

"Hedonism is very much the privilege of a select few," Rodmell offered up a bright platitude, until he saw that Osbourne himself had not been in the slightest bit embarrassed by his confession and was in no need of Rodmell's protective verbiage. "I mean, we all have to live, to make a living."

Osbourne looked at him and Rodmell looked at his hands. They were, he noticed, the hands of an old man.

"Yeah, I know that," said Osbourne. "I didn't mean that exactly."

A burst of gunfire stopped the conversation for a moment. Laughton continued to watch the smoke rising over the buildings. Osbourne was struggling to put his thoughts into words.

"I meant that somehow we don't seem to make an effort to be happy, do we? It's more something we expect to happen to us. It just sort of comes along, doesn't it? Like the monsoon. One day it's sunny, the next it's pissing down. One day you're bored and then suddenly you're happy. We never work at it, though, do we?" He looked at Laughton, a forlorn expression on his face. "I mean, do you know what's so stupid about all this?" He was not about to wait for an answer. "I'm just bloody starting, mate! I'm not ready to die yet. I haven't lived." His voice quietened a little, but he would continue. "Look, what I want to say is that I have spent all my life preparing myself for when I would be in a position to enjoy it. And what fucking happens? They come along and blow your bloody arse off!"

Laughton understood more than he would have liked to admit. "I had my moment, and it passed," he said, trying, in his embarrassment, to make his smoking, if not his words, thoughtful. "She was there and I sent her away."

Rodmell grunted. It was not clear that it was an agreement, but he said, "Maybe, had it not been for the war, it would have been failure that brought us together."

The other two men looked at him but said nothing, waiting for him to continue. But he had finished, it seemed, and so Laughton, drawn into speech by the proximity of silence, continued, "I sent her away. The only thing in my life that ever mattered."

This time, it was Osbourne who grunted. There was a tremendous desire to communicate, it seemed, but years of words snagging against incomprehension made them all wary of accepting the others' feelings. Instead, they held them at arm's length, or tried to find a dirty corner in which to drop them unnoticed and continue with the mundane and with themselves. But, at the same time, never had they clung before so tightly to the need to figure, to be a part of life, to put their little tragedies into perspective, into the solemnising of sharing. That none of them wanted to share the other's grief was immaterial, the only thing that mattered was the speaking, so, when Laughton said, "I sent her away," he was not expecting a response, rather he was trying to understand it for himself, trying to understand what had made him trim his life to make it fit into what he had thought he believed, when all he had wanted to do, he realised now, was to leave it all and be with her. Who did not love him. And so he said, "It wasn't so much the sending away as the not going back I mind now. I could have tried harder at least."

"It's never too late," said Rodmell, to say something.

"I saw a bloke once," said Osbourne, "His wife had died about six months before. You know what he said? I'm beginning to get over it now, he said." Osbourne looked at them and raised his eyebrows. "That's how you get through life. You get over things."

Rodmell shook his head. "You know you can't do that," he said. "Not always."

"What's worse than losing your wife?" said Osbourne stubbornly, although he wouldn't have known.

Rodmell shrugged, thinking of his life without Margaret. "That's what I mean," he said. "Some things you can't get over."

"But *he did.*" Osbourne was going to insist.

Before Rodmell could reply, there was an explosion at the end of the street, gunfire now coming too from behind them, the tireless drone of an aircraft overhead—the all too certain evidence of their mortality was all around them and made their feeble efforts to express themselves only too evident. But even so, it was their mortality which nudged their minds towards more succinct, if yet half-formed, sentences and emphasised their desperate need to communicate. But they were not friends, nor really companions even. Chance or history had thrown them together to live out what might possibly be their last minutes, hours or days together, who could not communicate, would not, they each knew, have communicated even had they been friends.

The need to speak and yet the impossibility of speaking was, thought Rodmell, like a blind man asking if it was night or day. It was the need to know and the impossibility of knowing. And so, giving himself up to the darkness of incommunication, and realising that he was, in fact, doing so with not a little sense of relief, Rodmell allowed his mind to race along with his fast beating heart. He had the eerie sensation that he could almost see his life drawing to a close. Everything that came into his head was past and done with, the future a blank wall before him. When he heard the gunfire, it was fire-crackers at Chinese New Year, standing in grey shorts on the waterfront and watching the lighted lanterns float past unsteadily on the waves, all his life before him, leading inexorably to this point, the water behind him now. He turned a pale eye to look over his shoulder. But there was nothing there. So much of life has been unnecessary, he said. Has been a waste of time. Has served only to move me a little closer to this point. And when I am gone, it will be as though I had never been. With no offspring even to remember me when they sense their own mortality creeping up out of the darkness in the loneliness of night. When everything is still except your fear. Because I could have done things differently. Even though this point would have been the same, the arriving here would have been different. Perhaps more worthwhile. Remembering now, suddenly, the deaths of relatives. Sound and then silence. Light and then dark. Movement and then stillness. That is all there is. No God even to come down from the skies and lift me up. Probably some Chink'll kick my lifeless body in the ribs while I lie in the gutter shot full of holes. Can't say I'd blame him either. Some anonymous Chogue adding insult to injury. If life were a book there'd be some kind of purpose to it all, there would be some kind of redemption. Finally some light at the end of all our tunnels. But here and now there is nothing. Except this pointless letting go.

Rodmell looked over at his two companions. Like him they seemed to have given up. Lost in thought and cut adrift, somehow the only escape from the horror which lay ahead. Osbourne was muttering the word *Bastards!* over and again beneath his breath. Bastards, thought Rodmell to himself with some abstraction. If only it were as simple as that!

"Life is all we have but we don't know how to use it properly." That's what Fletch said once, said Osbourne to himself. Only I needed things from life, he thought. I needed them to give me a stimulus. I couldn't do it on my own. Yet no one was prepared to help me. Who was always only crying out for help. All I ever needed was a hand to hold. But I couldn't tell them. I could never find it in myself to admit that I couldn't do it on my own. When sometimes it would have been so easy just to say, Please, help me. Not afraid that they would laugh at me, being used to it, it wasn't that. There was some larger impediment that prevented me. That always drove me on and away from whatever meagre help there might have been, so small I wouldn't have seen it anyway, even if I'd looked. Fletcher the only real friend I ever had. Killed for nothing. "To make a splash, Osbourne!" that fat git of an officer, Harland, had said. "Unrest." Rest for Fletcher and unrest for us, he might have said. Poor old Fletch. The ignominity. Head lolling in that rickshaw, mouth agape, with everybody looking on. That was probably written out for me, that death. If I'd accepted his invitation and joined in with that stupid fucking rickshaw race. It was probably meant for me, that. And Fletcher got it. Can't even get my own death right!

Osbourne looked up as another explosion came at them from over the roofs and another pall of black smoke rose into the air. "Could be going for the power station," he said aloud.

Laughton looked towards the smoke. "Could be," he said. "They've got a way to go yet though."

Osbourne sniffed. "Depends, don't it. If no one's in their way they'll be there before us."

"I hardly think, Osbourne, we're likely to have left them a clear run to one of our only sources of energy," Rodmell almost boomed, as though the force of his conviction coupled with the volume of his voice alone might be enough to stop the Japanese.

"I didn't think we'd let them get this far," said Osbourne.

"To hell with it!" said Laughton and moved away slightly to his left.

Laughton took out his packet of cigarettes, lit one, put the packet back in his jacket pocket, and squinted along the street towards the smoke and gunfire. He could see nothing other than the empty road and closed up buildings. He took another drag of his cigarette and leaned back, his read resting against the wall and his face turned to the sky.

And then suddenly it was raining. In no time, a rush of water tipping into the street from the gutter above him, and "Rain, now," he said, as though these two words somehow held a more definitive meaning than a mere description of the weather. For it was impossible now for him not to see Tung Nien in everything. The sound of the rain, the gushing torrent over the now intermittent cracks of guns took him back, not without his wanting it, to a night at the geomancer's at the beginning of their relationship when it had rained too, the waterfall of the stepped street and the guns now the spasmodic cracking of the blind across the alley from their room. She had wanted to try the whisky and he had got her drunk. And she had done a fashion show for him, leaving the room every few minutes to come back in wearing something new. Strange to think he didn't question that she should have clothes there. When, finally, in a small orange skirt that could only have come from a taxi-girl, they had started to dance, holding each other close, Laughton clumsy and she graceful through her drunkenness. He had slipped his hands up to her breasts and felt her pushing towards him, until he had moved his hand down her back and she had pushed him away and he had realised that the fashion show and the whisky had been instead of sex, that she had not known how to tell him the physical was sometimes above the emotional and the rain wasn't all that flowed.

Laughton looked up and let the rain fall onto his face. "I shouldn't be here," he said. "I shouldn't be here at all. I should be trying to find her. Because she is out there somewhere. Waiting, maybe. If not for me, for an escape. A way out. Which I could give her if I knew how to. But at least I could try. Find her and say I am here. I have come to take you away. As she did with me in the Floating City. Send a sign at least to say I am still alive and think of you."

Laughton looked across at his companions through the rain. "Lear, Edmund and the Fool," he grunted, "only with less grandeur." He pushed himself away from the wall and stepped into the street. He held out his arms and turned a slow circle, the palms of his hands upwards, "the centuries-old sign for pleading," he thought. As he turned his slow pirouette in the street, there was miraculously no shooting and it was with some surprise that he wasn't dead that Laughton made his way back to the shelter of the doorway where the others huddled. He put his hand on Rodmell's shoulder. "Lear," he said, much to Rodmell's surprise. He held a soggy hand towards Osbourne. "Poor Tom," he said and took a pace backwards. "This isn't for me. I'm off!"

"You can't desert!" hissed Osbourne.

"I'm a volunteer," said Laughton.

"Tacit desertion," Rodmell corrected.

"Fuck it!" said Laughton.

"They'll shoot you if you go," Osbourne might have been taking the decision himself.

"They'll shoot me if I stay," said Laughton simply.

Osbourne considered a moment.

"And what do you mean, 'Poor Tom'?"

Rodmell waved him into silence.

"I can understand," he said, "But I can't approve."

"There's nowhere to go," said Osbourne sulkily. As though he too had thought of running.

"She's out there," said Laughton. "I shall go to where she is."

Rodmell looked. The street was empty.

(iv)

Tung Nien was standing at her window, looking down over the city. She felt as though she had been standing there for days although it had been no more than half an hour since Chen Liew had said, "So, that is done. Everything is prepared." And she had turned her back on him and gone to her room. Everything was prepared meant their escape to Macao. Chen Liew had been in touch with her family. Their years of fishing from the island of Cheung Chau were over. It was time for them to repay their debt to Chen Liew. Tung Nien's father no longer looked after the Temple of the Jade Vacuity, having himself joined the Jade vacuity some years ago, but her two surviving brothers (one had been drowned doing an earlier favour for Chen Liew, an impromptu opium run into China which backfired and was intercepted by the Chinese Coast Guards) were even now preparing their junk to ferry Chen Liew and his troupe over to Macao before the arrival in Hong Kong of the Japanese Army.

"You bought them," Tung Nien had said, not even bothering to make the inflection of a question.

"As I bought you."

Tung Nien was silent.

"As I could have bought your Englishman."

She glanced up at him for a sign of emotion, of jealousy or anger, but he was just stating facts.

"I could have killed him, even. But it didn't seem worth it. He was self-destructive enough on his own. No threat."

Chen Liew stopped speaking to look through the window for a moment.

"And now the Japanese will kill him for me. As they will kill us, if we stay."

Tung Nien looked at his old, flat face.

"And Molly?"

Chen Liew rubbed his hands together and almost smiled. His lips quivered before he spoke.

"They would have paid me to take Molly. I did not need to buy her. It is a great pity she is not here. Now, you will get ready. Everything is prepared."

"You don't care what happens to her?"

Again his lips quivered.

"I know where she is and I know that she is safe."

There was, she thought, a kind of sad haste in his step as he walked off. She turned her back on him before he left the room to cheat him of the pleasure of her discomfort.

As she looked down over the city and watched the puffs of black smoke rising over Kowloon, Chen Liew's words came back to her. The Japanese will kill him now. It was like a death sentence. Chen Liew had spoken. A pact might have been made with the Japanese. Chen Liew had decided that Laughton would die and that was what would happen. Chen Liew was never wrong. The Japanese will kill him.

"I will not lose him a second time," she said. But before she was able to begin to think how she would escape from her husband, she noticed that various squadrons of 'planes were coming towards her. They were flying high over Kowloon, too high to be going to bomb it. As she watched, the 'planes flew past the mainland and out over the harbour where they banked and began to descend towards the city of Victoria. Tung Nien saw the first bombs fall on Central.

(v)

The city of Victoria lay exposed and defenceless on the north-western shore of the island. The so-called fortress was bombed systematically for four days and four nights. As the factories, oil storage tanks and paper thin tenement buildings went up in flames, the civilians fled into the streets and, as the streets crowded and filled, more bombs rained down until vast areas of the city became awash with heaps of mangled and blood-soaked bodies.

Laughton had wandered dazed and disgusted through the carnage until, forced on by the terrified pushing of hundreds of people he did not know, he took refuge with them in the granite hills behind the city. There he huddled with them and listened and watched the bombs raining down. His first initial surge of love, his hopes to see Tung Nien again had been slowly battered out of him as the days dragged on and the 'planes continued to come with their cargo of explosives. He felt empty, incapable of doing anything anymore.

Kenji was making his way north-east out of Victoria. He tucked sheets of propaganda into the pockets of the dead he walked past, urging them to turn against the British exploiters. It suited his feeling of useless, cocky triumph. During the four days of bombing, he had, like many others, hidden out in the firm, stone buildings of the commercial district. He had listened to the 'planes and the falling bombs with a sense of detached interest, and got some pleasure from observing the concern on the faces of his fellow refugees. He had, at one point, mentioned the fact that it was because the British had refused to surrender that they were being bombed, suggesting that the Governor, Sir Mark Young, was directly responsible for the air raids because he had given the Japanese no other solution, but his terrified Chinese companions received no solace from his words, nor did they manage to stir up any hatred. Now, picking his way over the dead bodies littering the narrow streets, he felt it served them right and so he stuffed his pages of propaganda into their pockets. More than death, what Kenji most noticed was how so many of the corpses had lost items of clothing—shoes and trousers, mostly—and the strange blue colour of their burnt legs.

The Indian soldiers came at them as soon as they'd stepped ashore. Wu had been expecting the English, or maybe even the Canadians, with guns, but not Indians with their bare hands. As he splashed ashore he had the strange thought that everybody, all races, looked the same in war. Everybody's face was grey. A taut, washed-out, bleary grey.

He had no time to think of anything else. A soldier wearing a blue turban leapt towards him as he reached the shore. Fell back suddenly as a bullet ripped into his stomach. Wu stood, paralysed. He watched the body as it floated face down in the water. Blood oozed at a small point on the soldier's back. Wu was pushed back into the sea. His mouth filled with slime and salt water. He sank beneath the water and opened his eyes to the bubbles of his own breath. Someone was sitting on his back, holding his head beneath the water. The water seemed to be exploding in his ears. Wu could feel himself moving, although he knew he wasn't. His heart felt like a clenched fist in his chest. The water pulled at his body and the heavy weight sat still on his back. He could taste blood in his mouth. He tried to turn but it was impossible. He could feel the soldier's hands tightening at his throat. The air was squeezing from his lungs. He gulped helplessly at a mouthful of seawater. He opened his eyes in the murky slime of seaweed and pushed his hands into the sand. Suddenly, the pressure was released from his throat. The weight was lifted from his back. Wu rolled over and sucked the fresh air deep into his lungs. It seemed to clog and choke him. He gagged and vomited a stream of seawater onto the face of the dead Indian soldier who had attacked him. He pushed himself onto unsteady, trembling legs. He felt that if he could just get out of the water, he would be safe, and so he focused all his energy on making his legs move him towards the shore. He tried to ignore the figures on the beach before him and the Japanese soldiers behind him. His first thought had been that the hand to hand fighting had been a result of the Indians' having no ammunition, but this idea was soon dispelled. A barrage of bullets tore into the Japanese beside him and he saw, from the corner of his eye, two bodies crumple into the sea. Wu refused to look round. But neither did he want to look before him. He knew he did not want to see the moment of his death. He knew he did not want to see an anonymous Indian looking at him along the sights of a rifle, knowing the bullet was coming and waiting for it to come. Better, by far, if it had to happen, for it to be a surprise. And so he ran, pulling his heavy legs through the sand, which clutched at his feet and the waves, which pulled at his legs. Until he was free of the water and stood shaking on the stones of the short beach which separated him from apparent shelter. He kept feeling that he was in the middle of a dream and that he would wake up dead. Then someone pushed at his back and he stumbled forwards, gashing his legs on a string of galvanised wire that was sticking out of an upturned and abandoned concrete block. The sound of gunfire was constant and deafening although, before him, among the buildings, he could see the soldiers fighting hand to hand.

When it was all over, Wu tried to relax. He didn't smoke but he was smoking a cigarette anyway. The beach was covered with dead bodies, both Indians and Japanese, and Wu tried to make himself remember that, although they were now dead, they had once been people with individual hopes and fears, with, until a few minutes ago, a past and a future, with, in short, a life which had been snatched away and which might as well have never existed. He felt guilty because he had thought only of himself and of survival. Not once had he thought of Molly. And he still hadn't fired his gun.

It was more than an hour after the battle when Kenji arrived. He walked out of the shadows of the narrow streets. He might have been strolling down for a swim. He was, it seemed, expected. Colonel Tanaka received him impatiently, but with respect. Kenji was distant and superior. They disappeared into Tanaka's makeshift office—a hurried tarpaulin strung over two kettledrums, one of the "chairs" the concrete slab which Wu had walked into on the beach, the other another metal drum. Kenji handed Tanaka some papers and sat forwards. He pointed his finger at the detailed map between them.

"Here," he said, quietly. "The Wong Nei Ching Gap. It's a deep valley to the South West of Mount Butler. There's a handful of Canadians there, defending the island's main North-South road. Once you've taken them out, it'll be on up to the reservoirs. You'll hardly even notice you've been in a war!"

Tanaka looked at the map. "And you?" he asked.

Kenji shook his head. "I have other things to do," he said. Noticing Tanaka was still looking at him, he added, "It's a private matter."

"There are no private matters now," said Tanaka.

Kenji laughed. "Oh?" he said. "In that case, it is official."

"May I ask what it is?" Tanaka did his best to give the impression that he didn't care.

"You may not," said Kenji.

"It will be a girl, " said Tanaka. "It always is."

"It is not a girl," said Kenji. "Although a girl is involved. It is just something I promised myself I would do when all this started. There is someone I have to kill."

Tanaka looked at Kenji slowly. Even now, killing, when it was personalised, was still killing. What he and his soldiers did, was institutionalised, it was different. But Kenji was talking about murder. Tanaka watched him coldly as he folded the map.

"Don't try to work it out, Colonel," said Kenji. "I am in a different war from you. Have been from the outset. What do *you* do with traitors, with deserters, in your war?" He raised his eyebrows.

"Why should it be any different in mine?"

And then he pointed across at Wu.

"He will come with me to help," he said.

Tanaka turned and looked at Wu.

"He's not one of mine," he said. "You're welcome to him."

(vi)

It was the lack of sleep that Laughton most noticed now. And with his tiredness, an awareness of time. How much of it had passed since he had relinquished his voluntary involvement in the fighting. Although his mind felt sluggish with exhaustion, it was, at the same time, light and elusive. It skipped from an unnatural regret at having left Osbourne and Rodmell to face their fate without him, to a natural despair at not having been able to find Tung Nien. Yet through it all, there was a tremendous desire to stop deceiving himself. He hadn't found Tung Nien because he hadn't tried. And as for the fighting, he was glad to be out of it. When he came out of the granite hills and walked back into what remained of civilisation, the battered city, he didn't even see how uncivilised it was. The dead bodies had, for the most part, been dragged away, and a convenient thunderstorm had washed the blood from the streets. What he saw was how far away he had come from the road up to Tung Nien's house.

He rounded a corner by one of the first stops of the funicular railway and a 'plane flew out from high over The Peak. Laughton didn't even look up. He was numbed. He didn't care if it was 'ours' or 'theirs'. There was room left in his mind for only one thought. Tung Nien. The rest, like the city, had been bombed out. And he wasn't even waiting for it all to come back to life. "If I don't find her, it can stay dead," he said to himself. And, once he had started, he had to keep talking. Only now, he spoke aloud, letting his crisp words fall like grenades into the empty houses and gardens he walked past. "Osbourne wouldn't desert because he was afraid of being alone." He tossed that towards a large white bungalow away to his left, all the windows shuttered. "Rodmell? Rodmell was just too tired. Although, to be fair, he felt a sense of duty too. Misplaced, maybe. But held back by his need to be respected to the last." This echoed flatly in a carless, grey garage with a crust of sand and debris from the bombs lying along the ridge of its half-closed door.

He pulled off his khaki HKVDF jacket, screwed it into a ball and tossed it up into the branches of a frangipani tree where it hung like the severed corpse of a dead paratrooper. He rolled up the sleeves of his shirt and felt in his breast pocket for the cigarettes he knew he had finished more than two days ago. Tung Nien," he said. "Just be there!" Then to himself, All the things I want to remember. To keep her alive. To keep me going. My mouth on her throat and her tasting of rose water. A line drawn by my finger down her spine. Her legs soft and her hands in mine, squeezing them tight, the knuckles hard promontories in a soft sea of flesh. Touching the tips of her fingers so as not to drown. When she lay back, I barely moved in the silence. As fragile and transparent as the warm breath of cows. All the things I need to remember to keep her alive, to not let her be dead. And gone without me. For what are we without a witness? We might as well not be. Keep thinking, then. Witness all the things I know.

Then, turning a bend in the road, he saw a body lying dead in the street before him, face down, a patch of dried blood leading from the mouth across the tarmac. Laughton walked slowly over to the body and looked down. It was Miss Dekyvere. The top of her head had been blown away and her brain nestled in the broken skull, the colour and consistency of a cauliflower.

Standing behind the sandbags that protected the Power Station, Osbourne read aloud from a grubby piece of paper which had been handed round the ranks:

"His Excellency summarily rejects the proposal. This colony is not only strong enough to resist all attempts at invasion, but all the resources of the British Empire, the United States and the Republic of China are behind us and those who have sought peace can rest assured that there will be no surrender..."

Rodmell listened in silence. Osbourne clapped the flat of his hand against the paper before passing it to another volunteer, Scholes, a sixty-five year-old retired dentist.

"His fucking Excellency's not doing much fighting, though, is he?" he said.

"Shut up, Osbourne," said Rodmell.

"What d'you mean, shut up?"

"Just that. Shut up."

Osbourne looked about him, indignant. Scholes was squinting at the paper. Osbourne looked back at Rodmell.

"The resources of the British Empire... those who have sought peace... It makes me feel a lot better, that does, I can tell you..."

Rodmell lost his patience.

"Oh, for God's sake, man! Don't you see what it means?"

His hands were shaking and his lip trembled.

"What it means?" he asked again.

"I know what it means, all right," said Osbourne sulkily.

Rodmell seemed to have lost control of his muscles. His whole face was trembling, his hands were shaking, his voice quavered.

"You don't know anything," he said. "I don't suppose you ever have."

Osbourne snatched the paper back from Scholes and waved it in Rodmell's face.

"I know," he said, almost crying with frustration. "I bloody know all right."

And he screwed his anger into a tight ball with Sir Mark Young's paper courage and threw them both onto the floor between them.

"I know," he said again.

Rodmell tried to change the subject, but their range of subjects seemed to have shrunk. There was nothing either of them wanted to talk about anymore.

"Got much ammunition left?" Rodmell asked finally.

Osbourne shook his head.

"They didn't really give us much in the first place, did they?" And he looked up at Rodmell, a mischievous smile on his face. "But I'm not worried about that," he said. "Not with the resources of three countries..."

"For God's sake, Osbourne!" Rodmell interrupted. "Does everything have to be so... so... bitter?"

"Yeah. Why shouldn't it be? Just give me one reason why I should feel any other way."

Rodmell had no answer and so returned to practicalities.

"What do they expect us to do when we run out?"

"Bayonets," said Osbourne with a purposefully bitter smile.

Neither Kenji nor Laughton knew it as they made their way up different sides of The Peak, but Tung Nien was no longer there. Taking advantage of the mayhem caused by the bombing, she had escaped. In the end, it had been quite simple. She had just walked out of the front door, down the long gravel drive of the garden and out through the gates. As the bombs fell, Chen Liew and Chan had been too concerned in getting themselves under cover. When they realised that Tung Nien was not with them, it was too late.

As she walked down to Mong Kok she watched the bombs falling on the city. She heard an enormous explosion from somewhere out in the middle of the harbour and saw the thick plume of smoke as a huge load of dynamite being brought on a barge from Green Island to Victoria was blown up by a shot from a patrolman who had not been told of its arrival. The explosion was so loud that it blew out windows all over the city and added to the confusion and the fear caused by the constant bombing from the 'planes. This was followed by a second explosion at Kowloon power station as employees disabled the main turbine. When Tung Nien reached Mong Kok, the cages were empty, the birds were gone and the old men were dead. She sat alone in the shuttered bar and cried.

(vii)

They had been holding off the Japanese troops for more than four hours. When the shooting had started, Osbourne had begun to fire off his rifle immediately, although he could see no one to shoot at. He had, though, he realised, in only five days got so used to the idea of death that it didn't bother him. He didn't care how many Japanese he killed or if he killed none at all. It wasn't that he hated them any more than he had done before. It wasn't even a question of survival, a question of killing them before they killed him. He quite simply didn't care. Rodmell, on the other hand, didn't like it at all. He had had to make a conscious effort to fire his rifle when he had someone in his sights. And when he had killed, when he had seen the Japanese soldier at the other end of the road jerk back a couple of paces and fall, holding his stomach, he had felt physically sick. Osbourne had shouted encouragement in his ear. "Got the little bastard!" he had said. Rodmell had crouched down behind the sandbags so as not to see. But now they had no time to think. All they could do was fire off endless rounds of ammunition into the advancing line of green uniforms. When one of them fell, it was impossible to tell who had killed him.

Their first casualty had been the old dentist, Scholes, followed quickly by Elderfield from the bank. Scholes had died silently. They had scarcely even noticed. He had just crumpled forwards onto the sandbags with a little sigh, as though everything had become just too much for him. There was no sign of an injury on his body. He just dropped his rifle, gasped and fell forwards. Elderfield, on the other hand, screamed out as he was hit in the shoulder, stood up, and the top of his head disappeared. Osbourne had been splattered by his blood, had even tasted it in his mouth. And before he fell, Elderfield had looked at him with a bewildered expression on his face, as though wondering why he hurt if Osbourne was the one covered in blood. When he had fallen back, Osbourne had snatched his ammunition and winked at Rodmell. "He won't be needing this," he had said. Rodmell had looked at Osbourne and thought, He is in his element. He has managed to adapt even to the horror.

A sudden burst of machine gun fire rang out from the other end of the street. Osbourne raised his eyebrows.

"Machine guns, now," he said, stating the obvious.

Rodmell crouched in the shelter of the sandbags and had time to wonder why everything had been organised so badly. The rounds from the Japanese machine gun whistled over his head and thumped into the wall of the power station. He scarcely noticed the noise anymore, would probably have missed it had it ceased. He looked to his left where Osbourne, a wild look on his face, was firing his rifle, reloading, and firing again. Beside him, the peaceful, dead body of Scholes and the mutilated pain of Elderfield. Rodmell felt tremendously heavy as he turned, pushed himself to his knees and poked his rifle through a gap in the sandbags at the Japanese. "Someone's gotta take out that machine gun post," Osbourne screamed at him.

Rodmell fired a solitary, ridiculous bullet, his last, in the general direction of the stuttering gunfire. His nerves had gone completely. Where Osbourne had grown with the mindless conflict, embraced it entirely without seeming even to question it, allowed it to buoy him up beyond the simplicity of his fear to such an extent that he no longer knew what he was doing, all powers of analysis gone, taken over by a blind fury of hate where he was shooting, not at the Japanese, but at all the failed opportunities of his life, Rodmell could only feel that every move would be his last. Where Osbourne seemed almost to have floated out of his body, Rodmell had become overly conscious of his; he could almost sense his heart, his liver, his kidneys as solid, vulnerable organs straining to keep him alive behind their ludicrous, paper-thin protection of skin. His whole body was fragile, on the point of breaking, and there was nothing he could do about it.

"Oh, God!" he hissed, his hands shaking.

The machine gun stopped suddenly. There was silence for a moment. Silence enough for them all to hope. Then the flat explosion of a grenade.

Everything happened very quickly after that. The Japanese troops began to advance slowly along the street and were met with only an occasional shot as the Hong Kong Volunteer Defence Force steadily ran out of ammunition. Someone told them to fix bayonets. That they were going to charge. Grenades were being thrown over the sandbags. Incredibly, Osbourne was scurrying from side to side, catching the grenades before they exploded and lobbing them back at the Japanese. Rodmell watched him with a numbed, detached curiosity. He couldn't move. He had not even tried to fix his bayonet. As he watched Osbourne throwing the grenades, he clicked the empty trigger of his rifle. Until a grenade dropped over the sandbags and rolled towards him, coming to rest some five feet away from him. Rodmell looked at the round grenade as though it were a harmless and exotic insect and then looked pleadingly towards Osbourne. Osbourne was standing some five feet on the other side of the grenade. Their eyes met. But their expressions were blank. Even now there could be no communication. Then, suddenly, Osbourne threw himself forwards and face down over the grenade. Rodmell turned away as the full blast of the explosion was smothered by Osbourne's disintegrating flesh.

Osbourne's sacrifice was as pointless and empty as his life had been. Three minutes later, at exactly 4 p.m., the volunteers fixed their bayonets and charged the advancing Japanese. Eliot Rodmell was one of the first to fall, his body riddled by more than eight bullets. The last thing he saw before he died was the red glow of flames from the conquered power station. They had managed to defend it for thirty-six hours.

(viii)

Kenji and Wu crouched in the evening half-light in Miss Dekyvere's garden. They could see Chen Liew's darkened house through the open gate in the wall. Knowing Molly would ask, when they arrived Wu had walked through the house looking for the old woman.

"She'll be all right," Kenji had said. "People like that always are."

On the other side of Chen Liew's garden, Laughton was also watching the house. He had no idea what he was going to do if he managed to get in. His only thought was that he had to get Tung Nien out. Neither did he know what they would do then. He did not allow himself to think that he might not be able to get her out. Instead, to make time, although he would not have been able to explain what he was waiting for, he turned to look over the city. He could see the burning power station, a thick cloud of smoke illuminated from below by the flames, and he could not prevent the stabbing, painful thought that he should have been there. He had been a coward and he had run. He had easily convinced himself that his flight had been, not away from the Japanese, but towards Tung Nien. He knew, though, that it had been both. He could not now imagine a life without her, but neither could he imagine not having a life, with or without her. You do not deserve to find her, he said. You have done nothing to deserve it. Ever. All the people you know have more of a right than you do to see their dreams fulfilled. Maybe that is what you have learned. Maybe that is why they have let you get this far. The bastards and wasters will inherit the earth, never mind the meek. The meek will die along with the heroes and the accidents. Miss Dekyvere. How can she have deserved it, the poor old sod?

"Why do you look at me like that? It's not my fault." Kenji loaded his pistol meticulously, looking at each bullet before he placed it into its neat slot.

"Someone has to be to blame," said Wu.

Kenji laughed. "Oh," he said, gesturing towards the burning city. "For that? I wasn't talking about that."

"What then?" said Wu.

Kenji shrugged and finished loading his pistol.

"We have to kill him," he said. "Your father's already paid for it. Blame him if you like."

"It wasn't necessary," said Wu, still looking at the city.

"What's necessity got to do with it?"

Kenji pushed the safety catch on his gun forwards and crawled on his stomach a little closer to the open gate. "No sign of anyone. I hope the bastard's not escaped."

"Does it matter now?" asked Wu, pulling himself over the grass.

"It especially matters now," said Kenji, and when he turned to look at him, his face was in shadow. The evening was creeping quickly down the hillside. "It matters now because now is precisely when many others would give up."

Wu crawled forwards in the twilight.

"You brought me to see it, didn't you?" he said. "To be your messenger. To report back to my father."

"Why else?" said Kenji quietly.

"I thought it was to protect me." Wu realised it sounded stupid. "I thought my father..."

He stopped speaking because a shadow, only slightly darker than the grey of dusk, had moved a blind on one of the windows.

"We're in luck," said Kenji.

"Don't keep looking, Chan," said Chen Liew. They had been sitting in darkness since the lights had blown two hours previously. "She won't come back now."

"I wasn't looking for her," said Chan.

"Who, then?"

"Anyone else," said Chan.

"This is not life anymore, Chan," said Chen Liew, after a long silence. "It hasn't been life, has it, for a long time? Let them come. Whoever it is, whoever calls, let them in. It doesn't matter anymore."

From Laughton's position in the garden, the house looked totally deserted. He felt a mixture of relief and disappointment. He was about to stand up when he sensed, rather than saw, some movement from the direction of Miss Dekyvere's garden. He pulled himself into the darker shadows of a bush and saw two figures creeping stealthily towards the front door. He couldn't make out who it was in the darkness, but he saw enough to make out the black shape of Wu's rifle. That was when he stopped thinking.

The door was unlocked and Kenji and Wu slipped unnoticed into the house. Kenji motioned Wu over to the side of the long corridor and listened. There was a murmur of voices coming from a room at the back of the house. Kenji smiled, visibly relaxed and reached his hand up past Wu's head to the wall. With a deft flick of his wrist, he turned Chen Liew's *pat kwa* mirror to face the wall.

They had left the corridor by the time Laughton reached the house. He pushed the door open slowly and strained his eyes to see more than darkness. He could hear the voices at the back of the house and he pushed himself into the vague protection of the wall. A window further down the corridor let a little moonlight fall against the blackout blind and illuminate a small corner of what he found to be an empty room. The voices mumbled still, but somehow with more urgency. Then there were two shots and then there was silence.

"Nooooo!" Laughton screamed out, unthinking but numb no more.

He ran towards the far room and burst through the door.

Before he saw Kenji, he saw Chan, a humped walrus of dead meat on the floor. Before he saw Wu, he saw Chen Liew, lifeless in an antique chair, now ruined by his own stain of blood.

"Where is she?" he asked, panting, addressing no one.

Until it all slowed down and he became aware of the pounding at the side of his head, the taste of metal in his mouth. When things end, there is a definite moment, and Laughton sensed it had arrived.

"Doctor Laughton," said Kenji, lifting his gun away from Chen Liew and pointing it at him. Laughton looked past Kenji, understanding nothing.

"Wu?" he said.

"Mao," said Wu, raising his rifle.

Perhaps because he had nothing else, Laughton raised his hands.

Kenji lifted his pistol still further and looked at Laughton along the barrel.

"Goodbye, Doctor Laughton," he said.

Laughton heard the shot and closed his eyes.

When he opened them again, Kenji lay dead before him on the floor and Wu was looking at him.

"Now, I want to go home," he said, quietly.

(ix)

There was chaos all over the island. People crowded into any accommodation they could find. Many of them were sleeping in the public rooms of hotels. The Japanese poured across the harbour commandeering junks and sampans. Behind the city, the bunkers, defended by D Company of the Winnipeg Grenadiers, finally fell after three days' resistance when the Japanese pushed their field guns up to their walls and opened fire at point-blank range. British troops fought the Japanese back then from Leighton Hill, in Victoria's eastern suburbs. Before long, they had to withdraw west to Mount Parish. The Winnipeg Grenadiers held back more attackers on Mount Cameron. But the Japanese had forced a path between them and split them into two widely separated areas, on the Stanley Peninsula, in the south, and around Victoria. The Japanese had captured all the island reservoirs and they had cut off the water supply to Victoria.

Tung Nien had been living for several days in the lobby of the Parisian Grill. Like everyone else, she was just waiting for it all to be over. She looked at every new arrival that walked wearily and bloodstained into the hotel but no longer really expected to see Laughton. Even so, she could not stop herself from looking because, no matter how hard she tried, she could not imagine him dead.

And for three days, Laughton sat alone in his darkened house, drinking everything he could find. When there was nothing left, he broke into the bungalow next door and found a crate of bourbon. And all the time, the guns were getting nearer and nearer.

When he was sober, he couldn't think. And when he was drunk, he couldn't stop. And so he tried to sleep. But when he closed his eyes, there was only nothing.

(x)

Molly stood on the walls of Kat Him Wai and looked towards Hong Kong. The sky was still lit up with a red glow although the guns had stopped. It was nearly dawn and Wu was sleeping. He'd said he hadn't fired a single shot in all the time he'd been away. A dispatch rider rattled past on a motorbike coming from Kowloon. He looked up at her, gave her a toothy grin and tossed a bundle of papers towards the walls. Molly went down to get them. The first thing she saw was a newspaper.

SOUTH CHINA MORNING POST

25th December 1941

DAY OF GOOD CHEER

Hong Kong is observing the strangest and most sober Christmas in its century old history. Such modest celebrations as are arranged today will be nonetheless light-hearted. There was a pleasant interlude at the Parisian Grill shortly before it closed last night when a volunteer pianist, in for a spot of food, played some well-known favourites in which all present joined in with gusto.

Bridge Game (Chapter 2):

♠—A 6 3 2
♥—9 8 2
♦—
♣—J 10 7 6 5 3
N
Ruth Dekyvere

♠—10 9 8
♥—A K Q J 10 4
♦—9
♣—A Q 9
W
Mary Laughton

♠—Q J 7
♥—
♦—A K Q J 10 8 7 5
♣—K 2
E
Eliot Rodmell

S
Alfred Laughton
♠—K 5 4
♥—7 6 5 3
♦—6 4 3 2
♣—8 4

Bidding:

A. Laughton	M. Laughton	Dekyvere	Rodmell
Pass	1♥	1 under	3♦
3 under	4♣	4 under	5♦
Pass	Pass	5 under	5NT
6 under	Pass	Pass	Double
Pass	Pass	Pass	

Game:

North plays and South is dummy

1:—W 9♦; N A♠; E A♦; S 6♦.
2:—E 7♠; S 5♠; W 8♠; N 6♠.
3:—W 9♠; N 3♠; E Q♠; S 4♠.
4:—E J♠; S K♠; E 10♠; N 2♠.
5:—S 2♦; W A♣; N J♣; E K♦.
6:—E K♣; S 8♣; W Q♣; N 10♣.
7:—E 2♣; S 4♣; W 9♣; N 7♣.
8:—W 4♥; N 2♥; E Q♦; S 3♥.

West is now left with the five highest cards in ♥